# DANGEROUS BOYS

## VOLUME 1

MAREE ANDERSON    VANESSA BARNEVELD
ROBYN GRADY    SARA HANTZ    EBONY MCKENNA

DANGEROUS BOYS: VOLUME 1
Copyright © 2016
Print edition © 2018
ISBN 978-0-9953839-9-9
by Sara Hantz, Maree Anderson, Vanessa Barneveld, Robyn Grady, Ebony McKenna
Published by Downunder Young Adult Authors

This book features the following Young Adult novellas:
Written in the Stars by Sara Hantz
Tangent by Maree Anderson
Live Fast, Die Young by Vanessa Barneveld
Raising Hell by Robyn Grady
Dangerous Honesty by Ebony McKenna

Thank you for respecting the hard work of these authors.

# WRITTEN IN THE STARS

## SARA HANTZ

# CHAPTER 1

"MOM SAID the ATV's deductible is seven hundred dollars," Tara says, as she charges into my dorm room.

"But I don't have seven hundred dollars."

My heart pounds against my ribcage and I drop down onto the edge of the bed. This is beyond crazy. I know Tara's mom couldn't start the ATV after I crashed it at the weekend when I drove on their ranch, but surely the damage wasn't so bad it cost more than the deductible.

"You'll have to tell your parents," Tara says, shaking her head.

They can hardly manage to pay my boarding school fees at the moment, thanks to the accountant screwing up their tax returns leaving them owing thousands to the IRS. I can't land this on them, too. They might decide to take me out of school. Which would be catastrophic. I love it here, even if some of the school rules are really annoying. And being here saved me from having to move school every three years when Dad was posted to yet another country, with the air force. It wasn't too bad when I was younger, but the older I got the more stressful I found having to make new friends.

But most important is leaving would mean losing Tara, my best friend. Also I'd never see Dan again.

Not that Dan even knows I exist, other than through Tara since he's a friend of her family. Dan's captain of the football team and is in the year above us. He's the hottest guy in school.

*And* he's not seriously dating anyone at the moment.

"No way am I telling Mom and Dad." I bite on my bottom lip. "You know the money-pinch they're in. We'll have to think of something else." I get up from the bed and walk over to the window. My dorm room looks out onto the quad, and I can see some of the ninth graders playing ball.

*Transport me back to ninth grade someone, please. Life is so much easier when you're fifteen.*

"When does your mom want the money?" I shift my gaze to Tara, who's staring in the mirror.

"Well, after your convincing sob story about not wanting to worry your parents, she felt really sorry for you and said she'll wait until the end of the trimester, which is ten weeks."

Tara turns to face me, grinning. Except I can't grin back. Tara's mom might have given me ten years to pay the ATV deductible and I'll still never be able to afford it. And where's that gonna leave me?

"That's like finding seventy dollars a week. You got any ideas how? Because I'm fresh out." My stomach clenches.

If only I could have a do-over day, then I'd see the hole instead of driving into it. No. Forget that. I'd refuse to take the wheel when Tara asked me if I'd like a turn driving.

Tara leans against my dorm room desk, her eyes full of concern. "Don't worry," she says gently. "We'll raise the cash. All we need to do is think of something,"

Normally I love her can-do attitude, but right now I'm not feeling it.

"Like?" I ask, a flicker of anticipation coursing through me.

She's usually more resourceful than me so here's hoping she can think of something.

"Um... um... like..." She twists her dark curls around her fingers and frowns.

"See. There is nothing. I'm totally screwed." Tears form in my eyes and I blink them away.

"Look, Megan. You've got to be positive. I've told you before, if you think about something hard enough, it will happen. Now let's will our minds to come up with a plan."

"You and your positive vibes." I shake my head then reach for a cushion from the bed and throw it at her. It hits her in the face.

Tara grabs it and throws it back, only it misses, slides across my desk and sends my favorite silver bangle flying across the room.

"Sorry," says Tara, as she scrambles to pick it up.

"Hey," I say, inspired by the bracelet. "I've had an idea. Why don't I sell some of my things on eBay to raise the money?"

"What things?"

"My bangle for starters." I reach over and take it from Tara.

"But your parents gave it to you."

"I know... I know." I bite down on my bottom lip. "Well, there must be something else." I open the drawer to my desk and stare in. "This?" I hold up my diamante key-ring shaped in the letter 'M'.

"No. I gave that to you."

"But Tara, everything I own was given to me by someone, seeing as I have so little money to buy myself anything."

I drop the key-ring into the drawer and push it shut.

*Why is this so hard?*

I sit down on my bed and rest my head on my arms. It's an impossible situation. My life is totally screwed. I feel the ball of hopelessness settle in my belly as I imagine being pulled from school and starting all over again.

"I'm sure we can think of something else," Tara says, sitting next to me and resting her arm around my shoulders.

I draw in a long breath. It's impossible.

"Maybe," I mutter.

"Come on. Let's go to Starbucks. I'll pay. We might bump into Dan."

I pause for a moment. "Actually, no. I don't think Dan is there today." I glance at Tara, who's staring at me with her mouth open. "What's wrong?"

"Watching that far-away expression on your face before you said about Dan just gave me an idea." She jumps up from the bed, a broad smiling crossing her face. "Psychic dating advice. We'll sell psychic dating advice to raise money. Cool idea, or what?"

"I don't understand. How can we offer dating advice, psychic or otherwise? Sure, we've dated guys in the past. But it's hardly enough to offer advice."

We've been best friends starting high school but sometimes I totally miss her point.

"You know how you always have feelings about things, and are always right?" I nod my head, slowly. "Instead of keeping these feelings to yourself, and only telling me, you can share them with anyone who wants to pay. We're going to make a killing. I'm telling you."

"But I'm not psychic."

Well, not in the traditional sense of the word.

"Okay, you're not psychic. So how do you account for all the times you know things that you couldn't possibly know?"

I let out a long sigh. She's only asking me the question I've asked myself hundreds of times over the past few years. I've had strange visions and feelings for as long as I can remember. It's like they just appear in front of my eyes. Sometimes the meaning is obvious, like the time when I knew my aunt had been involved in a car accident. Other times it's not so clear. No one knows, apart from Tara. I don't want people to think I'm a freak. And it's not like the visions happen on a regular basis. I can go months and months without having one, and then have two or three in a week.

"I don't want to. No."

"But why not? Just think for a moment. If you can give advice to girls in the boarding house about guys they want to hook up with, where's the harm in that? And if they pay you, everyone's happy. It's a win win situation."

Tara and her win win situations. I often wish I could be as positive about everything as she is. But I can't. Of the two of us, I'm the cautious one.

"It's too embarrassing. And what if someone wants to know something and I don't know the answer? Then what?" I lock eyes with her. "I'll tell you what," I continue before she has time to reply. "Everyone ends up hating me because they think I tried to screw them out of their money just so I can pay my bills."

Tara sits down on the edge of my bed. "Look, you're not thinking straight. For a start, if you can't get one of your feelings about someone, then make it up. No one will know. And, we needn't say the money is for the ATV. We could say it's for charity. Who's to know that you're the charity in question?"

My jaw drops. "I can't say it's for charity and then take the money. If I get caught I'll be expelled."

A shiver shoots down my spine as thoughts of Mom and Dad's reaction to that horrific situation careen through my head. The scenario seems as horrible as telling them about the ATV.

Somehow Tara's win win situation is looking pretty much lose lose.

"Yeah, I guess getting expelled is a risk. A *small* risk," she argues. "But apart from that?"

Small risk my backside. My school doesn't take things like that lightly.

"I don't know. Lying to everyone. Our friends. That's not good. Not to mention what Dan would think if he found out."

"You won't be lying. I bet you get feelings for everyone. You're offering a service—one they'd have to pay loads for elsewhere. That's if they could even find someone to do it. And all you're going to charge is... um... ten dollars. What do you reckon?"

"So, if the deductible is seven hundred dollars, that means I'll have to sell seventy readings. That's a lot. Maybe we should make it fifteen instead of ten."

A smile spreads slowly across Tara's face. "Does that mean you're going to do it?"

"I haven't decided."

"But you must have nearly decided, if you're thinking about the money. I'll help. I know I can't give the advice, but I can help spread the word."

"If Mrs. Johnson finds out, we're totally screwed. You know how seriously she takes being Head of Dorm Faculty."

"She won't find out. We'll only tell girls who can keep their mouths shut," Tara says.

I'm really not sure. If I've got *the gift*, surely I'd be more confident in its success. And I'm not.

"If I do agree, I'll have to practice first. I'm not convinced what I do counts as being psychic."

"Okay, I'll tell you what. During library study period tomorrow we'll plan it more. We can also get some ideas on how to channel your powers, you..."

"Channel my powers? I keep telling you I don't have powers. I'm not like those people on TV who get in touch with dead people. You're seriously overestimating what I can do."

I've Googled in the past about having visions, but didn't look too deeply. My way of dealing with it, I guess. I didn't want to know too much in case I didn't like what I learned. But even if I admit that I'm a bit psychic, it's not in the way Tara thinks.

"Let's just give it a chance. We'll do the research and then make a final decision," Tara says.

"I guess. I just can't help thinking that I'm heading toward the biggest freakin' mistake of my life."

# CHAPTER 2

"MEGAN. Tara. What are you doing? You're meant to be working in silence." Mrs. White, our school librarian, makes me jump with her question.

I quickly minimize the screen, leaving a page on worms. "Sorry, we were discussing our mid-term biology assignment," I reply.

"Oh." The shock in her voice is evident.

Hardly surprising, since our biology assignment isn't due in for ages. Which, under normal circumstances, would mean pulling an all-nighter a couple of days before the due date, like most others in our class.

"Yes." I wriggle in my seat and smooth out my skirt.

"Worms," she says leaning in between the two of us and making me gag her perfume is so strong. "Interesting. Do you know, if you cut a worm in half the head end will grow another tail?" Luckily she steps back from the screen and I manage to grab a breath.

"No. I didn't," I say.

"Well, I won't disturb you any longer." She turns and leaves us.

"Come on," I say to Tara, pulling up the psychic site. "There's a lot to read. And so many long words. I don't know what half of them mean." Unlike Tara. We may sometimes be slackers when it comes to school work but she has this amazing vocabulary.

I can't believe the number of websites there are on being psychic. And the way they talk, it's like everyone in the whole world is psychic. Just some are better at it than others.

"So, would you call yourself clairvoyant, clairaudience or clairsentience?" Tara asks.

I frown. "No idea. I didn't know there was a difference. I've only ever read about clairvoyance before."

"It says here: *clairaudience is the ability to hear or perceive sounds which are not normally audible.* Is that you?" Tara asks.

We've discussed my *ability* before but always in vague terms—I didn't want to come off as a freak to Tara, either. And I probably wouldn't have even mentioned it at all if she hadn't seen the way I act when I have one of my visions. This is the first time I've gone into any depth at all.

"If it means hearing voices, then no. That's definitely not me," I say, shaking my head.

Of course, I'm not counting the voices in my head, which sound like my mother when I'm up to no good. I don't know how she can make me feel guilty without ever having to be up close or actually speaking.

"Okay. What about clairsentience?" Tara asks, cutting into my thoughts. "That's to do with *knowing an event, past present or future through a feeling.* You definitely get those, don't you?"

"I guess."

"And we know you're clairvoyant, which is *extrasensory perception of an event which is not present to the five senses.* So I reckon..."

"Ohhhhh. Well, that explains it," I say, interrupting her, as I'm side-tracked by something I'm reading.

"What?"

"This." I point to the bottom of the screen.

"*In order to see future events,*" Tara reads, "*a psychic has to detach themselves emotionally.* So?"

"That's why I couldn't predict the crash. It says underneath that it's hard to be psychic about your own life." Not that I've ever tried to predict anything about my life before. Except maybe my future with Dan, which also came up relatively empty. I haven't consciously tried to predict anything else. Things come to me. I don't go to them.

Tara rubs her nose with her index finger and slowly nods her head, her brown curls bouncing from side to side. "You know, I wondered why you didn't know in advance about the accident. It also explains why you haven't managed to avoid any trouble we've got into over the years."

I burst out laughing. "It's probably more to do with me not being properly psychic. I'm totally untrained, and..." I pause, as suddenly it hits me. We're kidding ourselves if we think I can pull this off. All the sites talk about how it takes time to develop your psychic ability properly.

I pick up the pencil by the side of the computer and bend it until it snaps.

"Megan, what the..."

"This is stupid. I can't do it. All of these psychic people say you must practice. What chance have I got to do that?" I fold my arms tightly across my body, ignoring the jagged end of the pencil digging into my ribs.

"Look, how hard can it be? You're already getting feelings about people and that's with no practice at all."

"But I don't get these feelings all the time. And not to order, either..." The sound of the school bell, signifying the end of the period, interrupts me. "We'll talk at lunchtime."

I close down all the websites we've been in and reach for my bag under the chair.

As we stand Tara links her arm through mine. "Don't worry, it will all work out."

I wish she'd stop making it all seem so easy. There's got to be a catch in here somewhere. We just haven't found it yet.

---

"HEY, MEGAN." My heart skips a beat at the sound of Dan's deep, warm voice.

His dark blond curls are damp and frame his face, just covering his ears. I'm guessing he's just had sport. He smiles, and two of the cutest dimples form in the center of his cheeks. His hazel eyes have gold flecks and are totally mesmerizing.

"Hi," is all I can manage to say.

How does he do this to me? Would it be a crime if something witty came out of my mouth? He must think I'm so boring.

He holds open the door into the dining hall I walk in. Before I have time to say thanks, he heads to where a group of guys are sitting at the back. I scan the room to see if Tara's already here and see her in the corner sitting with Liv and Robyn, two girls from our year. She looks up and smiles when she sees me, beckoning for me to come over.

After grabbing my lunch, I make my way over to where they're sitting.

"Hey," I say, as I approach. "Are you saving this seat for anyone?" I look at Liv who's sitting next to the empty seat.

"Surely you already know that." She grins at me, and nods meaningfully.

My head jerks to the left and I lock eyes with Tara. She flushes and mouths *sorry*. It's meant to be a secret. How come she's told Liv, of all people? She may be our friend, but everyone knows she can't keep a secret, even if her life depended on it.

"Yeah, right." I give a half laugh and put my tray down beside her.

Quickly picking up my fork to hide my annoyance, I start to eat.

"Why didn't you tell us?" Liv's voice cuts into my thoughts. "Or is it another of your jokes?"

I can hardly blame her for thinking that. Tara and I are often playing practical jokes on people. Like the weekend we took out all the furniture in Casey's dorm room and hid it in mine. I still have the pic of her expression on my tablet.

"No. This isn't a joke," I reply.

"In that case, please will you do me first?" Her voice is suddenly like a hundred decibels.

"Sssh," I say. "No one's meant to know. And there's nothing to tell."

"Sorry. Tara said not to say anything, and I won't. Promise. Not even to Becky." Becky is her closest friend. And no way do they keep anything from each other.

"You can tell Becky. But no one else. Okay?"

"Sure. When are you starting? This is so cool. You know I read my horoscope every day, and now you're here... it's like..."

"Whoa, Liv. Nothing's agreed. Tara and I are still in the planning stage."

Liv frowns. "But... but... Tara said..."

"We're not ready yet, are we Tara?" I toss a glance in her direction.

"We are nearly," Tara replies.

"But there's still more to sort out." I rest my fork on the plate. "I'm going to the store. I need something decent to eat."

"Wait for me," says Tara, leaping up and causing her chair to scrape along the floor. "A chocolate fix is needed, if I'm to survive double accounting, followed by yawn-worthy math."

We walk in silence to where we leave our trays and plates and then head out the door. The chill wind whistles around my ears and I wrap my arms around my middle for warmth.

"I'm so sorry," Tara starts. "I didn't intend to tell Liv. She saw my notes when we were sitting at the table and started to question me about it. But if Liv and Robyn's interest is an indication of demand among the girls here, we're going to be a huge success." Her eyes light up as a smile spreads from ear to ear.

"I'm not sure asking two people is enough for us to predict success." I glance up toward the sky.

"Are you angry?"

"No. I just feel like we're moving too fast on this. We only came up with the idea last night. And I'm still not sure about announcing to the school that I'm some kind of psychic."

Though is it ever going to be the right time? Maybe I should just do it and stop being such a wuss.

"I understand, but the sooner we start, the sooner you will be making money." Tara has a point. Still...

"It's easy for you to say. It's not your cred that's on the line. You do know if I don't deliver then I'll be a total laughing stock."

And what will Dan think of me then—assuming he can get past the whole psychic thing?

"Give it a chance," Tara urges. "We'll try it on our friends and if it doesn't work out we'll pretend that we were kidding and give them their money back."

That makes sense. Nothing to lose by doing it that way. And how can I refuse seeing as the money is for Tara's mom. Especially after she was so good about giving me time to come up with the deductible.

"Okay. Let's aim to start in a couple of days."

She turns and looks at me, excitement etched across her face. "Cool."

As our eyes lock a thought comes rushing to the front of my head. I feel such an idiot not to have thought of it before. "And tonight I'll do a reading on you to see if we can really pull this off."

# CHAPTER 3

"L IV AT SIX, Becky at six-twenty, Robyn at six-forty, Jen..."

"Tara," I interrupt.

She looks up from her clipboard, the pencil between her thumb and finger dangling in mid-air.

"What?" She widens her eyes and looks all innocent. Except this time she's got no chance of it working.

"You know what." I shake my head. "We agreed on two. Three, max."

"But."

"No buts. We agreed that as we've no idea how it's going to turn out we won't do many the first time."

I'm feeling totally sick at the moment and the four walls of the small music practice room we're using seem like they're closing in on me. My reading with Tara was a disaster. Mainly because as hard as I tried nothing would come through. It didn't help that Tara couldn't take it seriously. We're too close, I'm sure that's the problem. Anyway, I've put it to the back of my mind.

I take a deep breath. Big mistake. The music practice room (actually, cupboard with small window and a few posters of old decrepit composers on the wall is a better description) is so musty it smells more like the boys' locker room than some place sweet sounds are made .

"I know, but I've agreed now." Tara fixes me with a pleading stare. "Please."

"Geez, Tara. You should be doing drama." I slowly shake my head. "Okay. I'll do all of them. But don't make any more appointments until these are over and we know whether it's working."

Tara punches the air and runs to the door. She opens it and sticks her head out.

"No one's here yet. Liv better not be late, or that will put the rest of them back, and we need to finish by seven-thirty so we're in time for roll-call." She pushes the door shut and sits on the chair by the piano, staring at her clipboard.

I glance at my watch. Ten minutes to go. Maybe I should try and get myself in the zone. Like, start meditating or something. I flop down on the floor, cross my legs and shut my eyes.

"Ommmmmmmmm..." my voice makes a buzzing sound in my ears.

"Megan, what the hell are you doing?"

"Ssshhhh." I half open one eye. "I'm trying to center myself."

"Excuse me?"

I draw in a long breath. "Ommmmmmmmmm. Ouch." My eyes shoot open. "What did you do that for?" I scowl at Tara, while rubbing the arm she pinched.

"I can hear voices. Get up."

She takes hold of my hand and pulls me up. Just in time, because there's a knock on the door and it opens.

"Hey, Megan," Liv says peering in and resting her eyes on me as I'm twisting my skirt back in place. "Where do you want me?"

"Over here, Liv," says Tara taking a step toward the two chairs in the corner that we'd positioned in a V shape almost facing each other.

Following Tara, I sit down on my chair (the one which I purposely left my purse on so I can face the clock on the wall) and clasp my hands, resting them in my lap. Except they don't stay there long, because they're so sweaty they keep slipping apart.

I can do this. I can. All I've got to do is relax. And smile.

"Thanks, Tara. We'll be okay now." I glance up at her and she surprises me with a frown. "Is there anything wrong?"

"You want me to leave?"

"Yes"

"You don't want me to stay?"

I shake my head in disbelief. Where did she get the idea she could sit in on the sessions?

"Of course not. You stand guard outside. This is between me and Liv. Right Liv?"

Liv looks up suddenly. I don't think she's been listening to a thing we've been saying.

"Whatever," Liv says. She half smiles at me, while wrapping her fingers around the long silver chain that's hanging from her neck, which she usually keeps hidden under her shirt. She seems as nervous as me. Though why *she* should feel like that I don't know. It's not like her entire existence is on the line if she screws up, is it?

But then again, maybe she's nervous about my peeking into her life.

"Okay. Let's start. We've only got twenty minutes." It amazes me at how confident my voice sounds.

I stare at Tara and nod at the door. She wraps her arms around the clipboard, pulling it toward her. She walks outside without saying another word.

"First of all, I need something of yours to hold. It helps me focus." And makes me look like I know what I'm doing. According to our research, lots of psychics use something belonging to their clients.

"Like what?"

"Your necklace will be good." Liv lifts it over her head and passes it to me, and I cup it in my hands.

Okay. This is it. As in *this... is... it.*

*Just think of the money.*

Yeah right. I'll think of the money and not be able to focus on anything else. That's not such a good idea. I'm going to think of warm sunny days, lazing by the beach, gentle waves...

"... Simon?"

Crap. I missed the question.

"Liv, I need you to ask the question again, only more slowly. That way I can concentrate on what's going on around you."

"Sorry. I didn't realize. You know, I still can't believe you're psychic. When I think of how you could have helped me last year with Mark."

It's probably not a good time to tell her I had a feeling that it would all turn to custard way before it actually did.

"Forget Mark. It's Simon you want to know about, isn't it?"

A dreamy look flashes across Liv's face. "I know he's going with Elle, but I want to know what I can do to get him to finish with her and ask me out."

*Come on Megan. Think. Relax. Think. Focus on Liv and Simon. Think. And while you're at it, think some more.*

Okay. I'm thinking. Now what?

*Clear your mind and let whatever feelings and thoughts you have wash over you.*

Why isn't anything happening? There's nothing in my head at all, apart from total dread at embarrassing myself. I can't believe that my very first attempt is turning out like this.

Tara's going to kill me. Her mom's going to kill me when I don't come through with the money. My parents are going to kill me when I have to tell them...

Wait. I have something. It's sort of fuzzy, but it's definitely something.

I gently shake my head to try and clear the fuzziness. Geez. Simon and Elle are in it for the long haul. As in, I can see babies. Uh, oh. I think they split up once though. And that's soon. Very soon.

But how does Liv fit into all this? This is *soooo* hard. If I tell her about Simon and Elle she's not going to thank me. Dating advice is meant to help, not shatter dreams. Then again, if I don't tell the truth I'll be found out when my predictions don't turn out.

Well, Liv," I say, trying to sound confident as I look at her. "I can definitely see a break in Simon and Elle's relationship. And..."

"You can," Liv says, while fidgeting in her chair. "When?"

"I don't know an exact date, my powers don't work in that way. But I think it will be soon. Like sometime this year."

"A year's a long time. Can't you be a bit more specific?"

"It's not that easy. Like I said things come to me in a general way."

Liv gives a sigh. "But definitely this year."

"Yes, I believe so."

I swallow hard as the enormity of what I've predicted hits me. What if Liv tells Elle or Simon that I knew they'd finish? How are they going to react to that?

"So what next?" Liv asks, cutting into my thoughts.

"What do you mean?" I ask

"You know. Once they finish, how am I going to get him to go out with me?"

I don't want to give her false hope by saying he's going to want to go out with her because I'm not sure that he will.

"There's nothing you can do. Just wait and see if he asks you."

Her face drops. "But I thought you'd help me. Tell something I should say, like a chant. Or suggest a potion. I've read all about them on the net."

"That's not what I do," I say gently.

That's all I need, people thinking I'm a witch. If I'm not careful she'll have me chanting over a cauldron in a high pitched squeaky voice.

# CHAPTER 4

MY HEAD's going to burst. Four readings, one after the other, has totally wrecked me.

"Come on tell me everything," Tara says.

"You know I can't do that."

"Why not?" Tara's bottom lip juts out.

"Because it's wrong and not fair."

I get that it's hard for Tara, because we've always shared everything in the past, but this is different.

"Well, were the readings a success?"

"I think so."

After Liv, the others seemed a breeze. Well, not a breeze exactly. There was one scary moment with Jen when all that came into my head was Mickey Mouse, but I think that's because a plastic Disney figure standing on the piano distracted me.

And Becky seemed a bit disappointed when she asked how long she'd stay going out with Rich and I had to tell her I can't see them together after school. But, I did say that just because I can't see it doesn't mean they won't.

You know, thinking on my feet is something I'm used to, but now it's taking on a whole new dimension.

"You're not sure?" Tara asks.

"We'll talk more later, after roll-call. Which if we don't hurry we're going to miss and then end up with a drill." And I've had enough litter collection to last me a lifetime. Why they can't find some other punishment, I don't know.

"Hey, Megan." I hear as I walk into the day room. I turn and see Kate beckoning for me to come over.

Tara and I exchange glances. Kate is the year above us, *and* Head of House. So, if she wants to speak to me that can only mean one thing... trouble.

As I make my way toward her she jumps up from her seat by the window and walks in my direction.

"Quick," she says. "Over here." She grabs hold of my arm and pulls me out of the door into the garden.

"What's wrong?"

A pink tinge creeps up Kate's face. "I need to ask you something."

"Me?" How weird is this. Kate, Head of House, Miss Popular, clever, sporty and everything else you could want to be, wants to ask me something that is causing her to blush.

"Sure." I lean against the wall and in an attempt to look relaxed.

"First, I need to know if it's true."

"If what's true?" I frown.

"That you can tell the future? Or is this just another of your tricks?"

What is it with everyone thinking it's made up? Rhetorical question. Our reputation goes before us. More to the point, how come I didn't guess that's what she wanted? Try because no one is meant to know apart from a few hand picked girls from our year.

"No it's not another trick. Who told you?" I fold my arms tightly across my chest.

"Emma."

Emma? And she knew how? Oh crap. She's Becky's cousin. That's how. Then again, it stands to reason that it would get around quickly.

"Sorry," Kate says. "I didn't realize it was a secret."

What planet is this girl on?

"I'm just doing readings for a few girls. To earn some money. Please don't tell," I plead.

Kate takes a step back. "Why would I do that?"

"Because that's your job?"

"Megan. I'm not like that. I might be Head of House, but that doesn't mean I have a hotline to the Principal or Mrs. Johnson."

"Thanks," I say, unable to hide the relief in my voice.

"Can I ask you my question then?"

"Sorry, no time at the moment."

---

"I HOPE you told her to come and see me, because I'm the one with the appointment book." After the meeting, Tara and I came back here to our block and we're sitting in the common room with a cup of hot chocolate.

"What appointment book?"

"Remember that locking diary my parents got me for Christmas?"

"The one you hated because it had rainbows and stars on it?"

"Yeah. Well, now it has a use. Look." She pulls out of her pocket a tiny diary with a padlock and puts her hand down the front of her shirt and lifts out a key on a string.

"Tara." I'm unable to contain the laughter. "It's only today's appointments. Not a list government secrets."

"You could be doing hundreds of readings so we need to keep track of them."

"Hundreds of readings? I don't think so. For a start I don't need to do hundreds. And there won't be hundreds of people wanting one. We did agree, remember, to keep it to girls in our year."

Tara looks away from me and takes a sip of her chocolate.

"That was before," she mutters, without looking up.

"Before what?"

"Before the buzz went around the day room when you were outside with Kate. Did I forget to tell you?" She turns her head and looks at me, the hint of a smile on her lips. "You, my girl, are hot. Thanks to Liv and Becky, who were so excited by what you told them, practically everyone in the house knows."

Excitement bubbles in the pit of my stomach. I'm doing it right. I thought I was but this is confirmation.

"I have to admit that it's cool how it's working out so well." A broad smile crosses my face.

"You'll have paid my parents back within a month, I reckon, and have money spare."

"Seriously?"

"As long as you do at least eight a week."

"Ah. That's what I wanted to talk to you about. I can't do four in one hit again. It totally wiped me out. What about if I do three, twice a week?"

Tara's face visibly falls. "But I've already taken appointments for Thursday and Friday."

"I can't do Thursday, because I've got a play rehearsal, remember?" I auditioned and got a small part in the school musical this year. Not because I have theatrical leanings or a spectacular singing voice, but Dan does drama. Which, in my opinion, is a good enough reason for anyone to audition.

"I forgot. Now I'll have to rearrange them." She places her mug back on the table and picks up her appointment book.

"I was thinking that because of all the work you've been doing I'm going to give you ten percent of the take," I say.

She's working so hard on my behalf, she deserves something. I know we're best friends and will do anything for each other, but I'd still like to give her some money. And I know she could do with it.

"Thanks." Tara jumps up from her chair and rushes over to me and gives me a big hug. "You don't have to."

"I want to."

"Okay, if you insist." She gives a huge grin. "Now, what about Kate? Aren't you dying to know what she wants?"

# CHAPTER 5

I SIT DOWN and glance up at the clock on the wall. Kate better hurry if she wants the full twenty minutes. Kate is the first person I'm seeing from her year, and if Tara's to be believed there are others waiting in line, depending on how she gets on.

No pressure then.

The thing is, I'm not sure I want to see the older girls. For a start, how seriously are they going to take me? And it's much worse to screw up in front of them than the younger girls, or the ones in my year. And if I do make a total hash of things then Dan might get to hear, which would be a total nightmare.

The thought of Dan makes me sigh. I wish someone could give me advice on how to make him notice me. Well, not notice me. He does know who I am, but he thinks of me as Tara's friend. And since he thinks of Tara like his younger sister I've got zero chance, if that. Maybe...

The sound of the door opening halts my Dan thoughts.

"Is it okay to come in?" Kate asks while peering round the door.

"Sure." I force my lips into a wide welcoming smile. I've been practicing it in the mirror, ever since reading that to have the best possible chance of reading someone it's good to get them to relax.

"Thanks."

"Come over here." I gesture to the chair next to me and watch her stride over and drop down onto it.

"I wanted to ask about... well..."

"Before we start," I say interrupting her. "Please can you give me something of yours to hold." She frowns. "It helps me focus."

"Oh, I see. Yes, of course. Is my watch okay?"

"Yes. That's good."

Kate hurriedly removes her watch and passes it to me. I cup it in both my hands and try to empty my mind of everything other than Kate.

Trouble is, it's really hard to concentrate because there's this sort of horrible feeling coming over me. And I'm finding it hard to breath. Kate will think I've totally lost it if I don't hurry up and get my crap together.

I take a huge breath and force this feeling to the back of my mind. "So, Kate. What do you want to know?"

"It's not for me exactly."

"Sorry, but the person needs to be here, otherwise it might not be possible to get an accurate reading." I hold out the watch for her to take but she doesn't. She just looks at me. Well, more like looks through me.

"It's my mom." What? She wants me to advise her mother? "She's going out with this guy and I want to know if it's serious."

"How are you involved, exactly?"

Kate furiously twists her hair around and around her finger, while at the same time going bright red.

"You see... it's..." Her voice is barely above a whisper.

I feel so sorry for her. Whatever it is, it's totally messing with her head. I concentrate really hard on her, and her watch, and her mother, but all that happens is that stifling feeling comes back. It's so scary. It's like something is pulling me into some creepy place. I've got to resist. Whatever it is, it won't get the better of me.

I shake my head and use every ounce of inner strength to bring myself back to the present. I glance at Kate but she doesn't seem to notice my discomfort.

"Please don't tell anyone," Kate adds after a few moments silence.

"Of course I won't. Everything you tell me is in confidence. You have my word." Kate's shoulders relax slightly and a half smile washes over her face.

"Well, during the holidays when I was at home with Stu − that's the boyfriend's name − and Mom was out, he sort of, like came on to me. I know he did. I'm sure I didn't get it wrong."

"What did you do?"

"Pushed past him, ran out, and went to my friend's house across the street."

"Did you tell your mom?"

"No. When I went home Stu acted as though nothing happened. And she won't believe me if I do say anything. Stu will just tell her I made it up, or misinterpreted what he did. They're very close. I'm sure she won't believe me over him. That's why I want to know if they're going to stay together. Because if they are, then I'm definitely going as far away as possible when I go to college. I can't live with them. I just can't."

I focus deep within myself for several moments.

Geez. I can't believe what's coming through. It all makes sense now. Now I know what those feelings before meant. I was actually experiencing how Kate felt when it all happened.

Poor Kate. What a jerk that guy is.

Well, I can help her.

"Kate. You have to tell your mom. He's done it before. To other girls in your position. She'll believe you. I think she's been thinking about ending it anyway. Speak to her. Don't worry. It'll be cool."

This reading has given me a whole new perspective on my gift. It's like it's validating what I'm doing. Except I don't think I could deal with many more like this. Feeling other people's pain is totally draining.

"Are you sure?" Her hands are tightly clasped in her lap, and she looks like she's barely breathing.

"Yes. And..." A loud thump on the door causes us both to jump in our seats and swing our heads around. "That's the sign someone's coming. Crap."

---

"WHAT DID MRS. JOHNSON SAY?" Tara asks, as I push open the door to my dorm room and find her sprawled out on my bed checking her cell.

"Thanks to my quick thinking, and Kate backing me up, Mrs. Johnson believed we were sorting out songs for the House Music competition. Lucky you were outside to warn us. But why didn't you tell me you were going to disappear if anyone came?"

"Because I hadn't planned on going. I saw her before she saw me, when she was peering in the windows of the other rooms, so it seemed a good idea to hightail it out of there." She swings her legs around until she's sitting.

"Anyway, what are we going to do now? We can't go back to the practice room in case Mrs. J appears again." I perch on the end of the bed next to Tara and take hold of my pink heart shaped cushion and hug it.

"Actually, I've been thinking about where we should go now. It needs to be somewhere private, where teachers can't find us and where you can't be overhead. And I have an idea which I think you'll like." She grins and looks unnervingly pleased with herself.

"Where?" Suddenly I find myself caught up in her excitement.

"Dan's house. His mom owns a fashion store in town, so she's out at work everyday. Am I a genius, or what?" She punches the air.

"Dan's house. You're crazy."

Not crazy in that if we go somewhere away from school it makes life easier. Crazy in that she's talking about me hanging out at Dan's house. As in, Dan's house.

"Hear me out. We can go for a couple of hours on Wednesday afternoon after sport and the same on Saturday afternoon."

"And his parents won't mind, of course."

"They won't know. His dad's overseas for twelve months and with his mom working every day, it's perfect."

"As long as Dan agrees."

"Details." Tara shakes her head. "He'll be cool about it. Ask him tomorrow."

My stomach dips. I wish the thought made me as excited as she sounds. Because at the moment I'm as far away from that state as is possible.

"I'm not asking him. It's your idea, you ask him."

# CHAPTER 6

"HE'S COMING," Tara whispers. "Act normal."

How, exactly? Ever since we decided to wait for Dan behind the school chapel after classes today—knowing he takes a shortcut past here to get home—the butterflies in my tummy have gone crazy, and I'm as far from normal as is humanly possible.

I know I'm being an idiot. It's not like we haven't spoken before, because we have. Lots of times. But I haven't asked him to do me a favor. Nor have I ever been to his house. Apart from when we had Tara's mom give him a ride home from the stadium one athletics weekend, after he twisted his ankle during a race and couldn't walk back.

"No pressure, then." I look up toward the sky and draw in a deep breath.

"Whatever," Tara says impatiently. "Now do you remember what we're going to say?"

"What you're going to say. I told you, if it's left to me to ask I'll choke."

Tara gives a loud sigh. "I suppose I can do your dirty work for you."

"Excuse me? My dirty work? Since when is it my dirty work? If I remember correctly, only last night you were reminding me we're a team. Well, fellow team member...." I pause, catching sight of Dan heading toward us. My nerve endings go all tingly and my fingers itch to slide through his blond curly hair, which hangs just over his collar and is swaying gently in the breeze.

"Hey, Dan." Tara's so cool when she wants. Who'd have guessed we were lying in wait for him.

"Hey." Dan nods and grins, his whole face lighting up. He's so cute when he smiles—in a broad, six foot, football-playing hunk sort of way.

"We were just talking about you. We've got a favor to ask," Tara says.

"Hmmm." A frown crosses Dan's face.

He doesn't appear very receptive, and that's before Tara asks him.

"I don't know if you've heard, but Megan, gives psychic dating advice," Tara continues.

"Psychic what?" Dan's jaw visibly drops.

"Dating advice. You know, girls come to Megan with their problems or wanting to know things and she uses her powers to answer their questions. And they pay, of course."

"You've got to be kidding." Dan looks from Tara to me, a look of disbelief shooting across his face.

I shake my head. "No. It's true. Really." My cheeks blaze. This is so embarrassing.

Dan throws his head back and lets out a huge laugh. "And they pay you?" he asks, and I nod. "And how do I fit into all this?" He asks, staring directly at me. His eyes, dark brown with gold flecks, sparkle. They're mesmerizing.

Well..." I force myself to break eye contact and glance at Tara, willing her to step in, since she knows him so well and will be able to say just the right thing. I hope.

"Because, don't expect me to come to you for advice, Megan," Dan adds. "Sorry, but I don't believe in all that psychic stuff. I've watched it on TV and it's all a fix." He shoves his hands in his pocket and scrapes the side of his shoe against the chapel wall, causing cement to spray onto the ground.

"That's not true," I say, panicked that the guy I've been crushing on forever thinks I'm a hack. Or worse, some kind of liar. Tara shoots me a glare, and I draw in a breath. "I mean, maybe some are fake but I'm not."

What happened with Kate proved to me that I can use my gift to help people.

"Anyway," Tara jumps in. "That's not what we want. We were holding sessions in our music room but Mrs. J caught us and now we need somewhere else. And we thought maybe we could do it at your house."

Dan's foot drops to the ground. "My house?" he asks, his voice slow and deliberate.

"Yes. While your mom's at work. We thought a couple of hours on Wednesday and Saturday afternoons. After sport. What do you reckon?" Tara asks, making it sound so simple.

"What I reckon is, why can't you find somewhere at school?" Dan shakes his head.

He's not going to let us.

"There is nowhere. Believe me, we spent all yesterday trying to find a place, but everywhere is too risky, isn't it Megan?"

"Yes. I can't focus properly, if half the time I'm worrying that someone might come in," I say, staring up at him. Our eyes lock for a few seconds and my knees go wobbly. I quickly lower my gaze, not wanting him to realize how he's affecting me.

"Please," Tara pleads.

I breathe a sigh of relief as the focus is now on her and not me.

Dan folds his arms across his chest and stares into space. "And what's in it for me?"

Tara and I exchange glances. We hadn't even thought he'd want something.

"Tara?" I ask.

"A free reading? I'm sure there's something you want to find out." She stares up at Dan, her eyes bright and sparkly. Then she collapses into a fit of giggles. "You're too funny. You should see your face. I was only joking," Tara adds.

"I don't really want anything." A lazy smile plays at the corners of his mouth, and my tummy fizzes. "I'm not sure. Then again..." He slowly nods his head.

"Are we cool, then?" Tara asks.

I hold my breath, while he deliberates.

"We'll have a trial." He says after about a minute. "But some days it might not happen. Like, when I've got an away game. I can't let you in the house without me being there. Mom might come home early and find you."

"Can we start this Wednesday, then?" I ask, hardly able to contain my excitement. "So I don't get too behind on my appointments." Out the corner of my eye, I see Tara smirking in my direction. Okay, I admit it, that's not my only reason.

"Sure. Meet me here at three and we'll go back together."

I love my life.

We stand in silence as Dan walks away. Once he's out of earshot we turn to each other grinning.

"Twice a week. You and Dan. Does it get any better? And all thanks to me." Tara takes a bow and nearly head-butts me. I quickly jump to the side and slam myself against a tree.

"Ouch." I rub my side. "Anyway, you're coming too, aren't you?" For all my excitement about wanting to be alone with Dan, my instincts tell me to wait. At least initially, anyway

"Of course I am. It will be just like before only a different venue."

"Except I don't need anyone to stand on guard. And you can't sit in with me. So, if he doesn't have a separate room for me to use then it could be difficult."

"We'll sort it when we get there. If it turns out you don't need me I'll stop going." Her voice is bright enough, but I can tell by the look on her face she doesn't want to be left out.

# CHAPTER 7

"I'VE GOT something to tell you and I'm not sure how you're going to take it," Tara says as we're heading toward Dan's house for the first time. A look of guilt shoots across her face and she steps away from me.

"What?" I fix her with my most intimidating stare and she lowers her gaze to the floor.

"Your first appointment."

"Yes. With Abby."

"She had to cancel, so I gave her time to someone else."

Why do I not like the sound of this?

"And this someone is?"

"Harry." Her voice is so quiet, it's barely audible. And her face is a delicate shade of pink.

"But I don't do readings for guys," I say, unable to hide the panic in my voice.

"I'm sorry. But he was so insistent."

"I don't know, Tara. It's not like reading girls."

"Guys are still people. It will be fine. Trust me."

*Yeah, right.*

---

"HI HARRY," I say.

I usher him into Dan's sitting room which is situated next to the kitchen. Luckily Dan is upstairs working. I don't think I could focus if he was too close.

"Megan." Harry's voice is strangely weird and low. And there's a bead of sweat running right across his forehead. I do believe he's nervous. Why can't I have this sort of power over guys in my normal life?

Harry flops down on one of the dark red leather chairs and starts to strum his fingers on the arm. I'd almost feel sorry for him, if it wasn't for the way he tormented me during the first year at school. Not that it matters now.

Harry coughs and I realize that I've been ignoring him.

"Right. If you can give me something of yours to hold, to help me focus, then we'll start."

He frowns then reaches into the pocket of his pants. "This okay?" He holds out a small flat stone. "It's my lucky pebble. I never go anywhere without it."

"Perfect." I gently rub the pebble between my two hands and a feeling of warmth floods through me. It takes me by surprise and I glance up from staring at my hands and rest my gaze on Harry. "What would you like to ask me?" My voice sounds different. All soft. It seems that we're going to become good friends. How weird is that?

"There's this girl." Tell me something I don't know. "And she smiles at me a lot. And I often see her looking in my direction. I want to ask her out, but I need to know if she really likes me, or is she just being... you know... just being friendly." He shuffles awkwardly in the chair, then crosses one leg over the other, stays in that position for about five seconds then uncrosses it.

"I sense a romantic involvement for you. And this girl feels close to you already. But you need to take the initiative. She doesn't know the extent of her feelings for you yet. And... hey... who is she?" I shouldn't really be asking. I mean it's my job to know everything. But I just want to double check, since what's coming through at the moment is weird.

"Tara."

He wants to date Tara. That's what I thought. And all my feelings are telling me that she wants to date him, too. Only she doesn't know it yet.

Shall I tell her? If I don't say anything and he asks her out, she'll know that I know and will hate me for not telling her. And if I do say something and Harry finds out he might not ask her. This is definitely not one of Tara's win win situations, that's for sure. More like a lose lose.

"Well, as I said, she does like you but you'll have to make the first move. Ask her out."

He leans forward slightly in his chair and his dark hair flops over his eyes. "Will you?"

"Will I what?"

"Ask her out for me."

"Look, I'm not running a dating service," I reply.

The corners of his mouth turn down and I feel really mean. It's not like it would be hard for me to do. Especially if I think they'd be good together, which I do.

A loud knock on the door makes us both jump and Tara pokes her head around the door.

"Your next appointment is here, Megan." She looks from me to Harry and back again. "What? Stop staring at me like that, the two of you. I'm sorry to interrupt, but Megan, you told me to let you know if you're running late."

I swallow hard and Harry flushes a deep red.

I'll ask her.

# CHAPTER 8

"SAY THAT AGAIN. SLOWLY." Tara's eyes are like saucers.

"Harry, who... came... to... see... me... wants... to... know... if..."

"Shut up," Tara growls. "Just tell me."

"But you know already." I try to suppress a grin but fail, and resort to covering my mouth with my hand.

"I need to hear it again. *Then* I'm going to pinch myself hard so I know I'm awake. *Then* I might pinch you too, just in case you're lying."

"I'm *not* lying."

"Lying about what?" Tara and I both turn our heads toward the door when we hear Dan's voice.

"Nothing," I say, feeling my cheeks heat and knowing that I've gone bright red, yet again.

"Nothing," repeats Tara.

"Whatever." Dan shrugs, and strides into the room, dropping down on the sofa next to Tara. "Don't either of you try lying for a living. You'd never cut it."

"Do you want us?" Tara asks.

"I just came to see if *Mystic Megan* has single-handedly solved the school's dating issues." He smirks, and two cute dimples appear in his cheeks.

He should come with a government health warning: *This guy will do dangerous things to your heart.*

"Just because *you* don't believe," says Tara, "doesn't mean that everyone else is skeptical."

"Sorry, Megan. I'm not saying you're making it up deliberately. Just that you know these people, so it's easy to help them." Dan's expression becomes more serious.

"I know what you're saying, but you're wrong." I say. "And the only way to prove it is for you to have a reading."

Tell me I didn't just offer to do a reading for him. I could no more read him than get an A grade at chemistry.

"No thanks," Dan says adamantly, shaking his head.

"You say that now," says Tara. "But one day you might need Megan's help."

Dan gives a huge laugh. How come he has such perfect teeth? Most football players' teeth are chipped and broken.

"If you say so," Dan says. "So, what were you lying about?" Dan asks, locking eyes with me.

"Someone wants to ask Tara out, and they came to me to find out if she likes them."

"A guy came to you for dating advice?" Dan sounds shocked.

"What's wrong with that?" I retort.

"Well, it's unusual. And who was it?"

"Harry," Tara says. "I couldn't believe it when Megan told me. You don't think he said it for a bet do you?"

"Why would he do that?" Dan replies.

"He wouldn't," I say. "I keep telling Tara that he wasn't lying. I'd have known if he was."

"Yes, but can you be sure? I don't want to agree to go out with him and then find it was all one big joke. How's that going to make me look?"

"Are you doubting my abilities?" I ask, arching an eyebrow.

"No. Of course I'm not. Sorry," Tara replies, waving her hand dismissively.

---

"WILL YOU GO OUT WITH HIM?" I ask Tara, after we leave Dan's house and are walking back to school. "He wants me to report back."

"Yes. I will. How cool would it be if Harry and I could double date with you and Dan?"

"Like that's ever gonna happen."

It was awesome spending time with him at his house, and it would never have happened otherwise, seeing as it's glaringly obvious he has no interest in me other than being Tara's friend.

"It could. It's not like he's with anyone. Maybe I should say something?"

"And maybe you shouldn't. We've talked about this before. I don't want you to ask him. If he knows I like him he might not let us use his home any more."

"I suppose. Especially as I've booked us up for the next three weeks."

# CHAPTER 9

THERE ARE two things of note happening today, both of which are scaring the pants off me.

The first, and most exciting, is I'm on my way to Dan's house alone, because Tara has to stay behind to work on her photography portfolio (teacher's orders) and won't make it here at all. Which means I have Dan all to myself.

Aside from my nerves, I'm okay with this because since we've been using his house he always makes a point of speaking to me at school, and even sat with us at lunch the other day. Although, I'm not sure if that was through choice or because there were no other seats left.

The second, and most scary, is my last appointment this afternoon is with Alice Grant.

Tara reckons I'm being paranoid. She reckons, because Alice needs my help she's going to be totally cool. Well, that's not what I'm feeling at the moment. And the closer I get to Dan's house, the more this feeling of impending doom is washing over me.

"Hey, Megan." Dan pokes his head out the front door just before I get to it.

My heart picks up its pace and I resist the temptation to smooth down my hair which, thanks to the wind, is flying across my face, and in severe need of damage limitation.

"Hi."

He goes back inside and I follow. Thing is, do I go through to the kitchen like we normally do for a drink and chat, or go straight to the sitting room and wait for my first client?

"I'll leave you to it," Dan says. "I've got an English assignment to finish."

"Sure." Crap. That's answered my question. Hopefully he'll be around later. I'll need someone to help with the Alice aftermath.

My eyes are drawn to his tight butt as he climbs the stairs.

Once he's out of sight I go to the sitting room and put my purse down. I also take off my watch and put it on the coffee table in front of me, so I can see it without making a show of what I'm doing. Tara's drilled into me the need to stick to our schedule and not overrun.

Before I have time to do anything else, the door bell rings and I jump up to go and answer it.

"Hey," I say, plastering a big smile on my face and pulling the door open. "Alice. You're not meant to be here." She scowls at me. "I mean, not yet. I'm seeing Sam and Ginny before you."

"We're seeing." She pushes past me and walks into the hall, where she stops and looks around.

"What do you mean?"

"I'm busy later so I swapped with them."

"Okay." There's not a lot to say. Alice gets what Alice wants. Everyone knows that.

"Is Dan here?"

"He's upstairs working. We'll be going into the sitting room."

I walk down the hall, assuming Alice is following, except when I get to the door and turn around she's not behind me.

"Alice?" No answer. I walk back up the hall and catch a glimpse of her in the kitchen looking through a pile of papers on the table. "What are you doing?" My voice is really sharp and she turns around and glares at me.

"Nothing. I went the wrong way."

"Sure." I take a few steps into the kitchen and see the papers on the table belong to Dan. Why on earth would she want to look through Dan's papers?

"The sitting room's this way," I say, walking out of the kitchen. I stop and wait for Alice to follow. This time she does, and when we get there I push open the door, step to the side and wait until she's walked in.

Her eyes are everywhere, scanning the photos of the family on the wall and all the surfaces. Yet, the huge wooden statue by the fire place, the one thing you think would capture her attention—as it's a six foot naked warrior with his tongue sticking out—she totally ignores.

Finally she sits on one of the chairs and stares at me. "Now what?"

My stomach is in knots and I draw in a deep breath to try and relax. "I'd like something of yours to hold, please. It helps me focus. Anything will do."

She pulls off a big silver ring, with an oblong mother of pearl set into it, and passes it to me.

"Don't break it."

"I won't. I'm only going to hold it." I cup it in both my hands and relax my mind. Easier said than done, under the circumstances. "How can I help you, Alice?"

She leans forward in her chair and fixes me with an icy stare.

"Dan. I want to know when he's going to ask me out."

"Dan?"

Dan as in *my* Dan? This is awful. How can she be crushing on Dan, too?

It takes me all my resolve not to lean forward and rest my head in my hands in despair.

"Why are you staring at me like that? He likes me. I know he does. It's obvious from the way he's always staring at me when he thinks I'm not look-ing. And you know he does, too. At least you would if you're not making up all of this stuff about being psychic. So tell me when he's going to ask me out?"

In an ideal world, that would be never.

But this isn't an ideal world. And I'm going to have to come up with something to satisfy Alice or I can say goodbye to earning any more money. Because she'll tell everyone I'm a fraud. And that will ruin everything.

The thing is, it's not that easy for me to tell if he likes her not. This reading is all about her, not him. And I'm finding it really hard to fathom anything. All that's coming through is indifference, verging on dislike. I don't know if that's connected to him or just what I feel about her. Or it could be what she feels about me.

I might have said I wouldn't lie in my readings, but all that's changed, because what's about to pour out of my mouth is exactly that.

What alternative is there? Other than tell her she's too difficult to read. And we all know where that will leave me. Clientless. With a huge debt.

"I'm definitely getting a good vibe about you and Dan. Yes, I think you're right. He does like you and he's planning to ask you out in the not too distant future."

That should do it. And if he doesn't ask her I can say that his plans changed and think up some reason.

"And that's it?" Alice's eyes narrow and her top lip curls. "I'm paying you fifteen dollars to be told something I already know. I don't think so, *girlfriend*."

What does she want, for goodness sake? Details about when and where? I swallow hard. She does. She wants me to tell her *all* about it. Now I'm seriously in trouble.

"It's difficult for me to pin point exactly when he's going to ask you out and..."

"Well try harder. I want details. Like when he's going to ask, and where we're going to go. So I can be prepared." She gives an impatient sigh, lifts up her hand and checks out her manicured nails.

"I can't get the exact day but definitely within the next week he's going to ask you."

"He is?" Her eyes light up, making her seem almost normal. "Cool."

"Uh huh." Why do I have a feeling that one day this is going to come back to bite me on the butt?

"And where will our first date be?"

Let's think. Where would I like to go with Dan on our first date? How about a picnic by the river, so we can cuddle up on a blanket, watch the boats drift by and enjoy the sunshine. And we'll spend the whole afternoon getting to know each other and planning our future.

"The movies."

*The movies?*

I'm not going to give her my dream date.

Anyway, it's all hypothetical because it isn't going to happen. Which means I have precisely one week to do something about it.

# CHAPTER 10

I CLOSE THE DOOR, and lean against the wall. How I ever managed to do the last two sessions is anybody's guess. All I could think about was Alice and that stupid, stupid prediction. And would you believe it, the only idea I've come up with to sort this mess out, is to try and persuade Dan to actually ask Alice out.

Like, he's going to do that for me.

And of all days for Tara not to be here, she had to pick this one. Maybe I should wait until I chat with her before asking Dan. She may even offer to do it for me. Except, the opportunity to speak to him might not arise again and then it will be too late.

"Finished?"

The sound of Dan's voice as he charges down the stairs startles me and I sort of give a half jump in the air. What is it with him that he makes me do the dumbest things?

"Just got some loose ends to tidy up."

"Do you fancy a coffee, before you start?" His lopsided grin sends my pulse into overdrive.

"I could certainly do with one."

We walk into the kitchen and he puts on the kettle. He takes two mugs from the dishwasher.

"Had a tough one?" He asks, while spooning coffee into each mug.

"You could say."

He turns round and stares at me. "Don't tell me, the voices didn't visit, so you had to think on your feet and come up with something."

Okay. How on earth did he know that? Maybe he's got the gift, too. Unless he was listening at the door, which means he knows exactly what the problem is.

"It's not voices, actually. It's kind of feelings and pictures. In a mixed up sort of way."

"Sounds very vague. Which makes it less easy to disprove." He arched an eyebrow.

"Look, Dan. I want to ask you something. I know what you're going to say, but honestly it's not like that. And it only happened this one time. I swear every other time it's been totally genuine, and..." I have to stop to take a breath as there's no air left my lungs.

I hold the back of the wooden chair at the kitchen table and inwardly order myself to relax. He'll never agree to my idea if I'm panicking, because he'll think it won't work. He needs to think it's no big deal.

"Megan, stop." He leans against the work surface and folds his arm. "What the hell is it?"

I draw in a deep breath and continue holding the chair. "Alice Grant came to see me today."

"Lucky you." His top lip curls into a sneer. Crap.

I'll just ignore it.

"Yes," I say in a pseudo-bright tone. "And you'll never guess who she wants to go out with."

"Which poor bastard has that pleasure? Because I wouldn't wish that on my worst enemy." A look of disdain firmly etches itself on his face.

Now what am I meant to do? And what's Alice done to make him so vehemently against her?

"You don't like her then?"

"You could say." He gives a hollow laugh, turns to pick up the kettle, which has just boiled, and pours water into our mugs.

After he adds the milk he passes one to me. The silence as we stand there is decidedly awkward.

"What did Alice do to you?' I finally ask, after deliberating whether to or not. But it's not like I have much of a choice.

"Nothing to me. It was Ben.

Of course. How could I have forgotten that? It was only the talk of the whole school last year. She went to the fair with Ben, and he caught her making out with one of the guys working on the Haunted House. What a bitch.

Maybe that's why I was getting such weird feelings when I tried to read Alice. Because Dan hates her so much. Now, I'm well and truly screwed. He'll never agree.

"I remember." I let out a huge sigh.

"So, who's the latest victim?"

"You," I whisper.

"What?" Dan bellows. "Did you just say *me?*"

"Uh, huh" I nod my head, painfully aware of the flush careering up my face.

"And what did your *special powers* tell her? That hell will freeze over first," He answers, before I have time to say anything.

"Not exactly."

He fixes me with an accusatory stare.

I lower my gaze and begin to fiddle with the ribbed edge of my sweater.

"What, *exactly?*"

"Dan, I'm so sorry. You know what Alice is like. I couldn't get anything that made sense. So, I decided to ad lib. And told her you will be asking her out..."

"Noooo," Dan says, spluttering into his coffee.

He quickly puts his mug down on the table, and I follow suit.

"I thought that when you didn't ask her, I could say sometimes things change between readings."

"That's helps, I guess." His face visibly relaxes. "Except, I'm not cool with what you said. Alice doesn't need any encouragement, and if she starts hanging round me..."

"Okay. Stop." I hold both hands up. "There's more to tell you. And I know you're going to hate me. I'm so sorry. But Alice asked me to give dates and times... and you know what she's like... so I had to say something or she would tell the others I was a fake... and then no one would want a reading from me... and I haven't got enough money yet to pay back Tara's parents... and so I told her."

The look on Dan's face is indefinable. It could be shock, or it could be that I spoke so fast he didn't have a clue what I was talking about.

"Can you say that again? Only slower."

Looks like the latter.

"Alice thinks you'll be asking her out next week, and taking her to the movies."

I bury my head in my hands and prepare myself.

Except it doesn't happen. I wait. And wait. After about ten seconds this huge sound comes from Dan. I jerk my head upward, open my eyes and am faced with him laughing. And not just your average laugh. This is like a huge belly laugh, which goes from head to toe.

I grin inanely at him. Then, caught up in the contagiousness of it, find myself joining in.

I have no idea how long we stand there laughing, but it feels good.

"What are we going to do about it?" Dan asks, once we're a little calmer.

"I was kind of hoping you'd take her out. Only once. I didn't say anything about it being long-term." Considering earlier, I'm sounding rather confident. "I'll pay for the movie tickets—no need for you to be stuck with that."

"You seriously thought I'd agree? Once word gets out Ben and the others will think me a jerk."

"I wouldn't ask if I wasn't desperate." I lower my eyes.

"And what's in it for me?"

What is it with this guy that every time we ask a favor he asks what's in it for him?

I glance up and notice he's grinning.

He's joking.

What an awesome guy. Perfect on the inside as well as the outside.

"You name it, and it's yours." I match his grin "Within reason. Of course."

"Of course," he repeats, his eyes glinting in the sun.

Wait, there is no sun.

"Are we okay, then?" I tentatively ask.

"I must be off my head. But, yes."

"Yes?" I screech.

"I said so, didn't I? Just tell me when and where and I'll do it. We'll talk payment later.

# CHAPTER 11

"AND YOU'RE sure he's really going to?" Tara asks, while she's staring in the mirror.

"Yep. Some time tonight. He has to come back to school for a debate team meeting."

I still can't believe he's doing this for me. If only it was because he likes me. As in *likes* me. That would be like all my birthday's coming at the same time.

"Is he going to text you once he's asked her?"

"I don't think so." It didn't cross my mind to ask him. Then again, knowing Dan he'd say they'd be no need because I should be able to tell.

"So how will we find out then? Unless Alice tells you. I hope so. I won't be able to sleep tonight until I know. This is soooo exciting. Well, not exciting for Dan, but you know what I mean."

To be honest, I'm not sure that I do. And *exciting* isn't the word I'd have chosen. My hugest worry is that he'll go out with her, realize she's a lot nicer than he thought and then want to see her again. And just having this worry is scary enough, because if it's actually one of my feelings then it's going to happen.

"Yeah, I suppose. As long as he doesn't suddenly discover that underneath her bitchy exterior she's really nice."

"Megan. You don't seriously think he'll fall for her, do you?" She rolls her eyes toward the ceiling.

"It hasn't stopped other guys, in the past. She's never been short of boyfriends, has she?"

"Agreed. But this is Dan we're talking about, and there's nothing she can do to sway him. He's too loyal to Ben. She's a cheater and guys like Dan don't go for girls like that."

"How can you be so sure?"

"Look." She picks up the half eaten bag of chips from my desk, sits on the edge of my bed and gives a sigh. "I have known Dan all my life, so if anyone should know it's me."

"How come you didn't know about him dating Kristin until I told you?"

"And how come you can't tell whether or not he's going to fall for her?"

"Don't start. It's Alice's belief that I know *everything* which got me into this mess in the first place."

Maybe I should give out a pre-appointment fact sheet, so all my clients know exactly what to expect, and what I *do* and *do not* know.

"Don't worry. Everything will be all right," Tara reassures. "And if you're so worried about it, we can always go with them to the movies."

"I bet Dan would love us to make up a foursome. You, me, Dan and Alice, it's so... ouch." I rub my leg where Tara prodded it with her foot. "What did you do that for?"

"Because you're being an idiot. I didn't mean go with them, as in *with* them. I meant we could follow them, and sit behind them to keep an eye on things."

"And if they sit in the back row, they'll see us."

"Okay," says Tara. "What about we just happen to be at the movies the same time as they are and we're with a couple of guys?"

"Like who?"

"Like Harry and one of his mates."

"And you reckon he'll be up for it?" I ask, after sitting back on the bed, unable to hide the surprise in my voice.

"Sure. I've already asked him." Tara replies.

"When? How come? And why didn't you tell me?" I fold my arms, and glare at her.

"Because it only happened earlier today, when you were at Dan's. And I didn't tell him it was to spy on Alice, because I didn't know about it then. We were chatting and he mentioned the latest Bond movie and I said you and I want to go too and why don't we go together."

"Just like that?"

"Just like that." She nods.

"And who's this other guy he's going to bring?"

"Craig," she says, looking embarrassed.

"As in Craig who you have the hots for?"

"Used to have," she corrects me.

"We can't tell them our real reason for going, though. No one must know Dan and Alice's date is a set up apart from us."

"I know that. But I'm sure we can trust them not to tell anyone."

"Yeah, right," I counter. "Which planet are you living on? As much as I quite like Harry, I'm not totally deluded into thinking he'll be able to keep quiet about something as gossip-worthy as this."

"I guess. So we're cool then?"

"Sure. As long as Craig doesn't think I'm going because I want to go out with him."

That's the last thing I need—for Dan to think I'm into someone else.

# CHAPTER 12

"Don't look now," Tara whispers in my ear, "but they're walking up the stairs."

My head swings around before I can stop it, and I make eye contact with Alice. She doesn't look happy. I give a sort of half wave and turn back to face Tara, who's shaking her head.

"Sorry. My head turned before my brain engaged."

"So much for us being discrete. Still, at least Harry and Craig didn't see them. Because it would be just our luck they suggest we all sit together."

The guys are buying the tickets, while we wait beside the door into the screen where they're showing our movie.

"You're right. That could have made things very difficult." I shudder just thinking about it.

"And we don't want Dan and Alice to think this is all a set up. Or Harry and Craig, for that matter," Tara says.

"That's hardly likely, though, is it?" I scrutinize Tara's face. "*Is it?*"

"No," she retorts. "And don't look at me like that. You know I'm not going to say anything. Why would I? I don't want to ruin everything between Harry and me. Not that there is anything between us, yet."

"True. Where are Dan and Alice now?"

"If I tell you, promise to keep your head facing in my direction."

"Promise."

"Dan's lining up for tickets and Alice is heading toward the bathroom. Oh crap."

"What? Tell me." The temptation to turn and look is so great, I have to use all my inner strength to stop myself.

"Harry's spotted Dan and is talking to him. Now Dan is looking over here." Tara gives a smile and waves in their direction.

"Can I look? Please."

"Do you think that's wise? Dan's certain to guess what we're doing if he sees you."

"He won't. Harry's probably said we're all together. So it's fine." Apart from totally ruining any chance I have of getting together with Dan because he'll think Craig and I are seeing each other.

"What's wrong?"

"Nothing, why?"

"You suddenly look all upset."

"Sorry. I was just thinking that if Dan sees me with Craig, he's never going to ask me out."

"We'll make sure he knows you're just friends. Leave it to me."

"Ready girls," Harry's voice brings our conversation to an abrupt end. "Guess who we've just seen?"

"Dan," Tara and I both say together.

"Man, nothing gets past you two. Well, you'll *never* guess who he's here with."

"Alice," we say together, then burst out laughing.

"But, why would he hook up with her?" Harry asks. A frown crosses his face. "After last year and Ben, there's no way."

"Well, she is hot." Craig says. The three of us look at him like he's totally lost it. "Isn't she?" he asks, tentatively.

"Come on," I say, not wanting to dwell on Dan and Alice's suitability any longer. "The movie starts soon and if we want to sit together we better get in there."

I don't wait for anyone to reply, just make a bee-line for the door into the movie.

More by luck than design, we manage to sit three rows behind Dan and Alice, which means I have a clear view of everything they're doing. So if he puts his arm around her I will know. I'm not sure what I'll do about it. Although, I am a good shot with the popcorn.

"Are you going to spend the entire movie looking at the back of Dan's head or are you going to watch." Tara whispers.

"It's only the trailers, and I don't want to see them."

Actually, I'm not so much staring at Dan, as wondering why on earth we decided to spy on him in the first place. I mean, what good is it going to do? We know he's taking her out, seeing as I arranged it with him. What's the point? Other than to give me a nervous breakdown. Tara would have been better off going out with Harry on her own.

---

"THAT WAS AWESOME," says Harry as we walk across the foyer to leave the movies.

I agree. At least I think I'd agree if I'd been able to concentrate on the movie instead of Dan and Alice. I said it was madness following them. But, one thing I'm happy about is that he kept his hands to himself and they didn't snuggle up.

"Starbucks, anyone?" asks Tara. "There's an hour before we have to be back."

I nod my head in agreement, while scanning the entrance to see where Dan and Alice are. Except they seem to have disappeared. Where are they? They weren't very far in front us when we left.

"Can you see them? I mutter to Tara when we get outside and start walking towards Starbucks. The guys are a little in front of us so don't hear me.

Tara shrugs. "No. But don't worry. They'll be going back to school."

"How do you know?"

"Trust me. My friend's a psychic."

"Ha. Ha. You're so funny." I temper my words with a grin.

"Okay, so you're not a psychic. Just don't tell anyone or they'll be demanding their money back."

"Don't even joke about it. We don't want to jinx everything."

Tara puts her arm around my shoulder and gives a squeeze. "Everything will be fine. Dan isn't going to do anything with Alice. No one is going to think you're a fake. Which, by the way, you aren't. We're going to have a fun time at Starbucks with Harry and Craig. And Harry is going to ask me out properly."

Once we're inside I ask the boys what they'd like to order. As they paid for our tickets it's only right we offer to get the drinks.

"I'll come with you," says Craig. "You two grab a table." He nods to Tara and Harry.

How sweet is that? Craig wants to give them some time together. Except, that's a girl thing and guys don't usually think like that. In which case, what's his game?

"Sure," I say, striding toward the counter.

"I've been wanting to talk to you alone," Craig says, quietly, while we're in line.

"What about?"

"Well, this seeing into the future you do. I sort of wondered if you'd..."

"Sorry Craig," I say, interrupting him. "Not in here. If you want a reading you'll have to book an appointment through Tara, like everyone else does."

"No I don't want a reading. It's just... I wondered if..." He reaches into his pocket and pulls out a piece of paper. "I wondered if you would choose the winning lotto numbers for me."

*Oh good lord. Now what have my abilities gotten me into?*

---

"What did you say?" Tara asks.

"I told him it wasn't ethical. I mean, really. If I could predict the lotto am I really going to tell him?"

"Exactly. Because if you could we'd have raised the cash you need a long time ago."

Our eyes lock and I can tell from the expression on Tara's face that we're having the same thoughts.

"Maybe we should try," I say

"You said yourself it isn't ethical."

"Well, it probably won't hurt to try." I shrug. "Anyway, do you think Dan kissed Alice goodnight?"

"No. Definitely not."

"But, can you be sure?" I ask.

"He doesn't like her. He only took her to the movies to help you out."

"I know." I let out a huge sigh. "Only I would be so dumb as to make everything up when dealing with the meanest girl in school."

"Not one of your smartest moves." Tara giggles. "Anyway, don't sweat it. He's taken her out, just like you *predicted*, so everything's fine."

"I just hope you're right."

# CHAPTER 13

"IT'S NOT HERE," Tara calls, from where she's peering into my closet.

"You're not looking properly."

"I'm telling you. *It's not here.*" She stands up, places her hands on her hips and sends one of her *don't-question-me* glares in my direction.

I jump up from the bed and stride over. "Move out the way."

"Be my guest." Tara takes a step to the side. "You won't find it."

I kneel, lean into the closet and proceed to fling to the side all the socks, books, and other stuff I'd strategically placed over an old toiletries bag housing the tin containing the money we've earned so far.

"I don't believe it," I shout, after frantically searching. My heart is pounding big time. This so can't be happening.

"Do you think someone stole it?" Tara asks.

"No, I think the money jumped out the closet all on its own and ran away. Of course someone stole it." I check myself and draw in a breath. "Sorry, Tara. I didn't mean to yell."

"How much was in there?" She crouches down beside me, and starts to move a few things in what seems like a half-hearted attempt to look for the money.

"Three hundred and seventy five dollars." In temper I pick up a math book from the floor and throw it toward the bed so hard it flies right over it and smacks against the wall. "Who would do such a thing? And how come they found it? It's not like it was on show for everyone to see. And no one knew the money was in there apart from you and me."

"Maybe someone wanted to borrow your clothes and found the tin while they were looking."

"Why would they look on the floor of my closet when my clothes are either hanging up or in my drawers? Anyway, who cares how they came to find it. The money's gone and there's nothing we can do about it." I sit back on the floor and wrap my arms around my knees. "I can't believe I was so stupid as to not put it in the bank."

"There must be something we can do."

"Like?"

"Go to Mrs. J, for a start. She can do a random search of all the girls' rooms. Remember, they did that last year when Gemma's iPad went missing?"

"And what will happen when she learns I had all that money in my room? I'll tell you. She'll totally freak because we've been warned not to keep large sums of money in the house."

"Okay, forget Mrs. J. We'll find the thief ourselves and get the money back."

"And how are we going to do that exactly?"

After all my hard work. I'll never be able to make up the money. Not by the end of the trimester.

Tara kneels next to me facing the closet. "First of all we need to examine the crime scene."

"Since when have you been a forensic scientist? Just forget it. There's nothing we can do. I'll have to admit to my parents what happened with the ATV, borrow the money from them, and forget about ever being able to afford to go anywhere again."

"Why don't you try and tune into the scene and see if you can find out who's been in here?"

"You know, that..."

"Ewww," interrupts Tara. "What's that?" She points to something on the floor to the left of the closet.

I lean across her and reach out to pick it up. "It's a fake nail tip. And it's not mine," I say, stating the obvious.

"Nor mine," Tara adds. "The thief must have broken her nail while she was in here. Which means, the crime scene has produced some *real* evidence." Her eyes are bright with excitement. "See. What did I tell you? Can you get anything from it?"

I tune into the nail in my hand, and a grey desolateness washes over me, followed by anger.

"I don't know who owns the nail. But I do know that they're very upset," I say.

"It's a start," Tara says.

"I'm not so sure. It means we need to check the nails of every girl in the house, focusing on the ones who look like they've been crying and we'll have our suspect. Forgive me if I'm not jumping up and down with excitement at the prospect. Because even if they do all agree to show us their nails, which we know they won't, no way do we have the time."

I'm totally bummed. There's no point in doing more readings. Not now.

"We'll be able to do it. It's almost time for dinner, so we can begin by surreptitiously checking girls out while they're eating."

There's no point in staying angry. That won't help matters. And who knows, we might get lucky. Stranger things have happened.

"Okay. Wait while I grab some paper and pen," I say.

Tara frowns. "Why?"

"So we can write down names as we eliminate them from our enquiries." I roll my eyes toward the ceiling.

"And if we find the thief, then what? Will you read her her rights, put the handcuffs on and march her down to the station?"

"Something like that." I laugh.

"Seriously, though," Tara says. "What will we do if we find her?"

"I don't know. Maybe enlist the help of Alice to make the thieving bitch admit what she's done, and to force her give back the money."

"Good idea. I mean, you and Alice are nearly BFFs after what you've done for her."

"Not so sure about that. She's hasn't spoken to me since the reading last week."

"Details." Tara gives a nonchalant wave of her hand before heading for the door.

"WE'LL SIT at the table in the far corner," I whisper to Tara while we're waiting in line for dinner. "You check out any girls who are sitting at the tables on the left and I'll take the ones on the right."

"You got it."

Tara is already eating by the time I get to our table.

"Well?" I ask quietly, when I sit down.

"No." Tara shakes her head. "You?"

"No."

"It's hard to be totally sure though," Tara says.

"I know. On the way out, I'll do your tables and you do mine and that will be a double check. Provided they haven't all left," I say.

"Good idea. And I've got an even better one," Tara says.

"What?"

"Let's ditch this." Tara screws her face up and nods at her plate. "I'll shout us a pizza."

"Done. Meet me at the entrance." I don't need to be asked twice.

My journey back through the tables is much the same as before. I scan the hands, and they all look normal. In fact the nails all seem very short. Which is a good point, seeing as school rules don't allow for tipped nails. I don't know anyone who has them, apart from when it's school prom time. Not that will stop some girls. If they can keep tattoos, tongue studs, and other piercings hidden, then keeping nails out of sight is a breeze.

"No," I say when I get to the entrance.

"Neither," Tara says.

We walk in silence toward the house. Just as we get beside the music block I notice Dan in front of us. As if sensing our presence, he turns and smiles. And my knees go weak.

"Hey," he says.

"Hey, Dan," Tara and I both say together.

"You okay?" Tara asks. "Survived the *date* the other night?"

Dan rolls his eyes toward the sky. "Just about." He grins. "You owe me big time, Megan."

"It was only the movies," I retort.

"That's true. But now she'll expect me to talk to her when I see her. She was in town earlier but I ducked into a shop entrance before she saw me," Dan says.

"Lucky she didn't come into the shop you hid in," Tara says.

"I guess. She went into some beauty place."

"Hair Salon, you mean." I say.

"I don't think it was hair. What was the name? I was staring at it while hiding from her. Unique something." He frowns. "Nails. That's it. Unique Nails."

# CHAPTER 14

MY JAW DROPS. "UNIQUE NAILS," I repeat slowly.

"Yeah," says Dan.

"And you're sure it was definitely Unique Nails?" Tara asks.

"Yeah," says Dan.

"Like, really sure?" I ask.

"Yes," Dan says, his voice getting more deliberate and louder. "I'm sure. Alice definitely went into Unique Nails."

"I don't mean to go on," I say. "But are you *really, really* sure."

"Yes. I am *really, really, really* sure. Now quit with the questions and tell me what this is all about." He folds his arms tightly across his broad chest and fixes me with a penetrating stare.

"Did she go to have her nail fixed?" I ask, after a few seconds silence.

I just need to make doubly sure before telling him. I know Dan's a friend, but we can't go around accusing someone like Alice of being a thief without being one hundred per cent certain.

"What else do you do in a nail shop?" He shrugs.

"You can have lots of things done. She could have gone there for a manicure or to have false nails put on," I reply.

"I have no idea. But she was walking with her middle finger in her mouth."

"That's it then. It's her. It's definitely her," Tara says.

This is madness. Since when has Alice gone around stealing money? I mean, we all know the girls you have to watch. Like, Dee. If you're not careful she'll steal your clothes and then claim them to be her own. Easy to do when you're a day girl and living at home, because no one is going to nip in and search your room.

But Alice. I just don't get it.

"Are you going to tell me what's going on, or what?" Dan demands.

"Sorry, Dan. My money. It's been stolen." Why am I sounding so calm?

"What money?"

"From doing all the readings." And just let him dare say anything about it serving me right for the lies I told Alice.

"How much?"

"Three hundred and seventy-five dollars," interrupts Tara.

"And you think it's Alice?" Dan asks, a disbelieving tone in his voice.

"We don't think, we *know* it's Alice," replies Tara.

"Not for sure," I add quickly.

I trust Dan, really I do, but it still feels dodgy to be accusing Alice like this.

"It is her, Megan. Now we know Dan saw her going into the nail shop, it can't be anyone else."

"Wait," Dan says. "Am I missing something? How can she be the one just because she's having her nails done?"

"Because the thief broke her nail and we found it by Megan's closet."

"Crap." He gives a low whistle.

"Quite," says Tara.

"So, where was the money?"

"In the bottom of my closet." I watch Dan's face as he slowly frowns. "But really well hidden." As the words come out my mouth, I realize how ridiculous they sound. "Not *well hidden* enough, though, huh?"

"Sorry, Megan. But that's such a dumb thing to do. Why didn't you put it in the bank?"

"Because I didn't. I thought the money would be okay in my room. And now it's gone and I'm in deep trouble." My voice breaks.

"Don't worry. Now we know it's Alice we'll get the money back." Tara puts her arm around my shoulders.

"Thanks," I give a watery smile.

"Why?" asks Dan.

Tara and I both look at him. "Why what?" replies Tara.

"Why did she steal the money? It makes no sense. It's not like she needs it."

He's right about that. Her family is so rich. And the allowance she gets each month is probably more than I get in a year.

"Maybe she did it for a dare," suggests Tara.

"No. Definitely not," I say.

"You don't know that," Tara retorts.

"I do."

"Is this one of your feelings 'know'?" asks Tara.

"Yes," I nod. "The dark feelings I got when tuning into the nail weren't those of someone just doing a dare. It was way deeper."

Dan makes a hmmmph noise, and Tara and I both glare at him.

"Sorry," he says.

"So you should be," says Tara. "We have enough on our plate without you questioning Megan's abilities."

"Sorry, Megan." He grins, sheepishly.

How am I expected to remain cross with him when he looks like that? He's way too cute.

"No worries. Just come up with an idea to get the money back and you're forgiven."

He looks thoughtful for a moment, then a smile slowly crosses his face.

"I've got it," he says. "Steal it back."

# CHAPTER 15

TARA AND I EXCHANGE GLANCES, and then both look at Dan. "Steal it back." I exclaim. "What an awesome idea." I pause as the smile on my face freezes. "I think. Isn't it?" I glance back at Tara.

"Yes," Tara says. "Assuming she hasn't spent it."

"I doubt she has. She's got enough of her own money."

"True," Tara says, nodding.

"Okay. What's the plan?" I say to Dan, who's leaning against the music block wall tapping his heel on the ground. He shrugs. "Tara?" I ask, turning my attention to her.

"We need to search her room, and the sooner the better, before she disposes of the evidence," Tara suggests.

"That's a bit risky. What if someone sees us?"

It would be just our luck for someone to catch us.

"We'll find a time when we know we won't get caught," Tara replies.

"Roll call," I say triumphantly.

"And then you both get a drill," says Dan.

"Well, that's where you're wrong," I say. "Because Tara and I are expert at getting out of roll call. Aren't we Tara?"

"We've done it once before." Tara says.

"Once?" Dan laughs. "That makes it okay, then."

"Twice, if you count the time we were accidentally locked in the drama storeroom," Tara adds.

"Whatever. We need to get out of it again. So no one's allowed to speak until they've got an idea." I cross my arms and lean against the wall.

"Sorry to spoil things," Dan interrupts the silence. "But I've got to go back home for dinner."

"Aren't you staying to help?" asks Tara.

"I can hardly search Alice's room can I?"

Good point, boys aren't allowed anywhere near the bedrooms. They can't go further than the day room.

"You could stand guard outside the senior boarding house and let us know when roll call is over."

"I can't go in the dayroom because that's where roll call will be, so how will I know? And if I'm seen hanging around I'll be expected to attend my own roll call."

"So back to square one then," I say, feeling deflated. "You better go then, Dan. See you tomorrow, if we decide to carry on with the readings."

"Why wouldn't we?" Tara sounds totally shocked. "You can't stop because we've lost the money. You need to do even more now in case we can't get it back."

"No. It's too much money to make up. I don't have enough time. Or enough energy."

I thought that once I had gotten used to doing readings that they wouldn't wipe me out so much, but they do. Deep breathing helps revive me and clears my energy fields. Which I only found out after researching on the net.

"I disagree. We still have plenty of time, and you're dealing with your energy issue." Tara shakes her head.

"Let's not worry about that now," I say, excitement lifting my feelings. "I've just had an idea. But it involves you, Dan, and..."

"You know I've got to go," Dan interrupts.

"It will only take five minutes," I plead.

"Go on then. What do you want me to do?"

"Go to Mrs. J and say you saw us in the park across the street and that we witnessed a crime. Say we saw someone stealing a purse. No. I've got a better idea. Tell her you saw us in waiting with someone who had collapsed on the sidewalk and we called the ambulance and were waiting for them and then we were going to the hospital."

"And you expect her to fall for that?" Dan raises an eyebrow.

"Wouldn't you?" I ask.

"I must be mad to get mixed up with you two. No wonder you're always in trouble. Okay I'll tell her. But don't blame me if she doesn't believe it," Dan says.

"Thanks so much, Dan." I rest my arm on his. And warmth floods through me. I quickly remove it before he realizes the effect he's having.

"Right," says Tara, taking over like it's somehow her idea. "We need to get our timing right. Dan, you can't go and see Mrs. J just yet because there's another hour before roll call. If you go and see her in twenty minutes and say that we'll try to get back but we're not certain we'll be able to."

"Sure. Don't worry about me being even later for my dinner."

"Let's just hope she didn't spot us in the dining hall," I say.

"She wasn't there," says Tara. "I didn't see any teachers."

"Good." I breathe a sigh of relief. "Let's go over to the park and wait. No one will see us there."

---

"READY?" I ask Tara.

"Yep."

"Okay, fingers crossed the back gate is open or we'll have wasted all this planning."

We walk stealthily along the hedge at the back of our house and after checking the way is clear make a dash for the side entrance. Normally being outside the house wouldn't set off any warning bells, but since we're ditching roll call, we need to be inconspicuous.

In the distance we hear the roll call bell being rung. I mouth to Tara 'wait two minutes', just in case there are any stragglers.

We then walk along the side of the house to where the gate is. I gingerly turn the handle.

Luckily for us, Alice is in Block C, which means we're heading away from the day room.

We creep into her block, up the stairs and along to her room, which is the last one on the right.

"Shall I keep guard and you look?" asks Tara.

"No. We both need to look or we'll run out of time."

"You take the closet and I'll take the drawers," Tara says

I open the closet and am overcome by feelings of guilt. I know it's madness, seeing as she's been through mine, but it doesn't feel right.

"Nothing in here," Tara says as she closes the last drawer.

"Or here." I sit on the edge of the bed. "Come on Tara, think. Where else would she hide such a large amount of money?"

We sit in silence for a few moments, during which time my eyes scan the room for clues. Finally, they rest on the mirror. It's different from mine. I just have a mirror tile that the school put up. Alice's mirror is in a frame. But it's not just the frame that's drawing me.

"There's no where to hide anything," Tara says. "Apart from under her mattress. Jump up and we'll look there."

"Wait. It's behind the mirror." I leap from the bed so fast I fall forward onto her desk. Steadying myself I step over to the mirror lift up the bottom and slide my hand underneath.

"Is it there?"

"I can feel something. I'll take the mirror down, from the wall."

With both hands I carefully lift the mirror from the hook and then turn it over. Taped to the back is my envelope.

"Gotya, Alice Grant. You thieving bitch," says Tara.

"Just watch who you're calling a thieving bitch," Alice's voice booms from behind us.

# CHAPTER 16

I TURN TO FACE ALICE, whose face is so distorted with anger that it's barely recognizable.

Well she can't intimidate me this time.

"You stole my money." I glare at her.

"I didn't steal it." She narrows her eyes and glares right back.

"So what did you do then?" asks Tara. "Because Megan's money didn't get here all by itself." She points to the mirror I'm still holding, which has the envelope dangling off the back.

"I took what's mine, and what belongs to all the others you've conned. Now, if you don't mind." She lunges toward me and grabs the mirror out of my hand. "Get out."

I lean forward and try to take it back from her but she holds on tight and manages to swing it to the side.

"Give me my money," I growl, surprised by the way I'm standing up to Alice. Maybe desperation has made me bold. "Or I'll..."

"What? Go and see Mrs. Johnson? And tell her how you pretended to be psychic and took all our money. Yes, let's do that, shall we?" Her venomous tone sends shivers down my spine.

"She *is* psychic, Alice. Just ask any one who saw her, and they'll tell you," Tara says.

"Yeah, right. Well funny how she can be psychic for everyone but me. With me she had to make it all up. Do I look a freakin' idiot?" Daggers shoot from her eyes.

"Look, Alice," I say softening my tone, because shouting isn't an option now she knows. "I understand how this might appear, but..."

"No you don't," Alice says. "If Gemma Ward hadn't overheard the two of you talking about how you'd set me up you'd have gotten away with it."

Gemma Ward, who left school last year, overheard us talking. I don't get it. Where could she have heard us? I glance at Tara who shrugs. It's crazy, we've been so careful when discussing everything.

Alice must be making it up. But how else could she know? Unless Dan told her. But why? He doesn't like her. I can't believe he would have told her. No. There's got to be another explanation.

"That's crap. We haven't seen Gemma for ages. Not since the beginning of the trimester when we saw her in town. Have we Tara?"

"That's right," says Tara, nodding. "Give us the money, Alice. We'll give you a refund if you're not satisfied with Megan's reading."

I'm not sure that's the right thing to say. Alice practically has steam coming out of her ears now. And let's face it she's right. Whatever we say, we all know I lied to her and that makes me a big fake.

"So, you weren't in Starbucks after the movies the other night, then?"

I feel the color draining from my cheeks. How does she know that? I certainly don't remember seeing Gemma in there.

"Yes, we were," I say quietly.

"And the pair of you didn't go to the bathroom together at all, then?"

She'll be offering psychic dating advice herself at this rate. How did she know that?

"Yes, we did."

"And of course you didn't check to see if anyone else was in there."

"It was empty," I exclaim. And I'm totally sure of that. Tara and I were the only two in there.

"And the cubicles, were they empty?" She scowls at me. "Do I have to spell it out?"

I think the cubicles were empty. I think. Actually I don't know. I don't remember checking them. Gemma was in one of the cubicles. That's how she overheard us. I can't believe we'd be so stupid not to check. And let's not even think about how, once again, my powers desert me when I'm in trouble.

"No. I get it. Gemma was in the cubicle and overheard Tara and me." I lean against Alice's desk, my shoulders sagging.

"Yes. I take it you don't want the money any more." She shakes the mirror in my direction, and I see the money in the envelope peeking out. It's so close. Maybe I should lean over and grab it.

"Of course she wants the money," Tara shouts, causing me to start. "The only person who didn't get a proper reading was you, Alice. And that was not Megan's fault. So you can have your money back and give us the rest."

"No. You owe me," Alice replies, clutching the mirror close to her. "I'll never forgive you for what you've done. And Dan better watch out too. Because he's just as much to blame."

For a moment, a look of raw emotion crosses her face. It doesn't last, but it's enough for me to see how much she's hurting. I feel really mean.

"No. He isn't," I say. "I persuaded him to do it. And he didn't mind. He was glad to go out with you, Alice."

Well, I can't get into any more trouble, can I? And if it placates Alice a little then it's got to be good. We've seriously hurt her. Then again, look what she did to Ben. Maybe it's like karma. And her time has come. And maybe I'm being stupid. Ben's hurt is not mine to seek revenge on.

"I don't care. If he was that keen he wouldn't have needed you to tell him to ask me out. You're just making it up to worm your way out of trouble. Nice try. But next time try harder. Now GET OUT."

Her words reverberate around the room, and even the candle on her table wobbles.

They also have the desired effect of bringing several girls down to her room, including Kate, Head of House. That's all I need. I forgot her room was in this block. What I don't understand is why roll-call didn't last much longer. It usually does. Not that it matters now.

"Alice, what's wrong?" asks Selma, one of her friends.

Alice blushes. Maybe she hasn't told them what happened.

"Alice stole Megan's money." Tara snaps.

All eyes focus on me, and I nod my head. In unison they turn back to look at Alice.

"Alice?" Selma appears really shocked, as do the other girls standing in the doorway. Well that confirms what I thought. She didn't tell anyone.

"It wasn't like that," Alice snarls. "This bitch has got one over all of us with this psychic crap. She makes things up, so I took the money to return it to everyone."

"She didn't make up mine," Kate says.

I flash a grateful smile.

"Nor mine," calls someone from outside in the hall, I can't see who, but I love her all the same.

"Well, she did mine." Alice yells. "And I can prove it."

The collective gasp from our audience, which now seems to have grown in numbers, causes my heart to plummet.

"There were extenuating circumstances," says Tara.

"Like what?" Alice asks.

"Yes," adds Selma.

There are also a few nods from the girls standing by the door.

"Tell them, Megan," Tara says. "Tell them what it was that made you lie to Alice, even though you didn't want to and you'd never done it before or since."

But what shall I say? Not that my feelings for Dan stopped me from giving her a proper reading, and I didn't want to let her down. No way am I going to admit that in front of everyone. It would be all round the school in about five minutes flat and then I'd be a laughing stock. Not to mention what Dan would think.

Also, technically I didn't lie because I said Dan would ask her on a date and he did. Though I don't think me saying that would go down very well.

"I'm so sorry, Alice. I shouldn't have done it. And I promise it was only you. But the day you came to see me I'd had this awful migraine earlier, and though the headache had gone I still felt a bit fuzzy. I think that stopped me from reading you clearly."

"And you couldn't tell me this, because?" Alice asks.

"I didn't want to upset you. Besides, I told you I couldn't see details but you kept pushing."

Alice gives a hollow laugh. "You didn't want to upset me, so you thought making something up, which resulted in me being embarrassed beyond belief, was better than being told you couldn't do the reading because of a headache? You can't be serious."

When she puts it like that, I guess it does sound really lame. Then again, it's not like it's the truth.

"I'm sorry, but..."

"What's going on here?" The sound of Mrs. Johnson's voice stops me in my tracks.

# CHAPTER 17

I GLANCE AT TARA, who unfortunately is looking exactly the way I feel. I guess she's thinks we're toast too.

"Well?" Mrs. Johnson barks. She is now standing in the room, thanks to the crowds parting to let her through. "I said, what's going on? I come over to see Emily, and all I can hear is your shouting, Alice, which is so loud it's disturbing everyone else in the block."

"Ask *her*," mutters Alice, nodding in my direction.

"Alice stole Megan's money because she made up the readings," calls a voice from outside.

"Alice, am I hearing right? You stole Megan's money?" Mrs. J sounds as shocked as Tara and I were when we first found out.

"It's not like that. I only took what's rightfully mine. Plus money Megan scammed from the others who went to her for *so called* readings."

Mrs. J inhales deeply through her nose. And we all know what that means.

"Megan, Tara, and Alice. My office, *now*. I want a full explanation. And I'm warning you," she glares at me, and not the others, which is par for the course, as she always picks on me, "it better be a good one." She turns on her heels and goes to walk out the door.

As we follow, I notice Alice placing the mirror on the table.

"Hey," I say in a low voice. "What do you think you're doing?"

"Shut up," Alice growls. "We'll sort this later."

"You can't leave the money there. Someone might take it. You can't leave it anywhere in here, for the same reason. Too many people know about it. Just bring it."

"Bring what?" Mrs. Johnson asks, her head peering over her shoulder. Oh, for goodness sake, has this woman got supersonic hearing, or what? My voice was barely above a whisper.

"Nothing," says Alice. She flashes a *look* in my direction.

"Just bring it," I say through clenched teeth and about as quiet as I can be without simply mouthing the words.

Alice gives a very loud sigh, pulls the envelope away from the back of the mirror and stuffs it in her pocket. Mrs. J seems oblivious to what we just did and carries on marching down the corridor. We follow in silence as she goes down the stairs, out the entrance and into the quad, where she walks around the edge, to avoid the grassy bit (school rule... keep off the grass), and heads toward her office.

Once inside she gestures for us all to sit down and she remains standing, leaning against her big dark wooden desk. She folds her arms, in a very threatening manner. I swallow hard.

"Right. Who's going to speak first?" She stares at each of us in turn, her gaze lingering a moment longer on me. I think. Unless I'm being paranoid about how she feels about me. Which is entirely possible. But my feelings are not without cause, when I remember her treatment of me in the past. "Megan. Let's hear from you," she says after a long pause during which time none of us had uttered a word.

"Alice took my money because..."

"Yes, yes, yes. We've already established that." She waves her hand dismissively in my direction. "Because you *scammed* her and lots of others. So tell me about this *scam* of yours."

"It's not like that, Mrs. Johnson, is it Tara?"

"No. Megan was giving readings, and..."

"Readings? From novels?" A frown crosses Mrs. Johnson's face.

"No," says Tara. "Psychic readings."

"*Psychic* readings?" Mrs. J shakes her head. "How can you give psychic readings, Megan?"

"Exactly," pipes up Alice. "She can't. She makes things up and then charges fifteen dollars for the privilege."

What a bitch. She knows it was only hers I made up. Now she's making me look even worse.

"Let me get this straight," says Mrs. J. "You pretend to be psychic and charge people when they come to see you."

"No," yell Tara and I at the same time.

"I *am* psychic," I say.

"Yes. She *is* psychic," Tara adds.

"And how long exactly have you had this *psychic* ability? Because it's the first I've heard about it."

"Years. I just haven't used it before." How lame does that sound? "I didn't want to use it until I was certain about doing it properly."

"It's true." Tara glares at Alice.

"So show me," Mrs. J says, standing upright and putting her right arm behind her. "How many fingers am I holding up behind my back?"

"My ability doesn't quite work like that. I tune into people when they ask me something and I can tell them what I see and how it relates to what they want to know."

"And I want to know how many fingers I'm holding up." Mrs. J demands. "If you're really psychic then you'll have no trouble. It's hardly rocket science, is it?" She stares at me, her eyes dancing menacingly as though daring me to defy her.

"Three." Okay, so I made it up. I've got a one in five chance of being right.

"Hmmph. Lucky guess," Mrs. J. growls.

I think she's made up her mind about me without even thinking about it. She's desperate to find me a fake.

"Now do you believe me?"

"If you correctly tell me how many fingers I am holding up twice more and then I suppose so."

*Twice more!*

I glance either side of me. Alice is looking smug and Tara is shaking her head.

I draw in a deep breath and focus as hard as I possibly can on Mrs. J and the hand behind her back. Nothing comes through at all, except something makes me look slightly to the side and suddenly I can see a reflection of her hand in the glass door of the trophy cabinet that's on the wall behind her.

"Four," I blurt out. A smile crosses my face before she even says anything.

"And now?" Mrs. J asks.

"Two." I say unable to hide the excitement in my voice. Screw you, Alice and Mrs. Johnson.

"Wrong." Mrs. Johnson snaps.

"I am not wrong," I say, hotly, jumping up from the seat.

"Are you doubting my word?" Mrs. Johnson leans forward slightly and glares at me.

"Yes," I shout. "I know exactly how many fingers you were holding up because I saw it in the reflection in the cabinet. And..." Tell me I didn't just admit to cheating. How can I be so dumb?

I glance at Tara. The hopeless expression on her face says it all. I'm screwed.

"Why am I not surprised by your behavior, my girl?' Mrs. Johnson positively glows with anger.

"But, Mrs. Johnson. Holding up fingers isn't the same as..."

"Enough,' she bellows. "I don't want to hear another word about your supposed psychic ability. And I forbid you to offer readings to anyone else. Do you understand?"

"But..."

"Don't *but* me. You had your chance. I will not tolerate being lied to."

"But..."

"Do you want the Principal and your parents involved? Because I assure you that can be arranged."

"No." I hang my head. Why on earth did we decide to look for the money? At least before I could still do my readings and make up some of what I've lost. But now.

"And after you leave here, you're to find everyone who has had a reading and refund their money."

# CHAPTER 18

"AT LEAST YOU got the money back," Tara says, as we're heading back to our block.

I glance down at the envelope in my clenched fist and feel the anger well up inside. This is *so* unfair. Mrs. Johnson is just getting me back for everything I've done in the past. Why should I refund all the money? It's not like I cheated anyone, not counting Alice. And she's got hers, as she took it from the money before giving it to me. The rest is mine and I should be able to keep it.

"I don't get you. It doesn't belong to me any more, so who cares if I've got it for a few more hours?"

"Try because the only people who know who's had readings are you and me. Which means we don't have to return all the money back. Who's to know?"

I come to an abrupt halt, turn my head and glare at her.

"*Try* the people who don't get their money. It's not like this thing is going to be secret. We'll have them queuing up before we can blink. In fact, knowing how the gossip works in this place they'll be waiting at my door as we speak."

"Yeah, I guess. God, this sucks." Tara gives a loud sigh.

"Tell me about it. There's only one thing for it."

"What?" Tara frowns.

"I'm going to phone my parents and tell them everything. Get it over with."

---

"HI MOM, IT'S ME."

"Megan? You don't usually phone during the week, what's wrong?"

*Hi Megan, good to hear from you.* How does she know something's wrong? Am I that transparent?

"Yeah, everything's fine. Sort of fine. Something's happened at school that I thought I ought to let you know about, before..."

"Oh Megan. What now?" She gives an extremely loud sigh, causing me to momentarily hold the phone from my ear. "I thought you promised not to get into any more trouble." Now I'm feeling even guiltier than before. "I'm *not* in trouble. Not really."

"Either you are, or you're not. Which is it?"

I lean back against the wall and draw in a deep breath. I've got to make sure this comes across as not that serious.

"You know how you've always taught us to take responsibility for our actions?"

"Yes."

"And you know when I went to stay at Tara's a little while ago?"

"Yes."

"I accidentally crashed their new ATV and..."

"You, what? How many times have we told you..."

"Mom. Listen." I pause a moment, to confirm she's actually stopped talking. "It's cool. They didn't blame me. It was an accident. And the ATV was insured, so all I have to do is pay the deductible. Which is why I was trying to earn some money. I wanted to take responsibility for what I'd done."

"Megan, when we say 'take responsibility' that doesn't mean you don't tell us. Especially something like this. You could have been seriously hurt."

"I wanted to sort it out myself, without getting you involved. You had enough to worry about with the accountant." My voice starts to crack and I force the tears back.

"So what's happened? Why are you telling me now?"

"I was earning the money to pay them back by giving psychic readings to people at school, and..."

"Sorry, can you say that again. For a moment I thought you said *psychic readings*." She giggles.

"I did."

"And people paid you for this?"

"Yes."

"But you're not psychic." She starts to laugh. "This is priceless. I have to hand it to you Megan, you're nothing if not inventive. Not that I approve of you taking people's money like this, you understand. But really."

Now *she* thinks I've been scamming people. This is getting worse by the second.

"Mom, I am psychic. I know things about people. It's been happening to me for years. I just didn't tell you."

"No. That's impossible."

"It's true. I'm not making it up. Whatever Alice Grant may say."

There's a silence that seems to go on forever. It's weird, I can almost hear Mom's mind mulling over my words.

"Your grandma used to tell me that her sister Dora could predict things. But I never met her, so I don't know if that's true. Dora lived in England and died when I was about your age." She draws in a breath. "And you're sure you can really tell the future?

"Yes. I promise I'm not making it up."

"So what's the problem?" she asks, as though suddenly remembering the reason for me phoning. "Is it something to do with the girl you just mentioned? Alice somebody?"

"Grant. Yes, it is. I made up her reading because..."

"You've just told me you're psychic and now you're telling me you made up readings. Oh, Megan. Why? You know that your father and I are..."

"Mom. Please, just hear me out. I have done hundreds of readings" Okay, maybe not that many, but I need to make an impact. "And they were all successful. Everyone was happy. This problem with Alice, I don't know why but I couldn't get anything. And she was asking about Dan, and you don't know her. If I'd have admitted to not being able to help she'd have made my life hell. She'd have totally ruined everything." The irony in what I've just said hits me. "Like she has already." My voice cracks.

"Megan it will be okay. We can sort this out. You'll be fine." The caring tone in Mom's voice makes me want to cry.

"It won't." I sniff. "Mrs. Johnson says I have to give all the money back, because she believed what Alice said, that I was just scamming everyone. Now I won't be able to pay Tara's parents the money I owe them, and everything's ruined." I start to cry again.

"Now, let's see how we can sort this out. How much money do you owe Tara's parents?" She's so cool.

"Seven hundred dollars."

"Seven hundred dollars. Oh, Megan." I can picture her leaning forward onto her hand and shaking her head. "And you made that much money from doing readings?"

"Not yet. Up until Alice stole the money I'd made..."

"Alice stole the money?"

"Yes. And when we went to get it back Mrs. Johnson caught us arguing with Alice about it."

"Let me get this straight. Alice stole your money and you're the one getting in trouble. That's not right. I'm going to see the Principal. I won't have you victimized like this."

"No. You can't. You know how the teachers all stick together. He'll only be on Mrs. J's side and that will make things worse."

"Here's what we'll do. We'll pay Tara's parents, and you can work for us in the office over the next vacation to pay back the rest."

Relief washes over me. Closely followed by guilt. Guilt for not going to Mom and Dad first. Guilt for risking getting kicked out of school. And even guilt for deceiving Alice.

"Thank you so much. I promise to work really hard and do anything you ask, and I won't moan about it."

# CHAPTER 19

"AND SHE DIDN'T TEAR you off a strip? Tara asks, sounding surprised.

"For once she thinks we're in the right. And I'm not complaining."

"Shame about having to work most of the vacation though, because you won't be able to come and stay. How long will it take for your to earn the money?"

"I'm not sure." The initial excitement about solving my problem is beginning to wear off.

"You could always do some more readings on the side."

"Very funny. I think my career as a psychic has definitely come to an end."

"It's a pity, though. Especially as I have a long list of people waiting for an appointment."

"I can't, Tara. If I get caught, it would be suspension at the very least, maybe even expulsion." I didn't even want to think about the hell Alice had in store for me for the rest of our high school career.

"Unless we do it in the vacation." She's nothing if not persistent.

"Well, we know that won't happen because I'll be working during the week. Plus, how can we if everyone lives all over the State?"

"Good point. There must be a way. We just haven't thought of it." She gets a faraway look in her eyes. "I've got it. You can do it online. Skype. And if you combine it with working for your parents you'll have enough money in a couple of weeks to pay the deductable. Then we can have some fun."

It's tempting. But I don't know. Then again...

"Okay. I'll do it."

We high-five, except suddenly a thought hits me and I leave my arm hanging in the air.

"It won't work," I say.

"Why not?"

"How am I going to get the money?"

I thump the bed in frustration.

"They could send you the money first and once you've received it you can get in touch with them. Or they could transfer it into your bank account. That makes it quicker."

"I don't know."

"Hey, Megan." Hearing my name makes me start, and we both turn our heads in the direction of the voice.

Standing at the door is Kate and behind her at least four or five others, if not more. It's difficult to tell from this angle.

I jump up from the bed and walk toward her.

"Hi, Kate. Is everything okay?"

"Yeah, it's cool. We've just come to tell you we think Mrs. J was wrong making you refund all the money."

My jaw drops.

"Thanks. After what I did to Alice, I don't blame her."

"She had it coming to her," says Lori, who's standing next to Kate. "I couldn't stop laughing for ages." The other girls nod and say yes in agreement. "And it's not like you did it to anyone else. You can't have done, your readings were so spot on."

"Thanks, guys. I can't tell you what that means to me." Warmth washes over me.

"Yes," says Kate. "Which is why we've come to give you back our money." She holds out her hand which has fifteen dollars resting in it. "Here," she says while I just stare at it.

"I don't know what to say." My voice is all choked.

"Don't say anything," says Lori, "except that you won't stop because I need to see you again, urgently." I frown. "Have you seen the hot dude who's just arrived in Braunston House?" I shake my head. "Well, when you do you'll understand my need for a reading."

Everyone starts laughing, including me. Though I think my laughter is so full of emotion it could turn into tears at any moment.

"Thanks, so much guys," I say after we've finally stopped laughing and they go to leave. That is, all of them except Kate, who hangs back until everyone's gone.

"Can I have a quiet word?" Kate asks.

I glance across at Tara who's standing by my desk.

"Don't mind me, I need the bathroom," Tara says, as she walks past us and through the door.

I close the door behind Tara.

"What's wrong?" I ask.

"Nothing. The opposite, in fact. I just wanted to tell you that my mom's boyfriend has gone."

"You must be so relieved."

"You bet. And it's all down to you. I can't thank you enough."

I feel myself blush. "It's nothing."

"It's more than nothing. You saved my life. Without your reading I wouldn't have had the courage to tell Mom." Kate gives me a huge hug. "Anything you want me to do for you, just say."

"You mean, like telling Dan Ross my powers are real and not made up?"

"He believes in you, I know he does."

"He doesn't. He thinks all psychics are fake. He told me. And the Alice incident just reinforced it."

"Megan," she rests her arm on mine. "Take it from me, Dan knows exactly how good you are. We were talking about it this afternoon."

I swallow hard. "You were? When? Why? What did he say?" My mind's a mass of incoherent thoughts. Surely she can't be telling the truth. He's never shown any signs of believing me before. So why would he start now. He was just saying that he did to Kate.

"During English, we were talking about Alice and I told him how good you'd been with me. Not the actual problem, obviously. Just that you were really good."

"And now he believes me. It's…"

"Wait," Kate says, holding her hand up. "He didn't suddenly believe in you because of me. When I told him he said 'I know, she's awesome'. You see, he doesn't need convincing."

"But. I thought..."

"Megan. He's a guy." She laughs. "He probably felt mean for not believing you right away so decided not to say anything at all."

"The warped male logic." I shake my head. But inside I'm feeling decidedly warm and fuzzy.

# CHAPTER 20

I CAN'T BELIEVE how everything has turned out. I've got most of my money back, thanks to Kate telling everyone what she did, and Dan knows I'm not a fake.

"For once in my life things are on the up," I say to Tara as we're skipping along the path near the football fields. "I mean, can they get any better? I'll have enough money to pay back my parents by the end of the first week of the holidays, there should still be some money left for spending, and my powers aren't in question."

"So there's nothing else you want?" Tara smirks in a knowing way.

"Like what?"

"Like a chat with Dan, maybe. You might want to stop clowning around as he's walking up behind you." My stomach suddenly goes into a total mass of butterflies.

"Hey, Dan," I squeak, as I turn around to see him.

"Megan. Tara." He flashes one of his drop dead smiles, that after all this time still send me crazy.

"I've got to go and speak to Mr. Timms about my photography portfolio," Tara says. "See you back at the house, Megan. Bye Dan."

I swear she just winked at him.

"But," I say, then stop as Tara runs away faster than I've ever seen her run before.

If I didn't know better, I'd say she's been up to one of her tricks. If she has then she better watch out.

"Megan," Dan's voice interrupts my vengeful thoughts.

"Yes." My heart is racing big time and beads of sweat form on my forehead.

"Are you free to talk for a moment?"

"Sure." Hardly an eloquent response but it's a major achievement when you consider the state of my insides.

"My Dad's coming back early. Which means you can't use my house for readings."

"Okay. Thanks for letting me know." For a moment I thought he just wanted to chat. Now I know the truth.

"I'm really sorry. I hope that's not going to ruin everything for you."

"I'm not sure I'll be doing it any more."

"You must carry on." Dan nods for emphasis.

"Excuse me?" I shake my head, not sure I heard correctly. "What did you say?"

"You must carry on."

"Because?"

"You have a gift," Dan says sheepishly, then looks down at his feet.

"So you don't think I'm a phony like you said before." I know I shouldn't be mean, but I can't resist a little teasing.

"I never said you were a phony. Just the ones you see on TV. And I'm still not sure about them."

"And what made you change your mind about me? Not the Alice incident, that's for sure."

I know Kate said he believed me, but hearing it from his lips makes it seem real. And makes me like him even more. If that's possible.

"Actually, it was the *Alice incident* and your reaction to it. I just knew you were telling the truth about it being a one off."

"Thank you," I say.

"What for?"

"Believing in me. Being honest and admitting you were wrong before."

He shrugs. "Any time."

"I guess I better go," I say, looking at my watch. "I've got to get ready for drama rehearsal. I'll see you there, if you're going."

"I am. But before you go, there's something I want to ask you."

"Yes."

"Remember you owe me for letting you use my house, and for the torture I went through with Alice?"

"Yes," I say, my heart thumping so loudly in my rib cage that he can probably hear it.

"It's payback time." He grins.

"Okay." I frown.

"I'd like you come to the Prom with me?"

I think I've died and gone to heaven.

# ACKNOWLEDGMENTS

Thanks, as usual, to my fabulous critique partners Amanda Ashby and Christina Phillips. Thanks, also, to my wonderful editor, Shannon Godwin, for your support and advice in getting this book together. Thanks to my fellow authors in this anthology. It's been great fun working with you.

Finally, a mention for my family. Thanks for all your support.

# TANGENT

MAREE ANDERSON

# CHAPTER 1

RIXON HOOKED his fingers into the sagging chain mesh fence, pretending to watch a ragged bunch of kids shoot hoops. The bravado that had sustained him until now had abruptly gone AWOL and the doubts were crowding in. If he failed....

His gut tried to crawl up his throat and he mentally kicked himself in the ass. Failure was not an option.

As he'd done time and time again in the weeks since she'd disappeared, he tried to get a lock on Lily's energy signature. But her unique pattern was still blurred and nebulous—like viewing a night-lit city through a body of water.

Fear prickled his spine. Shit. They must be shooting her full of drugs—

*Either that or she doesn't want to be found,* an insidious little voice whispered in his head. *She's blocking you. She's setting you free, man. This is your chance. All you need to do is walk away....*

Rix told that voice to go to hell.

He had cast himself in the role of Lily's protector and mentor from the minute he'd first spotted the shivering, half-starved waif going through a trashcan out back of the strip the locals called Restaurant Alley. He'd taken her under his wing, shown her the ropes—the eateries with staff that would dole out leftovers without expecting anything in return. The soup kitchens that turned a blind eye to underage kids and didn't report them to CPS. The do-gooders who handed over used clothing and shoes and stuff without getting preachy. Lily had been an integral part of his life for two years and damned if he would abandon her now... even if she had upped and left him without so much as a goddamn note.

Didn't matter what she'd done, or how she'd done it, Rix refused to give up on Lily until she looked him in the eye and told him to his face she didn't want him around, didn't need him anymore. Until then, she was stuck with him. And if she was in danger, Rix would do everything in his power to save her. Because Lily might view him as her savior, but the truth was *she'd* saved *him*—given him a reason to try'n make something of his life. It was cliché as all get-out for sure, but it was kinda like what the dude in that movie had said. How'd it go again? Yeah. Lily made Rixon want to be a better man.

He exhaled with a hiss, relaxed his jaw, rolled the painful tension from his shoulders. So far as plans went, it was the only one he had. So he wouldn't think about failure, refused to dwell on what those fuckers might be doing to Lily while he sat on his ass, freaking out and rehashing the past. No more delays. No more excuses. Time to do whatever it took to get her out of there.

But what if....

What if he wasn't as good as he thought he was? What if he got caught before he could get her out? Wasn't like he was a freaking superhero or anything. Wasn't like he had unique abilities either. There were others like him. *Liminals*—humans whose energy vibrated at frequencies outside the range that normal human senses could perceive. And sure, it could be useful to transport yourself someplace in the blink of an eye by slipping through realities, or planes of existence, or whatever the boffins wanted to label it. But phasing wasn't always reliable. Nor was it risk free.

Breathe, he chanted silently, just breathe. You're strong—off the freaking charts according to your mom. There're no ifs, buts, or maybes. You can do this. So man up and grow some balls, dude. It's time to rock and roll.

He pivoted on his heel, heading for the public restrooms where he wedged himself into a grungy stall.

It had taken a bit of doing but he'd finally pinned down Lily's elusive energy sig to a two-block radius. After that he'd hung with the locals for a bit and carefully asked around.

Turned out four local kids had been approached to take part in some kind of covert clinical trials. Three had shown up a week later flashing a tidy wad of cash. None of them knew for sure what had happened to the kid who hadn't made it back—a scrawny no-hoper addict who'd been tolerated but garnered little respect. But whenever they speculated on his fate, their obvious envy that he'd been "chosen for something big" clearly signaled they expected him to rock on up in the next couple of months flashing newfound riches.

They all thought he was one lucky prick. Rix wasn't so sure. He was betting the missing kid was a liminal, too, like Lily. So if you followed the logic, someone was looking for lims among the runaways and street-rats who wouldn't be missed. And Rix didn't need to be a freaking rocket scientist to realize that couldn't be a good thing.

Worry turned the energy drink he'd gulped down a half-hour ago to acid in his belly. Fingering the small wooden kiwi he always kept in a pocket, Rix smacked down his fears and locked them up tight. If he couldn't get his head in the game he would screw this up for sure.

A couple more deep, even breaths, and he could think clearly again.

He'd spent the better part of a week scoping out one particular high-rise with discreet gold "KP" lettering on its lobby doors. The building fit the descriptions he'd been given and so far as Rix was concerned, the whole setup screamed they had something to hide.

Next, he'd prowled the surrounding streets, orienting himself.

Phasing to a convenient alleyway across the street from the building was stage one of his plan—the warm-up. Rix closed his eyes, blocking out the illegible insults scrawled on the closed door of the stall, the stench of shit and urine and overflowing trashcans, directing his sole focus to visualizing that alleyway.

Three heartbeats later he cracked open an eyelid.

Recycling bins crammed into a corner of the alleyway. A moldering pile of newspapers beside them. Uneven asphalt beneath his boots. A distinctive tag by a local graffiti artist....

Success. The satisfied quirk of his lips flattened to a grim line. Because now came the hard part.

There were certain rules to being a liminal, and one of them was that lims could supposedly only phase to a place they'd been before. But there were tales of lims accidentally phasing someplace they'd been reading about at the time, or had seen in a movie—imagining the place so vividly, so completely, their hindbrains took over and transported them there. Fact or urban myth, Rix had figured that so long as he could piece together an accurate enough description from the returnees, there was no logical reason why he couldn't do it: phase directly to a place he'd never been. In this case, the place in question was a bathroom inside the KP building that all three of the kids had used at one time or another during their stay. One of them had even described a unique detail that Rix could use as a focus.

It had seemed so simple in theory. But now, faced with actually *doing* it? Yeah. Not so much. And Rix was forced to admit the bald truth: If it was *that* freaking simple, every liminal with half a brain would be skipping to exotic locales in the blink of an eye.

He cast a last critical gaze over the baggy, generic blue coverall he'd acquired, and adjusted the tool belt he'd slung about his hips. One last tug of the cap over his eyes, and there were no more excuses to delay.

Rix sauntered toward the main street, taking it slow and easy. At the mouth of the alley he halted, rummaging in the pocket of his coverall for a disposable lighter and the cigarette he'd bummed from one of the kids—just another overworked, underpaid guy, in no particular hurry to get to his shit job. He lit up, inhaled, steeled himself not to cough up a lung. Despite years on the streets, there were a fair number of things Rix didn't indulge in. Smoking was one of those things—he had more important things to spend his hard-earned cash on.

He took another drag and exhaled a curl of smoke, eyeing the silhouette of the big dude lurking inside the building's lobby. Rix had pegged the man as security from the get-go—hence the reason he couldn't bank on strolling right on in and charming his way past the pretty young thing manning the desk.

Too much to hope he'd catch a break and the guy would be off sick today. Looked like he'd have to do this the hard way.

Pinching off the end of his cig, Rix stowed it in a pocket, and ducked back into the shadows of the alleyway. And then, fixing every last detail the kids had described in his mind's eye, he phased.

Phasing had never been something Rix had to work at. He'd been a natural from a young age—much to the confusion of the various adults tasked with his care after his mom and dad passed. Those *caregivers*, for want of a better word, had believed Rix was somehow picking locks or escaping out windows. They'd tried all manner of disciplinary tactics to rein him in, including punishments that would shock the pants off your average social worker. But whatever they'd done to him had only made Rix stronger, more determined. And perhaps, a little too cocky for his own good. Because he damn sure wasn't finding things easy this time 'round.

The transition from this plane of existence to another started out smooth and uneventful, but the instant it occurred to him this phase seemed to be taking much, much longer than usual, it all turned to crap. Vibrating energy, previously a harmonious hum flowing though his body, began to buzz angrily... and then abruptly stall, as though smacking against an internal barrier. After a scary-ass pause that seemed to last an eternity, pent up energy burst through him again, pulsing and throbbing so intensely that, even in his subliminal state, the walls of his veins felt stretched to bursting.

Please God, his brain and body wouldn't give up the battle to stay subliminal and catapult him *Between*... where he'd be stranded until he regained enough energy to phase back to the real world. Between was a neither here nor there place that lay in wait for careless liminals who'd either expended too much energy or lost focus during a phase. Once ghost images of the last physical place you'd inhabited faded, the sensory deprivation was so complete, trapped liminals had been known to go insane. And while Rix was confident he could handle the mental stress of Between, he couldn't afford to sit there with his thumb up his ass—not when what seemed like a mere hour Between could equal a day in real time. Not when Lily needed him.

The energy flowing through him hiccupped again, this time twisting into a knot before surging onward.

Shit. He was on the verge of splintering apart and defaulting Between. Rix narrowed his focus to the message the kid had told him was scratched on the inside of the pale gray, toilet stall door. *Run, run, as fast as you can!* that message urged. Its author had signed off with the initials *GM*—Gingerbread Man. And although the kid who'd mentioned the creepy message had scoffed, it had spooked him big-time—Rix could tell from the way the boy's gaze had slid from his, the way he'd hunched and shifted uneasily.

He ran through each individual letter of the message, forming and shaping them in his mind, blending them into words, a sentence, a warning. And then, acutely aware he was out of time, and he'd either succeed or wind up Between and there was fuck-all he could do about it now, he quit fighting... and let his energy sweep him away.

# CHAPTER 2

RIXON UNDERSTOOD there'd been one big-ass hole in his logic the instant he came to, sprawled on the cold tiles of the toilet stall floor. If anyone had been using the stall when he'd abruptly become liminal, he would have been royally screwed. As it was, he could only hope no one had discovered him while he was out cold... and was even now sprinting off to alert security.

It took two tries to heave his butt off the floor, and he only made it as far as the toilet bowl.

When he'd finished emptying his stomach, he lay there for a bit, curled around the cold porcelain. Sheer willpower finally got him up and moving. Biting his lip to stifle a groan, he slumped atop the toilet seat, elbows braced on knees, head hanging, waiting for the pounding in his skull to ease. Blood throbbed hotly through his veins but his abdomen felt strangely hollow, as though cored by a raging torrent of electricity. His bones, his skin—even his effing hair follicles—hurt. And thinking logically was *so* not a good idea right now, either, but that didn't stop his stupid brain from chewing over why'n the heck he felt like shit.

Why'n the heck had *this* phase affected him so badly?

Huh. Maybe this was the reason lims weren't supposed to attempt phases to places they'd never been before—because once you exited the subliminal state and your body re-formed, you felt like you'd been steamrollered and turned inside out.

When he could focus without feeling like his head was about to explode, he squinted at the cheap men's wristwatch Lily had found a few months back. A mere ten minutes had passed but it sure felt like a freaking lifetime. On the plus side, he'd phased to the right place. At least, it was highly unlikely there were *two* dull gray toilet stall doors inscribed with a message from the Gingerbread Man, exhorting people to run like hell.

Rix climbed to his feet, steadied himself with a palm against one side of the stall, and then stumbled out. He checked the cramped shower stall next to the toilet, and found it empty... thank all popular gods. Hunching over the small washbasin, he splashed cold water on his aching face, and blotted his eyelids and mouth with the frayed sleeve of his coverall.

Better. Kind of. Because the mirror above the washbasin revealed hollowed eyes, ashen skin, and pain grooves etching the bridge of his nose and mouth. Looked like he'd been partying real hard all night and then some, and desperately needed to sleep it off—which, come to think of it, could work to his advantage, because right now he looked nothing like a stealthy intruder about to break someone out.

His brain revved up a gear, prodding him to quit stalling and move his sorry ass. The longer he lingered here, the more chance of getting busted.

He glanced around the bathroom. Yep, the kids had been right on the money. There was a floor-to-ceiling cupboard in the wall on the right—locked of course, but Rix had never let a basic locking mechanism stop him. He fished the lock picks from his boot, and had the cupboard open in thirty seconds flat.

Broom. Mop. Bucket. A few basic cleaning products. Dust cloths. Hardly worth the effort of locking up. Then again, in the right hands a mop could be a deadly weapon. And that metal bucket would sure do a bit of damage to someone's skull. Not to mention the unpleasant side effects of copping a faceful of ammonia. But Rix wasn't looking for weapons. All the kids had described guards armed with Tasers and God knew what else, and Rix wasn't arrogant enough to believe he could prevail over armed guards. His best bet was to fly under the radar and not get noticed. And, as he'd learned during a temporary stint to cover for a friend, no one took any notice of janitors. All he needed from this cupboard were a few props to beef up his disguise—kind of like strolling around an office building with a clipboard, looking all busy and shit.

He chose the bucket and mop. For good measure, he dumped a container of disinfectant in the bucket.

Geez! Wrinkling his nose at the nostril-searing, eye-watering smell, he filled the empty container with tap water, and dumped that in the bucket, too, swirling the contents. Nice. Anyone got too nosy, he'd accidentally on purpose spill some of this stuff at their feet. Or over their fancy shoes— whatever worked. Should be the perfect deterrent. The empty disinfectant container he refilled with water, capped, and stowed in the cupboard.

Rix grabbed his props, satisfied he'd done what he could. Ignoring his abused muscles and pounding head, he ambled from the bathroom, into the corridor.

His sources had told him where Lily was likely being held and as he walked, he consulted his mental map. Shouldn't be far now....

Yep. So far, so good. Here was the row of doors the kids had described— each one leading to a small room that served as sleeping quarters.

He eased on up to the first door and paused, making a production of squeezing out his mop and swishing it over the floor. And then he peered through the rectangular viewing window.

His heart galloped when he spotted a figure curled in a fetal position on the narrow bed, facing the wall. He couldn't see her face. Didn't need to: He would know her anywhere. Lily. The girl he'd sworn to protect... and failed to keep safe.

As though something inside him had called out to her, she uncurled, rolled toward the door, opened her eyes... and gazed up at him. Her eyes seemed clear. Which meant she wasn't fighting the effects of drugs. Relief washed through him and he mentally thanked whichever deity happened to be watching over him and Lily right now.

His confidence returning, Rix dumped his mop in the bucket, grinned, and gave Lily a cocky little finger-wave through the window.

Her deep brown eyes widened. And then, to his chagrin, she sat up and made shooing gestures, her lips forming the word *Go!* over and over.

Take off? Leave her in that sparse, cell-like room? Nyuh uh. Not gonna happen. Lily should know him better than that.

When he beckoned her toward the door, an adamant shake of her head told him she wasn't about to make this easy. Her eyes rounded as her mouth opened and formed that word again. *Go!*

Huh. Odds on she was yelling right now. The room must be sound-proofed.

Rix tried the door. Also locked. With a fancy keypad that needed an entry code. Typical. But hey, not an insurmountable problem. All he needed to do was phase in, sync his energy vibrations to Lily's, and phase them both the hell out of this place. And if they'd convinced her to stay—done some head-number on her—well, too damn bad. He'd force a sync and apologize afterward. Like, once he'd gotten her somewhere safe and she could be reasoned with.

Rix mouthed the words, *Stay put.* Last thing he needed was Lily careening off the bed and ending up in the exact spot he was trying to phase to. If that happened, his energy could instinctively react and catapult him Between as a protective measure.

He couldn't take that chance.

He held Lily's gaze, willing her to cooperate, projecting for all he was worth that everything was gonna be okay. He didn't know what he'd expected to see—happiness that he'd shown up because it proved she meant the world to him, perhaps? At the very least, relief that she was no longer alone. Instead her face kinda froze but her eyes flashed a fear so raw and stark, his stomach swan-dived to his boots.

What the eff? Lily had always seen through Rix's imposing physical presence. She'd never once been afraid of him.

Too late, he realized she was staring past him. The back of his neck prickled and Rix had just enough time to think, *Ah, crap!* before something jammed into the base of his spine... and all his nerve endings went supernova.

---

DAMN, but his skull was throbbing like some sadistic prick had hammered a spike into his brain. Rix cracked one eyelid the merest slit, and his limited vision was seared with bright white and deep-sea green. He let the eyelid droop shut, embracing darkness as he fought past the pain to interpret what he'd seen.

White-blonde hair. Intense green eyes....

A face. Belonging to a young guy, who was bending over him and—

Shit! The bastard was trying to force a sync. And the only thing standing in his way right now were the mental barriers Rix had honed in the years he'd been on his own.

Rix shored up those barriers, thankful for the hours he'd dedicated to erecting and maintaining mental defenses. No point being a badass during waking hours if you were vulnerable when you slept. Case in point, this guy might've succeeded in mapping his energy signature—meaning he could potentially yank Rix out of a phase, and even summon him if he were skilled enough. The mere thought made Rix break into a cold sweat.

"Don't bother trying to fake unconsciousness," a clipped, prep school tone advised. "I know you're awake."

Rix opened both eyelids, noting the strain etched into Blondie's too-pretty face with satisfaction bordering on unholy glee. He noted, too, the eyebrow piercing—a small personal statement that didn't gel with the expensive clothes or the fancy, born-with-a-silver-spoon-in-his-mouth voice. A wannabe rebel? Interesting.

"Thanks for the tip," he drawled. "And in the spirit of sharing and all, here's one for you: Don't bother trying to map me. Best case scenario, you'll give yourself one hua of a headache."

"*Hua?*"

"New Zealand slang for *helluva*." A loose translation, anyway.

Rix heaved himself up to rest on elbows and forearms, and couldn't help feeling gratified when Blondie jerked upright and took a hasty step backward.

Blondie covered his reaction with a quick-smart, "So you're from New Zealand—that explains the tribal ink."

Rix didn't bother to correct him. He happened to be a natural born American, but the tattoo ringing his biceps paid homage his mother's heritage—a Maori pattern called *pakati*, which represented courage and strength. Or at least, that's what Rix had been told it represented by the old guy who'd done it. He'd claimed to be a genuine Maori tattoo artist. Dude had seemed on the level, but for all Rix knew, his "tribal" armband could be a meaningless fake—

Hang on. How come Blondie knew about his ink?

Rix cast his gaze down the length of his body and found he'd been stripped of his coverall. His boots, too, had vanished.

Shit.

As though tapping into his thoughts, Blondie said, "I had the guards check you for weapons. Cool little carving, by the way. You do that?"

"Yep." No harm in admitting it, Rix thought. Maybe the guy would return it—

"Funny looking bird—what're they called again?" Blondie snapped his fingers. "Kiwis. It'll make a nice addition to my office desk."

Asshole. By stripping Rix of his disguise and leaving him barefoot and naked but for his boxers, Blondie thought to drive home how vulnerable Rix was—like, completely at his mercy. Well, if that's what Blondie thought, he had another think coming.... Just as soon as Rix's brain felt like it wasn't gonna explode and drip out his ears. And he could be reasonably confident his legs would hold him up.

"And the worst case scenario?" Blondie asked.

"Huh?"

"You mentioned a worst case scenario if I continue trying to map your energy signature."

"Oh. That. Burst blood vessels in your eyes. Blood dripping from your nose." Rix grinned wide enough to show his teeth—a gesture Lily called his "feral grin", designed to put the fear of God into any street-rat stupid enough to cross him. "If I'm lucky, maybe even an aneurysm."

Total BS, but Blondie couldn't know that. And with luck, Rix could get his shit together enough to—

He shook his head, banishing the temptation. The risks of exposure were too great.

Blondie rubbed his left temple before quickly lowering his hand to adjust the rolled sleeves of his white button-down, and the agonizing pressure in Rix's skull eased enough to make it bearable. "I presume you're speaking from experience?" Blondie asked, his tone intent, probing.

Excellent. Rix was getting to him. Now suck on this, Blondie.... "Presume what you like. It's no skin off my nose if you end up drooling down your shirtfront and wearing adult diapers for the rest of your life."

The pain ceased altogether, and Rix did his utmost to conceal his relief. He couldn't afford to show any weakness. Blondie was a talented lim, his strength on a par with Rix's own. He might look like some prep school graduate trying way too hard to be cool, but more often than not appearances came back to bite you in the ass. Pretty face aside, there was a ruthless gleam in those witchy-green eyes that indicated Blondie was used to getting his own way... and would do whatever it took to get what he wanted. If what Blondie wanted happened to be *Lily*, then Rix needed to conserve his strength and bide his time, because right now, even with his special little hidden talent, he wasn't at all confident he would come out on top.

"You need to work on your mind-fuck techniques," Blondie said, one hand whipping behind his back. And before Rix could summon enough brain cells to move to avoid the big bad headed his way, Blondie jabbed the Taser he'd secreted in the waistband of his chinos to Rix's chest, right over his heart, and let him have it.

# CHAPTER 3

THIS TIME RIXON came to sprawled on a single bed, in a room-cum-cell that could have been a twin to the one where Lily was being held. He groaned, stretching aching, throbbing limbs that felt like he'd put them through a week of abuse. Staring at the ceiling, determined not to give in to the despair that lay coiled in his gut, he muttered a heartfelt, "Well, shit."

"Got your arse royally Tasered, huh? Been there. Suffered a dose of that. Makes you feel like shite for sure."

Rix rolled off the mattress to his feet, fists raised, poised to inflict grievous bodily harm... except the room spun, and the tiny pulsing spots dancing before his eyes made him sway like a drunk on a major bender.

"Hey, easy there, mate. Give yourself a moment or three to recover, eh? Not to mention it's only polite to check whether I'm a friendly before you come out swinging. Just so's you know, I'm mostly harmless."

Rix honed in on the direction of that voice until he spotted a kid leaning on the wall by the bottom of the bed. He was barefoot, dressed in gray sweatpants and a white t-shirt. He was tall but lanky—all arms and legs—making it hard to gauge his age. A year or so younger than Lily, maybe?

"Take a load off before you fall over and knock yourself out or something," the kid advised. "Which would be a truly dumb-arse thing to do, considering I'm about to fill you in on how things work in this bloody hell-hole. Such as don't waste your time 'n energy trying the door. Ditto with phasing. Take my word for it, you're stuck here."

The kid nodded approvingly when Rix flopped back on the bed. Not that he'd had to think too hard about complying. For one, the kid wasn't brandishing a motherfucking *Taser* so there was no harm in chilling for a bit. Beat the heck out of falling on his ass, anyway. And two, knowledge was power. If this kid wanted to share what he knew, Rix had nothing to lose... and Lily's freedom to gain.

"Good decision," the kid said. "Cool dreads, by the way." His eyes were freaky—a light shade of blue that looked too bright and intense to be real—not to mention just plain weird paired with the black of his pupils. And his accent was English—like that vamp from *Buffy the Vampire Slayer*.

With the memory of the TV show that had been his mom's secret vice, came a pang of loss. If his parents had been alive, they could have taken Lily in, given her the stable home and love she deserved—

Rix clipped the thought before it could take root. This wasn't the time to mourn the past and get all wishful about what might have been.

"To be honest," the kid was saying, "when His Terribleness brought you in and dumped you here, it just about scared the bejesus outta me."

Rix stilled, his full focus now on the kid. "Did this guy wheel me in or—"

"He phased you in. Hence me being taken completely by surprise."

Shit. Shit! "Describe this guy to me. Was he around seventeen-eighteen, white-blond hair and green eyes? Did he have—?"

"A truly unoriginal facial piercing?"

Rix nodded, hiding his dismay. "Gold hoop through the left brow."

"That would be Liam Kincaid, AKA Terrible Twin Number Two. His father is the guy who runs this hellhole."

Well, hell. Looked like Blondie *had* managed to get through Rix's defenses to force a sync. Which meant that if Blondie was as good as Rix suspected, he'd mapped Rix's energy sig, too. Just his shitty luck to encounter an unusually well trained, strong-as-fuck lim.

The kid seemed to read Rix's mind. "If you're thinking you're royally screwed right now, you'd be right," he said. "Liam's strong as feck. And when it comes to all things liminal, he's been trained to buggery and back. Knows all the tricks, does Liam. His twin brother Reilly's the one you have to watch out for, though. Liam's got smarts but Reilly's a whole 'nother level of smart. Like, a laboratory, unlimited funds, and head of his own research team smart. Reilly's the 'good son' who's being groomed to take over KP from his father when that old fucker finally does the world a favor and turns up his heels—which isn't looking like it'll be anytime soon. More's the pity."

He scowled as he forked his fingers through his shaggy mop of hair. "Reilly's highly motivated to do anything Daddy wants. And just between you, me, and whoever's spying on us right now, some of the stuff Daddy wants will give you nightmares."

Rix grunted, trying to come across staunch and in control, like he wasn't borderline panicking about what Lily had gotten them both into. But he wasn't fooling this kid.

"Look, mate," the kid said, "if you want to celebrate your next birthday, you need to do what you're told, when you're told. They own you now. Get used to it."

"Who's *they*? And what do they plan to do with us?"

"*They* are Vaughn Kincaid, owner of Kincaid Pharmaceuticals, and his sons. The public face of KP is legit, of course. But the whole operation is just a front for Vaughn's real agenda."

"Which is?"

"Gonna blow your tiny mind. See, Kincaid Senior's not a lim but his wife was. He knows all about us. Far as I can tell, he'd give his eyeteeth to *be* one of us. He's jonesing to find out what makes us tick."

"So we're lab-rats."

"Gold star for you."

Rix scratched the stubble on his chin. "Why are you telling me all this? Even if you hadn't come right out and said it, I'd have to be a fucking idiot to think we're not under surveillance. Won't you be in deep shit?"

"Probably." The kid shrugged, and a weary acceptance that Rix had seen in old guys who'd lived on the streets for decades skated across those wolf-blue eyes. "Be worth it if you can talk some sense into Lily."

Unease stroked Rix's skin, raising goose-bumps. "What do you know about Lily?" He pinned the kid with a look that had him throwing up his hands in an "I surrender" gesture.

"Easy, mate," the kid said. "I'm on your side, remember?"

Rix just stared at him, stony-faced.

"All right. All right. I'd tell you to keep your pants on—if you were wearing any."

Rix fought the desire to grab the kid and throttle him to within an inch of his skinny, smart-mouthed life.

Some of what he was feeling must have shown on his face because the kid faked cringing and said, "Yikes. No sense of humor, eh?"

A low, rumbling growl escaped Rix's lips.

"Okay, I hear you. No sense of humor where your girlfriend is concerned. Fair enough." He heaved a sigh that was genuinely mournful so far as Rix could tell. And then he said, "Lily had no idea what she was getting herself into. And...."

"And?"

"Hate to tell you this, Rixon, but she's not doing so good."

Rix snatched a breath, held it until stars danced across his headspace. He exhaled slowly, painfully, insuring he could speak without losing his cool. "Define 'not so good'."

"She's on a hunger strike."

He clenched his fists, willing himself to calm, willing himself to think rationally. Much as he would dearly love to give in to his rage and fear, he couldn't afford to indulge. "How do you know about Lily and me?"

"She told me all about you. How you looked out for her—protected her from the pimps and druggies, shared your blanket with her at night when it got chilly. She thinks you're God's gift—it's so gosh-darned cute it'd bring a tear to my eye if I wasn't such a cynic."

The kid's light, flippant tone didn't match his thin-lipped, this-shit-is-serious expression, so Rix ground his teeth, clenching his jaw until it ached.

Keep him talking. The more information you get him to reveal, the more chance you have of figuring out where Lily's being held. And just when Rix thought he'd claimed a bit of Zen, the little voice in his head whispered, *That's if she's still alive....*

Panic clutched his chest, constricted his throat. He wasn't too late to rescue Lily from this... this... whatever the fuck this place was. He had to believe that.

"She figured you'd be all uptight over her going AWOL," the kid was saying. "But she hoped once you figured out she'd *volunteered* to become a KP lab-rat, you wouldn't be dumb enough to come after her." A long, drawn-out pause for effect. "Apparently she was wrong. And you are *that* much of a bloody idiot."

"How bad....?" Rix choked down the words that had clumped together to form a knot in his throat. "How bad is she?"

"It's only been a few days, so they're taking it softly, softly, you know?

Hoping she'll give in. But if it goes on much longer they'll restrain her and force-feed her."

"God. Why, Lily?"

Rix didn't realize he'd blurted the words aloud until the kid said, "Because according to her, you're smart enough to get off the streets and make something of yourself. And she thinks she's holding you back."

"Huh?" What the ever-loving *fuck?*

"She told me you turned down some awesome opportunity because you wouldn't be around to look out for her, or some shite like that. Bottom line, Rixon? She didn't want to keep on being a burden."

Ah crap. Lily must've found out about the offer from that fancy-ass art school. Someone on the board of directors had gotten hold of one of the carvings Rix liked to do whenever he could lay his hands on a decent piece of wood, and tracked him down via the café that sold the odd piece of his work.

Rix squeezed his eyes shut, blocking out the kid's too-knowing, laser-sharp gaze. He pinched the bridge of his nose, trying to get his head around the claim that Lily believed she was holding him back. But the kid's words rang true—too true for Rix to fool himself it was a lie. "Shit, Lily. You stupid little—"

"Don't be too hard on her. KP's got recruiters targeting lims living rough —kids who won't be missed, like Lily. They talk a good game, you know? Fed her and a bunch of other kids they brought in at the same time a bunch of shite about having a room of their own, regular meals—even a generous allowance—if they're chosen for a super-secret clinical trial. All the kids had to do was agree to let them run a few tests and take some samples." He shrugged. "Sounds totally plausible, right? Of course non-lims are never chosen for this—" he curled his fingers into air quotes "—super-secret clinical trial. Instead, they're given a nice little cash handout, and told to keep their lips zipped or else before they're shown the door. And by the time the lims figure out they're neck-deep in the crapper without a spade, it's too late."

The kid's story matched what little Rix had managed to unearth about the people who'd taken Lily. He swore beneath his breath and scruffed a hand over his dreads. "I'm guessing we're wanted for a whole heap more than blood tests and tissue samples."

"Yep. It's no picnic being a KP lab-rat. There's a reason this floor is off limits to all but a select few of KP's researchers. Didn't take Lily long to realize she'd made a big mistake. She's tried to escape a couple of times. Then she hatched this dumb-arse plan to refuse food until she gets so weak, next time she's forced to phase she'll default Between. She thinks she can hide out there until her energy is replenished enough to phase somewhere she can't be found."

That's my girl!

Hope surged through Rix, thawing the chill that had encased his heart. Now he needed to get a message to Lily so she'd know to hang tight Between and wait for him to find her.

As though he'd again tapped directly into Rix's thoughts, the kid threw him a pitying look. "It's a stupid plan. Liam and Reilly have mapped her energy sig—it's standard procedure. Even if she does default Between, they'll find her. And once they do, Vaughn might decide she's more trouble than she's worth and then it's all over, Rover."

Shit, that sounded ominous. Rix's heartbeat thundered in his headspace. "Meaning?"

"Meaning the old fucker'll put her on incubator duty."

"Huh?" Rix wondered whether he'd heard right.

"Harvest her eggs. Maybe artificially inseminate her."

Whoa. This was starting to sound waaay the fuck out-there. These people had to be dreaming if they thought they could get away with—

"I overheard them talking about her, Rixon."

From the kid's tone and expression and body language, Rix knew absolutely he wasn't playing games, wasn't trying to mess with Rix's head. He was dead serious.

Fuck. This shit just got mega-real.

"I need to get her out," Rix said. "There must be a way—"

"Forget it." The kid made a curt, dismissive gesture with his hand. "The last dipshit who tried to phase out of the building got his brain fried by the security system. Permanently."

"I phased in without any trouble."

The kid quirked a brow. "Bull. Fecking. Shite. I'd bet my most precious parts that phasing in here almost ended you. In my opinion—for what it's worth—the only reason you're not lying somewhere bleeding from all your orifices, is because they wanted you in one piece."

Rix's brain kicked up a gear. "You saying they gave me a free pass?"

"Yup."

What was this kid's deal? Why was he so darned eager to share?

The kid's freaky eyes drilled through him, and Rix got the uncomfortable impression that the kid was reading him like an open book.

"Of course I *would* say that if I was a plant," the kid said. "You know, make out like this place was Fort bloody Knox. Emphasize that the consequences for even attempting to break out are life-threatening." He shrugged again. "Take it or leave it, dude. Of course, Lily might be a little upset when she hears you're doomed to spend the rest of your days shitting into an adult nappy."

Man, if this kid *wasn't* secretly working on their behalf, then he was doing a fan-freaking-tastic job of convincing Rix to get with the program. And bringing threats made against Lily into the equation was a masterstroke.

"So you're not a plant," Rix said slowly, testing the waters.

The kid's blue eyes gleamed. "Nope."

"And you're not trying to manipulate me into being a good little lab-rat by ramming home how upset Lily will be if I'm punished for trying to escape, either."

Rix was rewarded with a toothy grin. "You got me there," the kid said.

The grin got a little crooked and foreboding slimed Rix's skin, raising the hairs on his nape. Seemed likely he might not appreciate what he was about to hear.

"If you think I have an agenda," the kid said, "you'd be right. Wanna hear it?"

Rix shrugged, channeling I-don't-give-a-shit-either-way cool. "Got nothing better to do right now."

"Another good decision. My agenda is getting you to put up and shut up, so you've got at least a shit show in hell of seeing out your next birthday. My agenda is to avoid daily visits to Lily while she's in an induced coma, all the while wondering if today's the day I'll be greeted by an empty bed. My agenda, Rixon, is doing everything I can to stay alive and mostly sane. Because one day, I'm getting out of this shithole. And when that day comes, Vaughn Fuckwit Kincaid better watch his back."

This little speech was delivered in such an inoffensive, conversational tone that it took a minute or so for the last sentence to wholly sink into Rix's consciousness. And when it did—

Whoa. The back of his neck prickled and he instinctively hunched in a vain attempt to make his big, linebacker-worthy body a smaller target. Rix didn't think it was paranoia to expect some goon to come bursting through the door to drag this kid out of here—punish him for trash-talking the boss.

The kid seemingly read Rix's mind again in that uncanny way he had. "Chill," he said. "Kincaid Senior doesn't give an arse what I think of him so long as I do what I'm told like a good little lab-rat. So far as he's concerned, if the tidbits I gab to the newbs scare the shite outta them, all the better 'coz they're less likely to try anything. So here's some more advice for you. Now Liam's mapped your sig, you'd better believe you'll be targeted the instant you try to phase. So don't waste precious energy trying to go subliminal unless you're given the all-clear. The effects in these rooms aren't as bad as if you try and phase out of the building, but they're still enough to fuck you up."

He shot Rixon one of those too-knowing gazes. "That's right, boyo. They've designed an energy-sig-targeted security system to prevent nosy lims from phasing in and spying on them. And I reckon someone tinkered with the security parameters in the expectation of you riding to Lily's rescue. Otherwise, as I mentioned before, you and I wouldn't be having this conversation."

Rix croaked an "Oh?" which the kid obviously interpreted as permission to continue. "Since you asked," he said, "if they'd been serious about keeping you on the outer, your brain would have been shredded. Meaning right now, you'd be on life support and one of Vaughn Kincaid's cronies would be milking your dick for swimmers. They're all about recycling here at KP."

"Thanks for sharing. I feel so much better now."

The kid ignored the sarcasm. "You're welcome," he said. "I'm Kade, by the way."

"My friends call me Rix." Rixon cocked a brow at his font of information. "*You* can keep calling me Rixon."

His sally met with a snort and a classic ceiling-ward eye roll, followed by, "Nice one." Pause. "Rix."

Rix absently scratched his chest. "How long have you been stuck here, Kade?" The instant the question left his lips, he wondered whether he wanted an honest answer.

"Got snatched when my parents were murdered." Hatred rippled across Kade's features, aging him from a kid with a smart mouth and attitude to burn, to a boy on the cusp of manhood who'd witnessed terrible things... and was more than capable of doing terrible things in return given half a chance.

Man. Rix wouldn't want to be Vaughn Kincaid if this kid ever got some alone time with him.

"I was a few weeks shy of my tenth birthday," Kade finally said. And apparently noting Rix trying to do the mental math offered, "I turned fourteen back in February. One of the researchers baked me a cake. Chocolate. My favorite."

Kade's smile didn't reach his eyes. He was putting on a good show, but this time Rix wasn't buying it. The kid had so much rage inside him that when he finally quit reining it in, the fallout would be epic.

Almost five years in this hellhole. Jesus. Kade was a survivor all right. "Feel like sharing what else to expect?" Rix asked. "You know, so I *don't* screw up and end up drooling into my pillow." Which wouldn't help Lily any.

The thought of her being stuck here for years, at the mercy of an entitled asshole who thought he had the right to snatch kids and do whatever the hell he liked with them.... Rix ground a fist into his breastbone. He had to get Lily out. Somehow.

"Best advice I can give is to be honest. Don't try'n hide the extent of your abilities, 'coz it'll only come back to bite you. Show off. Make yourself valuable. Convince Vaughn Kincaid you're worth keeping around." That arctic-blue gaze drilled into Rix. "You clear what I'm saying, mate?"

"I get it. Loud and clear."

"Good. Would rather not have the demise of your dumb-arse-self on my conscience." Kade tilted his chin toward the dead plant on the bedside table. "First thing you should do is come clean about *that*."

Rix's gaze dipped to his bare feet. Lily was in awe of his big feet. She ribbed him mercilessly about his long toes, calling them "prehensile", teasing him that he could curl them around a branch and hang upside down. He lifted his chin, meeting Kade's gaze. "Don't know what you mean," he said, keeping his tone even, his expression neutral, giving nothing away.

"Your funeral. They'll find out eventually. They always do."

Kade saluted and phased out of the room to God-only-knew-where. And only after the kid had vanished did it occur to Rix to wonder how come, after all the dire warnings, *Kade* could safely phase without being zapped.

# CHAPTER 4

Rix was well on the way to stir-crazy by the time Blondie—AKA Liam Kincaid—phased into the room-cum-cell. And if the curled lip and arched brows were anything to go by, he was expecting an epic-style, mega-shocked reaction to his abrupt appearance as he stood there, staring down at Rix.

Hah. In your dreams, douchebag. Rix gave the arrogant prick his best bored face.

Blondie sauntered over to lean against the wall, crossing his arms over his chest. And it was only then that Rix twigged what was bugging him. Blondie had changed clothes, sure, but his stance was subtly different—stiffer, more upright. The eyebrow piercing was missing, too....

"Might as well come clean, Rixon," Blondie said. "This room's monitored."

Different intonation. Different mannerisms....

Huh. This wasn't Liam Kincaid. Which meant this guy had to be the twin brother. Reilly. Liam's *identical* twin—a fact Kade had neglected to mention. Jesus. Talk about double trouble.

Rix yawned. Widely. Giving it everything he had. "Of course it's monitored," he drawled. And, figuring he had nothing to lose, cut right to the chase. "So how come the kid can phase without getting knocked on his ass? Or is all his talk of an energy-sig-targeted security system a load of shit." He paused for maximum effect. "Meaning I can phase outta here whenever I damned well please."

Reilly's brows rose. "I'd encourage you to resist the temptation to find out. But if you feel inclined to ignore my advice, please be aware that vegetative state or not, you're still of use to us. Your sperm, for instance."

If Reilly Kincaid was fondly picturing that statement totally freaking Rix out, he was right. But no way was Rix gonna let an inkling of his true feelings show on his face. You didn't survive long on the streets if you couldn't fake it when someone a whole heap bigger 'n meaner than you was all up in your face, eager to take you down and make an example of you. Not that there were many guys bigger than Rix.

He eyed Blondie II beneath his lashes, gauging how far he could push it before Reilly felt the need to assert his superiority. And whether Reilly, too, had a fucking Taser stashed somewhere to help him assert that so-called superiority. Too much to expect that an entitled poser like this guy would play fair.

Reilly sighed. "Entertaining as some might find it to encourage your mistaken belief you can phase without any ill effects, I'd rather not annoy my father by presenting him with damaged goods. So I guess it's time to come clean about Kade."

Rix refused to rise to the bait and clamped his lips shut.

Reilly huffed a snort that sounded almost admiring... or perhaps that was wishful thinking on Rix's part, and he almost missed it when Reilly said, "The kid's a really special snowflake."

"Huh?"

"Kade. Your eager-to-spill-his-guts visitor. A few months after he came to us he was—" Reilly's pause suggested he was choosing his words very carefully "—*participating* in an experiment, when he got a little... *distracted,* and phased. The consensus was he'd defaulted Between, but the guards found him in the lobby—a place he absolutely shouldn't have been able to phase to given the layers of security protecting this floor."

He paused for Rix to ooh and aah over Kade's antics, giving Rix time to debate how he was gonna play this. Cowed prisoner who would now say and do anything to survive, didn't sit right. Perhaps best to play cocky dude who lacked the smarts to realize he was out of options. A guy used to relying on his muscles, who went through life supremely confident he could bungle his way through whatever mess he'd gotten himself into. Yeah, that could work. It might annoy Reilly enough that he blurted something Rix could use to his advantage.

"You gotta be kidding me." Rix guffawed—quite convincingly, he thought —and shook his head. "That *kid* managed to bypass all your hot-shit security protocols? Man. Whoever's in charge of this joint needs to seriously look at the people he's hired. Seems to me they've been talking themselves up to the max, but when it counts, they can't deliver."

"Clumsy, Rixon. Very clumsy." Reilly crossed one ankle over the other and examined his nails.

Rix bit back a curse. Kade was right: Reilly was too damn smart for comfort.

He snapped his fingers, claiming Rix's full attention. "Kade wasn't exaggerating about the consequences of phasing anywhere within this building unless you're given express permission to do so," he said. "But if you're the kind of idiot who only learns by testing things out for himself, I guess there's nothing more I can do. Though I should think the difficulty you had phasing into that bathroom, and the length of time you were out cold—not to mention how shitty you felt when you finally regained consciousness—might give you pause."

Those incisive green eyes gleamed. Bastard was enjoying this.

"Kade's guess was pretty good, by the way," Reilly continued. "We knew you'd come after Lily—your protector complex made sure of that—and we bribed the kids to tell you all about a certain bathroom stall in the expectation you'd attempt that adventurous phase."

Reilly's tone was so matter-of-fact that Rix took a moment to comprehend the implications. And then his stomach performed a lazy somersault before bottoming out.

Jesus. He'd been led around by the nose and played like a fool. "Why not just snatch me off the streets if you wanted me that bad?"

"You're too well known, Rix. If the lone wolf everyone respects gets snatched, people talk. Now we can put the word out that you left town of your own accord and no one gets suspicious."

"What if I hadn't made it?" Rix felt compelled to ask. "What if I'd not been strong enough to get in?"

"There were other options available to us, of course, but we had every confidence you were talented enough to succeed. And just to be perfectly clear, our people have been watching you for a long time, Rixon. Ever since you were tragically orphaned, in fact."

Rix could barely contain his shock. Whoa. Consider my mind officially blown.

"In the interests of doing my utmost to keep you intact until my father decides he has no further use for you," Reilly was saying, "I assure you we employ the best and brightest in the field. But none of our researchers could have predicted that, in addition to other useful talents, Kade would manifest one that would prove so... inconvenient. Still, it's nothing that can't be overcome with time."

Or strong enough drugs and some sturdy restraints, Rix thought grimly.

"Kade's quirks are somewhat annoying, but we put up with him because there's so much we can learn from him." That witch-green gaze fixed on Rix, drilling through the protective veneer of fake confidence he'd built about himself.

The hairs on the back of Rix's nape stood on end and he fought the need to chafe his arms. Or worse, wrap himself in the navy blue comforter adorning the bed to ward off the chill seeping into his bones.

"If you want my father to keep you in one piece, Rixon," Reilly said, "you better pray you're a very special snowflake too. Unfortunately, my father has no patience for dross."

That blond eyebrow rose again.

Wait for it....

"*Dross* means—"

"I know what 'dross' means," Rix snapped before remembering he was supposed to be playing the dumb jock card. Ah, crap. Though, come to think of it, there was little point trying to censor what came out of his mouth when this guy already had his number.

"Good." Reilly rolled his shoulders, pushing off from the wall to saunter across the room. "Wouldn't want any misunderstandings. Coming?" he asked, keying a code into the keypad by the door.

Rix feigned surprise. "We're walking? And here I thought you'd grab the opportunity to demonstrate your awesomeness by forcing a sync, and piggy-back-phasing me to our destination. Color me sorely disappointed."

When Reilly stiffened, Rix knew he'd scored a hit. And before Reilly could dredge up a response designed to show Rix who was boss, Rix followed up with, "Mind you, if I were you, wanting to rub my nose in how powerless I am, I'd parade me down the corridor in my underwear, too. Nothing like a little humiliation to set the right mood." His gaze bored into Reilly's back. "Am I right?"

Blondie II glanced over his shoulder to shoot Rix a narrow-eyed gaze before playing his trump card. "I don't know what she sees in you, to be honest. But if you're as fond of her as she apparently is of you, I'd shut my mouth. I doubt you're the type to sleep well knowing you're responsible for anything unpleasant that happens to sweet little Lily."

There was nothing Rix could come up with on the spur of the moment to counter that—not when the risk of provoking this guy, or his twin brother, or their father, into using Lily as leverage was so very high. Reilly had Rix backed into a corner and they both knew it. Rix would never be able to live with himself if Lily was hurt to bring him in line. He would do anything they asked of him to keep Lily safe. Anything at all.

Since there was nothing more he could do for now, Rix contented himself with mentally debating whether trailing a guy down an eerily empty corridor in your underwear was humiliating, or just plain weird. He amused himself further by wondering what Reilly would have done if Rix had gone commando.

Reilly paused at yet another security door to input yet another umpteen-digit code, and when the door shooshed open, herded Rix into a room—a viewing room. With one of those room-length windows that resemble a mirror, but allow people to watch anonymously.

Reilly dragged out one of the fancy stools lined up before a narrow, black-lacquered counter, and indicated with a cursory wave of one hand that Rix should plant his butt. He then strolled over to a matching black sideboard, and retrieved a writing pad and a fancy silver pen.

To Rix's surprise, Reilly tossed pad and pen onto the table, and yanked out the stool next to Rix. Slouching atop it, he hooked his ankles around the legs of the stool, stuck one elbow on the counter, and leaned his chin on his hand—all the better to observe Rix. "There's a few questions I've been instructed to ask," he said. "It'd be best if you answer honestly but you and I both know that's not likely."

"Then why waste your fucking breath?" Rix snapped before his brain caught up with his smartass mouth. He mentally groaned. That screwed up phase, combined with stress and low blood sugar from lack of food, were taking their toll.

Reilly didn't bother retaliating. Instead, he started firing questions about

Rix's background, family, schooling, medical history. You name it, Blondie II asked it, allowing Rix around thirty seconds of stubborn silence after each question before moving on to the next.

Rix estimated he'd suffered around ten minutes of fruitless questioning when Reilly abruptly broke off the interrogation. "Showtime," he said, and jerked his chin at the viewing window....

Which was shimmering. Apparently Rix wasn't going to be *providing* the entertainment, he was going to be the audience. And as he watched, heart thumping the wall of his chest, the mirrored surface segued to a true window, allowing him to see into a large room.

"I'd like to introduce our least-promising test subject," Reilly said in a bored tone that chilled Rix to his bones.

Rix had never been one to rely on the power of prayer, but now he prayed for all he was worth to God and every Maori deity he recalled his mother ever mentioning.

*Please, if you're listening, if you care at all, please don't let the test subject be Lily....*

# CHAPTER 5

RIX HEARD the words "His name is Andy" and it took every ounce of self-control he possessed to strangle a shout of relief before it burst from his throat. Exhaling slowly through his nose, he released the terrible tension gripping his muscles and focused his attention on the "show".

Andy perched sideways, legs dangling and feet kicking, on a fancy reclining chair that wouldn't have been out of place in a high-end dentist's office. He was a scruffy, half-starved, scarecrow of a kid, with sagging, pock-marked skin and gray teeth. His restlessness was all the more off-putting given the vacant expression in his eyes when his gaze skimmed over Rix—who had to remind himself that Andy had no idea Rix was watching.

Andy's twitching limbs and jerky, back and forth rocking screamed "head-case" even before Rix noted the kid's lips moving, mouthing some silent chant over and over. Or perhaps it wasn't a silent invocation after all, because one of the white-coats said something that prompted Andy to swing his stick-like legs up onto the recliner and flop back against the semi-reclined seatback, but it remained eerily quiet in the viewing room. Apparently there was to be no soundtrack accompanying the disturbing tableau, so for all Rix knew, Andy could have been howling the place down.

While Andy wriggled in his chair, Rix's gaze roved over the three white-coats. The two guys were scribbling notes, but the third—a wholesome, girl-next-door type who looked barely out of college—was mucking with some-thing she'd taken from the drawer of a wheeled trolley.

Hmm. That trolley looked far too much like a portable med-unit for Rix's peace of mind. Hang on. Was that a—?

Yep. She held up a syringe, squinted at it, and did that flicking thing medicos did to remove air bubbles or whatever.

Well, shit. Rix gnawed the inside of his cheek and tried to ignore his racing pulse and clammy skin. Whatever this little "show" entailed, it could not bode well for Andy.

Reilly leaned across the counter, his thumb poised before a panel set into the strip of wall between the window frame and the counter. "Want to hear what they're saying?"

"Not particularly." That would make whatever they were about to do to the kid all the more real. At least this way, Rix could pretend he was viewing a silent movie. Or close his eyes and kid himself this was some nightmare he would eventually wake from.

Yeah, riiight. And you just keep on telling yourself that, Rixon.

"Too bad," Reilly said. And damned if the asshole didn't hit a button on the panel.

"—will feel like a little pinch. Okay, Andy?"

The lab-rat nodded enthusiastically. "Bring it on, bitch. Go on, poke me. You know you want to."

High-pitched shrieks of laughter filled the viewing room. Rix winced and hunched his shoulders. Man. The kid had some set of lungs on him.

"He's a real charmer." Reilly sounded ever-so-slightly amused rather than bored now. "Watch closely, Rixon. You don't want to miss this."

Somehow Rix doubted that. Odds were high that whatever happened in the next few minutes would haunt him the rest of his days.

"Ready, Andy?" the woman asked, her face bright and smiling, like this was going to be fun. Rix wished he could reach through the glass and shake her 'til her teeth rattled and the smile slid off her lying, deceitful face.

The men held Andy still while the woman swabbed his arm. And then she shot him up with whatever poison was in that syringe.

Rixon ground his teeth. From the corner of his eye he noted Reilly watching *him* rather than the test subject, and forced his jaw to relax. *Nothing to see here you little fucker....*

"I'm sure you're dying to find out what they've injected him with," Reilly drawled.

"Not particularly. When you've seen one walking dead druggie who's just scored a fix, you've seen 'em all."

"Not this time, Rixon. See, this isn't just any fix. This is an inhibitor."

"I'm sure you're dying to educate me as to what the ever-loving fuck *that* would be." A passably good imitation of Liam's scary-smart twin if Rix didn't say so himself.

Reilly didn't react, merely continued enlightening him as though Rix hadn't spoken. "We hope it will prevent lims from phasing." A pause for Rix to absorb this statement. And then he said, "I'm sure you're intelligent enough to understand the implications."

Oh, Rix understood the implications all right. And they were enough to shrivel his balls and dampen his armpits with sour sweat. It took every ounce of willpower he possessed to suppress a full-body shudder. Damned if he'd give Reilly Kincaid the satisfaction of knowing how spooked he was right now.

Rix tuned back in to Andy in time to hear him whine, "But I'm hungry." He thrashed against the restraining hands of the two men. "When do I get my burger, bitch? You promised me a burger. You promised."

"You know what you have to do, Andy."

"Yeah, yeah. Phase. All I have to do is phase."

"That's right. Very good, Andy."

"I can be good. Real good." Andy loosed that hyena-laugh again. "Then I'll get the knock-out drugs, too, right? The ones that take away the night-mares? You promised the drugs'd make the nightmares go away. You promised me, bitch!"

"Just as soon as you phase, you can have as much as you want to eat and the medication to help you sleep, too." The woman smiled down at Andy, projecting such benevolence that Rix was hard put not to puke.

"You can sit up if you like." She nodded to her colleagues, who released Andy's arms.

The recliner's backrest slowly rose. Andy shuffled forward, swiveling his butt to dangle his legs over the side of the chair again. Another chin-jerk from the woman, and all three backed off, giving Andy some space to—

To rock and scratch his arms and moan as it turned out. Not to mention screeching a bunch of crazy-assed crap about the "beautiful monster" that lurked Between, waiting to eat his energy. And, as the minutes ticked onward, Rix couldn't help wondering if Andy possessed enough functional brain cells to phase even without the inhibitor. The kid was a hot mess.

Reilly shattered the taut silence with a satisfied, "Excellent. Looks like we've nailed it this time."

"Oh, please." Rix snorted, secretly glad for an excuse to focus on someone other than Andy. "You and I both know the kid's brain is screwed. Reckon he's barely capable of phasing even when he's not half-starved and practically dead on his feet."

"You might be surprised. If he manages to phase, the building's outer security fields will bounce him straight back here. Should take no more than ten seconds, max. And if he goes Between, we'll locate him via his energy sig and haul his ass back. Watch closely."

Rix had opened his mouth to tell Reilly to go fuck himself when Andy screamed, and before Rix knew what was what, he was staring through the glass, gaze fixed on the kid, unable to look away to save himself as Andy clenched his jaw, followed by his fists, and every muscle in his body went rigid. His face contorted into an expression that would give little kids nightmares. Beet-red splotches painted his face, crept down his neck. His eyes rolled back into their sockets until only the whites showed....

And then he disappeared.

The experiment was a bust—thank all popular gods. Rix snatched a breath, released it slowly... and waited until he was mostly sure he could speak without his voice trembling and proclaiming his relief. "Guess it's back to the drawing board, huh? All that time, money and effort wasted. Pity." Not.

Rix couldn't bring himself to gloat over Reilly's lack of a response—not when he noted the perspiration beading Reilly's brow and the way he was working his jaw. His face had paled to sheet-white. And then he whispered, "Shit," and swallowed convulsively a couple of times, like his stomach was trying to crawl up his throat. Dude was doing a damn fine impression of a guy who was on the verge of tossing his cookies.

Aw, hell. This could not be good—

An anguished scream burst through the speakers and it was like some higher power took hold of Rix's body, forcing him to turn his head, forcing his eyelids to remain open, forcing his brain to make sense of the horror on the other side of the glass. And once he'd figured out what he was seeing, he dearly wished he could tear out the part of his brain that would force him to relive the nightmare Andy had become whenever he closed his eyes from now on.

God help the next person who got injected with that inhibitor. Because Andy hadn't safely defaulted Between when the phase had gone pear-shaped. Or if he had, his cells either hadn't been given enough time to re-form correctly before the chemicals swimming through his veins had taken hold and subverted the phase, or they'd gotten scrambled during the transition from subliminal to liminal. Or... or....

Fuck. Rix turned away, shutting down that loop of thought because honestly? It didn't matter what had gone wrong when Andy was beyond fucked up—so fucked up it would be a mercy to put him down. What else could you do for a human being with legs sticking out where his arms should have been and vice versa, and a torso that looked like it had been turned inside out?

Rix ground a fist into his churning belly, willing himself not to vomit. Leaning his spine against the countertop, he bowed his shoulders, an ineffectual attempt to ward off the screams of the wretched thing that had once been a kid named Andy.

Finally, after what seemed like eternity, the screaming abruptly faded to a gurgle... and blessed silence reigned.

"I hope that's not what you consider a success so far as experiments go," Rix told the stiff, pale figure of Reilly Kincaid, who was still staring at whatever was taking place inside the lab.

Reilly blinked and visibly shook himself. "We've made some progress. Father will be pleased."

"You gotta be shitting me." Rix shot the guy a disbelieving glance. Vaughn Kincaid would be *pleased* by this failed experiment? This was what he considered *progress*? "Damn shame your daddy's not a lim. If he was, and I had my way, I'd shoot *him* full of that poison and see if he'd like to redefine the meaning of progress when it fucks him up like it did Andy."

Rix couldn't be a hundred percent certain, but he thought he heard Reilly Kincaid mutter something beneath his breath that sounded suspiciously like, "And I'd be first in line to hold him down while you did it." And then, just when Rix was wondering whether Reilly might have some semblance of a conscience after all, he reverted to type by leaning forward and announcing loud and clear, "Bring in the next subject."

Jesus. They were going to try again?

Rix had to stop this, couldn't stand by and watch while Andy's fate was inflicted on another kid—not while he had a single breath left in his body. There was no time to think this through, no time to worry over the consequences. There was only a surge of desperation-fuelled, blind fury that coiled Rix's muscles, preparing him to launch from the stool. He would use Reilly Kincaid as leverage. He'd happily smash his fist into that pretty face and snap a few bones to show he was serious. Hell, he'd even resort to torture if that's what it took to call a halt to these experiments.

From what seemed like a world away, Rix heard Reilly ask, "Has she eaten anything today?"

And as one of the men's "No sir," penetrated his brain, something compelled Rix to turn back toward the viewing window in time to see a small, hollow-eyed figure in a baggy white tee and gray cotton pants being ushered through the door.

*Lily.*

His heart stuttered.

The adrenaline that had fueled his muscles abruptly drained, leaving him nauseated, weak and shaking. No. It wasn't Lily. It was only his brain playing tricks. It wasn't her, couldn't be her.

Please, let it be anyone but her!

Reilly's terse voice yanked Rix from his pathetic attempts to deny the truth. "Enlighten me: When was the last time she ate?"

"Monday, sir."

"Then what the hell possessed you to select her for this experiment, idiot? Do you have a morbid fascination with failure? Quit wasting my time. Take her back to her room and bring me Kade."

Rix exhaled in a dizzying rush that left him limp. Thank God....

And hard on the heels of intense relief that Lily was safe—for now, at least—came a wash of guilt over Kade's fate.

The kid was an exceptionally strong lim, Rix told himself. He would come through this intact. Now if only Rix could find some way to believe the lies he was telling himself.

Reilly stiffened and tapped his ear. "Duly noted," he said.

A teeny tiny mic, Rix guessed, watching intently, trying to get a handle on the gist of the conversation.

His breath hissed out as Reilly's face leached of color again. Shit. This could not be good....

Reilly's features twisted with something that might have been loathing before smoothing into robotic blankness. "Understood." He tapped his ear again. Without looking at Rix, he leaned toward the speaker panel. "There's been a change of plans. Take a seat, Lily."

And Rix could only sit there, paralyzed with horror, his gaze fixed on Lily's face as the researchers led her to the recliner.

# CHAPTER 6

RIXON'S weird paralysis ended when the female white-coat did her thing with the syringe. He lost it big-time, throwing himself at Reilly Kincaid, fists clenched, ready to pummel the guy into the floor and inflict some major hurt before someone called security and took him down. Instead, he scraped his ribs on the edge of the countertop, sent an empty stool flying, and skidded to a halt an instant before he slammed into the wall.

What the—?

The answer smacked him upside the head.

Well, duh. Of course Reilly's energy sig would be programmed into the security system, just like his brother's, meaning the bastard could phase without any ill effects.

And then something smacked into Rix's head for real, and he whirled, already knowing what he would see.

Yep. Reilly stood behind him.

"You've got a damn hard head," Reilly muttered, cradling a wrist as he tested his hand.

Rix knew when he was beat but it would be a singular pleasure to take the fucker down anyway. Because anything was better than watching Lily fighting whatever chemical cocktail they'd shot her up with. Anything was better than imagining what would befall her if she failed.

He had tensed, and was preparing to lunge again, when Reilly put a finger to his lips and beckoned him closer. Apparently for someone else's benefit he said loudly, "Well? Don't just stand there like an idiot. Pick up that stool you knocked over, sit your ass down, and shut the hell up."

Pretending to comply would make it easier to grab Reilly before he could go subliminal again. Rix took a step. And another. One more, and he was standing beside the guy, right up close and personal, body thrumming with the need to lash out, brain shrieking at him to wait until Reilly had said his piece, because whatever information he had to impart might prove crucial to getting Lily out alive.

Reilly grabbed Rix's biceps and hauled him closer, leaning in until his mouth hovered by Rix's ear. "If you care about the girl, calm the fuck down and zip your lip, or believe me, she'll be screwed sooner rather than later. I'm betting my father's intention is only to scare her into compliance. Unlike Andy, Lily is physically and mentally sound. She's too valuable to waste." A pause and then he spoke aloud for the benefit of whomever had bugged this room. "Nod if you understand the consequences of any more foolish behavior."

Rix registered that Reilly was waiting on a response and forced a nod. He didn't retaliate when Reilly shoved him away and sauntered over to resume his seat. What was the point when, while he'd been occupied with Blondie II, that baby-faced bitch with the glasses and freckles had emptied the syringe into Lily's veins.

He'd waited too fucking long. He could still hear that sweet, too-happy voice chirping, "Are you ready, Lily? This will feel like a little pinch."

Since it wouldn't help Lily any if he drove himself insane, Rix tried to empty his mind of lost possibilities—chief among them being that he should have smacked Reilly stupid, forced a sync with him, and then phased into that room. Hell, even low on energy as he was, he should have attempted what no lim to his knowledge had dared before—a three-way sync—and piggyback-phased both himself and Lily out of the building using Reilly's energy sig as a shield.

Better to go out trying, right? *Right?*

*Wrong* , that annoying inner voice told him. *Better to do whatever it takes to stay alive and fight another day.*

Fuck. He sucked at heroism. And if Reilly was lying about the inhibitor, there was shit-all Rix could do to save Lily now. All he could do was pray.

"Watch what happens to lab-rats who think they have choices," Reilly said, his tone signaling he'd resumed the role of bored bystander for the benefit of their unseen eavesdropper.

Rix did as he was told, focusing on Lily, who was shaking her head, lips compressed in a thin, white mutinous line. Shit. He knew that expression all too well. *She* wasn't going to sit there and shut up and do what she was told, even if it might be her best chance of saving herself.

"You know what you have to do, Lily," the female white-coat was saying, her tone cajoling. "And the sooner you do it, the sooner you can have those books you wanted. And ice cream, too. With chocolate topping and sprinkles. Didn't you tell Kade you missed ice cream and chocolate topping?"

Rix watched, cringing in anticipation of what would emerge from her mouth, as Lily turned her head to glare daggers at the woman. "You can shove your books *and* your ice-cream where the sun don't shine, sweetie. And don't bother trying to make out like Kade's running off his mouth. We all know our rooms are bugged and nothing's private."

"Lily, please. You know Mr. Kincaid doesn't like to be kept waiting."

Lily gave the window the middle finger, obviously believing Vaughn Kincaid was in this room, covertly watching her. Rix would have applauded her guts if he hadn't been so shit-scared about what was going to happen next.

"Very well," the woman said. "But please remember that you brought this on yourself." She paused, giving Lily time to reconsider. And then she sighed loud and long, as though truly regretful for whatever she was about to do. With a wave of her hand, she signaled the men.

Rix's heart kicked. Adrenaline burned through his veins, making his muscles twitch violently as his brain shrieked at him to *Move! Now! Take out Reilly Kincaid. Smack a stool into the viewing window until it shatters... take out the white-coats... scoop Lily from that chair... run and don't look back.*

He ignored the impulses needling his skin. And while he was mumbling another clumsy prayer beneath his breath, one of the men produced a thin rod with two protrusions on the tip.

"Is that a—?"

"Cattle prod." Reilly nodded. "No point in using Tasers. They disrupt the body's energy flows too extensively, making phasing impossible until the effects wear off."

"Jesus."

"If it's any consolation, it generally takes only a couple of prods before your hindbrain takes over and forces you to go subliminal to avoid another shock. It's an instinctive reaction. She won't last long. They never do."

Could Reilly be speaking from personal experience?

Rix gnawed the inside of his cheek so he wouldn't blurt the question, but Reilly answered anyway. "The highest number of prods I've ever endured before phasing is four. My twin, coldblooded bastard that he is, made it to five. Lily's tougher than she looks. Want to bet how many it'll take before she phases?"

"Fuck you."

"Now, now, don't be like that. It's not like she hasn't been given a choice. All she has to do is phase and this will be over."

Yeah. Until the next time Vaughn Kincaid figured on teaching Lily a lesson.

What kind of a man used a freaking cattle prod to force a teenage girl to do his bidding? What kind of man believed that torturing kids was okay—that any of this was okay?

The man approached Lily, weapon extended. She didn't cower, didn't try to evade the prod. But Rix, who knew her so very well, noted the panic in her eyes, in the set of her jaw, in the carefully still way she held her body.

The bastard jabbed the prod into her ribcage, held it there until she shrieked like a banshee.

Rix wanted to close his eyes, shut out the sight of Lily curling in on herself, hands clutching her ribs, chin lowered so the tangled sweep of her raven hair hid the tears spilling from her eyes. But he made himself watch. He knew what she'd endured as a child, understood how much fucking courage it was taking for her to endure this torture, too. He wanted desperately to tell her there was no shame in giving in if it meant avoiding more of the same. There was no shame in doing whatever you had to do to stay alive and sane. He wished he could be there, in the room with her, to tell her that.

"All you have to do is phase, Lily." The woman, whom Kade had concluded was the worst of the bunch, heaved another one of those fake theatrical sighs. "You know we don't want to hurt you if we can avoid it. All you have to do is phase."

Lily glanced up, her tear-drowned brown eyes spitting fire. "Here's an idea," she said, her tone so sickly sweet that Rix knew whatever came out of her mouth next wasn't gonna be pretty. "How 'bout you sit on that prod and rotate? Go on. Don't be shy. Reckon it'll be the only action you'll see for a while."

Rix muffled a groan. Yup. Bad as he'd imagined.

The woman's mouth opened and closed like a goldfish. The two men snickered, and beside Rix, Reilly gave a surprised snort. "Holy shit," he said softly. "That was all kinds of awesome."

The woman's face flushed crimson. She snapped her fingers at the guy with the prod. "Sorry, kid," he said, and jabbed it into Lily's thigh.

This time her scream was so loud even Reilly visibly winced. "For some reason it really hurts when you get it in the leg," he said.

"Dammit, Lily. Quit being so stubborn!" If she at least tried to phase, maybe they'd lay off with the prod. Please, God, let them quit with the torture soon because Rix didn't know how much more of this he could take without doing something stupid.

Lily glared at each of her tormentors in turn, saving the woman for last. Chest heaving, she swiped snot and tears from her face with the back of her hand. "Karma's a bitch, baby," she spat. "One day you'll get yours." And before the woman could respond, Lily phased out.

"Finally." Reilly sounded relieved. "Thought for a moment she was going to go another round."

"She could have handled it," Rix muttered.

"I'm sure you're right." Reilly barked a wry laugh. "She might resemble a delicate little Asian doll who'll shatter if you so much as look at her wrong, but there's nothing fragile about that girl."

Rix didn't much appreciate Reilly's opinions about Lily's character. Nor his appreciative tone.

Rix had always treated Lily like the kid sister he'd never had. He'd refused to consider anything else given her age, and his, and what he knew of her past. But now, faced with another guy's obvious admiration for the girl he'd sworn to protect, something primitive that couldn't be denied, rose up and snarled *Back off, she's mine!*

Reilly's gaze jerked to the lab. "She's back."

Rix slowly turned his head... and exhaled a shaky huff of sheer relief to see her whole and everything where it should be. But as he drank in Lily's features, vowing he would get her out of this hellhole or die trying, he noted the trembling, the wild eyes and hugely dilated pupils.

"Something's wrong," he said, as one of the white-coats approached her. And before Reilly could form a response, Lily went ballistic.

The two men attempted to subdue her but she fought like a wildcat, clawing and kicking, all the while screaming about monsters coming out of the gray to feed on her energy.

Frowning, Reilly tore his attention from the disturbing scene in the lab. "Can you figure out what she's going on about?" he asked Rix. "Because it sounds like she defaulted Between, but—"

"Something she encountered there spooked the living daylights out of her."

Reilly's frown got more pronounced and then his expression blanked, like something he'd rather not reveal had just occurred to him. "I think everything's gotten too much for her and she's finally snapped," he said.

Rix shook his head. "No. She's okay. She'll calm down when she realizes she's safe. She's scared, is all." Terrified out of her mind, more like.

Something niggled at him. Hadn't Andy been raving about energy-sucking monsters, too? Shit. Maybe the inhibitor also acted as a hallucinogen. He needed some alone time with Lily to coax her into revealing what had gone down, but the chances of that happening any time soon? Yeah. Not good.

Hang on. Maybe Kade could wrangle it. He seemed to care about Lily. Now all Rix had to do was find a way to contact the kid.

He was jolted from his thoughts by Reilly saying, "Better hope she snaps out of it sooner rather than later."

Rix narrowed his eyes at the veiled threat. "Or?"

"Or my father might decide to write her off." Reilly leaned toward the speaker. "How much longer is it going to take to administer a sedative?" he barked. "Some of us have schedules to keep." He forked a hand through his hair and muttered, "And fathers who don't take kindly to things not going to plan."

"I could go in and—"

Reilly cut Rix off with a curt slicing motion of his hand. "They've got her cornered. About time."

The two men had backed Lily against the wall and Rix watched, heart in his mouth, as they pounced, wrestling her to the floor.

If they hurt her again....

"Yes, that's right," Reilly said. "Hold her still so Little Miss Sunshine can administer the sedative.... Yes. Finally."

*Little Miss Sunshine*.... Yep. The nickname fit that smiling bitch to a tee.

The smirk slid off Rix's face as he watched one of the men plunk Lily's limp body on a stretcher, and wheel her from the room. He clenched his fists, wishing he could release the rage boiling in his gut, wishing he could surrender to the primal instinct that demanded he follow and protect Lily at all costs. Unfortunately he had to be smart. Little point escaping this room when he would be waylaid by security the instant he poked his nose out the door. Not to mention once he dealt with Reilly Kincaid, there was Liam to contend with, too.

Reilly stiffened again, commanding Rix's full attention.

Great, just fricking great. Looked like more instructions were forthcoming.

Foreboding prickled his spine when Reilly shot him a glance before saying, "Liam's not going to be happy about being kept out of the loop. Are you sure—?" A sharp exhalation that sounded all kinds of pissed off, and then he said, "Understood."

"Guess I'm next up." Rix stood, snapping the waistband of his boxers.

"You guessed right."

"Better not keep Daddy waiting." Rix sketched a flourish with his hand. "After you."

"A word of advice," Reilly said. "Don't try to hide what you can do. He'll find out eventually." His lips twisted, and when he said softly, "He always does," Rix could have sworn he hadn't meant to say the words aloud.

"You're the second person to tell me that," Rix said.

"Kade?" Reilly threw over his shoulder as he headed for the internal door that led directly into the lab. He jabbed a code into the security panel. The door shooshed aside, disappearing into a recess in the wall.

"Yeah."

"You should listen to him."

"So he tells me." Rix sure hoped Kade was as smart as everyone thought he was. Just like he hoped he could grab the opportunity to pick Kade's brains and come up with a new plan, because Rix was painfully aware he was in deep and sinking fast.

Reilly pointed to the recliner and clicked his fingers. "You know the drill."

As Rix made himself comfortable—or as comfortable as you could when you were wearing only boxers and your skin was sticking to the leather—another set of doors opened. A man strolled in, hands shoved in the pockets of his black pants, white shirtsleeves rolled up his forearms. He was average height, medium build. Bland, mild features—neither striking nor notably ugly. The sort of guy who'd pass unnoticed, or at least unremarked, in a crowd. And then his gaze found Rix's... and Rix just about swallowed his tongue.

Dark brown eyes weren't supposed to freeze you with a glance. Brown was a warm color—well, Rixon had always thought of brown that way, seeing as how his mother's brown eyes had always been warm, even when she'd been bawling him out for some minor misdemeanor. And if Rix were completely honest, Lily's cocoa-brown eyes could light up a room. But this man's brown eyes lacked any semblance of warmth. They were cold—the kind of biting, unforgiving cold that ate through the flesh on your bones. And those eyes made it abundantly clear Rix was merely a replaceable specimen that might live another day.... Provided he did something interesting.

The man jerked his chin at Reilly, who obligingly performed the introduction. "My father, Vaughn Kincaid, CEO of Kincaid Pharmaceuticals."

Rix waited a beat too long before responding with a curt, "Rixon."

"Surname." Reilly and Liam's father—who bore not the slightest resemblance to his blond, green-eyed sons—intoned the word like he expected to be immediately obeyed, or else.

Rix exhaled silently through his nose and kept his tone even. "Just Rixon."

"Best answer him, Rixon," Reilly said.

"What's the point? I'm sure you already know everything there is to know about me, otherwise I wouldn't be here right now. Instead, I'd be lying on some slab, waiting to be dissected in the name of whatever passes for research in this house of horrors." From the corner of his eye, Rix noted Reilly's eyelids drooping and his lips moving as though in a silent prayer.

Okay then. He might have gone a bit too far.

Vaughn Kincaid's lips stretched into something he doubtless imagined was a smile. "Here's how this will go, Rixon. You'll be given one chance to participate willingly, and showcase your unique talent to me, my son, and my eager employees. If you decide to waste my time further, you'll be injected with the inhibitor and we'll see how many times you endure the prod before instinct takes hold and you phase. Once you return, you'll be given another chance to be sensible. However, if you decide not to cooperate for a second time, the dose will be doubled before the cattle prod is administered. And each time you resist, the inhibitor dose will increase accordingly."

Vaughn paused to scratch his nose. "I'm sure you're intelligent enough to understand that eventually, even a resourceful lim such as yourself, will be so depleted of energy that phasing will become somewhat... perilous. How much more perilous when your veins are swimming with an untested inhibitor, of course remains to be seen."

He cocked his head, his cold fanatic's eyes gleaming with eagerness. "Shall we find out, Rixon? It would be a shame, of course, if you got a little— how to put this delicately? Ah yes—*scrambled* upon becoming liminal. But as you mentioned, even lying on a slab, waiting to be dissected in the name of what *I* fondly call research, you wouldn't be completely wasted." He tapped his lip with a forefinger. "Though I'm sure we could keep you alive for quite some time before putting you down."

As much as Rix wanted to resist and draw out the inevitable just to spite the fucker, dumbass ego games had no place here. Rix's sole priority had to be Lily. He was already low enough on energy that he would be hard pushed to prevent himself instinctively seeking the nearest energy source and revealing the full extent of his special little ability. And if he did manage to suppress that instinct for self-preservation, but came out of a phase too fucked up to help Lily? He couldn't risk it. Wouldn't.

This was it. He was gonna have to confess his biggest, darkest secret to Vaughn Kincaid—the one that he'd never confessed to anyone, not even Lily. The one that, if it got out, would slap a big-ass target on his back, because even people who dealt with all manner of woo-woo weirdness, who lived it every day of their lives like liminals did, would have no tolerance for someone like him. They'd treat him like the enemy. He exhaled with a hiss and put it all on the line. "I'm a siphon."

# CHAPTER 7

RIX WAITED for one of them to order him to elaborate. And when no one did, was forced to conclude his big secret hadn't come as much of a surprise. Someone—Kade, most like, if the kid's interest in the dead plant in Rix's room was anything to go by—had already put two and two together, and filled them in. Rix didn't have to like it but he couldn't really blame the kid for spilling his guts. In a place like this, you did whatever it took to make it through another day.

He met Vaughn Kincaid's gaze. "You already know about me—that I'm a siphon."

"Very good, Rixon." Vaughn beamed at him like a teacher proud of a good student. Or an owner praising a clever dog. "Although, in the interests of full disclosure, I must confess that until now we had no proof you possessed such a fascinating ability. And it is fascinating, is it not?" He paused expectantly.

"Fascinating!" Little Miss Sunshine dutifully enthused.

"I believe the term 'siphon' is rather apt for your ability." Vaughn rubbed his chin, playing at being human.

Hah. Rix doubted anyone in this room—including Little Miss Sunshine —was foolish enough to believe the act.

"*Siphon*. Yes, I like it. We'll keep it." *And you*, Vaughn's cold eyes seemed to say. "Now that you're prepared to cooperate, perhaps you would be so kind as to explain exactly what being a 'siphon' entails. It's always best to go right to the source for accurate information, don't you think, Rixon?"

Rixon smothered a wholly ridiculous impulse to start his explanation with "Once upon a time, a young boy named Rixon discovered he could kill things." Instead, he said, "When I get low on energy, I can take it from living things. Plants and insects and small animals—rodents and suchlike." He shrugged like it was no biggie. "Comes in handy sometimes. Have to be cautious how much I take, though. People start finding dead things around the place and it freaks them out."

He stroked his dreads, screwing up his nose like he was thinking real hard. "Don't know how I do it, exactly. Best I can describe, it's like when a lim partially phases—doesn't go subliminal all the way—and all the senses sharpen so you can see and hear and sense the energy vibrations of everything in range. Only I'm not partially phasing but I'm still hyper-aware of the energy a thing gives off. And then I kinda tap into that energy and you know, absorb it. Sometimes I can do it from a short distance. Other times, I have to be touching the thing I'm taking energy from."

He loosed a nervous-sounding laugh. And then, hoping to deflect suspicions that he was omitting something crucial, he volunteered another piece of information. "Tried it on a cat, once." Pause for a beat. "Ended up with a wicked migraine that laid me flat on my back for hours. I reckon cats are too smart. They sense what's happening and, I dunno, fight back or something."

The best lies always contained elements of the truth. Vaughn Kincaid didn't need to know that Rix *had* successfully siphoned energy from a cat—a poor little beast that he'd found badly injured after being clipped by a car. Rix hadn't been able to afford to take it to a vet. Draining its energy had been the most humane way he could think of to end its suffering.

And Vaughn Kincaid *definitely* didn't need to know that Rix had drained a human to death, too. But rather than keeping the energy he'd stolen, using it, he'd headed for the nearest park and fed all the energy he could spare to every bush and tree he could lay a hand on. He'd over-compensated, and afterward had been weak as a kitten, his head aching so bad he could barely focus. A small price to pay for insuring there was nothing left of that depraved scumbag inside him, though.

He had never told Lily that he'd tracked down her stepdad and lain in wait for him. All she knew was the official line: a fatal heart attack in the small hours of the morning. And that she would never have to be afraid of him again.

Rix knew in his bones that Vaughn Kincaid wouldn't be as discerning when it came to choosing victims, however. And right then and there, he silently vowed to end himself before allowing his talent to be used as a weapon—and not because taking out Lily's sadistic asshole of a stepfather kept him awake at nights, either. He'd felt no remorse whatsoever—still didn't. In fact, Rix suspected he could become rather good at killing. Too good. And although there were plenty of people out there that, in his opinion, needed killing—whose deaths would make the world a much better place—he didn't trust himself in the self-appointed role of judge, jury and executioner. He shouldn't be the one to decide who was irredeemable and deserved to die.

And neither should the likes of Vaughn Kincaid.

He gave his audience guileless, I've-told-you-everything eyes, and held his breath, hoping his confession would be enough. Hoping Vaughn and his cronies were satisfied—that he'd convinced them it was fruitless to waste their precious time and resources having him siphon energy from larger animals. Namely humans.

"Thank you for your honesty, Rixon." Vaughn Kincaid smiled that pitiless shark's smile again. "I trust you'll understand we must corroborate what you've told us—in the name of science, of course."

He clicked his fingers and Little Miss Sunshine bustled over, her lips pursed in thought. "A plant to begin with, perhaps?" she suggested, her tone and body language oozing deference.

Vaughn nodded. "Make it so."

She sashayed over to her remaining male counterpart, and the two went into a classic huddle. Rix concentrated on appearing tense and just the right amount of nervous about his situation, while deep inside he fretted over how much "corroboration" of his story they would require.

It wasn't like they balked at torturing kids. How far would they go? What would he do if they brought Kade in and insisted Rix take energy from him? Or worse, Lily?

The man broke away to bark instructions into a mic attached to the collar of his lab coat. Five minutes passed, and before Rix could work up to a full-blown freak out, a sharp buzz sounded.

Reilly sauntered over to admit the visitor—make that *visitors*. One guy carried a big leafy houseplant with flat white flowers that had stalk-like yellow stamens. The other hefted a tree that gave Rix a wicked jolt when he recognized it. He watched, stony-eyed, as the men were directed to place the specimens beside the recliner, and then to exit the room.

Vaughn clicked his fingers. "Rixon, please begin your demonstration."

"Yes, sir." Might as well do some sucking up of his own. Not to mention playing down his talent as much as he could without being obvious. "I'll try the plant first. Best if I touch it, so I don't end up accidentally taking energy from the tree and confusing the results or something. That okay?"

Vaughn regally inclined his head.

Man, talk about arrogant. Rix wisely kept his thoughts to himself. He crouched by the plant and gently pinched one shiny green leaf between his thumb and forefinger. In his mind's eye, the plant's energy flows gave a little hiccup, and then immediately reformed to accommodate Rix, flowing through him, making him a part of its circuit. He could take only a little energy, leaving the plant alive, but Rix didn't want Vaughn or his researchers knowing he could control how much he drained. Best they believed him a blunt instrument, lacking any finesse whatsoever.

Mentally apologizing to the plant, Rix blocked the circuit, setting up a one-way drain so that the energy circling through him was not returned to the plant. And, as he watched, trying not to reveal how much this process disturbed him, the plant drooped. Within seconds the leaves lost their sheen, crisping like a hothouse flower beneath a scorching desert sun.

If anyone had been monitoring his physical symptoms, Rix knew from experience they would note a slight rise in his core temperature—something he welcomed, considering he was still wearing only boxers. He darted a glance at Vaughn Kincaid... who was staring intently at the dead plant, his expression impassive.

All righty then. Time for the tree.

This one wasn't going to be as easy—not because he couldn't kill it like he'd done the houseplant. He could. Easily. And the energy it provided would ease the effects of weariness and hunger, and the constant stress he'd been under since Lily's disappearance. But did it have to be a *dracaena*—a dragon tree—that he was about to sacrifice for the cause?

Rix steeled himself to repel the memories but it was too late. They were too strong, too vivid. His mom'd had a really stellar specimen in the living room of their modest family home. She'd always insisted she had stolen it from a dragon, and carted it all the way to America with her. She'd regaled him with stories about the dragon, too. His mom had told the best bedtime stories....

"Whenever you're ready, Rixon."

Since he was very much aware "never" wouldn't be an acceptable response, Rix did his thing with the tree, reducing it to brittle, lifeless sticks that resembled some macabre sculpture. And, while he welcomed the energy boost, he couldn't help feeling a little sick to the stomach at what he'd done.

The sick feeling only worsened once he fixed his attention on Vaughn again.

Fuck. If the unholy gleam in his eyes was any indication, Rix didn't want to know what was going through the man's head right now. He ducked his head before Vaughn could capture his gaze, and for good measure, squinched his eyes shut and rubbed the bridge of his nose. If they interpreted the gesture as a worsening headache, all the better. Maybe they'd take him to a room, give him some space to figure out what to do next. Some food wouldn't go amiss, either.

On cue, his stomach rumbled. Loudly.

Vaughn beckoned Reilly over, and instructed his son to show their latest acquisition—Rixon—back to his room, provide him with some clothes, and organize a substantial hot meal.

Reilly didn't say a word until Rix was safely ensconced in his room. "Congratulations on not being deemed a waste of oxygen," he told Rix. "And if you know what's good for you, you'll work hard at remaining interesting." With that, he phased out, leaving Rix to contemplate the dead plant on the bedside table.

He half-expected the promised clothing and meal wouldn't eventuate, but in a very short period of time he was provided with both. First things first, he donned the sweatpants and t-shirt, mildly surprised to find they fitted him perfectly. When you were Rix's size, affordable clothing options were often limited to embarrassingly tight, or something that looked like a gaudy tent. He left off the socks. Without shoes it was better to go bare-foot—more traction if he needed to run. Safer if he needed to carry Lily, too.

Next, he checked out the food. Some kind of microwave-ready glop, its plastic seal intact save for a couple of small steam vents. He wasn't stupid enough to believe the food hadn't been doctored in some way, but if they were determined to drug him, there were a myriad ways they could go about it. Sleepy-type gas through the air-con vent, for example.

Experimentally he sniffed the air. Smelled normal, if a heap cleaner than what he was used to. But if they *were* going to knock him out with gas, odds were it would be colorless and odorless... and there would be nothing he could do about it in any case. He filled his belly. And then, popping the seal on the mineral water bottle, he guzzled half the contents. No point getting dehydrated, and he wasn't worried about being observed while relieving himself in the small toilet alcove. Let 'em look. You couldn't afford to be shy about bodily functions when you lived on the streets.

He prowled the confines of his room, and then flopped atop the bed to contemplate the ceiling... for all of five minutes before he was back on his feet. He knew he should try and get some rest but sleep was impossible when all he could see whenever he closed his eyes was Lily. Lying on a narrow bed, in a room identical to his. Maybe pacing the room, trying to wear herself out enough to sleep. Embarrassed as all get-out about the prospect of being watched whenever she had to pee. Lily was such a girl when it came to peeing—not that there was anything wrong with being a girl.

Especially when the girl in question was Lily.

And abruptly, Rix wasn't at all amused about the prospect of someone watching Lily's every move, maybe catching an eyeful of things Rix would rather not be seen by anyone. Except himself. Which was all kinds of wrong when he'd always treated her like the little sister he'd never had... at least, up until a couple of months back. He'd been standing guard while she washed up in a bucket of water he'd scrounged, and something had crawled over her bare foot. She'd screamed, and he'd reacted instantly, turning to snatch her into his arms. But as he'd patted her bare back, reassuring her it was only a bug—more afraid of her than she was of it—something had changed. He'd become hyper-aware of her smooth skin beneath his fingers, her small breasts mashed against his chest, her slim thighs gripping his waist, the way she quivered when he stroked her skin.... And then he'd become hyper-aware of his own body's reaction to hers.

Lily had wriggled from his arms, flushed pink, unwilling to look him in the eye. Things had been a little weird between them since then. And before he'd figured out what to do, how to fix things, she'd disappeared....

Ah, fuck this for a joke. Rix dropped to the floor and gave his unseen watchers twenty. Then twenty more. And he had just started on a round of sit-ups when it occurred to him that he'd taken far too much of what he'd been told at face value.

It was time to do a little corroborating of his own.

When he'd finished his third round of sit-ups, Rix sat cross-legged in the middle of the room. Might as well shoot for the moon. Fixing Lily's room in his mind, he gathered his energy, and phased.

He'd achieved a partial phase, and was cautiously hopeful he could do this, when his nerve endings lit up like firecrackers. And then it was like all his molecules compressed to a shrieking bundle of white noise. Next thing he knew he was flat on his back, staring at the ceiling, his veins hot and buzzing, and his body protesting like he'd been steamrollered by something huge and heavy and unforgiving.

"Dumb-arse idea, Rix. Real dumb."

Rix lolled his head to the right and spotted a Kade-shaped blur lounging on his bed, staring down at him.

"I told you what'd happen if you tried to phase outta here, remember?"

Rix tried to speak but all that issued from his throat was an incoherent mumble. His tongue felt far too big for his mouth. Even his vocal cords throbbed.

A bottle of water swam into his range of vision. Rix didn't like his chances of guzzling water prone—he'd likely end up half-drowning himself. He rolled to his side, then to his belly. And it took him three tries to coordinate his muscles to push up onto all fours. Slowly, painfully, he locked his knees, tensed his abs, and sat back on his haunches.

Kade proffered the water bottle again, and Rix gritted his teeth while lifting a shaky arm to grab it. Even that small gesture exhausted him. He rested for a bit before attempting to drink. And when he did give it a go, discovered his hand-eye coordination was totally screwed. Stubbornly he tried again. And again, missed his mouth entirely.

"Want some help?"

Rix started to shake his head, thought better of it, and grunted a negative. Fourth time lucky.... Yep. He confined himself to a modest sip, and managed to choke it down.

"Better?" Kade asked.

"Yeah." Rix capped the bottle and lifted his chin to glare at his visitor. "If you're still here in five minutes, I'm gonna wring your scrawny neck."

The kid quirked a brow. "For what? Snitching about your special power?"

Rix nodded.

"For what it's worth, I might have confirmed you *had* a special power, but they didn't need *me* to tell them what it was. FYI, it was Reilly, the scary-smart evil twin, who reviewed the security footage and figured out Rixon plus dead plant equaled energy-sucking vampire."

"Siphon."

"Eh?"

"I prefer *siphon*."

Kade rubbed his chin. "Siphon. I like it." He grinned at Rix. "But if you want to wring my neck, go ahead. Reckon you're strong enough that it'd be a nice, peaceful death—I can think of worse ways to shuffle off this mortal coil."

Rix narrowed his eyes, and was still trying to gauge the kid's mood when Kade sighed. "Look, I'm sorry my hinting dropped you in it, but better that than being pegged as one of the disposable lab-rats."

"Like Andy, you mean?"

Kade didn't flinch but his weird blue eyes darkened with an emotion that Rix didn't have to be Einstein to recognize as rage. "Yeah," he said. "Like Andy."

Rix heaved himself to his feet—all the better to loom over the kid. He needed information and he needed it now. No BS. No dancing around the truth.

He'd opened his mouth to demand an update on Lily but Kade beat him to the punch. "Lily's sedated. There's nothing either of us can do to help her right now, so best put any daft notions of riding to her rescue like a big scary dreadlocked knight out of your mind."

Not gonna happen. While there was breath in his lungs, Rix would never give up on her. His leg muscles had started to shake. Man, whatever they'd hit him with was no picnic. Unwilling to telegraph his ongoing weakness, he shoved Kade's legs aside and took possession of the bottom half of the bed. "Can I ask you a question?"

That sardonic grin was back. "Lemme guess," the kid said. "You wanna know how come *I* can phase in and out of this room at will without getting smacked out of phase and ending up limp as a wet noodle."

Rix wasn't in the mood to play games. "Yeah."

Kade scooted up the mattress to lean against the wall. His gaze fixed on the security cam's blinking red light. "Feel free to take ten and grab a nice cup of tea, ladies and gents. This ain't nothing you haven't heard before." He crossed his arms over his chest and laughed humorlessly. "Of course they'll stay glued to their seats for the duration. You know, in the vain hope I'll reveal something the Boy Genius hasn't already figured out."

"And the chances of that are?"

"Negative in the extreme. They extracted all my secrets a long time ago."

*Extracted....* Rix rubbed his arms. He wasn't a huge fan of that word choice.

"See," Kade was saying, "I've discovered I'm too fond of my skin and my sanity to bother hiding anything anymore. They ask, I spill my guts. They tell me to jump, I ask how high on the way up. And, I'm sure I recall mentioning earlier, they don't bat an eye when I tell the newbs the God's honest truth because brand new lab-rats are far less likely to do something stupid after talking to me." He tilted his head, owl-like. "To be quite clear, Vaughn Kincaid knows full well that if he was diagnosed with a terminal illness, or one of his employees decided to poison his coffee, I'd be the first to cheer. Ditto if some misguided animal rights activist succeeded in blowing Kincaid Pharmaceuticals to kingdom bloody come. We each know where the other one stands, so we get along swimmingly."

Rix had to give it to the kid: He was good—the perfect mix of resignation and trash-talking bravado you'd expect from a teenage boy. And if Rix hadn't spotted the rage Kade kept locked inside surfacing on more than one occasion, he might have bought it hook, line and sinker. But the kid wasn't as resigned to his fate as he appeared.

"Ready to find out why Vaughn's got such a hard-on for little ole me?" Kade asked.

"Not like I've got anywhere else to be right now."

"That's the spirit. For my first trick—" Kade phased.

So what? Aside from Kade's obvious ability to phase without getting his ass kicked, Rix couldn't help wondering what all the fuss was about. Kade was a lim, so simply going subliminal was hardly anything to write home about—

The kid phased back in again.

At least, *some* of him did.

Rix squeezed his eyelids shut, counted to three, opened them again. But he wasn't seeing things. And what he *was* seeing happened to be Kade's disembodied head. "Fuck me!"

"Sorry mate, you're not my type." The head's lips stretched in a wide grin. "Go on. You know you want to."

Rix waved his hand through the blank space that should have been Kade's torso. Nope. Nothing there.

And then, mind still struggling to comprehend what he was seeing, he reached out to pat the head's shaggy hair. Whoa. Not simply an afterimage imprinted onto his retinas. Real.

And too darned freaky for words. His mom had mentioned a lim back in her hometown who could go subliminal and then make only a part of his body liminal. He'd thought it just another one of her stories. But in his defense, this had to be seen to be believed.

Kade phased in the rest of his body. "It's not exactly a unique talent but it's rare. Reilly says it's usually only adult lims who can do partial phases, but I've been doing it since I was a wee chap."

"Whatever, it's pretty cool."

"You think so?" Kade's freaky eyes glowed with pleasure.

"Oh yeah. But what I really want to hear about is your being able to bypass this badass security system."

"I'm getting to that. Turns out they can't map my energy signature—not even if they try'n force a sync when I'm unconscious."

Like Liam had with Rix—leaving Rix screwed six ways to Sunday. He frowned, trying to recall long ago lessons with his mom. She'd told him "mapping" was kinda like taking a mental snapshot of a lim's energy during a sync, and memorizing the pattern. Unless the lim suffered some significant physical or mental trauma that would alter his energy pattern, the map would remain accurate. So....

So, barring significant physical or mental trauma, once he escaped this hellhole, Rix's best chance of preventing Liam from getting a fix on him was to erect a strong enough mental barrier to repel him. And looked like Kade was just the person to clue him in on how to do that. "How do you block them?"

Kade shrugged. "No clue. I'm mean, I'm strong and all that, but not strong enough to fight off the Terrible Twins—not yet, anyway. Liam let slip that my energy pattern changes before they can get a lock on it. There's speculation that's the reason why I can bypass the security nets."

Rix scratched the stubble on his chin, working through the logic. "Makes sense, I guess. And makes sense that until they figure it out, you're highly unlikely to become a disposable lab-rat."

Kade shook his head in a wry kind of way. "Thought Kincaid Senior was gonna crack open my skull and dissect my brain for a while there. Things got pretty fraught until Reilly got it through Daddy's thick skull that I haven't the foggiest flaming clue how I do it, meaning it isn't a skill I could teach to others. Hence I'm officially deemed more valuable intact—for now, at least."

Hang on. Things weren't adding up. Because if Kade could phase whenever he wanted, why'n the hell hadn't he made tracks? "And you haven't gone AWOL because... you have a thing for evil blond twins?"

Kade barked a laugh. "Only if they've got female parts." His grin soured. "There's a different security system that envelops the whole building and buggered if I can get through it. Though, between you and me and whoever's eavesdropping, I overheard one of the white-coats saying they reckon that by the time I reach full maturity, I'll be able to slip through any security system if I put my mind to it."

"And then you're gonna phase the fuck out of here and make yourself scarce, right?"

When Kade didn't respond, Rix leaned over to cuff him lightly on the back of his head. "Right?"

"Got nowhere else to go," the kid said. "Here, I have a room of my own, three meals a day, and I get to play all the video games I want. Beats the heck out of being a ward of the state and having to go to school and all that shite, right?" He eyed Rix, his expression revealing nothing. "Or roughing it on the streets, for that matter."

Rix was tempted to call him on the BS, but just then the door to his room buzzed and swung open. A guy stuck his head inside the room. "Mr. Kincaid's son wants you, Kade. STAT."

"Which one?"

"Liam."

"Be right there," Kade told him. Turning back to Rix he said, "You must be going nuts with nothing to do. I'll grab you a mag or two from the lunchroom. Any requests?"

Rix shrugged. He was too damn tired to read—not that he would be able to concentrate on written words right now anyway. His head hurt. His body ached. And his heart.... He didn't want to think about his heart. It was already battered and bruised but if anything happened to Lily it would shatter. Given his physical and mental state right now, even if he *could* phase without getting zapped, he'd end up defaulting Between. He collapsed on the bed and threw an arm over his eyes.

"A nap," he heard Kade say. "Good idea. Catch you later, Rix."

The door clinked shut. And when Rix peeled open an eyelid to check the room, he was alone.

RIX WOKE to find the promised magazine on his pillow. Huh. The food must have been drugged after all, because one thing he had perfected during years living rough was sleeping lightly and waking the instant another person invaded his space.

He scooped up the magazine. Over-priced men's fitness mags weren't exactly his reading material of choice but anything was better than nothing. He sat cross-legged on the bed to leaf through the mag, searching for an article to distract him from worrying about Lily for a bit.

He'd flipped through a third of the magazine when he spotted a slip of paper tucked between the pages. His pulse ratcheted up a notch. If Kade had managed to smuggle in a note from Lily, he would owe the kid big-time.

Ever-conscious of anonymous watchers, Rix flicked back a couple of pages and forced himself to read every word of some article that insisted personal trainers were a necessity rather than a luxury.

Hah. What a load of crap. *Food* was a necessity. *Clothes* were a necessity. For good measure he snorted—just a guy reading an article, unconvinced by the argument put forth.

One more paragraph before he could turn the page....

He scanned the note, heart leaping about in his chest like a jackrabbit.

It was from Kade. It was brief and to the point, and when he'd finished reading, Rix knew he couldn't fool himself any longer. The time for playing down his abilities and awaiting the perfect opportunity to get Lily out had passed.

Somehow, Rix kept turning the pages of the magazine like nothing had changed. Like white-hot rage wasn't circulating through his veins, taunting him to batter the walls, to smash and tear and destroy. Even his vision was infected, forcing him to view the pages of the magazine through a crimson haze.

Eventually, though, as a small part of his brain had instinctively known it would, his rage cooled and he could think and reason again.

Taking the magazine, he headed for the toilet cubicle, and made like a guy settling in for a lengthy sit. After ten minutes or so, he yanked a substantial handful of toilet tissue squares from the dispenser... and figured no one would be interested in watching him too closely right now. Only then did he risk palming the note and wadding it among the toilet tissue before pretending to wipe his ass. Pity he hadn't been able to take a crap for real. But hey, if they planned on examining whatever he flushed, good luck to the poor bastard who got that job.

After washing his hands and splashing water on his face, Rix settled back on the bed with the magazine to wait. While pretending to read, he chewed over the contents of Kade's note, committing each word to memory, using them to strengthen his resolve.

They planned to harvest Lily's eggs, fertilize them in-vitro with sperm taken from select male liminal subjects, and re-implant the viable embryos. Vaughn Kincaid was going to use her as a broodmare, force her to bear baby after baby until her body wore out. But Kade had a plan for getting her out of here. Tonight. He'd organized some sort of distraction, so Rix needed to be ready.

No problem. When the time came Rix would not falter. He would do whatever needed to be done. And if the opportunity presented itself, he would drain Vaughn Kincaid to a wizened husk and pummel his remains to dust.

# CHAPTER 8

AROUND MIDNIGHT, the lights in the corridor flickered and died. "And that's our cue," a voice by Rix's ear whispered. "Get your arse out of bed, boyo."

Rix rolled off the mattress. In the gloom, he could make out Kade rolling up a couple of blankets and stuffing them beneath the covers. The kid then plunked a dark mass of something on the pillow, and tugged the coverlet up until only the barest glimpse could be seen. "Mop-top," he whispered. "Dyed black. Nearest thing to your dreads we could come up with at short notice. Should buy us a bit of time."

Rix uttered a soft grunt of approval. And had just enough time to wonder who "we" happened to be, before Kade handed him a piece of clothing. "Lab coat."

Rix shoved his arms into the coat, and managed to hold still while Kade placed a pair of glasses on his nose. "Clipboard," the kid said, handing one over. "Can't do anything about the dreads, so we'll have to wing it. If anyone catches us, channel 'officious prick' and say Reilly Kincaid instructed you to bring me to the lab to run some tests. You got that?"

"Got it."

"Good. Now listen up." Kade reached for Rix's hand. "I'm gonna sync with you and piggyback-phase you, okay? So you gotta relax and trust me."

"I do trust you," Rix whispered back. And damned if it wasn't the truth.

"You done this before? Had someone sync with you, I mean."

"Nope." Rix had only ever synched with Lily—once, to get them both out of a tight spot. And he'd been the dominant one—the one doing the synching.

"Fantastic. Well, find your happy place and let me do the work. Oh, and fergodsakes don't panic and start siphoning energy from me or this is gonna turn to shite in a big hurry. Ready?"

"As I'll ever be."

Kade's hand squeezed Rix's. "Count to three. And whatever happens, don't freak out."

One. Two. Three—

Tendrils of Kade's energy probed, hesitant at first and then entering in a rush to circulate through Rix, now surging ahead, now lagging behind, and then matching his energy flows. He felt rather than heard Kade's thoughts: *So far, so good. Now for the tricky part....*

"The tricky part" being Kade synching his energy's vibrations to Rix's—matching the pattern exactly.

His mind drifted to his parents. They'd synched so effortlessly—like they'd been two halves of a whole....

Shit. He made a conscious effort to think about the good times—before his dad had gotten sick. Before his mom had fallen asleep at the wheel after an extra shift she'd taken to help pay for his cancer treatments, and never made it home. Before Rix had been outted as his father's sole caregiver, and placed in foster care, leaving his dad to die alone—

The energy that had been purring through Rix's veins buzzed and throbbed, and every hair on his body was standing on end.

*Whatever you're thinking, stop bloody well thinking it and think of something else!*

*Sorry,* Rix thought back. He let the memory of his parents fade and concentrated instead on Lily. Her beautiful eyes and expressive face. Her slim body thrumming with excitement as she'd presented him with a cake she'd baked for his birthday. She'd helped old Mrs. Hicks for a month when the old lady had a fall, and had refused to take any money. Instead, Lily and Mrs. Hicks had put their heads together and come up with a plan to bake Rix the cake. "Everyone deserves a cake for their birthday," Lily had insisted—just like she had insisted Rix blow out the candles and make a wish.

*Better. Keep doing what you're doing.*

Kade's voice was a distant murmur as Rix immersed himself in memories of Lily. Her smiles—all the more treasured because they were so infrequent. The day he'd taken her to a mall and the tears that had welled in those chocolate-brown eyes when he treated her to a new pair of shoes after selling a carving. Waking up in a derelict building to dawn's soft light creeping in from a broken window, and discovering that Lily had burrowed in close sometime during the night, and was curled beside him, nose buried in the crook of his shoulder, and thinking—*knowing*—that even though they were homeless, and had to struggle to hold on to what little they had, right here, right now, with Lily in his arms, he was happy....

He felt a "rightness" that was hard to describe, as though discordant notes had segued into perfect harmony, as Kade's energy meshed fully with his. And when Kade phased, rather than experiencing the slight lag of being towed, as Rix had half-expected, he was swept along, both of them sliding smoothly through this dimension into another.

It could have been a second, or a minute, or even an hour, when Kade disengaged and Rix found himself in a darkened room, beside a hospital-style bed.

Lily's bed.

He bent to whisper in her ear. "Lily, it's me, Rix. We're gonna get you out of here, okay?"

No response.

He brushed her cheek with the knuckle of his forefinger, discovered her skin was damp with tears. His heart knotted in his chest. Shit, Lily. How many times since you left me have you cried yourself to sleep?

His hand shook as he gently prised open one of her eyelids, and confirmed what he had feared. "She's out cold."

"Fuckwits have put her in restraints." Kade's voice was pitched so low it sounded like a growl. "I'll do the ankle cuffs," he told Rix, "you do the wrists. Quick as you can."

Rix worked loose the straps of the nearest cuff, and then reached across Lily to release the second cuff. "All done," Kade told him. "Pick her up and let's get outta here."

It wasn't until Rix had scooped Lily into his arms and her head lolled back that he realized her eyes were now open... but she was staring vacantly at the ceiling. Like the lights were on but nobody was home. He damped the panic before it could take hold. "What's the plan?" he demanded.

"Wait for the distraction, then head for the labs. My contact will piggy-back-phase you from there to the rendezvous point. I'll take Lily."

Kade's contact must be pretty high up the food-chain. Even so, Rix didn't like what he was hearing. "Thought you couldn't phase out of the building."

Kade started ticking off points on his fingers. "My sig status has been temporarily upgraded and we've weakened the protocols surrounding the labs, so phasing out from there should be doable. And because we like to cover all bases, we uploaded a sneaky little backdoor virus to temporarily expand—for want of a better word—the main security system's parameters, which covers you and Lily. Plus, I'm a heap stronger now than the last time I attempted to escape. Whatever happens, I'll get her out of here, Rix. I give you my word."

"I'm not entirely happy about this plan."

"Got a better one?" Kade's freaky blue eyes gleamed a challenge. And when Rix didn't answer, he gave a soft snort. "Too late to back out now. Trust me, it'll be fine."

"Tell me about this rendezvous point." A command, not an invitation. Rix wanted as much information as possible *now*. Before the shit hit the fan.

Kade moved closer, obviously not wanting to risk being overheard if anyone reviewed the security footage. "It's a place me and my folks stayed when we first arrived in the States."

"Describe it to me—as much detail as you can."

"It's a bit of a shithole, but it's permanently etched on my brain, so there's no risk I'll stray mid-phase."

"That's not what I'm worried ab—"

The boom was deafening. Rix's arms tightened around Lily. "What the fuck?" A blaring alarm cut through the ringing in his ears, quickly followed by shouts and the dull thuds of booted feet.

Rix shook his head, trying to clear the buzz from his ears. "*That's* your distraction? Blowing the crap out of the place?"

"FYI, that was Reilly's office. And yup."

The cocky grin slid off Kade's face and his gaze widened. The hairs on the nape of Rixon's neck stood on end as a voice behind him drawled, "Should have guessed *you'd* be behind this, Kade."

Kade moistened his lips with the tip of his tongue. "Reilly Kincaid," he said. "So nice of you to join our little party."

Kade's voice might have been steady enough to fool most, but Rix spotted the fear that chased across the kid's eyes before he got it under control. Kade was afraid of what Reilly would do....

Rix didn't stop to think, he reacted. He shoved Lily at Kade, whirled, and launched himself at Reilly.

This time Reilly was quick, but not quick enough. Rix smacked into him, forearm to sternum, bowling him over and following him down to pin him to the floor.

Dazed green eyes blinked up at him. Reilly's mouth opened, trying to form words, but Rix wasn't giving him an inch. "Don't worry," he told him, "I won't siphon everything from you unless you're stupid enough to come after us." And then he shoved claws of energy deep into Reilly.

His victim's eyes went wide, flaring with outrage. He bucked but didn't stand a chance against Rix's superior weight. Rix drained him until Reilly's eyelids drooped and he went limp.

"Well, that was... unexpected."

Rix pinched off the siphon and disconnected from Reilly. He climbed to his feet, swaying a little as his brain and body adjusted to the glut of energy roaring through him.

Kade was seated on the floor, Lily cradled in his arms. "You okay to take her, or do you need a moment?"

In answer, Rix dropped to his haunches and took Lily's limp form from Kade. He brushed the hair back from her face. Her eyes were still open, still blank, unseeing. It made his stomach curdle.

"Don't stress," he heard Kade say. "I've seen this before. She'll be fine when the meds wear off. Just give her time." And Rix wanted so desperately for that to be the truth, he simply nodded and pushed to his feet with Lily held snugly in his arms.

"Impressive." Kade's crooked grin was back. "Don't know many guys could do that without falling on their arse. You must work out."

"Yeah."

Kade headed for the door, jabbed a code into the keypad, and jiggled impatiently until the door opened. He peered through the doorway. "All clear. Follow me." He headed off at a trot, Rix hard on his heels.

Rix was too worried about the girl in his arms to fully focus on the route Kade took, and it was an unpleasant shock to be ushered into the same room where Vaughn Kincaid's cronies had tortured Lily. Even more unpleasant was confronting Kade's accomplice.

"You have got to be fucking kidding me," Rix snarled, rounding on Kade. "No way I'm entrusting Lily to *him*."

Liam Kincaid's eyes narrowed to slits, and the look he tossed Rix's way would have shriveled a lesser man's balls. "You've got five seconds to explain what the fuck you're trying to pull, Kade," Liam said. "And it better be good." The "or else" hung in the air.

Kade wasn't bothered by the implied threat. "Thought a siphon might be useful when you and your merry little band of outlaws go head to head with Daddy Dearest."

Liam scowled. "And the girl?"

"Package deal," Kade inserted before Rix could formulate a suitable response.

"Forget it." Liam's scowl segued into a sneer. "Her mind is broken. She's a lost cause."

Rix met his gaze. "Lost cause or not, I'm not leaving her for your asshole father to use as a breeder."

"Think about it, Liam," Kade wheedled. "Not only do you get Daddy's most valuable lab-rat—" he jerked a thumb at his own chest "—but you get Daddy's second best lab-rat, too. Imagine how pissed he's gonna be when he finds out you've got his siphon. And all you gotta do to keep Rix happy is be nice to the girlfriend? Sounds like an excellent deal if you ask me."

Rix was fed up to the eyeballs with negotiating. "Tell you what," he told Liam. "Shut the fuck up and get us all out of here in one piece, and I won't drain you and leave you for your father to deal with—like I recently did your asshole brother. How's that for a plan?"

Liam's attention snapped to Kade. "Thought he couldn't drain energy from humans."

"I lied," Rix said.

Liam ignored him, still directing his questions to Kade. "Is he on the level? Or exaggerating to convince me not to ditch his worthless ass?"

"He's on the level," Kade said. "Saw it with my own eyes, and frankly, it was full of awesome. Golden Boy didn't know what hit him."

"He really siphoned Reilly's energy?"

"Yep. Bro's out cold."

Liam's gaze fixed on Rixon again, speculative in a way that made Rix instantly suspicious. He didn't trust Liam Kincaid one iota.

"Tick tock," Kade said. "We doing this? Or we gonna sit here with our thumbs up our arses until security catches up with us."

Liam huffed a pissed off breath that made his nostrils flare. "Fine. We'll do it your way, Kade. But you owe me—both of you." His gaze flicked to Rix before settling on Kade again, and Rix could almost see the cogs spinning in his brain. He'd have to stay alert or next thing he knew, Lily would become a bargaining chip to keep him in line.

"Excellent." Kade wasted no time filling them in on how it was gonna go down. "Liam's energy sig's unrestricted, so he'll piggyback you," he told Rix. "He's strong enough to haul your arse through the net protecting the building even if your sig gets flagged during the phase. I'll take Lily. She's so low on energy right now I'm confident I can completely mask her sig during the piggyback if needs be. We'll meet up at the rendezvous point as planned."

Rixon reluctantly handed Lily over to Kade, wincing inwardly when the kid juggled her in his arms. "You sure you can do this, Kade?"

"Yep. That's not to say things couldn't still get a bit dicey—best laid plans and all that. Only way to find out is to do it. And I'd suggest we do it *now*, before we get busted."

"You and Lily first," Rix said. "We'll wait sixty seconds and follow you. And if things don't go to plan, you know what to do." Subtext: If Liam phases in alone, get Lily the hell out of there and keep her safe.

Liam snorted. "If you're worried I'll try something mid-phase, don't be. After all the trouble I've gone to, I'm not about to risk losing my prize asset."

Kade fluttered his eyelashes. "Aw, you say the sweetest things." The humor slid from his face. "I've already promised to keep Lily safe," he told Rix. "Now both of you shut up so I can concentrate on the sync."

Rix watched Liam observing Kade as though it might be possible, with enough effort, to physically see the synching process. Like his father, Liam had the ability to focus absolutely on his subject. It was unsettling as hell, and Rix was hugely relieved when Kade announced, "Got it." And then, in two breaths, he and Lily were gone.

Rix began silently counting down the seconds, his heart pounding like he'd run a record-breaking mile. This was it: crunch time. He kept a close eye on Liam, waiting for him to show his cards. Would he stick to the plan? Did he believe Rix's siphoning talent worth the effort, or would he hang Rix out to dry first chance he got?

Liam took a step toward Rix, hand outstretched, mouth open. "Dad is going to kill you," he said. "What the hell were you thinking?"

Huh?

Liam seemed as startled as Rix by what had come out of his mouth and—

Rix blinked. Please, God, let me be seeing things....

Ah crap. He hadn't wanted to risk accidentally killing the guy—just incapacitate him for a while. But apparently Rix was a total dumbass: He should have drained more energy from Reilly Kincaid while he'd had the chance.

"What did you hope to gain from blowing up my office?" Reilly demanded.

Liam crossed his arms over his chest and scowled at his twin. "Guess you better start sucking up to Dad so he'll replace it for you. Oh wait, you already do that on a daily basis."

Reilly's lips curled in a smirk. "Jealous, are we?"

"Of you?" Liam barked a harsh laugh. "In your dreams. You can have KP —or what's left of it once I'm done."

Reilly's gaze narrowed. "What are you planning, Liam?"

Rix interrupted before Liam could get a word in. "How about going public with your fucked up experiments on street kids for starters?"

Both brothers turned to him and in eerie unison said, "Are you crazy?"

Reilly shook his head emphatically. "The world's not ready to know about us lims."

"I don't agree with much my brother has to say," Liam said, "but right now we're in total accord."

A piss-poor excuse to justify letting a sadistic bastard like Vaughn Kincaid continue experimenting on lims if ever Rix had heard one. He didn't have time for this shit. God only knew how long Kade would stick around and wait for them. Time to take matters into his own hands.

Rix edged closer to Reilly, gauging the distance....

Perfect. "Watch out!" he yelled, jabbing a finger at a spot over Reilly's shoulder. And when Reilly instinctively turned to confront the supposed threat, Rix smashed a fist into his jaw.

Reilly's eyes rolled up in his head and he dropped like a stone.

Liam nudged his brother with his shoe. "Nice right hook. Pity. I really could have used you on the team but—"

"And here Kade insisted you were almost as smart as your brother. Synching with an experienced lim is a two-way street, motherfucker—even if one of the parties is unconscious at the time." Rix waited until he had commanded Liam's full attention before feeding him the lie. "Sure, you'll be able to track me via *my* energy sig, but I can track you, too."

Liam made a good show of not giving a shit but Rix had already noted the slow blink that indicated he was thinking hard about whatever he had planned.

"Oooh. I'm cowering in my boots at the thought of you coming for me in the dead of night," Liam drawled a beat too late.

Nice try, Blondie. "Wouldn't bother wasting my energy coming after you, though," Rix told him. "I'd simply tell your brother and your father where to find you. After this stunt I'm sure they'll be very interested in your where-abouts. Then again—" Rix made a show of snapping his fingers like he'd just come up with a brilliant idea "—I could drain you dry right this minute, truss you up with your fancy leather belt, and leave you here for your brother to find when he comes to. I should sell tickets to *that* encounter—would make a fortune, I reckon. Or—and this is my absolute favorite, by the way—I can suggest to your daddy that a suitable punishment for your betrayal would be for me to keep draining you of energy, leaving you so weak you won't be able to get out of bed. That'll be fun. For me, at least. For you, not so much."

Liam's eyes darkened. He opened his mouth, seemed to think better of whatever he'd been about to say, and shut it with a snap. Finally he said, "Let's do this."

Rix knew he had the upper hand but in case Liam was too dumb to realize it, he hammered home his advantage. "One more thing: If you're thinking of unsynching mid-phase and dumping me somewhere, think again. The instant I detect a fluctuation in energy, I'll drain you, and we'll both default Between. And you'd better believe I'll have the advantage. I can siphon energy from you and keep your ass there indefinitely if I choose."

"What about your little girlfriend? Who's gonna look after her while you're sucking me off Between?"

Rix refused to be baited. He didn't have time for another pissing match with Liam. "Kade will do right by Lily." Unlike you, you sneaky fucking bastard.

"You hope," Liam said.

Rix didn't deign to reply. He simply stared at Liam until that green glare slid away. Yeah. Kade would keep his word, and they both knew it.

Confident he'd made his point, Rix held out his hand. "Whenever you're ready."

Turned out Liam didn't need physical contact to initiate a piggyback-phase. His energy shrouded Rix's, paused for a split second, then slid through him like a hot knife through butter. Rix had just enough time to think, *Whoa, dude has some serious skills*, before he was swept away.

Whether Liam's intention had been to deliberately punish Rix, or whether phasing with an unauthorized passenger through the security net had taken a toll, Rix was shoved out of the sync the instant he became liminal.

Nice one, douchebag. He crawled to his feet and stood there, blinking, absently brushing grit from the knees of his sweatpants as he fought to re-orient himself to this new reality... namely a shadowy patch of asphalt in the lee of a dumpster.

"Took you long enough," a voice boomed. "Was beginning to worry you'd killed each other."

Rix pivoted on his heel, and nearly fell on his ass.

"Easy there, big boy." A hand shot out, gripping Rix's forearm to steady him.

*Big boy* ? Hugely ironic, considering the voice belonged to a massive black dude who made Rix feel small—not something he'd encountered before.

"Name's Simon."

"Rix." Rix shook off the helping hand and offered his own, hiding a wince when the guy obliged with a bone-grating handshake. Like the rest of him, the dude's hands were freaking huge. His deep purple suit screamed tailor-made: It was immaculately cut and fitted his big frame perfectly. And his shoes—expensive, and so shiny Rix could see his own reflection. The black shirt looked like silk, and Rix would have bet money the shiny black tie was silk, too.

Dude was seriously into dressing to impress, and Rix couldn't help but be impressed. One day, he promised himself, he would have enough money to kit himself out like this.

"Liam." Simon inclined his chin in what Rix took to be a gesture of respect. "Any trouble headed our way? And by trouble, I mean your brother."

"Handled," Liam drawled.

Shit. Rix's stomach somersaulted. While he'd been standing 'round, admiring Simon's fashion sense, Liam could have phased out again and been long gone, leaving Rix stranded, with no freaking idea where Kade had gotten to with Lily. The phase must really have screwed with his brain.

"The kids are inside," Simon told Liam. "Little girl's exhausted, though. I got a room and put her to bed—figured she needed to rest up." He turned to Rix. "She was asking for you."

"Lily's conscious?" Relief overwhelmed all worries about the future.

"Yep." Simon strode from the shelter of the dumpster and beckoned Rix to follow. Once Rix had joined him, Simon pointed to a row of motel rooms. "Room 110—the end room."

Despite the urge to sprint, Rix kept to a fast walk, still not quite trusting his balance. Last thing he needed was to trip and do a face-plant. The hot asphalt seared the soles of his bare feet and small sharp stones dug into his insteps. He didn't pay them any heed.

He'd taken a dozen steps when he heard Liam say to Simon, "We need to talk." Instinct told Rix to halt, manufacture some reason to hang around for a bit so he could eavesdrop on the conversation and get a sense of Liam's next move. But the need to lay eyes on Lily, see for himself that she was recovering from her ordeal, was stronger.

He didn't bother to knock. He barreled through the door. And the last thing he expected was to see a bare-chested Kade, perched on the edge of the bed... with his arm around Lily.

# CHAPTER 9

ROOTED TO THE SPOT, Rix stared at the couple. *Kade and Lily?* The breath he'd inhaled rasped painfully in his chest. He felt bruised inside and out, like he'd been pummeled to within an inch of his life. His gut pitched and rolled, and he ordered himself to calm the fuck down. He had no right to be angry or feel betrayed. Because Lily and Kade made sense—a helluva lot more sense than Lily and *Rix*. Lily couldn't be more than a year or so older than Kade. And Kade....

Kade had been her protector after she'd been taken. Kade had been the one she'd confided in, the one who'd helped her survive the nightmare. The one who'd been there for her.

Kade's eyes narrowed to blue slits and then rounded, eyebrows winging upward. His lips curved, his bark of laughter a spike through Rix's heart. Because there was nothing amusing about this whole cluster-fuck—about realizing he'd left it too late to tell Lily how he felt about her. That he loved her.

Only now could Rix admit the bald, unadulterated truth. He'd been lying —telling himself that he saw Lily like he would a little sister, refusing to admit his true feelings because she was so very young, had been through so much awful shit, and in any case, why would she ever be interested in a hulking great lummox like him in that way?

Kade groaned. "It's not what it looks like, dumb-arse. Lily's cute and all, but she's so not my type."

Lily's chin lifted and bruised, tear-drowned eyes fixed on Rix. "Rix?" Her brows knit as she worried her lower lip between her teeth. And then a choked gasp tore from her throat. "You can't think—? I would never— Me and *Kade*? Ewww! No way!" She pushed Kade away and edged sideways.

Kade pressed a hand to his heart, the theatrical gesture losing all impact given that he was grinning like a loon. "Charming. And after all I've done for you." He mock-punched her arm. "Ungrateful little sod."

Rix gnawed the inside of his cheek, hardly daring to hope—

Kade rolled his eyes. "FYI, dude, the only reason I'm sitting here without a shirt is because that gown thing they'd put her in gaped in all the wrong places. It was bloody indecent, so I felt compelled to do the gentlemanly thing and loan her my t-shirt."

"Oh." Rix blinked at stared at Lily's attire, for the first time registering that she wore a white t-shirt that was far too big for her overtop the gown. And his next thought was that he wanted to rip off the t-shirt and throw it at Kade... and then give her *his* shirt, wrap her in *his* scent and—

Don't be a dick, Rix. No need to act like a dog marking its territory. Kade was only thinking of Lily. Rix shrugged out of the stolen lab coat and handed it to Kade.

Kade's eyes glinted with amusement as he donned the coat. "I have something for you, too—I swiped it from Liam's office." He fished something from a pocket and tossed it at Rix.

Rix snatched the object from midair. His fingers closed about it, relearning familiar lines and curves. His carved kiwi—the one Liam had stolen. "Thanks." He shoved it in the pocket of his pants, too distracted by other things to truly appreciate the return of a talisman he'd put his heart and soul into.

"Again, no problem. Lily told me you always carried it around with you."

Rix couldn't stand it any longer. He needed to hold Lily, needed her in his arms, where she belonged. "Lily, come here."

She scowled up at him.

"I need to...." Aw, hell. He screwed up his eyelids, pinching the bridge of his nose. He was making a complete hash of this.

He opened his arms and stood there, not daring to move, like he was carved in stone. "Please?"

She launched herself at him. He scooped her up and wrapped his arms tightly around her. "Lily. Thank God you're safe. Thank God."

Rix closed his eyes, nuzzled her hair... refused to think about what could have happened to her. "If you ever run off and leave me like that again, I swear I'm gonna hunt you down and lock you up for the term of your natural life. Don't ever do that to me again. I couldn't bear it if you left me again."

She entwined her arms about his neck and buried her face against his chest, but her body was tense against his, like she didn't completely trust that she could relax. And then she heaved a huge, shuddering sigh, and all the tension drained from her limbs.

Rix knew exactly how she felt: like this was right—meant to be.

"If we've finished with the touching reunion, you two need to go." Kade strode to the window and twitched the curtain aside. He turned, his gaze meeting Rix's across Lily's head. "Sooner rather than later."

"But—"

Kade threw up a hand. "Now, Rix. Before Liam finishes giving Simon his orders. I know the way Liam thinks. To him, Lily's nothing but a pawn. He'll use her to convince you to work for him. And chances are mega-freaking-high once he's figured out how you do what you do, you'll be of no further use—either of you."

Shit. Kade was right. Rix's arms tightened around Lily until she gave a squeak of protest. "Sorry." He pressed a kiss atop her head and let her slide to the ground, barely registering her ducking beneath his arm to lean against his side. Despair clawed his heart. He'd been a fool to think he could keep her safe.

"We could go somewhere really far away," Lily was saying. "Like... New Zealand! That's where your mom came from, right? A new start for us both." Her face lit up at the idea. "Surely they wouldn't bother with us if we were on the opposite side of the world."

He couldn't protect her from the truth. "They know what I am, Lily. They've seen what I can do."

She peeped up at him, brows forming little question marks. And he couldn't bring himself to lie to her anymore. Even if the lie had been neglecting to tell the truth, it was still a lie.

"I'm a siphon." He forced himself to hold her curious gaze, even though it would gut him to witness her disgust when he explained what he could do. "I can take energy from other living things. Like plants and animals—"

"And humans, too. Duh. I'm not an idiot, Rix. I know you." She blew her choppy, uneven bangs out of her eyes—eyes that were clear and guileless. "I know what you did to keep me safe, too."

The walls of the motel room closed in.

She knew? She'd always known?

"God. Lily. I'm—"

She punched his arm hard, her expression cold and fierce. "Don't you dare apologize for taking out that piece of shit before he could hurt any other little girls. You hear me, Rix? The world's a far safer place without him." Her lips curled in a snarl. "I was planning on putting him down myself soon as I could figure out how to do it without getting caught. You simply saved me the trouble." She sniffed like he'd offended her, and finished with, "Now can we please move on?"

Rix blinked but Lily hadn't morphed into some ruthless, take no prisoners Amazonian princess. She was still the same slim, delicate-looking girl, only Rix was seeing her through new eyes. And it was then that another truth smacked him upside the head: Lily wasn't a little kid, she was his equal.

She rose on tiptoes to kiss his chin. And her smile was so sweet and loving, so full of affection, it almost brought Rix to his knees. "That's right, you big lummox," she said, punching his arm again. "You finally get it: I didn't stay with you because I *had* to, I stayed because I wanted to—because I love your big stubborn ass. But it royally pissed me off you've never seen me as anything more than a little kid. I needed to do *something* to convince you to ditch the big-brother routine, Rix, and I figured proving I could make it on my own was a good start." She huffed a shaky breath, all the feistiness draining from her. "My cool plan to return all triumphant with a bunch of cash for a down payment on a rental and shit didn't turn out so good though. Sorry 'bout that."

She loved him despite knowing what he was, what he'd done. She loved him... and she'd left him? Rix didn't know whether to paddle Lily's behind or kiss her senseless.

"Girls, huh? Too. Scary. For. Words."

Kade's wry comment yanked Rix back to the unwelcome reality of their situation. "You can say that again," he muttered, wishing he didn't have to be the one to shatter Lily's hopes of a fresh start. "Doesn't matter where we go, Lily. They've mapped my energy sig—yours, too. We'll spend the rest of our lives running, looking over our shoulders, wondering if today's the day one of the Kincaids catches up with us. And when they do—"

"They'll use us and then throw us away." She sagged against him, defeated.

Kade snapped his fingers. "Actually, there might be a place you can hang out for a bit—at least until the heat comes off so you can safely head for New Zealand."

"I'm listening," Rix said.

"Sedona. This article I read says the area is rife with energy vortexes that affect people by resonating with their energy centers. And not just lims, either. Meaning—"

"It'll be damn near impossible to track *our* energy sigs because of all the interference thrown off by everyone else."

"Gold star for you, Rix. Bet you could earn some cash selling cool little wooden carvings like that kiwi, too. You'll fit right in with the local scene—just don't get too famous or anything."

Rix glanced down at Lily. "How do you feel about a side-trip to Sedona? I remember my parents saying they stayed there for a bit—met up with a couple of dad's old school friends who were into all that New Age stuff."

Lily gnawed a thumbnail. "You've never been there, though, right?"

"Nope."

"Then how do we phase somewhere neither of us have ever been?"

Well, shit. Phasing from across the street into a bathroom that had been thoroughly described to him, was one thing. But phasing across the freaking country? If Rix had been solo he might have tried it, but he wasn't prepared to risk Lily.

"I think I might be able to help with that, too." Kade's grin was so full of confidence, Rix dared to hope they might have a chance.

"See, this article I read was in a travel mag, and it had pages and pages of photos. Lucky for you, I've got an excellent memory—almost photographic, if I don't say so myself. So I'm thinking I sync with each of you to project my memories directly into your minds. And once you've both got a good enough visual, you guys sync, and voilà, off to Sedona you go." He read the doubt in Rix's mind. "It's your best shot," he said. "Especially when you've got all that extra energy you took from Reilly to tap into."

Lily nodded. "It's the best chance we've got. We can do this, Rix. I know we can." She slipped her hand in his and squeezed.

He squeezed back. "Okay, we'll give it our best shot."

"What about you, Kade? Come with us," Lily urged.

"Can't, luv. I owe Liam big-time for getting me out."

Rix snorted. "You don't owe him squat."

Lily wasn't taking no for an answer. "What's gonna happen to you when Liam finds us gone?"

Good point. Rix knew it wouldn't go well for Kade if Liam learned he'd helped them escape.

Kade shrugged off their concerns. "Sure he'll be a little pissed he's lost his pet siphon, but he'll get over it. Bird in the hand and all that, right? He needs my special skills to help him take down his daddy, so don't worry about me, okay? Just worry about yourselves."

Rix waited for Lily's nod before saying, "Let's do this. Even if we both end up Between—"

He bit off what were meant to be reassuring words when fear chased across her face. But to his relief she nodded, again, short and sharp and fiercely determined. "We'll be together," she said.

Lily didn't need to add anything else because Rix got it: So long as they were together, didn't matter where they ended up. So long as they were together they would make it, whatever life, the Kincaids, or imaginary monsters lurking Between, threw at them.

---

THROUGH THE POUNDING in his skull, Kade heard a door slam. He stayed right where he was—sprawled on the floor beside the bed. More authentic that way. Not that he had to fake feeling like shite right now because man, getting booted out of a sync by a lim as strong as Rixon was a bitch. He couldn't blame Rix, though. Kade would've done the same if he'd been pressed for time, worried that at any minute Liam would come walking through the door.

He sensed someone looming over him and prised open his eyelids. Seeing a blurry form he recognized, he immediately closed his eyes again and groaned. "What the feck happened?"

"You tell me."

Liam's coldly furious tone matched the expression Kade had glimpsed on his face.

"Rixon and the girl are nowhere to be found," came Simon's deep voice, his tone carefully neutral.

Kade risked opening his eyes again. "Fuck. My head feels like it's gonna explode. Rix must've walloped me a good one, then phased with Lily."

"That your story?" Liam sat back on his heels, poison-green eyes fixed on Kade, drilling into his soul. "He knocked you out, when he could have simply drained you and used your energy to boost his own?"

"Sure feels like he drained my energy. Probably helped himself while I was out cold. That's what I'd have done if I were him." Kade attempted to sit up and flopped back to the floor with a heartfelt groan he didn't need to fake. It took two more tries before he managed to sit.

Liam stood without offering a helping hand.

Ah shite. He wasn't buying it.

Kade waited for him to pitch a fit, and while he waited, thought about how much he owed Liam Kincaid for busting him out of that hellhole. Yeah. Only his sanity. And quite likely his life, too, because he'd been thinking seriously about topping himself until Liam had promised to get him out, and give him the chance to help take down Vaughn's fucked up empire.

Simon skirted Liam and bent to grasp Kade's wrist, hauling him to his feet. "Give it a rest, Liam," the big man said. "All Rixon cares about is the girl. If you planned on keeping him around by using her as leverage, it was only gonna backfire and bite you in the ass."

Liam cocked an eyebrow. "Meaning?"

"Meaning that one day soon," Kade said, "you'll push him too far and he'll siphon your energy—maybe drain you of everything if you piss him off thoroughly enough." He stretched his arms over his head, wincing at the soreness of his muscles. "Take it from me, Rixon doesn't play well with others."

"Kid's right." Simon ran a palm over his shaven head. "Let them go. Sure, a kid with Rix's ability would be damn useful, but we haven't got the resources to chase them both down right now."

"Point taken."

Kade's relief eked out in a slow sigh that left him limp.

"Before you start congratulating yourself, I have a job for you, Kade—a way to show your gratitude to me for busting you out."

Liam's grin reminded Kade of a wolf—all teeth and unspoken threats. "Whatever you need," he said. "Whatever you need to take Vaughn down, just name it."

"Music to my ears." Liam's tight grin relaxed, turning lazy. "There's someone I need you to watch for me. She's a couple of years younger than you—should be no problem for a lim of your abilities to keep tabs on her."

"What's her name?"

"Wren."

"Cute name. She a lim?"

Liam shrugged. "That's what I need you to find out." He clicked his fingers at Simon, who obediently pulled a photo from the breast pocket of his jacket.

"She's a pretty little thing," the big man said. "Can't imagine it'll be too much of a hardship to watch her, eh, Kade?" He winked as he handed over the photo.

"You in?" Liam asked.

Kade nodded, gaze still fixed on the photo of the girl. "Yeah. I'm in."

# ACKNOWLEDGMENTS

Dear Reader, I hope you enjoyed this novella-length prequel to the *Liminals* series. Kade and Wren's story continues in *Liminal*, the first book in the *Liminals* series.

# LIVE FAST, DIE YOUNG

VANESSA BARNEVELD

# CHAPTER 1

MOLLY

WHEN IT COMES TO ALEX, my best friend and study buddy, lately every little thing he does gets me steamed up. Not to mention frustrated. Confused. Sad.

All of the above.

I stop off at Burger Deluxe after school. The diner's in a pocket of coastline south of Malibu that used to be popular with tourists. Last year's wildfires scared a lot of people off for good.

My stomach rumbles because I haven't eaten lunch. Couldn't touch that cafeteria meatloaf special I mindlessly ordered. The only thing "special" about that stuff was that it resembled three-day-old roadkill.

But my main reason for coming here is not to fill up on chili fries. It's to hunt down Alex and find out why he's been avoiding me. I already checked San Marco Cove, his favorite surf spot. So this is the next logical place.

Lo and behold, the first person I see when I walk through the doors is Alex. He's facing the wall, head down. I'd recognize the line of his shoulders and the shape of his head even in a dark room. He shaved his hair off when he was on vacation as part of some charity fundraiser. It's growing back now. Much as I miss his wavy brown locks, this crew cut looks kinda sexy.

Wait a second. I'm mad at him. We need to talk. Straightening my back, I stomp to the far corner of the dining area, bypassing the order counter.

"Alex, what are you doing here? Why weren't you in school today? You realize that's two days you've missed. In a row."

"You realize you sound like my mom right now, don't you?" But there's no real snark in his tone. Clutching his phone, he gestures for me to hop into the booth seat opposite him. His face has that weary, just-tumbled-out-of-the-surf look. He runs a hand over his cropped hair. Grains of fine white sand fall onto his shoulders.

"I'm worried, that's all. It's not like you to skip school and go to the bea —" My lips keep moving but no sound comes out, because Kip interrupts me merely by sliding into the booth beside Alex.

That's Kip as in the infamous Kip Jones. He graduated a year ago, got into community college, then dropped out after two weeks—allegedly to apply his newfound agricultural skills to growing weed. It's common knowledge that he's the go-to guy for pot.

The guys fist-bump each other. When did Kip and Alexander 'The Geek' Gibson become pals? Alex is straight as an arrow, focused on gaining early acceptance into Yale. He wants to be a pediatrician, not a pothead.

Yet here he is, his hazel gaze vacant, spaced-out. I narrow my eyes at the remnants of burgers and chili fries on his tray. It looks like a pack of wolves tore the meal apart.

Now I'm *really* worried.

On top of steamed up, frustrated, confused, and sad. Let me add angry to that list. The two of us made plans, and now Alex seems determined to break every one of them.

Kip stares over at me and gives a slow, lazy smile. His long fingers scoop up fries. "Hey. You're Miss Molly, right? Kip."

"It's just Molly. And I know who you are," I say, my voice as frosty as Alex's untouched milkshake.

"My reputation precedes me." Kip grins, showing yellow-stained teeth.

*More like your police record speaks for you,* I want to say. Kip's tongue flicks out and laps sauce off the corner of his lips. Could this guy be any more reptilian? I shudder.

Turning to Alex, who's staring at his food like he's trying to figure out what planet it came from, I say, "Are you ready to go?"

He snaps out of his trance and blinks at me. "Go?"

"Yes, go." My appetite is totally out the window. Okay, I wouldn't mind swiping a fry or five. I don't do well when I skip meals. "We've got those college applications to write, remember?"

"Quit trying to micromanage me!" Alex snaps.

My jaw drops. A month ago, *he* was the one nagging me to sort out our applications. Now it's the other way around. What has gotten into him?

Kip belches and steals another handful of fries. He stares at us the same way people stare at car crashes—with morbid curiosity.

I try to ignore him. "I'm not micromanaging you. We agreed to draft our essays together weeks ago. It was *your* idea."

Alex's mouth twists. "I'm uncoupling myself from that agreement."

Rolling my eyes, I say, "Since when?"

"Since right now." He bites on a soggy fry for emphasis.

"I cannot believe you're doing this."

"It's not a big deal in the grand scheme of things," Alex insists.

"Yeah, not everyone goes to college," Kip adds. He sits back, hands behind his surf-tussled blond head. Grit is stuck to his elbows, making his skin look like sandpaper. "Look how I turned out. I'm livin' the dream here."

Even Alex's eyebrows rise a little at that. From where I'm sitting, Kip's living my worst nightmare. No job. No legal one, anyway. Still living with his parents. Drifting through days and doing God knows what when the sun goes down.

"I'm happy for you, really," I tell Kip, then fix my gaze on Alex. "Are you coming?"

Alex shifts his weight, but doesn't make a move to get out of the booth. His shoulders heave halfway up to his earlobes as he sighs. Suddenly, the rivers of blood-red chili on those fries are the most fascinating things in the world to him.

"Alex?"

Finally, he looks up. His gaze goes over the top of my head. "I'll see you later."

Kip chortles.

To stop my lips from quivering, I clamp them tightly together. I'm not going to blow up or cry in front of these clowns. Although... I'm close to it. In this one moment, it feels like Alex is not only rejecting our plans, he's rejecting me. And that hurts in a way I never thought possible. Like someone's rubbing salt *and* chili into a wound. Without a word, I pick up my backpack and walk out.

LATER THAT NIGHT, a gentle knock on my bedroom door disrupts my seventh—or is it eighth?—attempt to write a college essay.

"I'm still not hungry, Mom," I call out while staring at my blank screen. What if I write Alex's essay instead? To get the creative juices flowing? Great practice for an English lit major-to-be—

The door opens. It's not my mom at the threshold. It's the devil himself —Alex. My lungs seize.

He smiles at me sheepishly and holds up a DVD. "How about a movie? And gourmet popcorn for dinner?"

Getting over my surprise at seeing him here, I stalk to him and grab the DVD. "What's this? *Rebel Without a Cause?*"

"You've never seen it before, right? James Dean. Natalie Wood. Classic movie."

Alex snatches it back before I can read the synopsis. He crosses to my entertainment set-up—gadgets he found at garage sales and fixed up. He's useful that way. Sometimes I wonder if Alex is a genie. He won't accept a dime or even credit. I've snuck some bucks into his piggy bank when his back was turned. One day, he gave me an iPad. An iPad. And it was brand-new. Lord knows where he got it.

He gets the movie cued up to the studio's logo and takes a bag of popcorn from his backpack. Opening the bag, he waves it under my chin.

"Sweet and salty!" he singsongs. "Your favorite!"

Ugh. He knows me so well. I shove a handful of popcorn in my mouth and sit on the bed, back against the wall. "So is this your apology? Stale popcorn and a fifty-year-old movie?"

"If it's stale, why are you eating it like there's no tomorrow? And *Rebel Without a Cause* is not fifty years old. It was *made* in the fifties." He settles next to me, not close enough to touch. But I wouldn't have to lurch very far if I wanted to put my head on his shoulder. If.

"Oh, that makes it all right, then." I aim popcorn at his mouth and shoot it in. Score! This is as far as I go in terms of athletics.

"One point." He claps. "You are gonna love this. This is *the* best James Dean movie. Do you know he only made three movies?"

"Why only three?" I ask, clueless about last century's rich and famous.

Alex's voice turns flat. "He died. Car wreck. He was pretty young. Twenty-something."

"Wow, poor guy."

"Yup. He made the most of his short life, I guess." Picking up the remote, he asks, "Are you ready?"

I sigh and point to my iPad. "We should probably do those applications first."

"After the movie." He studiously brushes salt off the buttons.

"Really?" I stare at Alex. He refuses to look at me. "See, that bugs me, because I *know* how much you want to get into Yale. And to do that, you've got to apply."

"I will. Later," he says in dismissive tone. He starts the DVD.

"But college is everything to you! What's changed? Tell me!"

Finally, he faces me. "At this time, in this place, college isn't the most important thing. All we need is now."

Shaking my head, I say, "What does that even mean?"

"It means we watch this movie and forget everything else."

"But, Alex—"

"Please. Do this one little thing for me. Watch the movie. Okay? It's about kids like us. Delinquents."

"We are not delinquents. We're straight-A AP students." I cross my arms and sit ramrod straight against the wall. I'm determined to not enjoy this movie because, as far as I'm concerned, it's the one thing standing between us and the Ivy League. But as the film stretches on, I fall in love with James Dean. Long dead now. Back then? Hot. And Natalie Wood? Well, she was hot, too, in an innocent, vulnerable way. Beautiful as they were on the outside, both characters had major flaws gnawing away at their insides.

When James Dean, playing Jim Stark, gets into a huge, long, intense argument with his father, I watch Alex out of the corner of my eye. I'm sure he's thinking of his own dad, who moved back to his native Australia a while ago. Alex has stepped up his visits to "Big Dave" in Sydney lately. Each time, Alex comes back just that little bit weirder. He's starting to become a stranger. Did he and his father get into a fight during his last trip? One that the ocean-wide distance between them made even worse?

"Alex," I whisper, noticing him clenching and unclenching his fists. I inch my hand closer to his side. "Are you okay?"

His head snaps toward me. "Why are you asking me that?"

"You look sad." I pull my hand back and press the pause button. "What are you thinking about?"

He sighs and turns to me. "I'm thinking that is the worst question ever. Guys hate being asked what we're thinking."

"And gals hate resorting to reading guys' minds. It's tiring. We've got enough things to do. So to save time, why don't you just spill? Is this movie making you miss your dad?"

His hazel eyes blink. "I always miss Dad. But right now? I'm thinking I want to be like James Dean. You know, live fast, die young. Do things at full speed and go out with a spectacular crash."

"Please tell me you're joking," I splutter. Alex looks away. "Oh, God, you're serious. My friend, you are not living fast. You are sitting in one place, vegetating here slowly. And I do mean vegetating."

Squeezing his eyes shut, he puts his fingers to his temples. "Trying...to read...Molly's mind... Nope, not getting what you're saying. Spill."

"I'm talking about Kip Jones. I hear he has a particularly green thumb, if you know what I mean."

Now it's his turn to splutter. "You think I'm buying weed off Kip?"

"And smoking it? Baking with it?"

Alex laughs. "No, no, and you know I can't bake."

"Then why are you hanging out with that loser?"

"He's not a loser. He's just lost. And he looks out for me out on the waves, so..."

"Why would you need looking after? You've been surfing since you were three years old."

"Look, he just does, all right? It's the bro code." Alex turns his attention to the screen. Natalie Wood and James Dean are looking angsty at Griffith Park Observatory. Funny—that's about an hour's drive from our neighborhood.

"Before you met Kip, you were not running around saying idiotic things like 'bro code.'"

His smile is sardonic, twisted. "This is the new me, Molly. A rebel without a cause. Better get used to it."

# CHAPTER 2

ALEX

I LEAVE Molly's bedroom feeling sick. Not just physically sick. The way she looked at me every time I snapped at her, it was like I'd killed a kitten with my bare hands. She doesn't deserve to be disrespected like that.

When I get to the end of Molly's driveway, I look up at her bedroom window. One second it's a blazing rectangle of yellow. Next second, it's pitch-black. I know it's dumb, but the way that light goes off, it's like she's disconnecting herself from me.

Maybe that's a good thing. Maybe that'll make things easier in the future. For her, anyway. Not seeing Molly ever again? Yeah, that's going to hurt me for an eternity.

Molly's pretty smart, but there are two things she doesn't know:

1. I'm dying. Stage IV melanoma.

2. I've been in love with her since kindergarten, since before I even knew what love is.

And there are two reasons why I don't want her to know:

1. She'll feel sorry for me and make a big fuss of things. I hate pity as much as I hate having cancer.

2. She'll say ninety percent of high school hook-ups don't last. In our case, she'd be a hundred percent dead right.

According to the docs, I *might* make it to my next birthday. So that's roughly six months to live. A hundred and eighty days. Fifteen million seconds. Still doesn't sound like much when you put it like that.

Hence all this "live fast, die young" stuff. I want to go out my way. No one, not even Molly, has the right to dictate how I should spend those fifteen million seconds.

Don't get me wrong. I don't *want* to die. Who wants to die at just seventeen?

Not me.

------

AROUND SIX THE NEXT MORNING, I find Mom sitting at the island bench in the kitchen. She looks pretty chill for someone who just laid on a breakfast of fruit salad, yogurt, sautèed mushrooms and kale, unbuttered whole-wheat sourdough and two eggs, sunny-side up. A thick, football-field-green smoothie sits in a tall glass by the blender. Great. More kale.

"Hey, kiddo!" She smiles over her coffee mug and pats the stool next to her. "Sleep well?"

I shuffle onto the seat and stare at the food. "Have I died and gone to buffet heaven?"

My mother winces at my choice of words, then makes a big effort to put on a happy face like she always does. "I want you to keep your strength up. You don't have to eat all of it. Just most of it."

"And you don't have to go out of your way to make this for me. I mean, thanks. A lot. But I don't have much of an appetite."

"Oh, I'm having some, too," she says in an overly bright voice. With her fork, she scoops up a tiny portion of kale, hardly enough to fill a mouse's belly.

Since my diagnosis a few months ago, Mom hasn't been eating much either. This doesn't stop her from testing all the "cancer-fighting" recipes she finds on Pinterest. Baking is therapy, she says. I call it a waste of food. Fortunately, the family next door is more than happy to take excess lentil loaf off our hands.

Every hour of every day, I wonder what will happen to Mom after I go. She'll be all alone. Dad moved back to Australia after the divorce. He's making custom surfboards, connecting with old friends, so I know he'll be okay. Mom's literally got no one. Except the perpetually hungry neighbors and her five employees. Yet another reason why I shouldn't die so young.

It's crazy. Why does it have to be like this? Maybe the doctors got it wrong. They're not infallible. They're not gods. They can't predict the exact number of months, days, hours, and seconds a person has left on Earth.

Then again, I've peeked at my medical records. I know it doesn't look good for me. With the help of a counselor I've gotten to the stage of mostly accepting that I'm headed for a dead end. I've even started giving some of my stuff away. The iPad Dad gave me is now Molly's. Mom won't have to go through boxes of my middle-school clothes after I'm gone because I've already dropped them off at Goodwill. The cobalt-blue board I learned to surf on? I'm giving that to a kid down the street whether he likes it or not.

Noticing I haven't touched a single morsel, Mom says, "Will you at least have the kale, broccoli and goji berry smoothie? You don't even have to chew. Close your eyes and drink it."

Speaking of acceptance... Yeah, Mom's adamant that five doctors on two continents are wrong and that I'll make a miraculous recovery. All we need is faith and love and kale.

I would rather eat broken glass mixed with cyanide, but for Mom, I guess I can manage this. Forcing a smile, I sip chunks of raw broccoli that slipped by the blender's blades. I'll check over the blender later, make sure it's working okay.

"After breakfast, I'm taking you to that appointment you missed yesterday," she says quickly.

Feeling guilty, I look away. She didn't hammer me for skipping out on seeing this "amazing herbalist-slash-psychic-healer." Still, I know she was disappointed in me. "What about work? You've missed a lot of days because of me."

"It's fine. Things are slow anyway." Her voice is two octaves higher than usual. She's lying. The real estate biz in this corner of SoCal is booming. Foreclosures have brought in the flippers—the people who swoop in on bank-owned properties and fix them up for a profit.

"But you need those commissions." Silently I add, *To pay my medical bills.*

Another reason to feel guilty. I'm aware of how much my cancer is costing my parents. Flights to a melanoma specialist in Sydney and more hospital follow-ups here don't come cheap. My folks tell me not to worry about that, but ironically I'm old enough to figure out that dying young is expensive.

And now Molly's pushing me to apply to Yale.

I can't blame her. She knows it's been my dream since forever to go to

Yale, get a medical degree, become a pediatrician. But it'd be a waste of time and money for me to even try to follow that dream.

I grimace at the olive oil oozing from the barely touched kale and mushroom thing.

*Waste.* Sure is the theme of the day. Of my life, even.

"Alex, look at me," Mom says in a much firmer tone. "I don't want to lie to you. Money is tight, but we will manage. We always do. I have investments and savings. Your last days should not and will not be about how we're going to pay for things. So for the last time, money is not your problem. Dad and I have got this."

"Mom, I—"

She puts up a palm to stop me from going on. "Nope. Not another word about this. What I do want to hear from you is that you'll make this appointment. Today. Ten-thirty."

Glancing at the clock on the oven, I say, "So I've got time to surf."

"Or go to first period," she suggests carefully.

"You really want me to spend my final days at school? The doctors said I don't have to go."

My teachers, the principal, they all know what the deal is. Pretty soon I'll be too weak to even get out of bed let alone make it to homeroom. My parents have argued about this over and over.

Mom cups my hands in hers. I can tell by the look in her eyes that it rips her up inside to make me choose between enjoying the time I have left and doing what normal kids should do. "You love school, remember? You can hang out with your friends. Including Molly."

"People will know something's wrong when I can't do stuff like P.E. anymore. They'll ask questions. And there's another thing. I don't want people to watch me die slowly." Or quickly. 'Cause six months is pretty fast no matter what kind of spin you try to put on it.

I catch my reflection in the shiny glass of the oven door. My cheeks look less full than they did a few months ago. I've lost muscle, but apart from that I look okay. I'm over the shock of losing my hair. Everybody fell for my excuse about why I shaved it off. All in the name of charity. That was Dad's brilliant idea. Course the truth was it fell out in clumps during chemo. Shaving off the wispy leftover bits of hair was a necessity. And because I was in Australia at the time, none of my friends got to see me without eyelashes and eyebrows. I looked like an alien. Had she seen me looking like that, Molly would have figured everything out.

"Tell them the truth. The people who love you would want to help, honey. If you let them."

"No." I swig more of the craptastic smoothie. "I don't need anyone's help."

She sighs. "Does Moll-Moll know yet?"

"Mom, she's the last person I wanna tell."

"I think you're making a mistake. Please confide in her. She's your best friend." Her voice is barely audible. "You need all the support you can get."

"I'm handling it, Mom." To prove how well I'm handling it, I take a double hit of kale—first in sautéed form, then in smoothie form. The stuff tastes like bile. "You know, this kale is really giving me a ton of energy."

Mom beams at me.

"So I'm going for a surf down at the cove now."

The smile wipes from her features. "Alex..."

"Mom..." I flash her a smile and slide off the barstool. "I've gotta do this while I can still stand up on my board."

Looking defeated, she nods.

"All right, but pick the closest surf break to the lifeguard tower. Meet me back here at no later than nine." She has to yell because I'm already halfway upstairs. "And remember to put sunblock on."

At the stair landing, I hesitate. It's too late for sun protection now. Too late for everything.

# CHAPTER 3

MOLLY

"UNBELIEVABLE!" I glare through the windscreen with such intensity that it's entirely possible the glass will crack under the strain.

"What's unbelievable?" Suze Carlisle asks.

We're heading to school early because we have a dance committee meeting before first period. I've signed up for four extra-curricular committees this year, all in the name of college apps. As far as I know, Alex hasn't signed up for a single thing. It's so unlike him.

"Alex! He's skipping school *again*. Look!" I watch his silver Toyota streak across the intersection on the Pacific Coast Highway. His passenger? A distinctive aqua-and-black surfboard. Strapped tightly onto the roof. No prizes for guessing where Alex is heading. His words about James Dean haunt me: *live fast, die young.*

"So he's going on a surfing safari. Why do you care so much about what he does?" Suze presses the radio's volume button, muting a song I barely heard in the first place.

The subject of Alex Gibson is a touchy one for Suze. She's been my neighbor since the sixth grade and watched him come and go from my house. She used to "coincidentally" stop by for homework help while he was scrounging cookies from my mother. To call her obsessed with Alex back then would be an understatement. She badgered me to ask Alex if he liked her. That bugged me because, if you like someone, why not cut out the middleman and do the asking yourself?

Anyhow, I sounded him out, and he told me he was interested in another girl. He wouldn't say which girl, no matter how hard I needled him. At a guess, she was probably an Aussie girl he met on his regular vacations down under. I didn't tell Suze any of that. I simply told her Alex didn't have a girl-friend, which was true. Next thing I knew, she asked him out to a party.

He said no.

She didn't speak to me for a week. Like it was my fault. That was freshman year. Suze forgave me, but not Alex. Now, no matter how many other guys Suze has dated since then, every time I mention his name, she goes stiff and aloof.

"I care because we're supposed to go on this tour of colleges together, and he's completely bailed on me," I fume.

Suze's mouth falls open a little. "What? You're going away together?"

"With my mom as chaperone. It might not even happen if he keeps blowing me off. And absolutely not if his GPA goes into free fall." The Toyota is long gone. I swivel back to Suze. Her brown eyes are huge and full of curiosity.

She nods. "I knew it. I don't know how I missed it before."

"What do you know? What have you missed?"

"You've got a thing for him."

"Wh-what?"

"Come on. Don't even try to deny it."

"Suze, he's a friend. No, wait, he's like a brother because he's *extremely* annoying." The light turns green and I ease the car forward, trying to keep my attention on the road.

"Annoying, huh?"

"And he teases me too much. Like... like a brother." But do I really think of him as a brother? Not so much. I may be his best friend but that doesn't make me blind to his obvious hotness. He's tall and sinewy. Got a friendly face with high cheekbones and a strong chin. A nose that isn't too broad, isn't too long, isn't bent out of shape. Then there's that mega-wide, mega-watt smile. It hasn't been as bright lately.

"Right."

"Plus, he's never talks about dating. Not when I'm around anyway."

"Okay, how does he react when *you* talk about dating?" she asks. "What happened when you went to see the new *Star Wars* movie with that sleazy guy from your chemistry class? What was his name, Declan? Deacon?"

"Deacon," I say with a shudder. Deacon who turned into an octopus at midnight. Hands. Everywhere.

"Yeah, that guy."

"Alex hit the roof. I think it was because I ignored him when he said Deacon's got tentacles for hands." I didn't tell Alex how badly the date went or that I almost kneed the guy. I knew he'd singsong "I told you so" when that was the last thing I wanted to hear.

Suze shakes her head and groans. "Ohhh, Molly. Don't you see? Alex has the hots for you. And you're annoyed because deep down you really like him, too, but you *tell* yourself he's like a brother."

"That's the craziest thing I've heard today." So many reasons why this conversation is super uncomfortable. "He doesn't have the hots for me. I'm not totally blind. I can sense when a guy likes me. Or doesn't like me, which is the usual scenario."

"That's not true, Moll."

I don't know what it is about me, but I seem to have a built-in boy repellent. Oh, they'll be friendly with me and ask for my calculus notes. I've been on a sprinkling of dates, nothing too serious. It doesn't help that Alex is *always* hanging around, I guess. Maybe people think we're a couple.

"Anyway," I continue, "even if I did have a 'thing' for Alex, which I don't, there's no way I'd act on it. That'd be the kiss of death for our friendship. Plus, lately he's been a complete oddball. One minute he's ignoring me, next minute he's barging into my room like nothing happened."

I nose the car into a prime parking space right near the door. The janitors unlock the school at seven, and it's only six forty-five now. Maybe I'm wrong about Alex skipping classes again today. San Marco Cove is only a few blocks away. There's enough time for him to catch a wave or two and then show up here before the first bell. At a stretch. Second bell, definitely.

Suze sighs. "He's cute, though. I'll give him that."

"Mm-hm." I want to say hot, but I don't. Freshman girls practically fan themselves when he grins and his dimples show. But for me it's what's on the inside that counts. I've watched him grow up into nice, dependable, smart, thoughtful Alex.

At least, he used to be.

We get out of my car and lounge on the stucco balustrades lining the entrance steps.

"Maybe he's going through a mid-teen crisis." Suze gets out an emery board and see-saws it across her black-painted nails.

"Is that a thing?"

She shrugs. "If it isn't, it should be. Some boys are off the planet. There has to be a scientific, physiological explanation for it."

"Or maybe a psychological one." I gaze into the distance thoughtfully. It hurts that Alex no longer confides in me when something's *really* bothering him. After all, I was there for him when his parents split up, there when his dad moved countries, there when he and his mom had to move to a smaller house. He didn't cry and he didn't always talk about what was happening, but he never pushed me away. How did I lose his trust?

What scares me most is that we'll grow apart and lose each other. And he's already distancing himself from me.

Suze looks up and frowns. "Now that I think of it, he hasn't been as cheerful in our Asian Studies class as he usually is."

"When he bothers to come to school, you mean." Again, so not like my Alex.

Nodding, she puts away the emery board. She runs her fingers through her blonde hair, separating the carefully constructed curls. "And he's lost weight. Have you noticed?"

"He's eating plenty of popcorn, I know that," I say, picturing his lean frame. He could eat junk food three times a day and not gain an ounce. "But he's always been on the skinny side, even though he lifts weights."

"He told me he was really sick when he was little. Maybe that's why he's naturally thin. You know, going through that might've stunted his growth."

I purse my lips. "So you know about the...?"

"Cancer?" She nods grimly. "Yeah."

Alex had a type of lymphoma when he was eight or nine. Not the terminal kind, but still... Alex missed about six months of school back then. I shake my head. "Poor guy. He spent so much time in the hospital. He hated missing school more than he hated being sick."

"That's awful. I'd hate to be cooped up like that, too."

"He didn't want anyone to feel sorry for him." I watch ants crawl over my sneaker toe. They crash into each other like bumper cars, then go on as if nothing happened. That's what Alex did when he was sick. He kept on going, kept on fighting until he beat his illness. "I remember him as the ringleader of the kids' ward, always rounding up the others for games and whatever.

Sometimes they'd pretend to be in classes, because school sounded like more fun than being stuck in the hospital."

"Let me guess. He'd play the role of teacher. I bet he gave really tough tests," she says with a crooked smile. I sense a shift in her attitude toward Alex. Usually she tries to steer the subject away from Alex if I bring him up.

"Pop quizzes, research assignments, you name it." I chuckle, then grow serious as memories surface. "I can still picture some of those kids' faces. There was one girl named Caitlin. She was a couple of years older, but she looked like Alex's age then. Huge blue eyes in a tiny little face. Her skin was so thin you could see every vein."

"Was she terminal?"

I nod. A big lump forms in my throat. "I don't know about most of the kids in that ward, but Caitlin was definitely aware she was going to die. There was no hope left. This is what she'd tell Alex and me, 'The angels are singing to me. Listen!'"

"Oh. My. God. How freaky." Dipping her head, Suze dabs tears. "I can't imagine being that young and knowing it was all going to end."

"Yeah, her life hadn't really started." My throat constricts even more. "All she knew was the inside of a hospital. That was her world. Like, the staff did their best to turn the place into some kind of wonderland. Bring in clowns and musicians. Make it seem colorful and fun. But when you looked closer and saw the IVs and the machines those kids were hooked up to, well, no amount of glitter was going to hide what was really going on."

Suze gulps audibly. "What happened to Caitlin?"

"Alex tried to 'cure' her," I say with air quotes.

"Um, how?"

"Well, Alex being Alex, thought he knew everything there was to know about wizardry." I smile at Suze's puzzled look. "Because he'd read all the *Harry Potter* books three times, you see. So one day, he ordered the other kids to donate their fruit drinks. All different flavors. Mixed it up with whatever food was left over from breakfast. So it was this gross, sugary, gluggy mess. He chanted spell he'd found on the Net and fed the potion to Caitlin."

Suze makes a face. "Ew. Cue projectile vomiting."

"Fortunately, that didn't happen." Poor Alex. He was only eight. And it wasn't like he'd mashed up other kids' medication into his potion. At least he had some common sense. Along with good intentions.

"Then what? Did she spit it out?"

"She loved it. Said she'd never felt better in her whole life and that it made her angels dance in a circle around her." I blow out a shuddering breath. "And then she died. The next day."

"What?!" she screeches. "Oh, please don't tell me it was because of Alex's magic. It couldn't have been!"

I give her a bittersweet smile. "No, it wasn't anything Alex did. It was just an awful coincidence. No one could tell Alex that. He was inconsolable. Truth is Caitlin was even sicker than he or any of the kids knew. The doctors knew, of course. And her family."

"That is the saddest thing ever!"

"I don't think Alex got over Caitlin. If I can't forget her, chances are he can't either. He spent months with her." I wonder if she's the reason why he doesn't date anyone. Could he be holding a torch for a ghost? "Best day of *my* life was when I found out he'd been cured. No more hospitals. No more spells. No more gross cocktails."

"I'm sure it was the best day of his life, too." She cracks a tiny smile.

The rattle of wonky wheels and metal grabs my attention. I look over my shoulder. A homeless man in a tattered trench coat slowly pushes his shopping cart across the school driveway.

"Oh, there's Bobby Lee. Wait here for a sec, Suze." From the trunk of my car, I take a bulging laundry bag, then run to the sidewalk. "Bobby Lee? I got your clothes here, freshly laundered."

Bobby Lee walks on as if he doesn't hear me. I tap on his arm. He jumps a little, then recognition crosses his weary features. "Molly! How you been?"

"Good. And you?"

"Oh, can't complain," says the man who's been homeless for more years than he can remember. We've been buddies since I first saw him wandering around school back when I was a freshman. He was trying to get in the main building to use the bathrooms. I snuck him in. How could I not? The man had no home. There's a shelter nearby, but it's filled to capacity most days.

I hand him the laundry bag. "There's a big bottle of water in there, too. And hand sanitizer and toothpaste. And those rice crackers you like."

"Thank you, Molly. Appreciate it," he says gruffly. His face twitches as he passes me a bag of dirty clothes from the cart. He's a proud man, but he knows not to argue with me anymore about doing his laundry. I'm happy to do it. A simple thing like clean undies goes a long way to help restore a person's dignity.

"You're welcome. I'll see you next week?"

He waves and keeps walking. I stash his dirty clothes in my car. Back at the school steps, Suze is fixing her eye make-up.

I sit beside her. My thoughts turn to Alex. Like Bobby Lee, he's a proud guy. Despite the warmth of the morning sunshine, a shiver rattles my bones. What if Alex is sick again? If so, why wouldn't he tell *me* about it? What if he needs me?

No, of course, he needs me. I'm his best friend.

"It's been so hard to talk to Alex lately," I begin. "But I have to get to the bottom of what's bothering him. Maybe I should drop by and see his mom about—"

Vigorously, she shakes her head. "No, no, a thousand times no."

"Why not?" I ask, wide-eyed.

"What if she doesn't know he's been skipping school?" She slaps her forehead. "What am I saying? Of course his mom wouldn't know. Nobody skips and tells their parents. If you go behind his back, he'll hate you."

"But what if he needs my help?"

The door unlocks behind us, startling us. Inside, the janitor waves and goes back down the hall.

"Trust me. It's not worth tattling on him like some kindergartener. Talk to him face to face." Suze tugs on my arm. "Now, come on, let's get this meeting set up. I didn't get out of bed at five AM for nothing."

# CHAPTER 4

ALEX

I GLANCE around the biology lab. The session with the herbalist/psychic healer was okay. I don't feel any better. Then again, I don't feel any worse.

Seems like it's been so long since I last came to class. It's really only been less than a week. For extra college credit, I got a gig assisting Mr. West. It fits in well with my spare period on Fridays.

But I couldn't care less about the credit now.

In front of me, three rows of sophomore kids contemplate the dead rats pinned to boards on their benches. Joel Baker looks like he's going to throw up. Andy Redfern? Yeah, as I suspected, he's looking like he can't wait to cut out the rat's heart. Maybe unravel the intestines to measure their full length, too. He's that kind of kid.

I glance at the white rat I'd placed on West's bench. Stiff arms and legs spread out. Paws permanently curled. Pink tail in a straight line except for a tiny kink at its tapered end. Two slightly yellow teeth protrude from a vee-shaped mouth.

Gently, I prod its rib cage. Dead. I knew that. Mr. West took care of euthanizing the animals.

My stomach roils. Does this rat have a soul? Is it in heaven, looking down on its cold, dead corpse? Are we—or me, specifically—going to hell for carving up its body in the name of high school science?

*Six months to live.*

Six months to find out whether I'm damned for eternity.

*What am I doing here?*

Joel and I run out of the class at exactly the same time. He races down the hall and skids around the corner toward the bathrooms. Me, I run straight into the one person I didn't want to see.

"Alex!" Molly squeaks as she bounces off my chest.

I grab hold of her wrist so she doesn't fall backwards. "Hey, are you okay?"

She clutches her iPad tighter. "I'm surprised."

"About what? Bumping into me in school?"

"Yes, of all places!" She flashes a wry grin, then pushes long brown bangs away from her eyes to peer at me. I turn my head the other way. "Maybe I should be asking *you* if you're okay. Why are you running out of class? Did the teacher spring a quiz on you and you're running 'cause you haven't studied?"

I hook my thumbs into the back pockets of my jeans. "It's D-Day. Dissection day."

Molly winces. "Oooh, not pretty. I always opt out of those. I suppose that's what you're doing now?"

"Yeah, I'm opting out."

She leans against a locker. "Speaking of opting out, I really need to know, are we going on our college tour or not?"

Groaning, I try to stall her. "Don't you have a class now?"

"Free period," she says smugly. "Do you really think I'm so easily distracted that I'll forget I'm in the middle of hounding you?"

"Nope, you're persistent. Always have been." I glance down the hall again. Joel's ambling around the corner. His face is as white as beach sand. We stay silent as Joel gives us a tight, sheepish smile before going inside the lab.

"Alex, help me out here. You can't keep avoiding my questions." Molly's voice quivers. "You can't keep avoiding *me*. Something's wrong and you're not telling me what it is."

I stare down into Molly's big green eyes. I know her so well. It's almost like I can see the confusion building up inside her. Sooner rather than later, she's going to blow her stack.

But I'm not ready to tell her. Probably never will be.

"Look, I know I've been...strange lately. But it's nothing to do with you.

I'm dealing with something." I take a deep breath. "And I need to deal on my own."

She steps forward. Her hand flutters onto my arm. "Whatever it is, you can tell me. I won't judge you."

Flinching, I tell her, "Really? You won't judge me? What about the way you acted when you saw me with Kip yesterday?"

"That's way different. Kip's a real-deal delinquent. He's not the type of person you need to be hanging out with."

"There you go, judging people again."

"What if he ruins your chances of getting into Yale?" she continues.

"You don't know Kip like I do. He won't wreck my chances." *I can do that myself.* "Don't you trust me to make my own decisions? What are you afraid of?"

Her face contorts a little, then she finally whispers, "Losing you."

Those two words knock all the air out of me. Does she *know*? Did Mom tell her?

Molly steps forward, mouth open like she's about to say something else. But suddenly, she spins on her heel and sprints down the hall.

Quickly, I try to hold onto a bank of steel lockers for support. Stupid slippery lockers. As soon as Molly's out of sight, I slide down to the floor and clutch my stomach.

This is what dying feels like. When your heart pounds hard enough to crack a rib. When loud, squealing noises echo from an unseen source. When you look around and the world distorts, fades to black. When the last thing your brain registers is the thud of your head hitting the linoleum.

*I'm dead.*

---

A FAINT BELL RINGS. Behind my eyelids, I sense a bright, flickering light. Something hard supports me. A bench. With super-thin padding. My body feels weighted down. Lifting a finger takes so much effort that I give up.

"I think he's awake."

Mom. That's my mother's voice.

Slowly, I open my eyes. Directly above me, a fluorescent light burns. Flickering. At the end of its life span.

*I am not dead.*

"Alex? Honey, it's Mom."

The room seems to spin as I turn toward her. The worry lines on her forehead and around her eyes go in and out of focus. I lick my dry lips. "What happened?"

"You fainted outside your classroom." The school nurse nudges my mother aside. She takes my blood pressure. Mom and I stare silently as she checks over me.

"Who found me?" I ask in a thick voice. *Please don't say Molly. Don't say Molly.*

Concentrating on her work, the nurse replies flatly, "Mr. West."

"Did anyone else see me?"

"Alex, you're lucky anyone saw you at all! Stop worrying about that!" Mom says, exasperated.

"You know why I can't stop." Humiliation. Exposure. Everyone will know I'm weak. And after that, they'll treat me like a freak.

The nurse frowns at the LED display. "Another teacher saw you. They brought you to the infirmary."

When she's done looking me over, I take a few deep breaths and try to sit up.

Whoa. The room's spinning again. More deep breaths.

The nurse turns my mother. "His blood pressure is a little low, but otherwise he seems okay. I would recommend you take him to his regular physician as soon as possible, given his status."

My status. My almost-dead status, she means.

"I can still call the ambulance, if you want, Mrs. Gibson," the nurse continues. "But I don't think it's an emergency, per se."

"No, no ambulance. No doctors," I insist. "And especially no hospitals."

Mom nods. Her grip on my arm is vise-like. "I'm taking you to see Dr. Hobart now. I'll call ahead to make sure we can get an appointment."

"I'm okay. My status is fine. Let's go home." I sit up. On the inside, I scream like a drill sergeant, ordering every muscle to keep me upright. Mind over matter and all that. I glance at the nurse. "Are classes in session right now?"

"The fourth-period bell rang a few minutes ago," she says. "There shouldn't be many people in the halls."

"Great. Thanks." I feel anything but great as I walk through the deserted main corridor with Mom. She tries to put her arm around me for support. "I can move on my own."

"Of course you can." She bites her lower lip and nods. "Will you be fine to drive home, though? We can leave your car here and pick it up tomorrow."

"No, Molly will see it and wait for me, I'm sure."

"Alex, you have to stop being so stubborn about this. Molly's your friend. And she seems to be your only friend. You'll lose her if you keep alienating her."

I stare at posters lining the walls without really seeing them. Their colors and words blend into an abstract mess. "What does it matter if I lose her now or later? At least if it happens now, she won't have to see me turn into a walking corpse before I actually become one."

"Don't talk like that." She grimaces. "And despite what you think, it matters a whole lot to be surrounded by people who love you when your time comes. I know it meant a lot for both my parents when they passed on."

A pang of guilt strikes me. Like me, Mom's an only child. Grandma and Grandpa Atkins died within weeks of each other when I was twelve. They lived in a nursing home and all they had left was their daughter. Mom was really strong through the whole thing. She had to be.

Impulsively, I reach out and hug her as hard as I can. "You're right. I'm sorry. I'll tell her. But leave it up to me, okay? I'll do it my own way, in my own time."

She nods and squeezes my hand.

We step out into the bright afternoon sunshine. Heat radiates off the concrete and cars surrounding us. Hottest February ever. Would it kill anybody to plant more trees? The spindly date palms dotted around the school aren't doing much to shade the place. But the fresh sea breeze revives me a little more.

"I'll follow you to the clinic," Mom says when we reach her car. "Give me a minute while I call Dr. Hobart's office."

I sigh. Do I really want to spend what's left of my life hanging around a doctor's waiting room?

"Can we go home? It'll be a waste of your time if we go there and can't see him," I say. "Besides, I feel all right."

She looks conflicted. "Are you sure?"

Flashing her a high-wattage smile, I say, "Yeah, I'll rest up for a while."

"You'll rest? You promise?" she asks like she doesn't believe me.

"Promise. I'll wind down, relax. Think about how I'm going to tell Molly everything."

Mom still looks skeptical, but eventually she nods. "Okay. Let's go home. I'll drive slowly so I don't lose you in the traffic."

"Pretty sure I'll find my way home if that happens, Mom."

I wave as I overtake her after the first intersection. I get to the house minutes before she does. And I didn't even have to break the 35-mile-an-hour speed limit.

"Show-off." She scowls at me when she pulls up in the double driveway. I unlock the front door and wait for Mom to go in first. "Listen, I need to check in with the office. Why don't you have a nap and I'll fix lunch in the meantime?"

Shrugging, I head to the living room and flop onto a sofa. The *Rebel Without a Cause* DVD is on the TV cabinet, right where I left it. Molly seemed to really get into the movie after a while. As for the "live fast, die young" motto? It's clear she doesn't understand where I'm coming from. How can I fix that?

Absently, I stroke the rectangular scar under my left arm. The docs cut out a chunk of tumor-riddled flesh. They said there was a chance some rogue cells migrated to my lymph nodes. They were right.

*Six months to live.*

Mom's right. If I have such a short amount of time left, shouldn't I spend it with people I care about? I need to fix things with Molly before she stops caring about me.

I fish my phone out of my back pocket.

*Hey,* I write.

*Hey,* she texts back. *Make it quick. I'm in class.*

I wait half a minute, then type *I'm not.*

*Why???!!!*

*Didn't feel like hanging around.*

*Say goodbye to your high school diploma!!!!!* After a pause, she continues. *I don't understand why you've changed since u came home from Oz.*

*You can't fix me.*

*If I knew what's wrong, maybe I could.*

My fingers hover over the screen. I start tapping a message, then delete everything. I'd be a class-A jerk if I told her the bad news in a text.

*Have to go. Rly can't text in class. Talk later.*

*K.*

I scroll back up the screen and read the conversation again. It isn't always easy to know what people really mean in a text. But I know Molly. She's mad.

In the other room, Mom talks on the phone. "I'll see what I can do, Bob. But I don't... Okay, yes, yes, I get it. Okay. See you soon."

She walks into the living room and peers over the sofa. "Alex, how are you feeling?"

Wish she'd stop asking how I'm feeling. Isn't it obvious? "Fine."

Mom flicks a look at her phone. "I'm so sorry, but I have to get into the office before Bob bungles this deal. If you're hungry, there's lots of ingredients to make yourself a salad."

"Mmm, salad. Just what I feel like. Said no dying teenage boy ever." I grin to convince her it's okay to leave me alone. Mom playfully throws a cushion onto my chest.

"Please. Eat and drink something. I don't care what it is. Then rest. Love you!" She flutters away toward the foyer, purse slung over her shoulder.

"Love you, too, Mom," I say after the front door shuts. Pretty soon, I'm snoozing on the couch, dreaming about trying to break the cancer news to Molly, but being too paralyzed to speak.

A text alert rings in my ear. It's Kip.

Funny. When he was in school, we never really talked much. It wasn't until I started moping and surfing at the cove with him that I've gotten to know him a bit. He's *always* there. He doesn't pressure me. At least not about college.

*Hey, man. Wanna come to the cove? Nice set of waves coming through.*

My gaze falls on the DVD case again. Natalie Wood's face morphs into Molly's. She's looking at me and shaking her head in disapproval.

*Hell, yeah.*

# CHAPTER 5

MOLLY

Alex's front door swings open less than ten seconds after I press the doorbell.

"Mrs. G, I'm so sorry to bother you."

She opens the door wider and waves me inside the house. She hugs me. Really, really tightly. I can feel her ribs. "Moll-Moll, you're always welcome here. You know that."

"Thanks." My chin is jammed against her bony shoulder. Everyone seems to have a nickname for me. Only she calls me Moll-Moll. I let her cling on for a fraction longer and pull away. Her hazel eyes look puffy. Red lipstick barely coats her lips, settling into fine, dry lines. "Is everything okay? You're so thin right now."

Mrs. Gibson pastes on a bright smile. "Oh, everything's fine, fine! Come into the kitchen. I'm making a kale, broccoli and cucumber juice."

"Oh. Yummy." I do my best to sound super enthusiastic about the super juice. As I follow her to the rear of the house, I peek left and right into the dining and living rooms. Alex and his mom recently moved, so now they're only three blocks from my house instead of four. The rooms are smaller than those in the old hacienda-style place. Their furniture looks huge and clumsy in this ranch house. Not once has Alex complained about the downsides of downsizing. "Is Alex here?"

"He'll be back. Soon. I think," she says, striding around the timber kitchen island. There's that bright smile again. Quickly, she turns on the blender. We watch green blobs whiz around in the glass chamber until they liquefy. "Do you like coconut water?"

Shrugging, I say, "I've never tried it before."

I've never seen her act this crazed before, either.

"Never?" Mrs. Gibson gasps. She gradually adds the slightly opaque coconut water to the mix. "It's wonderful. So incredibly nutritious."

"Are you on a health kick, Mrs. G?" I've always called her Mrs. G. But she hasn't changed her last name, and I feel weird about calling her Jill.

"I'm trying to stay healthy. Do you know that one cup of raw kale contains eighty milligrams of vitamin C? That's almost as much as a whole orange!"

"Wow!" I'd much rather eat an orange, but I don't tell her that. "I can't wait to try it. I'll get the glasses."

"Thanks, sweetie. You know where to find them."

I pace around the island and grab a pair of tall glasses from an upper cabinet. On the counter beside the fridge, amber prescription bottles stand lined up like bowling pins. It's an awful lot of pills. A cat calendar stuck on the side of the stainless steel fridge. Days are marked off with thick red marker pen. Appointments with Dr. This and Dr. That.

A cold, shivery feeling overwhelms me. Only sick people need that much medication. Are they Alex's? Or his mom's? I steal another glance at Mrs. G. Her pencil skirt is practically falling off her. She keeps hitching it up at the waist. And her cheeks look hollow, like she hasn't consumed anything but smoothies in months.

If she *is* sick, that could explain why Alex has missed so much school lately. He's probably staying home to look after her. And surfing is the only thing that takes his mind off his problems, so he spends whatever precious time he's got left at the beach. That *has* to be it.

Before I get a chance to peek at the labels on the pill bottles, Mrs. G swoops over and takes hold of my arm.

"Moll-Moll, it is *such* a lovely warm day. Let's drink these outside." She leads the way through a set of sliding doors onto the patio.

We recline side by side on redwood garden chairs under the shade of a pergola. Long tendrils of a wisteria vine curl down through the rafters, tickling my head. But all I can think about is the pill stash. My heart twinges. Alex shouldn't have to deal with his mom's illness alone.

"Cheers!" says Mrs. G, reaching out to clink her glass against mine.

I lift my glass, and the tip of a vine dunks into the drink. Gingerly, I remove the vine and take the tiniest of sips.

"What do you think?" Mrs. G asks. Her glass is now half-empty. "Refreshing, huh? Alex can't get enough of this stuff. He practically begs me to make it for him every morning."

"He should be making it for *you!*" I blurt. Mrs. G doesn't respond. In fact, silence sets in pretty fast. There's only the sound of birds tweeting, a mower whirring in the distance, and us breathing.

All of a sudden I feel really awkward. It's not that I'm uncomfortable around her. She's like a second mom to me. But right now it's like she's wound up tight like piano wire and trying so hard not to snap. At the same time, she's pretending nothing's wrong.

Question is, do I ask her what's on her mind? What would be the harm? Maybe I could help. Unless relationship problems are the cause of her scary weight loss. I'm not the best person to talk to about romance. If she goes into too-much-information territory, then the awkwardness level would be off the scale.

No, I should just be quiet until Alex comes home. Concentrate on something else. I put my glass on the chair's armrest and set about twisting some of the wisteria vines out of the way. Once that's done, I pluck three varieties of weeds from the gaps between flagstones.

"You don't have to do that!" she exclaims. Talk about a delayed reaction. Something's *really* up with her.

"It's totally fine, Mrs. G," I reply in a super-cheerful voice. "Weeding is therapeutic."

"Absolutely. I should do it more often," she says after a long pause. Mrs. G stares at my hands, but in an unfocused way. As if she's thinking about something completely different. Her face is pale. Way too pale for Southern California. The make-up she's wearing is doing nothing to cover the purple smudges beneath her eyes. Spindly fingers continuously spin a ring on her right hand. It's her wedding band, I realize.

Tossing the weeds on a patch of hot concrete, I sit back on my heels. "Mrs. G?"

She clears her throat. "Yes, Moll-Moll?"

"I don't mean to pry, but..." She looks away. Probably because she's aware I'm going to do just that. Pry. She knows I like to make everything my business. Some people think I'm nosy. I say it's because I care enough to help people deal with their problems. My pulse gallops. I've started this conversation and now I can't stop it. "Are you unwell?"

She stares at me eyes wide. Her fingers work that ring even faster now. "Me? Sick?"

"I, um, saw all those pill bottles on the kitchen counter and I wondered..." I drop my gaze and rip out a few more weeds around my chair's legs.

Mrs. G looks uncertain for a split-second. "They're, uh, hormone pills. You know? For menopause."

"Oh." I blink. Mrs. G is forty-something, around the same age as Mom. Granny Corbett, my paternal grandmother, was almost sixty when she went through "the change." Believe me, everybody knew about it. The mailman. The packers at the grocery store. My ballet teacher. Everybody.

Mrs. G picks up her glass and knocks the rest of her monster-green drink back in one hit. Her hand trembles. Enough for me to notice without looking too closely. "The kale smoothies really help bring some relief to those hot flashes."

So Alex is okay, then. That's a relief. His cancer isn't back. Of course it isn't. He beat that thing into submission years ago. But...*all* those pills are for menopause? Really? Sheepishly, I say, "Sorry for pushing you into telling me something so personal."

"Don't be sorry," Mrs. G says, patting my now dirty hand. She stands and collects our glasses. "Will you excuse me? I need to make a phone call. Stay right here, and I'll be back soon with another smoothie, okay?"

I smile. "Sure. Thanks, Mrs. G."

"Stay right here." Her smile is bright and white and overly perky.

Mrs. G can't get inside fast enough, almost tripping over the threshold. I bet she's as embarrassed as I am. She shuts the French doors. Some clunking and rattling echoes through the kitchen, then I hear the sound of high-heeled shoes hurrying across hardwood.

Five, ten minutes pass. There's not a lot of shade under the pergola now. I could really do with a drink. Something crystal clear and old-fashioned. Like water. I wander into the kitchen. After scrubbing dirt and weeds off my hands, I help myself to the fridge's ice and water dispenser. That's when I notice not only is the cat calendar gone, so is the cache of pills. Totally obvious that Mrs. G thought there was a high chance I'd try to get a closer look at those things.

She was right, of course.

Her soft voice floats down from her bedroom. It's hard to make out her conversation, but I hear Alex's name at least three times. Discreetly, I head back to the patio. Minutes later, Mrs. G returns. And without the promised kale concoction.

She sits prim as a princess, then leans back, then fidgets wildly and stands up. Her face is a picture of worry, all lines and creases.

"Tough phone call, Mrs. G?"

My question seems to startle her. She practically jumps out of her skin. She settles down enough to nod a couple of times. Looking down at her lap, she says, "You ever get frustrated with someone? Someone you really love and adore? And you know you have a right to be angry with them, but at the same time, you don't want to upset the balance because life's too short?"

"Oh, yeah," I say, thinking of Alex. Who else? I love him to death, but sometimes his secretive nature makes me crazy. Have to wonder if Mrs. G is talking about her ex, Big Dave. "Only in my case, I *so* want to upset the balance. I'm ready to start throwing furniture around."

Mrs. G stares at me in surprise. "I've never known you to lose your temper."

"Don't worry. I won't set fire to your lovely outdoor setting here, Mrs. G. It's safe. Today anyway."

She laughs. "Maybe not. Might find me lobbing this chair into the neighbor's pool if you stick around long enough."

"You've had your super juice. I'm sure you'd have the strength," I say with a grin.

"Oh, that reminds me." She rises. "I meant to fix you another glass."

Standing, I put a hand on her arm. "Thanks, but I should get going. It's Friday night. You've probably got something planned, and I have to sort my bookshelves in accordance with the Dewey system."

"Believe me, your plans sound more exciting than mine." Mrs. G giggles as she walks me out to the front door. She leans on the doorjamb. "So tell me, how should I deal with this person who's frustrating me so much?"

Wide-eyed, I stare at her. "You're asking me?"

"Sure, Miss 5.0 GPA. I trust your opinion."

Shaking my head, I say, "I may have good grades, but I still can't figure out what makes human beings tick. The best thing to do is tell them how the situation makes you feel and that you want to work together to make it better."

Mrs. G looks into the distance. "That's good advice. It's not putting blame on them. I like it. Really like it."

"I'll try it myself and let you know how it goes." I wrap her in a quick hug. Again, her bony ribs ring alarm bells inside me. "Please eat more. And I don't mean kale. Text me if you need anything."

"I will, Moll-Moll. Thanks," she whispers.

As I trudge along the sidewalk, guilt pings me. What I didn't say is that I *have* been trying to tell Alex how I feel about him throwing his life away, but he's not listening to a single syllable. Am I doing something wrong?

I've made plenty of mistakes. But nothing that couldn't be fixed. In my mind, there's a solution to everything. You've got to spend time figuring it out, that's all.

A car horn honks just before I reach the T-junction. Throwing an annoyed look to my right, I keep walking. The car follows me and honks again.

"Listen, jerk. Can't a person walk in peace?"

"No one walks in L.A. Get in," comes the swift reply. Alex grins from the passenger window of a newish black pickup that has dents and scratches in virtually every panel. "And who are you calling a jerk, anyway?"

My face burns, then I smile, "Sorry. Make that *delinquent*."

"Yep, that's me." Alex laughs. I peer at him. He looks pale. I really don't think the kale diet is doing him or his mother any favors. They need real, solid food. Maybe I should invite them over for dinner at my place.

"Hey, Miss Molly!" Kip shouts from the driver's seat.

"Hi, Kip." I can't muster up a smile for the guy at all.

"Where are you going?" Alex asks. "Do you need a ride?

"Home, and no, thanks." I continue down Sycamore. Kip crawls along-side the curb.

Alex reaches an arm out, but he isn't close enough to touch me. "Katie Hansen's having a party at the cove tonight. Wanna come along? There'll be popcorn."

"Among other things," Kip chuckles.

"I'll bet," I say in a cool tone. Flipping my brown ponytail, I fib, "I'm busy. Suze is coming over and—"

"Oh, yeah, we bumped into Suze at the mall. She said she'll be there," Alex says.

Great. Fabulous. I tell one little white lie and it backfires. How do I get out of this?

# CHAPTER 6

ALEX

"YOU'VE GOTTA TELL HER, MAN," Kip insists.

"Nope."

"She'll hate you." He lies back on my floor and tosses a foam basketball up and down.

"But I'll be dead, and I won't give a flying fuck." I grab the basketball mid-throw and send it to the hoop on the back of my bedroom door. We didn't end up surfing. Once we got to the cove, I made the mistake of telling him what happened outside the biology lab. So he dragged me to the mall instead. He ate two burgers. I watched.

"Think about your life *before* you die, then. Both of you will be miserable. Do you really wanna spend your last days feeling like crap?"

Most people don't associate Kip—college dropout, sometime weed dealer, contender for title of Laziest Guy on Earth—as being the reasonable type. But he is. He doesn't let anybody see that side of himself. A lot of people, including Molly, think he's the classic juvenile delinquent.

When Kip and I first started hanging out at the cove, the only things we talked about were the surf and barometric pressure. Seriously. Then one morning, he pulled me out of the water when I had a blackout.

He saw some of my surgical scars. Like the one on my right shoulder blade, where the docs carved out a big-ass malignant mole. I got around to telling him about the cancer. He told me his twin sister died of leukemia years ago.

Her name was Caitlin.

Well, that hit me like a billion volts of lightning. She was the same Caitlin I met a long time ago when I did time in the kids' hospital. We were both being treated for cancer. Before Caitlin, I'd never had someone close to me die. I still think about her a lot.

Even more now I'm in the same canoe that she was in then. Sailing to the edge of a mile-high waterfall and knowing we're going to plunge right off. I don't know where *I'll* end up, but I'm pretty sure those angels Caitlin used to talk about swooped down and took her somewhere safe.

"No question, Kip. Near the end, I'm going to feel like crap, look like crap, probably say a lot of crap. Why would I want anyone to see me like that? Especially Molly. I don't want her to remember me as some broken-down wreck."

"Yeah, I get that." He stands and does bicep curls with my ten-pound dumbbells. I make a mental note to give those to him. Haven't lifted weights in months. "But you don't wanna be alone either."

"I can deal." I shove my biochemistry textbook hard into a bookcase. Pain jags down my arm. I wince and turn away.

The dumbbells thump on the rug. "Hey, are you all right? Want me to get your pain meds?"

Keeping my back turned, I say, "I took a couple of pills. It takes a while to kick in sometimes."

Not sometimes. Most of the time. Wasn't that long ago that all I needed was aspirin. Rarely at that. My doctors prescribed a bunch of medications to help numb me temporarily. What am I going to do when even the maximum dose won't kill the pain anymore?

Lowering my voice, I ask, "When are you getting me the stuff?"

Medicinal marijuana is legal in California if you're over eighteen. My eighteenth birthday is more than a year away, so, yeah, that's a problem for me. Even though Mom puts all her faith in the power of green vegetables and green fruit, she's not convinced about a particular green herb when it comes to pain relief. So she won't give her permission for me to try it, even under strict supervision.

Which leads me to Kip.

Surprisingly, he's as much of a roadblock as my mother, but for his own reasons.

"I told you, man. I really wanna help you. But I had to break my old connections. I'm trying to get clean. I *am* clean," he says. For the past few months he's been going to an AA-type of group for teens. I turn around and see turmoil written all over his face.

In the old days, Kip was in high demand, so to speak, at parties. Holding court in a dark corner of a basement or a backyard. Supplying weed. Molly and I never went near him. We wouldn't admit it to each other, but we were actually scared of him.

*You can't help out a dying man just once?* I want to say now. But I get it. Mostly. I haven't got much to lose, unlike Kip. He's got his whole life ahead of him. The guy's made mistakes. Mistakes he doesn't want to repeat.

"There's bound to be a joint or two at this beach party," he says, sounding like he's trying to make it up to me.

"Yeah, true."

Kip checks his watch. "Let's get going."

My mother traps us at the bottom of the stairs. "Oh, good. I was about to call you down to see what you wanted for dinner."

"And we were about to head out to a party." I glance at the door, hardly able to look at her face. When I finally do, I see her lips are pressed together so tight they almost disappear. "But, um, we can stay for a snack. Right, Kip?"

"Sure, sounds great," he replies, giving my mom an angelic smile.

Later, having stuffed our faces with grilled cheese, chicken and—surprise! —kale sandwiches, Mom pulls me aside while Kip's in the bathroom. "I haven't had a chance to talk to you all day. I really don't want you to go out tonight. You *fainted* today."

"Mom, I'm all right. I feel good," I say. And I do. There's something magical about melted cheese. "I need to go to this party. It's on the beach. It'll make me feel alive."

Her eyes well up and she blinks rapidly. Turning, she says in a dejected voice, "I want you home at ten, okay? Not a minute later."

That's crazy. My usual curfew is eleven. "But—"

"That'll give you four hours. Plenty of time. It's the least you can do for missing your appointments."

Another round of guilt stirs inside me. It doesn't go so well with that gooey cheddar clogging my stomach. "Okay, okay."

"Oh, I've got an idea. Why don't I pick you up?"

"Why don't I catapult myself into the sun?"

"I get it. You're embarrassed by your own mother." She digs into her purse and sticks a twenty-dollar bill in my hand. "Use that for a taxi in case you can't get a ride home."

"I'll get an Uber." I smirk. "Sounds like you don't exactly trust Kip. He's been a really good buddy to me, Mom."

She shrugs. "Yes, but I know how things work at these parties. Your ride hooks up with someone and the next thing you know, you're hitchhiking home."

"Yeah, maybe when you were young," I groan.

"Hey!"

Kip comes back to the kitchen and lifts his brows at me. "You ready?"

"Yep." Turning to Mom, I give her a quick hug. "Thanks for dinner. See you later."

"Have fun," she says faintly.

We head out to Kip's car. As I click my seatbelt on, I look up and see the living room lights dim. The silhouette of Mom's thin, lone figure is visible behind the curtains. More guilt sloshes inside me. What if that was the last conversation I ever had with my mom? A stupid semi-argument about curfews and hitchhiking?

I unsnap the seatbelt. "Hey, one second, okay?"

I don't even wait for Kip to reply. I run as fast as I can into the house. Mom's standing in front of the TV, studying the *Rebel Without a Cause* DVD cover. She looks up at me with wide eyes.

"Did you forget something?"

"Yeah." I cross the room in three big strides and scoop her into a rib-bruising hug.

She laughs. "What's gotten into you?"

*What's gotten into me? A bunch of tumors and the thought of imminent death, that's all.*

"Love you, Mom." I squeeze her one more time and then sprint back to the car.

———

By the time we get to the cove, what's left of the sun is a thin strip of orange and pink on the horizon. Still enough light around to see the faces in a group that gets bigger and bigger by the minute. Kip veers off to catch up with old buddies standing by the beginnings of a bonfire. Out of habit, I scan the crowd, looking for Molly. She's not big on parties, but maybe Suze convinced her to go. Then again, if Molly doesn't want to do something, it's hard to change her mind.

In a way, I'm glad she isn't here. There are a hundred different reasons why I can't be with her now, all of them very good. I let my shoulders relax and watch a couple of surfers ride one last set. Both seem to know what they're doing out there, but they're taking a risk. Twilight is not only happy hour for vampires. It's prime feeding time for sharks.

I kick my shoes off and head to the shoreline. Cold water laps my toes. I stare down at the froth easing over and back until I'm sort of hypnotized. I've eaten a lot of fish all my life. It'd be poetic justice if a great white snapped me up whole like a piece of sashimi. No more waiting around for the cancer to pick me off. Question is, am I brave enough to tempt a shark into taking me as a main meal? Stupid enough? A few months from now, will I be desperate enough?

Course not much goes to plan in my life. Sharks probably wouldn't come near me. The more likely scenario is I'll go out into the water after dark and the worst thing that'll hit me is a piece of slimy seaweed. Right in the kisser.

Then it'd be back to square one.

"Alex?" a voice calls out behind me. "Alex! Hey!"

Molly. Guess Suze has incredible powers of persuasion and managed to drag her here. Squeezing my eyes shut, I take a deep breath and steel myself. No way will Molly pass up a chance to hassle me about college and skipping school and God knows what else is on her mind. When I open my eyes again, she's right beside me, taking off her flip-flops.

"How are you?" she asks with so much concern I almost fall over. I expected anger from her. Maybe nostrils flaring in defiance and flashing, indignant eyes.

But not *concern*.

She's looking at me like I've got a "fragile" sticker on my forehead. I turn my gaze back on the surfers. They're paddling in, not far from the relative safety of dry sand.

"Me? I'm fine. Just thinkin' up ways to die," I say, partly to scare her off, but mostly because it's the truth.

"Morbid much?" She arches a brow. "What's on your list so far? Drowning? Getting hit by a boat propeller?"

"Look who's morbid now? Not to mention gruesome." I pretend to shiver. After a few beats, I tell her, "Shark attack. How would you rate that as a way to die?"

She frowns. "Apparently, sharks don't even like the taste of human flesh. That's why, in a lot of cases, people get a chunk taken out of them or a limb bitten off. Sharks take one bite and realize it's not a seal they're chowing down on and spit you out. You, of course, would know this if you'd—"

Bristling, I stop her. "I know what you're going to say. I'd know if I'd been in school."

"No," she says with a smirk. "You'd know about all that if you'd watched Shark Week."

I let out a laugh, grateful she's not hammering me about skipping classes for once. Lying to her about my impending doom is one of the hardest things I've ever had to do. The more we skate around the topic of school, the better.

Molly swishes her foot from side to side in the water. Music and excited voices float down the beach to us. The sun's all but gone now. We watch the two surfers finally climb out, looking exhausted but exhilarated at the same time. I know that feeling. I live for it.

Finally, Molly speaks up. "There's a, um, rumor going around about you."

My back stiffens. God. Somebody found out about the cancer? How? Kip wouldn't tell. I trust him. I try to focus on the sea, 'cause if I look at Molly, I'll crack. The winds are whipping up a little more. If only those surfer dudes had stayed in a few minutes longer. I work hard to keep my voice even. "Oh, yeah? Whatever it is, I didn't do it."

She steps closer to me. Her long silky hair brushes against my arm. "So you didn't faint in class today?"

Still trying not to look at her, I say, "No, I didn't faint in class."

That's not exactly a lie. I fainted *outside* the biology lab. In the hall.

"Oh," she says simply. She looks a little more relieved, a little less concerned. "But you would tell me if something like that happened, right? We're still friends, aren't we?"

This time I turn to Molly. Wide-eyed, freckle-faced Molly, who has no idea how cute she really is. I don't even remember the exact moment I fell in love with her, but I can't imagine being *out* of love with her. Yet I don't want Molly to fall in love with *me*. Not when I've got a death sentence.

The words of Mom, of Kip, of my conscience echo inside me. *Tell her the truth. She deserves to know. She deserves the chance to prepare herself.*

Would it be so bad if we made some good memories together before I get too sick, though? And then, when I can't hide the cancer from her any longer, I'll tell her. Everything.

"Moll, of course we're friends. That'll never change, no matter what." It takes every ounce of strength I've got to not blurt out the truth—that I want to be more than friends with her.

She looks at me sheepishly. "Even if I say I went ahead and reserved plane tickets to Connecticut? For spring break?"

"What?! I can't just get on a plane to visit colleges. Are you crazy?" I yell. She shrinks back in shock and immediately I feel stabs of guilt. She's probably thinking, *Well, why the hell not?* "I'm sorry. Sorry."

"Relax!" she shouts back. "The tickets are refundable."

Breathing deeply, I try to get ahold of my emotions again. "Good."

"And why is it good? You've always talked about going to Yale. This is your chance to see it for yourself. I wanted to get you inspired again."

*Keep breathing, Alex. Keep breathing. Yeah, until you literally can't breathe anymore.* Fighting for composure, I force myself to say, "Thanks, Moll. Really. But now's not the right time."

"I can change the reservations. How about May? The weather'll be fantastic."

I swallow hard. My body will not be fantastic three months out from death. Will it withstand a five-hour-plus flight? Nope. And for what, anyway? I'm not going to survive long enough to graduate from high school.

Tentatively, I put a hand on her shoulder. She jumps like she wasn't expecting me to touch her. "Molly, do me a favor?"

She brightens. "Anything. What do you need?"

Roaring, snarling engines tear my attention away from Molly for a second. They sound like they're closing in on the cove, ready to join the party.

"I need you to cancel the tickets." I start walking up the beach, sand squeaking between my wet toes. "I'm not going to Yale. Stop asking me why."

"Alex! ALEX!" she shouts after me. "You're an ass, you know that? And you can go jump in the ocean with a million rabid, hungry sharks for all I care!"

# CHAPTER 7

MOLLY

"I HEARD you scream at Alex. What happened?" Suze asks when I plunk beside her on a log. In front of us, the bonfire rages. Some kids are setting marshmallows on fire and running up and down the beach with flaming sticks.

My gaze sweeps over the partygoers. "Is he still here? I'm not actually done screaming at him."

She puts a hand on my arm. "Whoa there. Maybe you should cool off."

"Is he here?" I repeat crisply.

Suze sighs and jerks her thumb toward the parking lot. "A couple of seniors rocked up in their tricked-out cars. Alex went that way along with half the other boys to kick tires or get high on fumes or something."

A revving engine punctuates her words. I make a move to stand, but Suze pulls me down. "Hey! I was only going to get a drink."

"No, you weren't," she says, rolling her eyes. "You were going on the hunt for Alex. Stay with me a while. You're my date tonight, remember?"

Heaving a sigh, I say, "Fine, but don't expect me to make out with you."

She throws her head back and laughs. "It's okay. I know you're saving yourself for someone else."

"What are you talking about?"

Suze offers me a chip, then digs into the bag. "Not what. Who. Alex. You've conveniently avoided admitting you liked him."

"Is all that processed cheese affecting your brain?" I point at the Cheetos she's stuffing into her mouth.

"Stop lying to me. No, better yet, stop lying to yourself." Suze dusts off her hands. "You, my friend, should no longer deny your total, raging crush on Alex Gibson. You'll be a lot less grumpy if you just say it."

I squeak in protest.

"Don't pretend for my sake. My thing with Alex... Well, you can't even call it a thing because nothing happened between us. So don't even think of telling yourself he's off limits."

"Suze, you've got it all wrong—"

"Nope, not this time." She holds up an orange-stained palm. "Life is short. Girl, if you want him, go after him!"

"But I don't want him!"

"Riiiight. You only talk about him 24/7."

I wince. So I'm a broken record. That must be beyond boring for everyone else. It's a wonder Suze sticks by me. "I'm not *that* bad, am I?"

With a laugh, she says, "You are that bad. But it's adorable. You two are adorable together, and you obviously care a lot about him."

I gaze at the crackling fire. The flames reach ever higher toward the stars. "I don't want things to change between me and Alex."

"They won't have to. Well, some things will, and for the better." She nudges me. "I'm sure you'll have fun making out with *him*."

A strange feeling buzzes around my stomach. Kissing Alex. Feeling his arms around me. The thought of being close to him—physically—isn't that foreign. Or as gross as the thought of kissing Jared Christie over there chugging beer. It's pretty clear to anyone who gets close to Jared that he doesn't brush his teeth and often wears the same T-shirt two weeks running.

No, Alex has got the personal hygiene thing down pat. That's a plus. And he's got a really nice smile. I always feel like he could brighten the gloomiest day with that wide grin. And the way he fixes broken gadgets and gifts them to me is completely awesome and thoughtful.

"You shouldn't let him get away," Suze says, echoing what I'm thinking at the same time.

Then my chest deflates. "I don't want him to, but there's one problem. He's had it with me interfering in his life."

"He said that to you?"

"Not in so many words, but he's pulling back from me. Maybe I've been too obsessed with the college thing and it's scared him off." I glance over at the cars. A group of kids moves and finally I spot Alex and Kip. They're running their hands over a black Porsche like it's a thoroughbred horse. "Plus, I've pretty much told him he's dead to me, so I don't think it's meant to be. Not romantically, anyway."

Suze shrugs. "Apologize to him. Then see where things go."

"Oh, and he'll forgive me just like that?" I click my fingers.

Holding out her hand, she says, "Fifty bucks says he will."

"You're on." I shake on it, then fold my arms and stare at the fire till my vision goes blurry. I can't help but think Alex is the one who owes *me* an apology for being a general jerk during the past few months.

She lightly shoves me off the log. "No, lady. *You're* on."

"What?" I scramble to my feet.

"I mean, the spotlight's on you. Get up there and make things right between you and your soon-to-be-boyfriend."

"Let's take one step at a time. We need to just be friends again." I frown and shake sand off my skinny jeans. "I cannot believe you pushed me."

"You're welcome," she singsongs, batting her long eyelashes.

I pull her up. "And you're coming with me."

"Fine, fine." She stashes the Cheetos into her purse and links arms with me.

We trudge past clusters of seniors and juniors from school, including the birthday girl, Katie.

"Don't go!" Katie leans toward us. Her eyes are glazed and round like doughnuts. She points to a cooler at her feet. "Party's just starting."

"We'll be right back," Suze calls out as we pass. "With boys!"

"For my birthday?" Katie slurs and grins. "You two are the best!"

We step off the cool sand onto hot asphalt. Kids are swarming around cars, whooping every time a car engine revs. The smell of rich gas and burning rubber competes with the fresh air.

"Why does this turn guys on?" I ask, fanning my nose.

"They're weirdos from Mars." Suze tugs my arm. "Come on, I see Kip and Alex. Oh, look. They're talking to Tom. We can bring him to Katie later."

I saw them from a mile off, too, but I wanted to take my time getting closer. What the hell am I going to say to Alex? Is he even going to hear me apologize over these obnoxious engine noises?

I take a couple of steps, then stop dead. "Are you implying you want Kip for yourself? *Kip?*"

Under the solar-powered parking lot lights, Suze's blush is plain to see. "I mean, Katie can choose between Tom and Kip."

Rolling my eyes, I continue walking. What is it with this Kip guy? Why is he so magnetic to everyone but me?

Alex turns his head and meets my gaze. I falter. And so does Alex's smile. He turns back to Tom.

"Come on," Suze mutters. "You can be the bigger person here. Apologize. Tell him he's the best thing that ever happened to you and kiss him senseless."

"Do I have to do that in front of you? And everyone?"

"Maybe only me, so I know you've successfully carried out your mission." She winks and propels me forward.

"So what do you say?" Kip is asking Tom when we reach them. "A little street race for my boy here?"

Tom leans against his gleaming, black, and very expensive Porsche. A little something his movie producer parents gave him for his eighteenth birthday. It was a replacement for the BMW sedan he'd gotten for his sweet —ha!—sixteenth. Both cars cost more than all the contents of my house. In our school, there's a big gap between the haves and have-nots. It must be hard for Alex, who fell swiftly into the have-not group when his parents divorced after the longest separation in history.

"I don't know..."

"It's for a good cause," Kip cajoles. Alex stands by the car, looking like a kid in a chocolate factory.

"Which good cause is that?" I ask, walking up behind Kip.

He jumps.

Tom angles toward me and Suze. "Hey. How you doing? Long time no talk, Suze."

Studiously ignoring Kip, she replies, "Oh, you know, been busy. Nice wheels."

He grins. "Kip's trying to convince me to let Alex drive it."

"Why?" I ask warily, thinking of James Dean and the way he drove fast and died young. In a freakin' Porsche.

Alex shrugs without looking at me. "YOLO."

I turn to Tom. "You're not seriously thinking of giving him the keys, are you?"

Tom scratches the back of his neck. He rakes his gaze over the car. To me, it looks like a coiled rattlesnake ready to strike. "Well, I know Alex is pretty cautious. He tutored me in calculus."

"Um, math and Porsches are two different beasts," I point out. "Formulas and equations are predictable if you know your way around them. Alex, you don't know your way around a car like this."

Alex finally looks at me. "Did somebody call the fun police?"

His words are like poison ivy, making me itch like crazy. But, most of all, making me plain crazy. I am not going to be making out with Alex Gibson tonight. No way.

"Playing NASCAR games on your PlayStation does not count as real driving experience," I insist. *James Dean. Car crash. Porsche. Dead.* Those words keep jumbling up in my brain. If Alex gets behind the wheel and wraps that car around a streetlight, I'll never forgive myself.

"Hey, come on, Miss Molly, that's all the more reason to try the real deal," Kip speaks up. "Stop busting his ass all the time."

Steam practically vents out of my ears. "I'm not busting his ass! I'm looking out for him."

"And so am I!" Kip takes a couple of steps closer to me.

Suze grips my arm tightly. She whispers, "We should get out of here. This is all getting a little nutty."

I stand my ground.

"Kip, don't," Alex warns.

"But Miss Molly, you're so busy thinking about yourself that you can't see Alex is—"

"Kip!" Alex moves between me and Kip, whose eyes are getting wilder by the second. And scarier. But I will not be intimidated by that loser. Judging by the way Alex is glaring, standing over him, maybe he finally gets it. Kip is bad news.

Kip peers around at me and starts waving his arms. "Alex is—"

"No!" Alex roars. He grabs Kip by the collar and throws him against the Porsche's driver's side.

"Hey, hey, watch it!" Tom pulls Kip away from the shiny paintwork. He lovingly inspects the undamaged door. "You know what? I'm gonna leave you guys to it. I'll take you for a ride some other time, Alex."

Tom gets into the Porsche. He theatrically guns the engine and makes the tires spin before peeling away in the direction of Malibu. The four of us left behind choke on the thick stench of burning rubber.

Kip shoots a look at me. He opens his mouth like he's going to say something terrible.

Alex glares at Kip. In a menacing tone, he says, "Not one word."

Shaking his head violently, Kip swings around toward me. "I used to think you were good for Alex. Not so much now."

"Alex and I have been friends since we were four. I know him better than anyone!" My chest puffs indignantly. I cannot be*lieve* I'm having this conversation with Kip Jones, of all people. "What gives you the right to pass judgment on me? You don't even know me or Alex."

Kip settles down a little. He looks at the ground, hands on hips. "I know more than you think."

Putting a hand on Kip's shoulder, Alex practically begs, "Don't say anything else, man. How many times do I have to tell you? I'll do this my way."

His voice is low. I'm sure he didn't mean for me to hear. Do *what* his way?

"This is getting boring. Let's go back to the party." Suze tugs on my arm again. I know she's not being superficial, though. She's trying to be a good friend, trying to steer me back to the relative safety of the beach.

Like a bad friend, I ignore her. I stare first at Kip, then at Alex. There's an undercurrent between them. It's palpable, pulsating. Something is *definitely* up. "What's going on? You're both acting weird."

"Nothing." It seems to take a lot of effort, a lot of control, for Alex to utter that one word. He won't take his eyes off Kip.

"Tell her." Kip's jaw clenches. "Or I will."

Alex turns into a statue. Immobile. Unable to talk. He won't meet my gaze, but he keeps staring hard at Kip.

Suze lets out an enormous, annoyed sigh. "You two are the worst drama queens ever. I'm here to have fun. Moll, are you coming?"

"No, I'm staying right here." Something deep inside warns me that I need to be around for Alex. Who knows what Kip's capable of?

"You have no right to tell her, Kip," Alex says. "Just like you had no right to tell Tom. You don't get to do that."

"Will one of you, I don't care *who*, tell me what the hell is happening here?" My voice carries over the revving of engines. I feel the weight of a dozen gazes on me. Kip shifts from foot to foot, and looks up at the sky. His lips purse.

Slowly, Alex swivels to me. Clearing his throat, he says, "Molly, come with me."

"Where?" I whisper. The cold feeling returns as he shakes his head. I throw a glance at Suze, who looks confused and scared.

Alex takes my hand and leads us away from the glare of the parking lot lights, away from the stares. It's strange to feel his palm against mine. Warm and firm. At the same time, it feels right. Natural. Calming. Some of the coldness inside me goes away.

But I'm still worried. "Alex, I can't wait anymore. Please talk to me."

"Everything's going to be fine," he says in a reassuring voice.

A three-quarter moon sheds enough light for us to see the path ahead. Alex takes me along the top of the beach, then down to the jagged edges of the cove. His hand grips tighter as he approaches a flat boulder overlooking the sea. We sit side by side. Salt water sprays our faces, cooling us down.

"You want to know the truth?" he asks.

"No, go ahead. Tell me more lies."

He laughs. It's a rough, weary sound. "You're right. I have been lying to you."

My spine goes rigid. It's hard to hear those words come out of his mouth. We've always confided in each other. Till very recently. Now I know for sure he's been avoiding me. Lying to me. "What about?"

"Everything. My life." Alex swallows hard. He stares into the distance. A line of oil tankers inches across the horizon, lights blazing. "I'm going to lose you."

"Why would you think that? Because you've told a few lies? I'm not *that* unforgiving."

"It's not that." He shakes his head. "I'm...leaving."

"Are you moving to Australia?" I whisper. My insides churn. I miss him already, and he's right here with me. "It's not for forever, though, is it? You *have* to come back, because Yale's going to accept you in a heartbeat."

"Molly, I'm sorry." He grabs both my hands and squeezes like we're riding ten-foot ocean waves together and can't get separated. "What I said about living fast, dying young..."

"Yeah." I ignored it till now, but an intense fear is making my bones shake. It's the way he says the word *dying* that makes me feel the worst pain.

"I may not be living all that fast." He strokes my hand with his trembling thumb. "But I'm gonna die young. For real."

"What?" I stare at him uncomprehendingly, unable to move.

"Molly?"

"No." Tears blur my vision. "It's not true."

His voice cracks. "Molly, I have stage IV melanoma. I'm dying."

"Stop it. Don't joke about it." *Not true. Not true. Not true.* He's beaten cancer once, when he was a little kid. Now he's bigger and stronger. He's invincible, dammit.

My heart and my mind start to make the connections. Missing school. Losing hair. Losing weight. Losing interest in the future.

*Oh, God.* How could I have been so blind? What kind of best friend am I?

I put an arm around him. Try to weld myself to him.

"I'm not joking, Molly." He shudders as he breathes deeply. Connected by his touch, I shudder along with him. It's like the earth's shattering beneath us. Cracking wide open. Ready to swallow us whole. "I'm dying. And there's nothing anyone can do about it. Not even you."

# CHAPTER 8

ALEX

"No!" Molly gasps as if she took a direct hit from a sledgehammer. A tidal wave of tears spills over her lashes. Seated on the boulder, she wobbles sideways. I reach out to bring her back to me, but she pushes against my chest. "You're lying. If you're not joking about it, you're lying. Again."

"Trust me, I wouldn't lie or joke about something like this. Not to you." I clench my fists, partly to stop myself from touching her again. "But God knows I lied to myself. Tried to tell myself it wasn't happening."

She draws in a shaky breath. "I won't let you die."

"It doesn't work that way," I say, shaking my head. "Death doesn't bend to Molly Corbett's wishes."

Her voice pitches higher. "And what about Alex Gibson's wishes?"

"My wishes? There are so many I can't prioritize them anymore. And none are ever going to come true." I bite down on my lip. The salty sea taste is actually a welcome change after weeks of subsisting on Mom's bitter kale smoothies.

"Oh, my God," she breathes. "You've given up. That's why you haven't been going to school and why you've been avoiding college applications."

"Well, Molly, you tell me," I snap. "If you were given six months to live, would you want to spend it cramming for pointless exams and being forced to attend pep rallies?"

Her jaw goes slack. "Six months? That's all?"

"Okay, five months and twenty-seven days. Give or take."

She doesn't smile at my attempt at a joke. Even in the weak light, the hurt on her face is easy to see. "Why didn't you tell me? When did you find out?"

I look away. "Last year. When I was in Sydney visiting Dad."

Molly lets out a sob and struggles to compose herself. "I don't understand how this happened. How you could have cancer a second time. It's so unfair!"

It was sort of easier finding out when I was half a world away. Easier to hide the news from Molly, that is. It gave me time to clear my head. When the doctors told us the rounds of chemo hadn't worked and there's nothing else they could do, my head got completely clogged again.

"My dad has had a few carcinomas cut out over the years," I say, trying to keep my voice from shaking. "Growing up by the beach in Australia, he worshipped the sun, you know? And I wanted to do everything he did. Stayed out on the waves from dawn till dusk if I could. Ignored my mother when she lectured me about using sunblock and all the rest of it.

"Anyway, I went along with Dad for one of his regular check-ups. A nurse at the clinic didn't like the look of a mole on my neck. I got a biopsy right away. The rest is history." I breathe in sharply. "You should have seen my dad's face when the docs gave us the diagnosis. He looked so guilty. But I don't blame him for anything. He gave me the love of surfing. I never feel more alive than when I'm out there on my board."

*Or when I'm with you.*

Molly weeps silently. "I'm so sorry I wasn't there for you, Alex."

Shrugging, I say, "There's nothing to apologize for. My parents went into full-on Papa Bear and Mama Bear mode. Did everything they could to get me the best treatment. Meanwhile, I was numb. Just a piece of driftwood getting tossed around. I went in whatever direction they told me to go. Even if you were there, I don't think it would've been good for you to be near me."

"But that's crazy!"

"Not really," I tell her. "A counselor talked to me about grief and loss. You know how they talk about those stages? Denial, anger, bargaining, depression, acceptance. I didn't want you to see how angry I was."

"And your new buddy Kip? When did you tell him?" There's a shade of accusation in her voice. Envy and pain, too.

"Look, I know now I should have told you, but at the time, I didn't know the right way to deal with all this."

After a while, she says quietly, "I don't know if there is a right way."

"I'm sorry Kip found out before you did. It happened by accident." I tell her about my blackout here at the cove and the connection to Kip's sister Caitlin.

"Wow. That's...that's amazing. I'm sorry. I didn't mean to get all bent out of shape about who knew first. I can't believe this is happening!" Her gaze drops to her fidgeting hands. "Were you ever going to tell anyone?"

I sigh. "I had this grand plan to fade away without anyone knowing."

"What, and not allow anyone to say goodbye?" There's that accusing tone again.

"Yep. No funeral, no memorial. It's not like I've done anything important in my sixteen or so years on the planet."

Molly gives me a doubtful look. "You've been my best friend since forever. Always bringing me gadgets and making me laugh. I think that's pretty important."

I squeeze her hand as hard as I can. "Hey, you've been my BFF. You *are* my best friend."

Best friend. What would it be like if I kissed my best friend now? Kissed her like I've wanted to since our first day as Palisades High freshmen? I'd been away all summer and instead of coming home to tomboy Molly, I found grown-up Molly with curves in places that weren't there before.

Molly eyes me thoughtfully. Is she thinking what I'm thinking? Will she ever dream of kissing me, knowing I'm going to die anyway?

"What stage of grief are you at now?" she asks.

My shoulders slump. I guess kissing is the last thing on her mind.

"I'm at the unofficial 'I don't give a shit' stage. But sometimes I go through *all* of those other stages in the course of an hour." I look over at the ocean. White-capped waves roll one after the other. The sea has been the one constant thing my whole life. Whether here in L.A. or in Sydney, I've never lived more than a few blocks away from it. "There'll come a day when I won't be able to grab my board and paddle out. And I'm okay with that. Today, anyway."

Her gaze rakes over me, lingering on my chest. "But you look so good."

"Stop it. You're making me blush," I say in a flat voice.

"I mean it. Apart from being kinda pale, you still look fit and muscly." Her voice trails off. She stares at my biceps. They're covered by my sleeves, but anyone can tell they're not as bulgy as they were at the start of the year. And that really blows because I worked so hard to build those suckers up.

"Must be the smoothies Mom makes for me. I'm surprised my skin isn't green right now."

"Alex, listen." Molly jiggles my arm. "We can fight this with kale, with positivity, proactivity, hyperactivity! You beat lymphoma, for God's sake. You can beat this, too."

Numbly, I stare into her eyes. In the moonlight, they're dark and stormy instead of their usual calm green. "Yeah, I did beat cancer the first time around, but the odds are not in my favor now."

"Who says?" Her tone's defiant. She is really not going take this sitting down.

And I can't blame her. I felt the same way. Once.

"Because I've had second, third, fourth and fifth opinions!"

"Then get a sixth one," she says, exasperated.

Despite everything, I smile. "Find one for me, and I'll go."

"Okay, then." Molly pulls out her phone and starts googling.

"I didn't mean right now." I chuckle. "Are you for real?"

"Yes, I'm for real! We're talking life and death. There isn't a second to waste." She yelps when I rip the phone from her grip and toss it safely aside on a patch of sand.

"Let's chill here now and come up with a list tomorrow." I say the words, but secretly I hope she'll forget them in the morning. Soon she'll understand that *terminal* really does mean *beyond hope*. Besides, we've gone to the very best oncologists we could find. They all pretty much said I'm doomed.

"How do they even come up with that deadline?" She stops and winces at how literal her words are. "I mean, does anyone *really* know?"

"If I'm still alive and kicking after six months and one day, you get to come over and badger me about not sticking to timetables."

Darkly, she says, "Do not even kid around with me right now."

I swing my leg over the boulder. "I don't know what else to do anymore except make stupid jokes."

After a few minutes of thinking, she says, "You know what you've got to do now, right?"

"What?" I say uneasily.

"Make every word, every action, every second count."

"Does that mean I have to stay awake 24/7 for the next six months? Can I at least get a siesta in the afternoons?"

She doesn't even crack a smile. I hope she gets her sense of humor back soon. She'll need it.

"No, it means we are going to carry on as if you haven't been given six months to live."

I stare at her, dismayed. Didn't I tell her bluntly that I'm a dead man walking? Maybe joking about death isn't such a good idea after all.

Molly goes on. "What if the five or six doctors are all wrong? What if you defy the odds and survive? Where will that leave you?"

"You're saying I should pretend everything's hunky dory and keep going to school? I've already told you, the Yale dream has crashed and burned. Why would I even want to apply? I'd be wasting everyone's time. Plus, I might be in the way of someone who really deserves to be there."

"*You* deserve to be there. We'll research drug trials," she insists, clearly not listening to a thing I'm saying. "What if someone finds a cure or—"

"Don't you get it?" I cut her off. "There's no future for me. No miracle cure. Nothing."

"You've still got a future that's at least six months long," Molly mutters. She squeezes her eyes shut. When she opens them again, she looks determined. "I'll take six months off, too."

"No! You can't put your life on hold for me." I'm floored. She'd seriously do that?

Looking defiant, she lifts her chin. "What's six months when I have to face the rest of my life without you?"

# CHAPTER 9

MOLLY

I WATCH Alex jog from his front door toward my car parked alongside the curb. My brain still can't process what's happening. How is it possible that my best friend is *dying?* It can't be true. But Mrs. G confirmed it, admitted all those pill bottles were for Alex and not for managing her menopause. A part of me aches because Alex didn't tell me about the cancer sooner. I know where he was coming from now. I'm just not sure I'd handle things the same way if I were in his sneakers.

"Welcome to T-minus seventy-nine days," Alex says cheerfully, strapping himself into the passenger seat.

"Ugh, do you have to say that?"

"Yep. My last words will be *blast-off!*"

On cue, I fire the engine. I came through on my threat to take a leave of absence from school. With parental blessing, of course. How could they or the school admin refuse my perfectly reasonable request to help take care of a dying friend? When I'm not spending as much time as possible with Alex, I'll have to continue my schoolwork at home. Small price to pay.

"What are we doing today?" I press a button to wind down his window. In a robotic, GPS-lady voice, I continue, "I'm awaiting your instruction. Just tell me the coordinates. Or a rough address."

Alex laughs and rests his elbow on the windowsill. "I hadn't really thought this thing through when I texted you last night. We could go cruising."

Concentrating on the thickening traffic near the beach, I suggest, "How about a road trip? I hear there's a quaint little university about three thousand miles away that you might want to see."

"Isn't it enough that I wrote the essay you've been bugging me about?"

I smile. "Not quite. Next step is to actually send it."

"Sure. You know I'm signing it off with Alexander 'Six-Feet-Under-By-the-Time-You-Read-This' Gibson," right?

"Alex!" *He* may be deep in the acceptance stage of grief, but I'm still wallowing in the denial phase.

"What's your problem? It's full disclosure."

"You *might* be gone," I growl. "There's always hope."

"We'll see," he mutters. Further down the PCH, he points to Burger Deluxe. "I'd kill for any type of food that isn't green right now. Are you hungry? My treat."

"This must be the shortest cruise in history. We haven't even seen a single girl for you to hit on."

"No girl will want me now." Before I can protest, he adds, "Besides, we haven't got a second to lose. Isn't that what you said? Let's do everything in double-time."

Quick as a flash, I find a parking spot, and we soon have steaming coffee and breakfast sitting in front of us. There's nothing green or anything else that resembles a vegetable on either of our plates.

I dress my pancakes with maple syrup and swirl it into the whipped cream. Alex jabs at his bacon, but leaves it sitting on the plate. There's a definite change in mood. Mouth full, I mumble, "Why aren't you eating?"

He winces at his mountain of scrambled eggs, hash browns and crispy bacon strips. It all looks and smells so good. "I'm not hungry anymore."

My fork freezes halfway to my mouth. I'm suddenly reminded that he's sick. He's dying. People lose their appetites when they're close to death, don't they? Tears start to well. Impossible to think I have any left. I wore out my tear ducts that night at the cove when Alex told me everything. "What's wrong? Are you in pain?"

He shakes his head like he's trying to remove something lodged in his brain. "I didn't mean to put a downer on breakfast. It's just that I feel fine a lot of the time. Then suddenly it hits me. When I'm trying to sleep. Brushing my teeth. Sitting in class. I'm fucking *dying*."

Fighting tears, I reach across our booth's table and lightly cover his hand with mine. "It's okay. Listen, I don't want you to hide anything from me ever again."

Alex stares at my hand. Finally, he lifts his hazel gaze and gives me an intense look. Two spots of red glow on his cheeks. "I can't promise you that. There are some things I don't want you or anybody else to know."

"Oh." Removing my hand, I sit back and breathe in deeply. My heart feels like it's shattering into a million tiny pieces. I tell myself he's totally within his rights to keep to himself. It's his life. His death. "Alex, are you scared?"

He looks out the spotless plate-glass window. Discarded fast-food wrappers roll among the parked cars. Tumbleweeds of the city. "See, if I were scared, that's definitely something I'd hide from you."

Peering at him, I find fear etched over every square inch of his face. "I'm guessing it's normal to feel scared in this situation."

"How would you know?" he snaps.

Refusing to flinch, I say in a calm voice, "I don't. I need you to tell me."

"There's nothing normal about what I'm going through," he says through grit teeth.

"You're right."

"I haven't *lived* yet." He takes two long gulps of coffee. I notice a faint tremor in his hand. He follows my line of vision and plunks down the sturdy cup. "And I'm only going to get weaker from here on out."

Pushing aside my plate, I take hold of his hands. Firmly this time. He doesn't squirm away. Maybe, I note with a marble-size lump in my throat, he doesn't have the strength. "Okay, I've been thinking about this 'live fast, die young' mantra."

He lifts an eyebrow. "Yeah?"

"We should totally do it. Live fast."

"We?"

"Yep, tell me what's on your bucket list and we'll strike each item off. One by one. Starting now." I let go of him and check my imaginary wristwatch. I press its imaginary button.

"But what if..." he lowers his voice and gives me a loaded look. "I want to do dangerous things?"

"Define 'dangerous.'"

Seemingly speechless, his mouth flaps open and closed. "Dangerous things are the kinds of things that make me *feel* something, you know?"

"Wow. So specific." I pour another sachet of sugar into my coffee.

"You're making fun of a dying man?" He gives a bittersweet smile.

"Hey, I'm not going easy on you now. No more feeling sorry for yourself." I'm carrying enough pain and pity inside to last two lifetimes. With my fingernail, I tap his phone screen. "Type five things you've never done before but have always wanted to try."

"Do they have to be legal things?"

"That's up to you," I say. "But if you need to be bailed out, I'll have to sell your car, my iPad and every other gadget you've given me so I can raise the cash."

Alex taps and swipes on his phone. "Do I have to tell you what these things are in advance?"

"That's also up to you."

His lips twist thoughtfully. "So, I can surprise you. Even though you hate surprises."

"When did I ever say I hate surprises?"

"Come on, Moll." He snorts. "You organize your life right down to the minute, allowing for every contingency. I got you good once, though. Remember your fifteenth birthday? *You* threw a tantrum when *I* threw a surprise party for you."

"How could I forget? You told me to come over for a study session. I turned up in mismatched sneakers and a rat's nest for hair. Plus, I had ketchup stains on my unicorn T-shirt."

"And a smear on your cheek. Can't forget that. You looked cute, though." He laughs, then stops abruptly.

"Cute?" Alex thought I looked cute? My stomach does a weird little jump. Somehow. I press a hand on my chest. Maybe I scarfed down those pancakes too fast. Or maybe it's a reaction to hearing Alex say I once looked cute—the same Alex who never comments about my appearance unless I'm red from heatstroke or green from eating bad shrimp.

"In...in a Little Rascals kind of way," he stammers. "Okay, I'll shut up now."

"No, please, do keep telling me how cute I used to be."

"Used to—" He breaks off. I throw the empty sugar packet at him. "Stop throwing things at me so I can write this bucket list before I actually kick the bucket."

Sitting back, I watch him tap with those long, lean fingers. He bites his bottom lip, deep in concentration. While he's busy, I swipe some of his bacon. He doesn't even blink. Finally, he puts his phone screen-side down on the table.

"You've finished your list?"

He grins enigmatically and fishes bills from his wallet. "You've finished my breakfast?"

I smack my lips. "The bacon was divine."

"Glad to hear it. Give me your car keys. Let's go."

# CHAPTER 10

ALEX

A PACK of cyclists zooms by us on the trail. Dust whirls after them and kicks up into our faces. Apart from that, it's a clear morning. In the distance, the stark white walls and dull copper domes of Griffith Park Observatory stand out.

I glance over at Molly. She's trying to balance on a rented mountain bike while pushing dark bangs away from her eyes. The bike's front wheel wobbles as she fights for control. It's an uphill battle. Literally.

"Maybe we should stick to the newbie trail," she says. "This one is for experts and show ponies."

"Nah, not dangerous enough." I try to control my breath. My lungs are close to bursting. We're supposedly on the intermediate trail. But for someone who hasn't ridden a bike since middle school, even the gentle slopes here seem like deathtraps. I know it must be killing Molly to not be in charge of this excursion. She'd find the paths of least resistance, paths that didn't have razor-sharp bushes and bone-jarring ruts.

"Are we close to the top yet?" Molly pants. Sweat pours down her forehead. Her face is as red as Mars. And still she looks beautiful.

She would hate to know her face is an open book. Every emotion, every feeling, shows in those big green eyes. I could tell it shocked her when I said she was cute. It's something I've always thought, but never said out loud. Question is, do I have the guts to say it to her again? Molly didn't exactly fall at my feet. She only had eyes for the bacon.

"Less than a mile," I call out. "Piece of cake. You can do it!"

She flicks a look at me, then gives a firm nod. I know what she's thinking: If a half-dead guy like me can ride this trail, she can do a half-mile, too. Her short legs pump a little bit faster. "Come on, Alexander the Geek! Double-time!"

Within minutes, we're at the top of a ridge amongst groups of tourists, looking out across the L.A. basin. A bit of the marine layer clings near the horizon. Otherwise, the sky is wide and clear blue. Right in front of us, the Hollywood sign stretches out across a hill.

"Wow," Molly says simply. She shares her bottle of water with me. "I've lived here all my life and have *never* seen the sign up close."

"Same." I grin at her and pull out my phone. Molly has no clue that I'm taking shots of her as well as the sign.

Before, I thought it was weird that out-of-towners put this at the top of their sightseeing list—stare at a friggin' sign made of ordinary steel. Now, I wish *I* had more hours and days to take in those giant white letters.

We spend a while mixing around with the tourists and taking selfies. Molly subtly tries to find places in the shade where we can get a good view.

"Ready for the best part, Mollywood?" I drag her away from yet another vantage point.

Hope springs into her eyes. "What, are we going to climb the sign?"

I make an obnoxious buzzing noise, the kind heard on game shows. "Nope. We're going on a race to the bottom. Bonus points if you go hands-free for at least ten consecutive seconds."

She gives me a double high five. "Let's do it."

Molly gets a head start on me. But, thanks to her shortage of coordination, almost immediately loses ground. Her left foot slips from the pedal, and it takes a few spins of the wheel to get resettled. I zoom past her, whooping triumphantly. The breeze whips my skin, but in a good way. I don't even mind the heat of the sun on my face or the effect of the bumpy terrain on my butt.

"Hey, Alex?" Molly calls out behind me. Her voice vibrates. "I think we took a wrong turn."

"What makes you say that?" I yell back.

"Look down to your left. See that smooth path everyone else but us is riding?"

My seat judders under me. I glance further ahead and spy deep ruts in the worn asphalt. I could avoid them. If I'm careful.

"Alex, we should turn back."

Over the rush of wind, I hear her tires skid on gravel. Alarmed, I throw a quick look over my shoulder. She's okay. Just standing with the bike stationary between her legs. And looking furious.

"Alex! Stop!"

I face the trail in front of me. Brambles whack my legs, but I don't care. My heart bashes against my ribs. Maybe it's the heat. Maybe the bumpy track's damaging my brain. But something tells me to keep going. Keep daring myself.

Molly's voice is far, far away.

I shut her out. Words from the past echo through my head.

*"You're such a brave kid."*

*"What a trouper!"*

*"I know it hurts, but you've gotta be brave for your mom now."*

Tears stream from my eyes. I want to think they're caused by wind blasting my eyeballs, but of course that's not exactly true.

"Come on, Alex," I bite out. "Let's see how fucking brave you are."

I pedal faster and faster. The harder I ride, the harder it is to control the front wheel. I wrench the bike left and right in order to stay on the trail.

"Alex!" Molly's voice is shrill and clear in my ear now. Did she catch up to me?

I turn my head slightly, and I catch sight of the sharp drop next to me. It's got to be fifty feet down into the canyon at least. My wheels spin inches away from the edge. One wrong move and I could go right over. Break my neck. Die.

It'd be so easy.

Chest pounding, I adjust my grip on the handlebars. The rhythm of the bike and the blur of the landscape put me into a trance.

And Molly's screams take me right out of it. "Alex, you maniac! Are you trying to kill yourself?"

I squeeze the brake levers. The back wheel fishtails over the edge, but the rest of the bike—and my body—stays on the trail.

Panting, I turn to Molly. She's on foot, her bike nowhere to be seen. Wouldn't be surprised if she tossed it off the cliff. "Yeah. And so what if I am? It doesn't matter."

She stomps up to me and puts her hot palms on my shoulders. "It matters to me. *You* matter to me. You are not going to die. Not on my watch."

# CHAPTER 11

MOLLY

THERE'S one thing I've never, ever told Alex, and that is I hate swimming in the ocean. Pools I can handle. A calm lake is fine. But to me, the sea is an untamed, unchained animal. The idea of being caught in a riptide and dragged into the middle of the Pacific is nothing short of terrifying.

Surfing has always been Alex's thing. Just like going vintage clothes shopping has always been my thing. I couldn't care less if he knocks back a chance to try on seventies bellbottom jeans with me.

But I know he'll care very much if I back out of a surfing lesson.

Touching my head self-consciously, I step out of the cove's public restrooms. The short-sleeved, thigh-length wetsuit Alex bought me clings in all the wrong places. Now that the sun's on the move above the horizon, people will actually see me wearing this get-up. Not only do I feel like a seal, I look like one, too.

"Hey, there you are!" Alex calls out and jogs toward me.

For the first time, I notice he's acquired a limp. I hope to God he isn't in pain. But if I know Alex, he wouldn't want me to make a big deal out of it. Pushing away dark thoughts, I wave, then gesture at my back. "Help. I can't reach the zipper."

"Sure." When he reaches me, his sunny expression fades. "Whoa. What happened to your hair?"

"Attack of the stylist. She chopped twelve inches of hair. It's called a pixie cut. What do you think?" Channeling a catwalk model, I put a hand on my hip and show off an exaggerated pout.

"Pixie, huh?" He studies me for several long seconds. "You look like a little fairy penguin in that wetsuit."

I push his shoulder. Gently. Because that limp of his worries me.

His voice roughens. "I like it. Suits your face."

"High praise coming from you." I laugh.

"So what's with the big makeover?"

Trying to keep my tone light, I say, "I figured I had plenty of hair to share around."

His eyes bulge. "You donated your hair to charity?"

"Uh-uh. I found a company in Orange County that makes wigs for chemo patients." Tears begin to sting my eyes. I blink them away and quickly change the subject. "Can you zip me up now? I'm getting a chill here."

Alex spins me around. One hand curves around my neck, bringing warmth to the bare skin right there. He zips the last couple of inches and spins me again.

"So this is T-minus seventy-eight." Grandly, he sweeps his arm toward the beach. In the distance, a couple of surfer dudes sit up on their boards watching the sunrise. "Good thing we're here early, 'cause we've got a lot to do today. Starting with teaching you how to surf."

"Um, fabulous." I want to say I'm scared and want to go back to bed, but I bite my tongue. This isn't about me. And, really, I'm happy we're here. Alex said the ocean makes him feel alive. Yesterday, on the bike trail, he was *this* close to launching himself off a cliff. The longer we stay around the water, the safer he'll be.

Overnight, he'd somehow found a board that was the right size for me. And the right color—cobalt blue. The leg rope drags on the ground behind me as I follow Alex. Halfway to the shore, he drops his board on the sand, fins down.

"Okay, best place to learn how to surf is not out there." He points at the Pacific. A low swell rolls toward the shore. Then he points at the white sand under our toes. "It's here."

"Fine by me!" I say cheerfully.

Alex gives me a funny look. "Don't worry. As soon as you get your technique right, we're heading out."

I gulp and avoid looking at the waves.

"I'll demonstrate first." He jumps down. It might be my imagination, but *his* wetsuit isn't as clingy as mine. He's lost more weight than I realized. "Float your board on the water, then climb onto it on your stomach. Paddle, paddle, paddle with your arms. Head out past the breakers. Hang out with your buddies until a worthy set comes along. Angle your board to the beach, let the wave's momentum push you." He pauses. "You look spaced out. Are you getting all this?"

"Yep, keep going." The only thing on my mind is getting caught in a riptide. Oh, and then being taken by Jaws.

"Cool." He lightly grips the board on either side of his chest. "Now, as the wave's starting to roll, put your palms flat on the board. Push up. Then jump into a crouching position, feet about shoulder-width apart. You'll figure out which foot feels more natural to lead with. Rise up a little more. But keep your knees bent. You want a low center of gravity. Stick your arms out for balance. Head up. Eyes forward. And you're surfing. Well, standing up on your board anyway. Fancy stuff comes later."

"It's all really quick." I bite my lip.

"Try it. Double-time." He grins.

I perform the whole sequence so well the first time that he makes me do it six more times "to make sure it's not a fluke."

Unfortunately, once we're out on the water, the landlubber in me sabotages my performance. The swell isn't even half a foot high, but I can't keep my balance. I spend more time treading water than I do paddling on the board.

"I'm not meant to be a creature of the sea," I pant. Alex looks at me with the patience of a saint. "Who knows? I could pioneer sand surfing instead."

"Yeah, I can totally see that as an Olympic sport some day." His smile brings dimples to his cheeks. It's really quite adorable the way that happens. Forget bulging pec muscles. Dimples really get my heart pumping.

*Um, Molly? Focus on not drowning, okay?*

"Should we call time for today?" I ask.

"Sure, but I'm telling you now," he says. "I've finally found my life's purpose. Teaching you to surf like a pro."

My heart pumps again, but this time painfully and sorrowfully. Six months is not a lot of time. It'll take me six months alone to learn how to stand up on a surfboard. Looking away, I nod, unable to utter coherent words.

Exhausted, I wade to the shallows and collapse on the sand with the board. I don't care about the sand coating my hair and neck. I'm just grateful to be alive. Alex flops beside me, breathing hard. We lie there for what feels like forever Nothing to bother us except the sounds of waves constantly approaching and retreating, squawking seagulls, and traffic building on the PCH behind us. I doze off long enough to dream of Alex, of him staring into my eyes with an intensity that makes my heart swell.

The sensation of something warm gliding along the back of my hand wakes me. I open one eye and find Alex gently rubbing my skin. He's staring at my fingers like he's trying to commit every line, every freckle to his memory.

I'm not sure if it's all the salt water I took in, but my throat's suddenly dry. I want to get some water, but even more, I want Alex to kiss me.

I want my best friend kiss to me right here, right now.

Talk about out of the blue.

"Hey," I whisper. Before I can talk myself out of it, I hook one hand around his neck and kiss him. Lightly. Enough to gauge his reaction. His warm, salty lips linger on mine, pressing gently at first, then with more delicious pressure. I can't get close enough to him. "Alex, this is—"

"Wait." Alex sits up. His cheeks are virtually on fire.

"What's wrong?" I thought he was enjoying the kiss. I sure as hell was.

"We should get going," he says without looking at me. "I've still got a bunch of things to do before I die."

He leaves me staring after him in shock.

I kissed my best friend.

And he walked away.

———

"Did you see the looks on those little kids' faces?! So worth it!" Alex says gleefully. We half-skip, half-walk down the corridor toward a waiting area and elevators. Visitors and hospital workers take one look at our woolly brown costumes and can't help but laugh out loud.

"They were totally confused." I twirl my long, curled tail. "I'm not so sure the kids bought our story about being Christmas kangaroos who got lost on the way to the North Pole. But they loved it. And they loved you."

"I don't know about that. Might've had something do with the toys we took out of our pouches." He waves goodbye to the oncology nurses one final time. They'd all been great about us coming in to read stories and hang out with patients. Of course, somehow Alex found the time to organize our visit to the unit in advance. We showed up looking like mutants from down under, and the staff didn't bat an eyelid.

I cast Alex a sidelong glance. Yesterday's kiss on the beach was yesterday's news. He hasn't mentioned it since. And I'm too cowardly to bring it up. I can only guess that he doesn't want to move our relationship to the next level because he doesn't see a future for us.

Why does life have to be this hard? Without warning, I start crying silently. I turn my head so Alex can't see.

"Alex? Wait." A nurse chases us down the hall.

"Did I forget something?" Alex squints and pats his marsupial pouch. While he's doing that, I discreetly wipe my eyes.

The nurse shakes her head. "One of the doctors peeked in when you were reading to the kids. Dr. Khan? She said she knows you from way back."

Alex breaks into huge grin. "Dr. Khan's *still* here?"

"She did a long stint in Britain, but she's been back for a couple of weeks," the nurse explains. "If you're okay with waiting for a few minutes while she finishes a consult, she'd love to come by and say hi."

Alex raises his eyebrows. "Is that cool with you, Molly?"

"Absolutely!" I say after clearing the husk out my voice.

We sit side by side on armchairs. Big plate-glass windows look out onto Ventura Boulevard and a row of pawnshops. Not the greatest of views from a children's hospital. But inside, the walls are painted a sunny yellow and enhanced with framed finger paintings.

Alex's knee jiggles uncontrollably. Beside him, I wage an internal struggle. I could tell him to stop it or I could put my hand on his leg. Or both. Until the past few days, I'd never thought too much about touching Alex. Now I feel like I can't keep my hands off him. When he was reading to the kids, I found myself sneaking looks at him and not being able to tear my gaze away. The kids were completely bewitched by him and the funny faces he pulled as he read.

I clamp a palm on his hyperactive leg. "Hey, are you nervous about meeting up with your old doctor?"

"Yeah." He gives a weak smile and puts his hand over mine. "Dr. Khan was *the* best. She's the one who inspired me to grow up and become a pediatrician. I even told her that I wanted to go to Yale, her alma mater. Now I know it's never gonna happen."

"But this could be great, Alex. She could have that sixth opinion we were looking for!"

A small woman with sleek black hair and a white coat gets out of an elevator. She glances around the waiting room and makes a beeline for Alex.

"Dr. Khan!" Alex practically hops toward her.

"Alex Gibson! It really is you!" The doctor widens her smile. She hugs him, but her short arms can only get halfway around his costume.

"I can't believe you remembered me after all this time!" he says in a voice that carries the slightest of tremors.

"You have changed some since I was last here as a resident, but I never forget a face." Dr. Khan laughs. "The tail is new."

"Stranger things have happened during puberty." Alex beckons me. I struggle out of the chair and pad over on my giant paws. "This is my best friend, Molly."

"Hi, Molly. It was really nice of you two to come down and cheer up the kids. The nurses told me all about it." The doctor shakes my hand and smiles warmly. "So tell me, what else have you been doing? You must be close to graduating from high school."

Alex looks down at the purple carpet. I can almost tell what's running through his mind. For some reason, he's balking at confessing to a cancer doctor that he has cancer. In a super-bright and chipper voice, he says, "Yep, in my junior year. I've been working really hard in my AP classes so I can get into Yale. Follow in your footsteps, you know?"

Dr. Khan looks from Alex to me, then back to Alex. "Oh, my goodness. Really? Alex, I know you'll get there. You have such drive and determination. Listen, let me have your email address. I'd be happy to write a character reference for you."

The doctor types Alex's address into her phone as he recites it. A disembodied voice calls her name over the P.A.

"I'm so sorry, Alex. Duty calls." She gives both of us quick hug. "It was so wonderful to see you again. I'm really proud of you. I'll send that reference this afternoon, okay?"

We watch her hurry to the nurses' station, then disappear around a corner.

"Alex, why didn't you tell her?" I feel itchy and sweaty not just from the costume, but from anxiety.

He gulps and shrugs. "I wanted that character reference. If only to get into heaven or whatever comes next."

Tears prickle my eyes. Again. "But she could help you stay on earth a little longer."

Slowly, he turns to me. "Molly, I'm not going to get better. I can feel it in my bones."

"You can't give up hope. I know it's easy for me to say that."

"Yeah, it is." He looks down at me sadly, his little kangaroo ears flopping as he moves. "But the reason why I can feel it in my bones...is because it *is* in my bones."

"What?" I whisper.

Alex draws in a shaky breath. "When you were out getting these stupid costumes, I got a phone call."

"No..."

"It was opinion number six." His hazel eyes are dull and tired. "The cancer's in my bones."

# CHAPTER 12

ALEX

"How did you pull this together so fast?" Molly gapes, clearly impressed by my work. Her pixie face, framed by that short crop of shiny dark hair, radiates joy.

"Not bad for T-minus 62, huh?" I smile. Head tilted to the ornate ceiling, she spins around and around. Chrome and frosted glass light fittings on the walls give the room a soft yellow aura.

Tom really came through for me. Or rather, his movie mogul parents did. They pulled a helluva lot of strings so I could use their big-time studio's screening room. It was less risky than having me get behind the wheel of Tom's 911.

"Some day, we're going to be saying T-*plus* 62, et cetera, et cetera," she says, waving a hand dismissively. I love her show of optimism, I really do.

Things have settled in the past couple of days. She freaked out about the bone cancer diagnosis. Freaked. I know she's trying hard to keep those feelings under wraps now. Me? I'm back at the acceptance stage and am done with freaking out.

"Speaking of positive figures, whew, you look incredible." I told her to go vintage-dress shopping and find something that screamed HOLLYWOOD! She dug up a slinky, silky gold number Natalie Wood would've worn back in the day.

"Oooh, you're so smooth! Thanks." Almost shyly, she adds, "You look red-carpet ready yourself in that suit."

"A present from Dad." It's a special night, so I don't tell her I plan to be buried in this suit. But I'll go to my grave knowing she approves of it.

Her eyes glisten. "Must be great to have him back in L.A."

"Yeah, at last. He says he can easily run his business from here. Even Mom's happy to see him again. I think they'll need each other. You know, after I'm gone." I quickly clear a lump from my throat and put on my best TV personality voice. "Did you know this is where the bigwigs and actors used to watch the rushes? The stuff they shot that day? So watch where you sit. Might find James Dean's fifty-year-old chewing gum under an armrest."

She laughs like it's the most hilarious thing ever, and that makes me light up inside. "If I do, I'll auction it off for charity."

When she kissed me on the beach, at first I was stunned. After all these years, I finally got to kiss Molly. But at the same time, that kiss tore me up. Did she do it because she felt sorry for me? In the end, I had to get away, because it seemed pointless to start something that's got zero chance of surviving.

That was a mistake. I've been punishing myself ever since that day.

"So it's just us tonight?" She sweeps her arm across the ten-seat theater. Red velvet curtains with gold tassels hide the movie screen. The whole place is no bigger than my living room. Cozy and intimate. Perfect for tonight.

Pointing to the back of the room, I say, "You, me and the projectionist. He promised to leave us alone for the most part."

She claps her hands together. "What are we watching?"

"An oldie but a goodie. I think you might know it." I catch sight of the projectionist through the portholes as he laces film over and under rollers.

Molly's eyes go round. *"Rebel Without a Cause!"*

"I know. Again. But maybe this time don't talk all the way through or chomp on popcorn, okay? It's not like we can press rewind here."

Molly swats me playfully.

"And it's an old print, too. Scratches and everything. Makes it even more of an old-Hollywood experience." I lead Molly to a seat in the center of the room, in line with speakers on the walls. A silver bowl filled with salty-sweet popcorn rests on the empty chair beside her.

"Alex, this is perfect. You've thought of everything."

"I've learned from the queen of organizing," I say. "All settled?"

"Yeah, let's get this show on the road. Double-time." She giggles.

"Watch this." I press a button on my armrest. "Mr. Grant? My starlet here would like the movie to roll now."

"Sure thing, boss," comes the projectionist's gruff voice over an intercom.

The lights dim and the velvet curtain parts. Dramatic orchestral music crashes into our eardrums. I glance at Molly. Her skin glows red, the color of the letters shouting the movie title on the screen. She gets deeply engrossed within minutes like she'd never seen it before. After a while, her head drops onto my shoulder and stays there. Every breath, every sigh, every gasp she makes seems louder than the dialogue.

I stare at the screen, but the images are a blur. I'm not interested in the teenage angst up there. I'm thinking about *my* inner teen angst. Exactly when is the right time to tell someone you're in love with them? Is there a wrong time? When James Dean is crying in a scene? When the Grim Reaper is hot on your tail?

I've prepared myself for all possible reactions. Molly doesn't have to say she loves me back. She could even walk out on me if she wants to. But I need her to know how I feel before I die.

Molly shifts suddenly. Her right leg angles closer to mine. I hesitate for a few seconds, then close the gap with my thigh so we're touching. Feeling bold—'cause what have I got to lose, right?—I inch my hand over and hold hers. She doesn't move away. That's good.

In my head, I rehearse the words I want to tell her after the movie: "I love you."

Then something weird happens.

Molly stops breathing.

That's not good.

I sit up quickly, my grip tightening around her hand. "Molly?"

In a stunned whisper, she asks, "What did you say?"

Dumbfounded, I stare at her. "I...I said your name. I wanted to check you were still alive 'cause you stopped breathing for a second."

"No, before that." Her green eyes lock on me, and I can't look away.

"I didn't say anything. Or at least I don't think so." I frown. Did I actually say the words aloud instead of in my head? Am I that much of a doofus?

"Are you sure? I could have sworn you said, 'I love you.'"

Looking down, I realize I'm still holding her hand. Her pulse matches mine. Fast and pounding.

This is it. *This* is the right time. While there's crazy shouting going on in the movie. While I'm buzzing with nervous energy. While I've got Molly right here beside me, where she's been practically my entire life.

I take in as much air as my lungs will hold. She watches me intently. "You didn't imagine it. I said I love you, Molly Corbett. I always have loved you. I'll love you till the very end."

Holding my breath, I wait for her to throw the bowl of popcorn over my head. Run out on me. Or worse, laugh.

"Ohhh, Alex!" Two tears roll down each cheek. One drop for her, one for me. "I love you, too."

"You do? Are you sure?"

"Don't ask me dumb questions at a time like this," she murmurs. "Kiss me."

Leaning forward, I kiss her tears away, then trail my lips down to Molly's. Her arms wrap around me, and I squeeze as hard as I can without strangling a vital organ. All I want is to keep her as close as possible for as long as possible.

Then a jarring thought distracts me. I pull back and she squints. "This could be another dumb question. Did you say you love me just because I'm dying?"

"Yes, that's a really dumb question," she says solemnly. Linking her fingers around my neck, she drags me close again. Her kiss is light as a feather, but the impact is huge. "I love you because you make me happy even when you're infuriating. You make me happy by walking into my room with a bag of popcorn. Wait, you don't even have to bring popcorn! Just yourself. You're lovable, adorable and, I'm very, very happy to report, a thousand times kissable."

Orchestral music swells around my ears. Our lips dance together. Moving fast, moving slow. Yes, *this* was the perfect moment to tell her how I felt.

The next time we look up at the screen, the words *The End* appear. Gradually, the lights go up. Hands entwined, Molly and I stare at the curtains as they glide shut once more.

A strange peace settles over me, and not just because the chaos in the movie is finally silenced.

Mr. Grant's voice crackles over the intercom. "Hope you enjoyed that, folks. I'm gonna wrap a few things up here and I'll meet you out in the foyer in fifteen minutes."

Molly leans over and presses the button. "Thank you!" She winks at me. "Do you think he saw us making out for the entire movie?"

"Nah. He was probably checking Facebook the whole time." I clear throat. "So, Molly...telling you I love you, that was number five."

"From your bucket list?" Her eyes widen. "It's not going to be the last time you tell me, is it?"

"No. I'll tell you every hour, on the hour, from now on."

Molly angles her head in confusion. "Let's go over this list. One, getting gravel rash on a bike trail. Two, teaching me to surf. Three, the hospital visit. Four, confessing you're madly in love with me, and I'm glad you did because I'm mad about you. Five...?"

Sheepishly, I tell her, "Go back one step. Four. I sent my application to Yale."

Molly squeals. "You did?! I'm so proud of you!"

I silence her with a kiss. This is how I wanted to kiss her on the beach. Slow, fast, hard, soft. For a very long time. But I was saving myself for tonight.

What the hell was I thinking? Short answer: I wasn't thinking.

"Can I make another confession?" I take her soft moan as a yes. "Technically, 'Kiss Molly Corbett' has been number one on my bucket list since we were thirteen."

She grins. "It was worth the wait. For me anyway."

"And me." I stroke her cheek.

"We'll make up for it." Molly leans her forehead against mine. "You know what we're gonna do? Make another list of five things we haven't done before. And then another list when we get through those."

Hugging her tightly, I say, "But no more of this double-time, double-speed stuff. Too dangerous. From now on, we take things extra slow."

"To make it last," she whispers, her lips hovering near mine.

I meet those lips and kiss her extra slowly. "To make it last. As long as we both shall live."

*Thank you to Elvis, Anna Campbell, Annie West, Kim MacCarron and Pintip Dunn (YOLO!) for being my loudest cheerleaders.*

# MRS G'S KALE RECIPES

Dear Moll-Moll,

I was so pleased to see how much you enjoyed my kale and broccoli smoothie. Don't you feel healthy and energized now? I thought I'd send a few special recipes for you to try. You're welcome.

## Faith & Love & Kale Smoothie

*Ingredients:*

1/2 cup broccoli florets, raw

1 cup kale, raw

1/2 medium-sized cucumber, sliced and diced

1/2 cup chilled coconut water or coconut milk if you're feeling adventurous

1/4 cup goji berries

*Method:*

Whizz the broccoli, kale, cucumber, and goji berries in a blender. Gradually add the coconut water or milk until, well, smooth and drinkable. Pour into a tall glass. Alex tends to down this while melodramatically pinching his nose, but I know he secretly adores this smoothie.

## Slippery Sautéed Kale & Mushrooms

*Ingredients:*
1 tbsp butter
2 tbsp olive oil
1 clove garlic, crushed
1 cup button mushrooms, sliced thinly
2 cups kale
A small splash of balsamic vinegar
Salt & pepper to taste

*Method:*
Heat the olive oil in a frying pan or wok. Add the butter and allow it to melt. Then toss the garlic to this shimmery golden pool. As the garlic begins to brown, throw in the mushrooms. Stir until soft. Splash in the balsamic vinegar and kale. Keep stirring. Lob in more butter if necessary. When the kale is wilted and "slimy," as Alex would say, season with salt and pepper, and serve. This is divine on sourdough toast or with scrambled eggs.

## Kale Ice-Cream Dream*

*Ingredients:*
2/3 cup condensed milk
1 1/4 cup heavy cream
1 cup kale, cooked and pureed (ensure you squeeze as much liquid out as possible)

*Method:*
In a large bowl, whip the condensed milk and cream together until soft peaks form. Fold in the puréed kale. Pour the blended green mixture into a 2-pint container or two 1-pint containers. Freeze overnight. Enjoy for breakfast.

*All right, I admit I'm only kidding about this one. But I think it'd make Alex smile, so I beg you to give it a try.

Much love,
*Mrs. G.*

# RAISING HELL

## ROBYN GRADY

# CHAPTER 1

"This is not a day for venturing out," Ruarc Bae growls in his best *prince of darkness* voice. "You should stay here," he says. "Stay here with me."

I ease out a breath. Who knew immortals had abandonment issues?

Warlocks are supposed to be evil creatures who care only about themselves—kind of like my mom. Which is probably why I connect so strongly with Bae. People stick with what's familiar, even if it makes no sense. Even when it hurts.

Except, I'm convinced Bae isn't evil. He's more protective than putrid. More megaton hot than hideous.

Right now he's sitting by the porch steps, butt on floorboards, back against a post, closest leg bent. Before I came out to join him, he was staring at a gemstone—a ruby the size of my fist. He says that stone is the only thing that can get him home some day. Back to a place Bae calls *The Realm*.

"Just be careful," he says now. "Careful of who you talk to or touch."

"Because you'll get jealous," I tease, "or because I'm a five-year-old?"

He looks at me, mortified. "Because I care."

"I need to go to school," I remind him gently but firmly. "That's the whole reason I came back to Hellaway, remember?"

"To finish your senior year," he groans, like saying it's a chore.

"Because Hellaway High has the best AP psychology class around," I add. "I need that credit for college."

I'm desperate to get into that field. Maybe then, sometime in the future,

I'll be able to explain an insane childhood that only ended when my mother slit her own throat and I went to live with Aunt Lilia in Boston. Four years later, my life swung full circle when I applied and was accepted back at Hellaway. Lilia and I talked about me boarding in. Finally we decided on wiping away the cobwebs and taking advantage of this creaky old Victorian that Mom left me in her will.

Lilia helped set me up for when summer break finished and the new school year kicked off. That's today. Just as soon as she wraps up her current project (my aunt is a kick-ass bio-archaeologist no less), she'll move here for the duration, too.

*And warlock makes three.*

A rumble of thunder shakes the porch floorboards a second before ominous clouds block out the sun.

"A morning storm," I murmur, moving to the railing to examine the sky.

Bae is up and beside me in a flash. I'm not sure if he dematerialises and appears somewhere else in a blink or if he's simply super-fast like a vampire from some cheesy horror flick. I do know that Bae has this amazing scent about him, like musk crossed with everything paradise. When he stands this close, I want to reach out, melt in and totes surrender.

"It's a bad omen," he says, glaring at the heavy sky.

*Ugh.* "You are so superstitious." So totally paranoid.

He cocks a brow. "Am not."

"What about the black cat you shooed away the other night?"

Bae's luminous gaze narrows on mine. "I didn't like its eyes."

The same day Lilia had hugged me tight and driven back to Boston, I found Bae in the attic. Sounded like monster squirrels were slam-dunking coconuts at the rafters. Cloaked in shadows, he'd looked oddly withdrawn or uncertain. Beautiful in a not-of-this-world type way. Even now he won't say how he came to call Hellaway home, only that he likes the weather (often bleak), the atmosphere (old-world). Go figure—he likes *me.*

And, sadly, when I say *like,* I don't mean *boyfriend hearts girlfriend*—although he has mentioned that I'm the mirror-image of a witch he crushed on a few lifetimes ago. And, sometimes, when a certain effervescent feeling ripples up my spine, I turn around and Bae is there, a curious smile tugging on his lips, his amazing chest heaving on each breath.

Obviously I can't kick him out. Firstly, a nuclear explosion couldn't shift him. Secondly, my warlock is *the* most delicious looking hybrid demon ever created. I'm talking coal-black bed-hair and lidded eyes that glimmer like cut sapphires dipped in moonlight. He's in awesome shape, too. First time I saw him sans shirt, I drooled.

Thing is, he's here, and—*fine, okay*—he cares. A *lot*. In fact, lately, he struggles to let me out of his sight.

Bae needs a hobby. An interest. A *goal*.

"I have an idea," I say. "Tag along. You're not doing anything for the next few hundred years. Might as well get your GED." He's ancient as far as years go, but, physically, Bae looks my age. Eighteen tops.

His head angles and dark hair flops over his brow as he contemplates. "I should go with you to school?"

"If you promise not to hang around every single minute."

His winged eyebrows swoop together. "I can't promise that."

I flick a glance over the tatty jeans he's wearing—the ones he must know I adore. His white button-down shirt is open, revealing his bronzed chest and hard-muscled abs. His gaze is pleading, begging me, *please don't go*.

I sigh. So darn hard to resist but... "I can't hole up here with you forever."

"I could insist," he says, lifting his chin. "Maybe conjure up some manacles."

I give a cheeky grin. "I'm listening."

He leans in, obviously tempted, before whirling away in frustration. I'd love to see that move in a long, sweeping cape. He's gotta have one—I mean, he's a *warlock*, right?

"Vow to me," he says. "If you get in trouble, you'll call. Just call out my name. Even *think* it. I'll come, no matter what. No matter when."

"What kind of trouble? Catching ebola from cafeteria meatloaf?"

When I snort, his gorgeous lips twitch at the same time moonlit eyes penetrate mine. "I like your sense of humor."

"That's because it's bent," I smile, "like you."

As I finally head down the porch steps with a book bag in one hand, an umbrella magically appears in the other—Bae's gift against the threat of rain. I smile (*so sweet*), but when thunder rumbles again, a shudder creeps up my backbone and I give in to the urge to look back one more time.

Bae's face is tense, poor guy, like he's sure he'll never see me again.

# CHAPTER 2

"GOOD MORNING, class. I'm Professor Gerard Hinkley."

"Also known as Professor No Nose."

Sitting toward the back of the class, I glance across and recognize the girl responsible for the whispered jibe. From what I recall, Dita Jenkins-Smith was always a bitch. In middle school, she'd worn too much makeup and not nearly enough underwear. Nothing's changed, except maybe the skirt's gotten shorter.

Another girl slips in the back door and into the seat alongside of me. Behind thick-rimmed glasses, her close-set eyes sparkle, she's so eager. Settling in, she fumbles and drops her planner. After swooping it up, she preens her Gap dress and pale red hair, which is flat on top then crimps down to a pair of meaty shoulders.

She smiles across and speaks softly. "Hey. I'm Kellen Winters."

"Kellen?"

"Yep, with a K, like Krispy Kreme."

I introduce myself. "Brinley Stone."

"What'd I miss?" Kellen asks as she focuses fully on the Professor and then winces. "*Geez*. What's wrong with his face?" She sinks into herself. "Sorry. That's mean."

I'm familiar with the professor—his work as well as the legend. I whisper back, "When he was in college, he sliced off his own nose."

Kellen gags as Professor No Nose—I mean *Hinkley*—addresses the class again, rubbing his hands together, clearly relishing what's to come.

"Let's kick this off with a bit of an icebreaker," the professor says. "We'll each announce three facts about ourselves and one lie. The rest of the class will decide which is real and which deception."

As my cheeks heat, I steal a furtive glance toward the door. This is high school psych, not sixty freaking questions. I promise myself, not one word about horror childhoods or suicidal moms.

"I'll start." The professor rubs his hands again. "I'm fifty-four-years old. I love pecan-nut ice cream, have spent time as a psych ward resident and my dog's name is Sigmund."

A dude in the row behind me pipes up. "You don't like ice cream."

Turning, I check the guy out. Delectable dirty-blond hair. Dark eyes that shine like polished onyx. His focus drops from the professor onto me and those intense eyes smile even more. My heart gives a running jump before I turn back fast to face the front.

Professor Hinkley is strolling up the aisle. "The young man is correct. I don't suffer from a sweet tooth. Only grandiose and paranoid delusions."

A gasp goes up around the room while I grin. The professor and my warlock ought to swap stories sometime.

Looking amused, the professor holds up a quietening hand. "No need for alarm. I'm on a suitable cocktail of meds. I haven't been Archangel Gabriel for over thirty years." The professor points at me. "You there. You first."

I push up in my seat. "*Me?*"

"Your name," he goes on, "and then one lie hidden among three facts."

*Oh crap*. Here goes.

"I'm Brinley. I hate the color purple, I'm addicted to Sudoku, I was born with two pinkies on one hand." I take a breath. "And I live with a warlock."

No one makes a sound. Then the professor grins, so wide a gold filling in his eye tooth flashes beneath the artificial light. The room lets out a collective breath. A few people even chuckle.

Kellen whispers close to my ear, "Anne Boleyn had six fingers on one hand. Guess you know that."

Anne B was supposed to have been a witch, too. Not sure either story was true.

"Who's next?" the professor asks.

Cute guy behind me puts up his hand.

"Name's Nick King. I'm one of ten kids, my father was a CIA agent, my middle name is Morris," he pauses, "and I'm into black magic."

A debate ensues, some pointing to a CIA lie, others coming down on the witchcraft tip. All the while Nick King sits back, looking like the cat who put a hex on the canary. Like me, he doesn't admit which statement is false and which is cross your heart, hope to die.

---

AFTER PSYCH, Kellen and I head off to grab a bite. Her every look and word is saccharin sweet, which is way better than histrionic. With a surly warlock waiting at home, I want to avoid complications wherever I can—that includes staying clear of I'm-so-freaking-hot (*not!*) Dita Jenkins-Smith.

In the busy cafeteria, Kellen chooses pasta and a shiny red apple while I opt for a decent looking chicken salad and OJ.

"I like your hair," Kellen says, as we claim a table. "Is that your natural color?"

My hair is blond, like brushed corn silk my poor deranged mother used to say. "I get darker highlights sometimes."

"I had a perm last spring. My hair takes forever to grow out."

"It's pretty."

*It's not.* But behind those glasses (and forgetting the mono-brow), Kellen's eyes glitter like jewels. Her smile is bright, too. Genuine. When we get to know each other more, maybe I can help her do something with those crimps. Any makeovers would need to happen at her place though. Not sure how Bae would fair with guests at the house. If warlocks are anything, it's territorial. Which begs the question... what happens when Aunt Lilia finally comes to stay?

Too hard to think about.

"Do you live with your folks?" Kellen asks, twirling linguini onto her fork.

I start off slow but go on to tell her pretty much everything about my mom, including how she used to scream at me so hard, sometimes she'd turn the color of a beet and spit. Maybe it was because my room was untidy, or I'd given her the 'wrong look.'

After her death, I cried non-stop for a month. But Mom's departure from this world was the best thing that could've happened. For me. Most definitely for her. "Tortured" didn't come close to describing our existence.

"I'm sorry about your mom," Kellen says. "I lost mine when I was five. Don't remember much about her except she was always smiling, always kind. Up until this week, I lived with my dad and stepmom, Leena."

"Nice people?"

She blinks twice, hard, and then her lush lips curve a little. "They're good to me. They live in Jordonson, a town north of here."

My mother and I visited Jordonson when I was young. Can't recall the reason for the trip—just that it was fall, and the breeze was fresh, swirling with colorful leaves.

Kellen turns serious. "We have a pretty famous corn cob eating contest in August."

I nod. "Cool."

"I'm boarding here this year," Kellen goes on, twirling more pasta. "Finally gives my parents some time to themselves, you know? They deserve it."

*Hmm.* Why do I feel that's 'Leena Stepmom' talking?

Bursts of laughter pull my attention to the far end of the room. Nick King is regaling an attentive group with some story. Our gazes connect and he smiles that wicked smile. As my cheeks heat up, I instantly drop my focus to my plate. The group is mainly girls. Fair bet Master King has flashed that Colgate smile around all morning.

"Brin, do you remember me?"

I look up. Dita Jenkins-Smith flicks back her long, dark and, yes, glossy hair, gifting me with a smile as fake as her lashes.

The question is how well does she remember me?

Mostly everyone used to call me *Looney Brin.* I didn't mix much. Probably always looked spaced out. Gloomy. While Dita was the life of the party.

Now she takes a seat. "I'm Dita."

"Oh. Right." I go back to my salad. "How you doing?"

"I'm in between."

"In between what?"

She looks at me like I have steamed cabbage for brains. "Boyfriends."

Kellen offers over her hand. "Kellen. Hi. I'm dorming in."

Dita glances across like she hadn't realized we had company. Then her jaw drops. "What's with the hair?"

Kellen draws her hand away at the same time her peachy cheeks turn crimson.

*Way to go, Dita*. Once a bitch, always a bitch.

Dita tips closer, conspiracy style. "I just might have to introduce myself."
Arching one perfect eyebrow, she blatantly checks out Nick King.

There's a measure of arrogance associated with a person who knows
precisely who they are, why they're here, where they want to go. Nick comes
across as relaxed and yet inherently prepared. While his looks are Hollywood
hunk in a Chace Crawford kind of way, his body isn't quite as buff as Bae's.
Still, the dimensions are impressive. Athletic. Super fit.

It's as if Nick senses my thoughts. He ends the story and without skipping a beat, heads toward our table. Of course, he could simply be off to grab
another soda. Either way, my stomach flutters big time. If we strike up a
conversation and he asks me out to catch a movie or something, I might
even say yes, if only to stick it to Dita.

But now my childhood nemesis is gazing off in the other direction,
toward the cafeteria entrance. I watch as Dita's cappuccino eyes flash and
then grow heavy, like she's auditioning for a porn flick.

"Oh my freaking god." Dita sighs. "Who *is* that?"

An odd, crystal-ball feeling bubbles up inside of me, like I just caught a
glimpse of the future.

Any girl in this room with half her quota of hormones would find my
roomie irresistible. Half the guys, too. But Bae shudders at the thought of
leaving the house. And, even after my suggestion this morning of coming to
school, would he actually rock up here unannounced?

But as I turn my head, in my heart I already know.

Sure enough, Bae is standing in the cafeteria doorway, wearing those
amazing jeans, looking more delectable than any man, or warlock, has a right.
*Shoot me now.*

I'm bracing for his next move when a vibration hums through the air, at
first icy-cold like a breeze off a North Atlantic berg then hot enough for
sweat to break out down the dent of my spine. As hairs stand up on the back
of my neck, I know I'm not the only one affected. Every person in the room
has stopped eating, talking, as gazes are pulled toward Ruarc Bae. One by
one, heads turn and people seem to stop breathing, including Nick King.

So much for avoiding complications.

# CHAPTER 3

FOUR YEARS AGO, TOWARD "THE END," Mom started talking to herself—*non compos mentis* babble mainly. Certain sounds, smells or even colors would irritate the bejeezus out of her. The last couple of weeks, she ceased to feel physical pain. Bumping into doors. Stepping on broken glass. The bruises and cuts literally made me vomit.

But she wasn't tripping out *all* the time. Certainly no one, other than yours truly, realized she'd gotten so bad. She refused to see a doctor or call Aunt Lilia. She warned me I'd better not, either.

Schizophrenia, dementia, some form of late onset autism... Doesn't really matter what was wrong with my mom. Except it does. Apparently she was totally "normal" before she gave birth to me.

So, do I feel responsible for her problems, her decline?

I'd be lying if I said no. But, mainly I worry that I might have inherited her whacko gene. I want a family of my own one day. Dear lord, I want to *belong*. But I'll avoid all that like the plague if there's the teeniest chance that I'm somehow infected.

After I went to live with Lilia, my mental health was evaluated. Talking with my psychiatrist, Doctor Phoebe Damon, is the best. When I admitted to feeling invisible most of my life, she softly smiled like she understood. Even now, sometimes I need to remind myself that I exit. That I'm real.

That I *am*.

Dr. Phoebe wasn't wholly against the idea of my returning to Hellaway.

Facing old surroundings and fears might help shift ingrained perspectives to healthier spaces in my mind, she'd said. I need to accept that I am no longer a frightened, confused child. I'm an almost-adult with a bright future, not simply a suckish past.

Somehow, Bae helps affirm that. Although his level of protectiveness is nuts, his concern also validates me. Bae cares about me deeply, and, yeah...

I care about him, too.

Just not enough to have him swoop into my school cafeteria unannounced and create a full blown crisis. Because, sure as snow is cold and wet, this can't end well.

Bae scans the room. When he spots me, tension eases from the sharp-angled planes of his face. It's like he's found a survivor at a crash scene.

My heart is beating so hard, it's about to leap out of my chest. I pray he doesn't do that superfast vampire trick and magically appear right in front of us. Instead, his impressive shoulders press back. With his cross-hairs fixed on me, Bae prowls over with the stealthy grace of a demon jungle cat.

Every eye in the place is still glued as he stops before me, or, more correctly in front of Dita; my chair is closest to the wall. While Dita and I both get to our feet, Nick King is still negotiating his way over. Looking curious—wary—he's nearing our table now.

In full seduction mode, Dita flicks her hair again. "Wow. You don't fool around, do you?" she says to Bae, all breathy.

I expect Bae will ignore her, or even physically sweep her aside if she refuses to get with the program and move. I haven't seen him interact with anyone else. If I go out for supplies, he stays at home. He *always* stays at home. Now, his concentration shifts from me onto Dita. A line furrows between his brows, his head cocks and that sweep of black hair falls forward.

Bae is well over six foot, a good eight inches taller than me. Dita is perhaps 5'9". As she peers up into his eyes, her lips part and, understandably mesmerised, she tips in. The word *hypnotic* was created for this guy.

"You're new," she says, and I imagine her sultry smile. "I'm Dita."

"*Dita*..." Bae elongates the "*eeeee*" as if tasting it.

"You're obviously not a science geek," she goes on.

One dark brow slowly lifts. "Geek?"

"I'm into biology. *Physiology*." She curls hair behind one ear. "You know... anatomy...     cardiovascular..."     Her     gaze     rakes     his     shoulders. "Musculoskeletal..."

I groan. This woman knows no shame. Worse, Bae seems vaguely interested. Is it possible he might shift his fixation onto someone else, and so easily? And I thought he had taste.

"Do I know you?" he asks Dita.

"Would you like to?" Dita returns.

"Excuse me." I push around in front of her and tug on Bae's sleeve hard. "I believe you were looking for me."

Dita gives me a patronizing glare. "I'll handle this."

As Bae focuses on me, the inky darkness in his gaze lifts. His eyes are shimmering again—sapphires mixed with swirls of shifting light. I know they're pretty, but away from the gloom of that house, his lidded gaze is flat-out breathtaking.

He catches my arm. "We need to leave," he growls under his breath. "You need to come *now*."

I flick Dita a *no hard feelings* look and then try to put out the imagined fire in Bae's mind. Paranoia is the pits.

"I'm fine," I say in a calm, soothing voice.

But his grip only tightens. "This is *not* a discussion."

"I'll be home after my last class," I say more firmly, hating that everyone's focused on us. "We'll talk about it then."

His chest inflates on a deep breath and then that hot, cold tremor ripples through the room again. I cast a look around. But I'm not seeing straight. Tables, people... everything is coming to rest on a fuzzy undulating wave at the same time Bae's voice drops. His cool intensity vibrates through me.

"You need to come," he says. "You need to come *now*."

Something drops through my center from the tip of my crown to the soles of my Keds. Each cell tingles and then my stomach falls, like I'm standing in an elevator plummeting from top floor to basement. The room and its contents zooms back and fades. All I see is Bae, his troubled, handsome face right in front of me. All I feel is his presence, and so acutely, it's as if...

As if he's *inside* of me.

Then a sound breaks through the daze. Or is it a trance? Nick King is standing beside us. From his expression, he's ready to give Bae exactly two seconds to step the hell away from the girl before he breaks someone's jaw.

Good luck!

# CHAPTER 4

"Hey, creep, the girl said to back off."

As my tingling, swooping feeling fades, I focus on Nick King's voice and scowl, which are aimed directly at my warlock. Nick is almost as tall as Bae but of a slightly narrower build. Beneath his T-shirt, the strength in Nick's chest is obvious. Muscles and veins bulge in his arms as fists clench by his sides. He's ready for action. Ready to defend.

Bae, on the other hand, is only now becoming aware of this other presence like a Rottweiler might notice a flea. I swear, the second his eyes lock with Nick's, hair lifts on Bae's head—the alpha wolf preparing for a fight. So, does he view Nick as a threat to my person, to my attentions? Either way, Bae looks set to kill.

Before the underdog is fricasseed supernatural style, and Dita hyperventilates with excitement, I step in.

"I'm fine. Nothing to worry about," I say to Nick.

But he only curls his lip at Bae. "Dickwad there needs to tell me that."

Bae literally growls at Nick—very low, very mean. Before he swoops and rips this mortal's head off, I set my jaw and glare so he knows I mean business. *Bad Bae. Very, very bad.* While I have half his attention, I enunciate each word clearly.

"I need to speak with you—*alone.*"

When Bae continues to growl, Nick gets in his face. "Want your teeth knocked down your throat here, or will we take it outside?"

*TIME OUT!*

"I don't know about you," I tell Nick, "but I'm not keen to be kicked out of school on my first day."

"Better tell Conan the Barbarian that." Nick waits a heartbeat for Bae to react. "What's your problem, Mac? You can only talk tough to the chicks?"

Bae's menacing grin comes slowly. Nick doesn't know it, but there's an apocalyptic firestorm coming his way.

I grab Bae's big, hot hand and am stunned that he lets me lead him out. I don't look back. Nick King has no idea what he's up against.

Outside, I drag Bae behind a massive tree and try to shove him up against its trunk. I'm so mad right now. After such a public pissing contest, how will I ever show my face here again? I'll be ostracised. *Looney Brin* all over again.

And yet, from the slant of Bae's lips, I can tell he's enjoying himself. Is this his idea of a joke?

My fist thumps his chest, which is like granite only warm and rhythmically breathing. "You actually find this funny?"

"I love when you're filled with fire."

I drag a hand down my face. "That is so not healthy, Bae."

He eyes my book bag, which I'd swiped up on our way out. "All set to go home?"

"You cannot appear out of nowhere and demand that I leave with you. Not here, not now. Not *anytime*."

He leans back against the trunk, crosses his burly arms over his buttoned white shirt and rests the heel of one boot against the wood. "Did you feel what happened in there?"

I frown remembering lots of weird sensations, like the world was dissolving and I was fading away into vapor. I shift uncomfortably. "What was that? What did you do?"

"That will happen more and more often, the occurrences closer and closer, unless... until..."

With my heart beating in my ears, I wait.

"Until *what?*"

He looks bereft now, like he might have to say goodbye to his closest friend. Say goodbye to *me*.

Okay. Never mind that he's from another world. Bae and I have known each other a matter of weeks, which is a hiccup in an immortal's frame of reference to time. I love waking up and finding him in the room next to mine. I adore his dazzling, lopsided smile. I get off on fantasies that one day he'll fall madly in love with me (as opposed to being freakishly obsessed) and we'll embark on a relationship that will culminate in a little hybrid warlock or two.

That's going too far. I don't even know if warlocks and humans can mate. Don't guess there's any empirical data to either support or refute it. Nevertheless, I bet we could have fun trying.

And I'm way off track...

"I don't understand," I tell him. "I don't understand any of this. Unless..." I cringe at a thought and then ask the unimaginable. *This will happen more and more until...* Trying to get my head around it, I shrink away from him and wince.

"Is this all some kind of threat? Are you threatening to hurt me unless I stay with you at the house?"

Before he can answer, Kellen appears, walking with her shoulders up and head down like she's not sure she ought to intrude. I try to gather myself. Kellen's a sweet kid. She doesn't need to be freaked out any more than she already is. I need to speak with Bae alone and...

And then what?

How in god's name do I fix this?

"Hi, guys." Kellen's green eyes sparkle through their lenses, first at me then at Bae. "Everything okay?"

I let out a shaky breath, tack up a fragile smile. "Everything's fine."

Kellen grazes her teeth over her lower lip. "I'm Kellen," she says to Bae. "Brinley's friend."

Bae concentrates on Kellen as if she's some kind of rare and delicate, possibly dangerous creature. Where are his manners today?

"Kellen, this is Ruarc Bae." Kellen already knows most of the colossal cock-up that is my life. She might as well know the kicker. "Bae and I room together."

A smile lights her eyes. "So *this* is the warlock you were telling us about in psych."

Bae's focus zaps over to me. I sense uncertainty—his doubt, maybe a little pride—at the same time spots of rain begin to tap on, and fall through, leafy branches overhead.

As far as Kellen's question goes... I wave off the warlock thing. *Haha.* Big joke. "Remind me to show you the scar where they took off that extra finger," I tell her.

Interested, Bae takes my hands and studies each in turn. I should wrench away, but it's not often we actually physically touch, and this time the warmth radiating through his flesh feeds me like nothing else in this universe can.

Kellen pushes her heavy frames back up the bridge her nose. "You all caused a stir in there. That guy... Nick King... he was asking questions after you left. Then Professor Hinkley stuck his nose in..." She bites her lip. "I mean, he wants to know what's going on."

The wind has whipped up, running wheels of leaves over the ground, and Bae is telling me with his eyes that we really, really need to leave. I think again about whether this is all manipulation, but for now, I need to err on the side of caution.

"I have to go," I tell Kellen.

She purses her lips and then slips Bae a dubious look. "Brinley, maybe you could give me your number and I'll call later to make sure you're okay."

"I'll be back tomorrow." I gently squeeze her arm. "Honest. It's all good."

A thick bolt of lightning rips open the sky at the same time thunder explodes and rain suddenly dumps down by the buckets full. The storm that has threatened all morning has arrived with a vengeance.

As Kellen and I jump like girls, Bae grabs both our hands and runs with us to the entrance of a nearby building, so fast, I feel as if we're flying. As we reach shelter, that earlier *plummeting, dissolving* feeling consumes me again, only this time I'm racing down a rollercoaster's sharpest, scariest dip with no brakes.

There's just no stopping it.

One second I'm at school, cold and wet, the next I'm gone—I have no idea where.

# CHAPTER 5

"BAE? *BAE!* WHERE ARE YOU?"

I wait a few clamouring heartbeats and then shout so loud, my lungs hurt.

"WARLOCK! *This is freaking me out!*"

One minute, I'm at school. It's raining. The next I'm here. *Nowhere.* Totally alone, standing in a thick spooky mist. My bones are lead pipes but I feel as if my heels have grown wings. I'm so heavy and yet... somehow floating, too.

In a dreamy, slow-mo pan, I look around. In the distance, a foggy outline fades up... a shape, tall and built like Bae. As the outline grows clearer, comes closer, my chest aches. I'm not normally a wimp but, this minute, I need to reach him. *Hold* him.

*What the hell is going on!*

But the shape is only a tree. Bare, gnarly branches and needle-sharp tips scratch my hands and arms before I can writhe away. As more trees form, crowding me in, I call out again, only the void swallows my words and steals them away. The mist is so dense that moisture has filled my lungs, robbing me of air, making my head grow light. I stumble slash slow-mo-float backward and then trip.

As I keel slowly over, zigzags of lightning crack open the bleak space above. Rain falls, a cold gauzy screen. But in the distance I see a shadow weaving between tree trunks—zapping fast then slow, fast then slow again. It's a horse, midnight black coat with red coals for eyes. Vapor jets from both nostrils each time a set of hooves thunders down. As it draws nearer, I know the future like it's already happened. Those hooves will trample me. I will cease to be. And yet I'm not afraid—not anymore. I can't see the rider, but soon I will. Somehow, weirdly, that's all that matters.

The horse's heavy chest is almost upon me when something hooks around my waist and I'm swept clear. As wind blows my hair over my head, strong arms crush me in. Dazed, I look up. Bae is peering down at me, concern stamped all over his darkly handsome face.

For a long, giddy moment, we simply hang there, suspended in time and place. His gaze is so intense, penetrating mine like he's trying to tell me something mega important. Then the trees and mist begin to swirl around our hanging bodies, faster and faster, until everything outside of us is spinning out of control.

But Bae's arms don't leave me. He holds me tight against his chest. So tight, I can barely breathe. My eardrums are bursting with what sounds like the screech of a thousand cats being swung by the tail. That's when the realization strikes like a super nova streaking through my brain. Soon it will be over.

This is the end.

# CHAPTER 6

W HEN I REGAIN CONSCIOUSNESS, either fifty years or a split-second later, I'm at home, lying face up on Bae's four-poster bed. My warlock is hovering over me. Aside from his dark hair falling toward my face and dusting my cheeks, only the tip of his nose touches mine.

I blink, and then the mother of all headaches cracks open my skull. Groaning, I press a palm to my brow. I'm soaked through and so is Bae. He's dripping all over me. With one eye shut against the scarlet sunset slanting in through the window, I focus on the troubled gaze searching mine. My voice is threadbare and my thoughts are pretty much paralysed.

"That wasn't a dream, was it?" I croak.

He shakes his head and then adds, "You're trembling."

*No shit.* When the vibration of his voice penetrates my skin, warming me a little, my fingers twitch. I need to drag his otherworld heat closer still. But my body feels as if I've reached max g-force capacity. I can't move.

As Bae rolls off to one side, I grunt.

"Where did we go?" I ask, aching all over. "I remember trees... mist..." A horse with a rider I needed to meet, even knowing that when I do...

I shudder so much that my teeth chatter.

"Bae... was that *hell*?"

In a blink, he's on his feet, standing by the bed. A pulse is pounding in the angle of his shadowed jaw as he stares down at his feet, dark hair hanging toward the ground.

"That," he said, "was the Realm."

*Jeez Louise!* Creepy as. "No wonder you like it here."

I struggle to sit up and swing my legs over the edge of the mattress. One eye shut against the pain stabbing my temple, I cast my blurry mind back.

"We were at school with Kellen running from the rain." And then...? "Did you cast a spell? Twitch your nose?" A black thought rises and I'm even more confused. I feel my cheeks burn with disbelief. With anger. "Why did you drop me there all alone?"

His chin pulls in like he's offended. "I didn't drop you anywhere."

"Well, someone did."

When his brow furrows more and he crosses to the window, peering out over the street like he's keeping watch, I set my teeth and growl. *Enough.*

"Whatever's going on, I need to know, Bae, and I need to know *now* because I am never, *ever* doing that again."

"Yes." His expression grave, he glances back over one big shoulder. "It's time."

Suddenly my heart is crashing even harder against my ribs. I have that feeling like when you're about to leap into something that can either turn out to be the biggest thrill ever or screw things up big time. The same feeling I had at six when I thought I could fly, jumped off the top of my slide and broke my leg. Compound fracture. Major pain, infection, months of downtime.

"What do you know about warlocks?" he asks.

Off the top of my head and to be totally honest... "They're sexy and stubborn."

"And *lethal*." He wanders back from the window. The mattress dips as he sits beside me. "Currently we have three strains of warlock."

"Strains? Sounds like a virus."

"Three families then. Warlocks are solitary creatures. But we defend our own."

"To the death?"

"And beyond."

I guess my expression says, "*Aaaannnnd??*" because he stares up at the ceiling and exhales.

"Let's go back a few thousand years," he says. "Back to the beginning."

I flop back flat onto the covers, fold my hands over my stomach, take a deep breath. "'kay. I'm ready."

"Warlocks are conceived via a union between demon and human," he says in that deep rumbling voice that makes me feel safe, even now. "With or without the human's consent. The offspring may or may not acquire powers, which may or may not be strong and or survive throughout time."

*Getting this straight...* "Demon and human..." I'm thinking pitchfork tails, scaly skin, putrid breath. "It's a little—" *(rank)* "—hard to imagine."

Bae lifts his right hand. Two fingertips touch the middle of his forehead and, just like that, an entire bedroom wall and part of the ceiling becomes a movie screen. I sit bolt upright as two-dimensional images come to life, holograms projected here and now from another, looks like, hellish time. The pictures are full of static... scratchy and yet goose-bumpily vivid. Terrifying depictions of creatures that might torment a little kid's darkest dreams. Even darker than my dreams growing up.

Long, pointed teeth. Gaping, drooling mouths. Something that looks like an ancient centipede eating a—

Wincing, I turn my head away. "Geez, Bae. *Gross*." I'm shivering uncontrollably now. I know I asked for this, but, "Let me get out of these wet clothes first."

His hand touches his forehead again. In a blink, my wet clothes are gone. His, too. Now he's wearing a long-sleeved crew-necked shirt that covers his upper dimensions to perfection. His pants are fitting low-waisted breeches with badass boots that'd make Bluebeard jealous. I'm rocking a cardinal-crimson sheath dress that smells like rose petals. The neckline's a little low, the fluted sleeves a little long, but overall, nice!

"Better?" he asked, looking beyond delectable all in black.

I run both palms over the heaven-spun velvet hugging my hips. "It'll do."

My attention hooks back to the 'movie screen'. Mesmerized maidens are being seduced. Then abused. Women, with abnormally swollen pregnant stomachs like they're having a litter, appear. Muted screams fill the space as mothers give birth to...

I cock my head and then shrug. "Those babies look normal."

"If they chose, warlocks will go largely unnoticed in this world. They will always carry a distinguishing feature, however."

"Like pig trotters for feet?" When his jaw shifts to one side, *not impressed*, I apologize. "Over the top?"

"Warlocks will have a deformed ear or cat eyes..." He arches a brow. "Extra fingers or toes."

Well, that's not *so* bad, especially considering I hadn't been lying in Professor Hinkley's class about my eleventh digit. It's not as uncommon as people might think. Mom had my extra pinkie surgically removed not long after I was born. Now there's barely a scar.

I look Bae up and down, over two long masculine legs, a barrelled chest, the hard line of his mouth with its kissable plump lower lip. I haven't noticed a snake's forked tongue, or a birthmark resembling the number 666.

"So, what's your distinguishing feature?"

Without a second's hesitation, he lifts the hem of his shirt until it's off over his head. With that scratchy horror reel still playing behind him, he displays a big, bronzed chest which is free of hair and thrumming with muscle. He turns around; arms and dynamite shoulders gleam and bulge with mouth-watering strength. My eye line travels across the powerful expanse of his back before tapering down to a pair of lean hips. His long strong legs in those breeches and boots are so hot, it's criminal.

Then I remember. I'm supposed to be searching for some deformity. Only testosterone fused excellence as far as I can see. Then again... I haven't seen all of him yet.

The big brass knocker on the front door booms three times, echoing up the stairs and into the room. Like the film has been ripped from an old-style projector, the movie on the wall clatters and spins off. At the same time, Bae whips his shirt back on.

"Wait here," he says.

Before he can vanish to investigate, I hold up both my hands. "I appreciate that we're in the middle of something, but I reserve the right to answer my own door."

"You don't know who it is."

"Which is why I'm on my way to find out."

I don't know where this is all headed, but of one thing I am certain. I will *not* be locked away from the outside world. I will *not* hideaway like my paranoid mother did for most of her tormented life. Dr. Phoebe taught me that positive behavior begets action that evolves into healthy habits. If I *behave* normally, I'll likely *be* normal.

Or that was the plan before Bae rocked up on the scene.

Anyway, down the stairs I go and open the door.

"*Ew!*" Dita recoils as she runs an eye down from my décolletage to my toes. "Are you going for a 70s vampire look?"

I rest my forehead against the door frame's timber edge. Do I really need more of Dita Jenkins-Smith today?

"What's up?" I groan.

Barging straight past, she checks out what she can of the questionable decor.

"This is so..." She visibly shudders, "*Dark*."

I smile prettily. "The spiders and I don't mind."

Her heavy lashes blink twice before she dismisses it. "I wanted to make sure you got home all right," she says, scouting around, edging deeper inside.

"This isn't a good time," I say at the same moment she gasps and steps back.

Bae has graced us with his company. Because he senses danger? Maybe because he finds Dita intriguing. Attractive. At least Dita will see it that way.

Recovered, Dita slinks toward my sexy demon houseguest. "We meet again. And what's this?" she asks with a curious smile in her voice as she checks out Bae's dashing garb. "You two like to play dress up, huh? I have a mermaid's outfit, if anyone's interested."

"Anyone" meaning Bae.

She's practically pressed up against him now, and I wonder. Dita was, is, and always will be a sluz-bucket. But remembering the debased movie reel that played upstairs earlier, I wonder... is something else at work here? Those women were under demon spells. Defenceless.

So, do warlocks exude some kind of supernatural pheromone that attracts mortal females like bees to an ocean of honey? Am *I* under that kind of influence where Bae is concerned? While infuriating and a little warped, I'd like to think that our connection is real. No hocus-pocus.

Whatever. Point is there's no room for Dita in my, *or* Bae's, life right now, thank you very much.

"Dita," I cross my arms, "you have to go."

She eyes me, half playful, half Dita nasty. "You always were an antisocial type. You really need to stop that." Then, breaking into I'm-so-hot mode again, she returns to Bae. "Which brings me to the other reason for this call. *Party*. Weekend after next." She rattles off her address and gives a wink when she says her folks will be out of town. "Bring your own alcohol."

"I don't drink," I say.

She gives me a *what the?* look. "Seriously?"

I skirt around and herd her toward the door. "Bye, Dita."

Bae's deep insistent voice interjects.

"*Wait.*"

I shoot him a death glare that says, *Let her go already.*

But, no. He wanders over, his steps gliding like he's moving across a sheet of ice. Dita doesn't seem to notice. Clearly, she's engrossed by his eyes, which are suddenly far more moonlight than sapphire. With a smoldering frown of concentration, Bae rests a hand on Dita's shoulder and she begins to visibly, but subtly, vibrate. Her eyes drift shut and she makes a sound in her throat like she's making love with a sex god.

I'm almost embarrassed. Definitely jealous. Bae has never touched *me* like that before.

Then his hand draws away. Dita's eyes open and she looks around like she's just woken from a very pleasant dream. Without another word, she heads for the opened door and sees herself out.

I fix my fists on my hips. "What precisely was *that?*"

I hear the door shut by itself as Bae closes the distance separating us and gives me his best 'trust me' look. "We'll walk and I'll tell you."

"A *walk?* You *never* want to go out."

"I went out today."

"And wasn't that a mistake."

A breeze whirls around me and I look down. Now I'm dressed in the clothes I wore to school that morning, dry and clean. Bae remains in his bone-melting black gear. Fine by me.

I glance out the window. "It's practically dark."

"Good."

"Because we won't be seen?"

"Because it's best that we talk among shadows."

He takes my elbow and ushers me out the door... I mean, literally *right through* the timber! What a weird sensation. Cool and yet, in a thousand other ways, not.

---

"TWO QUESTIONS I need answered right now," I say as Bae and I round the corner of Wilsted and Marsh five minutes from the house. A series of streetlights blink on and our shadows grow along the sidewalk.

"If you didn't sweep me up and drop me in that Realm place," I go on, "who did? And," just as importantly, "what did you do to Dita? Coz it looked like she really enjoyed it."

"I'll get to all that."

My lips tighten. "You know you'll never get rid of her now."

"Your friend won't even remember."

*Ha.* "Bet she will."

Bae sends me a bone-melting grin. "Trust me. She won't."

"Dita was always the popular one," I say. "She let everyone know that she was wearing a bra before anyone else in our grade. Padded, mind you, but it made a difference in our sport shirt—"

"Brinley, I'm not interested in that girl." He stops and smiles into my eyes. "I'm interested in *you*."

Blushing, I fight the urge to link an arm through his. He is so yummy. So wicked and yet not. "Really?"

He looks at me the way I like best... like he totally *gets* me. Hell, like he even *admires* me. But then his mischievous look fades and it's back to warlock business.

"When you were in the Realm," he says, walking again, "you saw a black horse. Did you see the rider?"

"No. But I felt... It sounds crazy, but I felt as if I knew him. Or wanted to, even though I sensed he could hurt me. *Would* hurt me." I shrug. "Like I said. Crazy."

"The rider... the warlock Strauveer..."

I repeat that name in my head. "Sounds French. Maybe German."

"He comes from an ancient land. A place you don't know of... yet." Bae holds my hand and hesitates before he speaks again. "The warlock Strauveer... Brinley, he's your father."

# CHAPTER 7

MOTHER USED TO PAINT. Watercolor, which isn't easy. The combination of intense focus and creative release seemed to calm and nourish her. Some of her pieces still hang on the walls.

One Christmas, alongside soft-centered chocolates and a pushbike with a wicker basket, Santa left me a set of paints. A wooden easel, too. The following week spent with my mom was the best of my life. There was art lessons and laughter. A real bond formed. I'd looked into my mother's smiling face, her sparkling grey eyes, and finally recognized joy. A sense of peace.

As a child, I felt responsible for her happiness. I simply had to try harder. Find the key. Be a better kid. At last, I seemed to be doing something right. That week, she held my cheeks and dabbed kisses on my brow. She was *so* proud of my wobbly lines and splodges of color. Standing together on the porch surrounded by scented pines and powdery fresh-fallen snow, she would talk about 'negative space' and 'contrast hues'. Soaking up every drop of attention and advice, I made a wish. More a prayer.

*Please, please, please, let it always be this way.*

If a person lives a miserable existence, they adjust to the misery; no one misses what they never had, right? *Wrong*. Being deeply unhappy most of the time sucks monkeys' balls. Feeling loved by someone who counts, however— truly feeling present and worthwhile—is a euphoric state of being.

That Christmas, I had felt reborn.

I didn't think about my father. Not once did I hide under the covers at night sending out magical thoughts, begging to be rescued from my often horror-filled reality. Whatever demons had been poking rotting holes in my mother's mind for so long had suddenly packed their smelly bags and moved on.

Then New Year's morning, I wandered downstairs, rubbing sleep from my eyes, and all that anguish hurtled back in a heartbeat... like a dump truck had collected another mountain of crap to unload at my feet. On my head. During the night, my mother had painted a picture. The image left me standing frozen in fear. It was of a deformed, putrid man-slash-monster. The most horrific looking being I'd ever seen.

I wondered... was that the kind of picture my mom would have me painting next? What would she do if I refused?

A bolt of panic sent me stumbling up to my room. I destroyed every one of my own paintings, even my favorite—the one with a baby reindeer, her head tilted up, kissing snowflakes as they fell. It was too painful to be reminded of what happiness looked or felt like. Downstairs was *my* reality.

Christmas was definitely over.

As Bae looks into my eyes now, his masculine frame silhouetted beneath a streetlight and his delicious natural scent filling my lungs, that memory shoots through my head and I wince at the bittersweet pain. I hold my churning stomach, my clammy brow.

The abomination my mother had painted that night... was that my father?

Impossible. *Obscene.*

My voice is strangled. "That's the most insane thing I've ever heard."

Bae nods like he understands. "You never met your father."

"Mom said he up and vanished before I was even born."

And now the question isn't, *will I ever meet him?* It's *do I even want to?* Being abandoned was bad enough.

And then another thought comes barrelling out. A realization that turns the blood in my veins to ice. If my father's a warlock, who—and *what*—am I?

Angry doesn't come close.

"So now, after all these years," I go on, "he finally decides to front up?"

"It's not that simple." Bae seemed to struggle to find the right words. "After your mother died, Strauveer ended his own existence, too."

Nausea rises in my gut. Bending over, I dry retch. I do have a father, and then I don't. A *double* suicide. *I'm not okay with any of this!*

Strong arms loop around me before Bae guides me to a bench set outside of the streetlamp's light. My knees buckle and I plop down on the hard timber slats.

"Why did I see him riding toward me on that horse?" I croak out.

"He wants to protect you, too."

"Wait. You just said he was *dead*."

Bae tugs me closer. "It's a lot to take in, I know."

*Massive understatement.* "I've just learned my mother was raped by a warlock—"

"Not raped. The act was consensual."

I could be smug and ask, *What the hell was she thinking?* But I only have to look into Bae's incredibly beautiful, concerned eyes to know precisely how she might have felt. Which begs the question I'd only ever asked *myself* before now.

"I wasn't sure warlocks and humans could conceive."

"As far as we know, in all cases, bar this, warlocks are infertile. That's why you're so special." His glittering gaze roams my face. "You are one of a kind. Part of our strain... of our family."

I'd always wanted more extended family but this news only makes me feel faint. I take a deep quivering breath, and another.

"And the other strains?" I finally ask. "How do they feel about me?"

"They are incredibly... curious."

I make the obvious connection. "That's who snatched me away from school today, isn't it? That's why you're always so paranoid."

In the shadows, I see his jaw flex and the line of his mouth harden before he nods once.

*Okay. Breathing extra deep now.* A panic attack will get me nowhere, other than maybe a psychiatric ward. No one, including Dr. Phoebe, would ever swallow this story. I'm not sure I do.

"So, what's their plan?" I ask. "These other strains want to throw me a surprise *welcome to the other side* party?"

He looks pained. "Not so much."

"They want to hold me prisoner? Cut me up into little pieces to see how I tick?"

When Bae slowly pushes to his feet, his shadow envelopes me whole. "That's enough for tonight."

Luckily there's no one around because my voice is high-pitched, loud and desperate. Pieces of the puzzle are falling into place, and the picture I'm seeing leaves me feeling stone cold.

"Stauveer was the reason my mother went mad, wasn't he? He drove her crazy."

"Not intentionally."

My throat closes up. Is that what Bae is doing to me now? Screwing with my brain even if it's not 'intentional'?

"We're going home," he says.

When he reaches for my hand, I shake my head as tears well in my eyes and my chest aches. "I want to know, *damn it*. All of it."

"You will. In time."

I shoot to my feet, bunch my fists and yell. "I need to know *now!*"

Overhead, that streetlight blows out. Sparks arc, showering down. When a couple burn pinpoints into my skin, I growl.

"Don't show off, Bae. I'm not in the mood."

"That wasn't me. I didn't blow that streetlight." Through deepening shadows, his gaze pierces mine. "Brin, that was you."

# CHAPTER 8

AMID THE DARK and the quiet, I study the pattern of streetlight shards glinting across the sidewalk.

*I did that? Seriously!*

Then, like I didn't have enough to deal with, I suddenly realize that Bae and I are standing in front of a spiked iron fence outside of a cemetery. And not just *any* cemetery. My mother is buried in there. Clear as day, I see her headstone... the carving of a winged-angel beside her name. As the sour scent of forgotten bouquets drift across, I try to get my bearings. This makes no sense. No sense at all.

Hellaway's only graveyard is on the other side of town, on the long road heading out. I glance over my shoulder and across the street. It's a familiar view of an elm-lined sidewalk and family homes. Peering back at the cemetery again, I tug Bae's sleeve.

"Is that another creepy movie reel?" Like the one he'd played in his room earlier?

Before Bae can answer, I hear scuttling... like stiff broom straw brushing over gritty stone. Then I catch a movement. Something is shifting in the shadows behind my mother's headstone. When the scuttling sound comes again, louder this time, my pulse begins to thump. I feel so sick, I want to puke.

"*Bae*," I whisper and coil myself into the rock pillar of his side. "Tell me that's not real."

He hesitates before replying, sounding puzzled. "What's not real?"

I see questions as well as concern darken his eyes. Arching a brow, I tip my head very carefully toward the spiked cemetery fence.

"You don't see that?" *Can't smell it?* I mean, totally rank.

The line of his mouth shifts. His nostrils flare a heartbeat before he grabs my hand—so hard and unforgiving, my fingers feel squashed. "We need to leave."

He'd said the exact same thing earlier today at school. He had *insisted* that we go. I'd tried to fob him off then. I want to be strong now, too. But that prickly feeling is filling me again like it had in the cafeteria, and then later in the rain. I don't need to wake up a second time in that misty, creepy nowhere that Bae calls the Realm.

I swallow and nod deeply. "Let's go."

Bae sweeps me up in his arms like I weigh as much as a bag of leaves. Next second—as if I'd snapped my fingers—we're back inside the house. The front door is shut and I am shaking uncontrollably, like I'm coming out of insulin shock. Massive overload on every one of my systems, I suppose.

Holding me tight, Bae seems somehow bigger, broader. *Badder.* Beneath his black shirt, muscles have grown muscles. He is flawless sculpted marble left in the midday sun to warm through.

His eyes narrow, penetrating mine. "What did you see?"

I get my rubbery mouth to work. "A cemetery with my mother's headstone. And something else..."

Carefully, he sets me on my feet and then squares his shoulders. "Now it's begun," he says, "they won't stop."

*They* meaning the other 'strains' of warlock? Crazy! Seriously warped.

My laugh is a little maniacal. "Bae, I'm not interested in your stupid warlock world."

There's not only pity but also a look of pride on his face. "You're a part of that world."

When his palm brushes my cheek, delicious warmth swirls through every fibre of my body. His touch immediately calms me. Sooths me. *Feeds* me. But it won't change my mind.

I set my jaw.

"Just tell your friends, or whatever the hell they are, to *back off.*"

"They know now you have capabilities."

As in shattering that light? Big hairy deal. "I have my own life. I want to be a regular girl whose biggest worry is getting a date for prom."

"That's another thing."

My jaw drops. *There's more?* "Now what?"

"I'll need to go to school with you from now on."

Holding up my hands, I back away. "No, no, and *no*. Clearly you forget the scene you caused this afternoon appearing out of nowhere to drag me away."

"I haven't forgotten. But everyone else already has. Just like Dita earlier, their memories of that time have been wiped clean. No one will remember me being there. Just like Dita won't remember being *here*."

I stop and absorb.

"Not Kellen or Nick King, either?"

"You mean the mortal who wanted to lock horns with me?" Bae's lip curls. "He should learn to keep his mouth shut."

"He was trying to help."

"He'll help himself into an early grave," Bae mutters before getting back to the heart of our conversation. "I'll go with you to school every day," he insists. "I'll be invisible to everyone but you."

I'm shaking my head, wanting to laugh. This is all so Buffy-esque. "You're not listening."

"We'll also need to change arrangements here. I need to keep you close. *Always*." He draws up to his full intimating height. "As of tonight, you will share my bed."

I'm about to get tough, tell him he has to leave and find someone else to haunt. But his last statement grabs me. I clear my throat as my stomach fills with butterflies.

"You and me... In the same *bed?*"

His chest expands as he siphons in a determined breath. "Every night."

Beneath my shirt, the tips of my breasts begin to tingle. Deep inside, the sweetest kind of kindling starts to glow. Intimacy is the last thing on Bae's mind. Should be the last thing on mine at the moment, too. Only I can't control the urge to imagine us together, under the sheets, his hard long limbs nudging mine... his warm breath only a whisper away.

Every. Single.

*Night.*

One obvious question needs to be addressed.

"Can I ask... what do warlocks wear to bed?"

He arches a brow, almost grins. "You tell me."

"I'm not a warlock." But then I blink.

*Am I?*

His gaze softens as it brushes my cheek, my throat. "You're tired," he says. "Let me do something for you."

During my next intake of air, surroundings go fuzzy... dreamy. My taste buds hum with a fresh mint flavor. Suddenly my skin feels cool, smells divine... like it's been lathed in lavender oil. When my eyes drift open again, I'm standing in Bae's bedroom. My tongue runs over smooth, freshly brushed teeth. Every inch of my body radiates a just-stepped-out-of-the-shower glow. Best of all, I'm dressed in my blue bunny T-shirt and matching pyjama shorts.

Bae is lying under the covers, his mouth-watering chest on display like it's no big deal. With fingers thatched behind his head, he's propped up against a bank of soft white pillows. He glances across at the bedspace waiting vacant alongside of him.

He asks, "Are you okay with this?"

*Trick question.*

I edge closer, deliberately eyeing his chest. "You, uh, don't do pyjama coats?"

His expression is all integrity. "Don't worry," he says. "You're safe with me."

Out of nowhere, I yawn... the exhausted type that floods my body with the need to hibernate until spring. My bare heels and then toes leave the soft carpet floor. Then I'm lifted up at the same time the covers on 'my' side of the bed magically peel back. As Bae brings his arms down to his sides, his knitted eyebrows say that he's taking this ultra seriously. He needs to know I'm okay with this move.

My body levels out horizontally, and then I lower onto the sheet at the same time the covers float up and settle around my waist. Content, I exhale quietly. A ghost of smile lifts one side of his mouth, which suddenly looks more kissable than I can handle. I can't help but wonder...

Who was the witch he'd crushed on so many years ago?

Can a warlock truly fall in love?

No sooner am I settled than his body heat drifts across. Not too warm. Not even too drugging. Amazingly just right. And if by chance his mouth were to cover mine, what defence would I have? I'd remember my mother's torment and melt into his kiss anyway.

That frightens me more than anything. Not because I'm a virgin, which I am. Because I might not regret anything until it's way too late.

I bundle the sheet up under my chin, hunch my shoulders. "You never did tell me about your warlock mark."

He looks at me for a long moment like he could lie there drinking me in for eternity. He is so absurdly sexy, I could die.

"So..." I continue as I focus on the pulse throbbing on one side of his throat. "What's yours?"

"I wonder..." He rolls onto his side to face me. "What's yours?"

As the light magically fades in the room, I recall that sixth finger. I thought my mother had agreed to the procedure so kids wouldn't call me freak. Did she know from the beginning I wasn't like other boys and girls?

But I can't think about that now. Sleepiness has gotten a real hold; perhaps Bae is controlling that, too, making sure I have a good night's rest.

As my heartbeat steadies and my eyelids grow heavier still, I gaze around the quiet shadowed room. My gaze drifts to the far corner, to a chest of drawers where Bae's ruby sits as if waiting... as if calling.

From its core—from its *heart*—that stone is glowing blood red.

# CHAPTER 9

I WAS nine-years-old the first time my mother slit her throat. Finding her lying on the bathroom floor, not breathing, I screamed and ran into the bedroom to snatch up the phone receiver. I was dialling 911 when cold fingers gripped my shoulder and I spun around.

Mom stood before me. No gash on her neck. Color in her face. She was even smiling, asking me what was wrong. The blood was gone, too. Every drop.

'Confusing' doesn't come close. Back then, I only knew that I'd woken up from the worst nightmare ever. Mom was alive and she hadn't looked this sane since that beautiful Christmas six months earlier. When she asked what I'd like for lunch, I wrapped my arms around her and wept.

I'm thinking about those feelings now as I sit in Professor Hinkley's class, which is about imagination versus reality. About dreams.

"While we are yet to understand why we dream," the Professor says, "there are theories. Freud posited that dreams are mechanisms of wish fulfilment related to latent sexual desires."

Sitting beside me, Kellen moves like she's uncomfortable at the S.E.X. reference. Over the last couple of weeks, we've become close. She is super friendly and sweet and, from where I sit, naïve. She misses her dad a lot. Reminisces about things they did together... hike and play tennis and what not. She has some brilliant memories. Obviously some crap ones, too. But I have the deepest feeling Kellen's life will work out well. Someone's watching out for her.

Like someone's watching out for me.

Professor Hinkley ends by flashing his silver-tooth smile and making a suggestion. "Humans are capable of experiencing various levels of consciousness throughout any given day, ranging from alertness, to daydreams to psychotic episodes with visual, auditory and even olfactory hallucinations."

Remembering the other night with Bae, I grin to myself. *Creepy graveyards anyone?*

"Before we meet again," Hinkley goes on, "think about your own unique states of awareness. Consider the roles of individual memory and sensation. Deliberate on the possibility of parallel universes. After all, reality is perception." The professor's gaze connects with mine. "And perception is reality."

He smiles again, a curious grin, before his focus shifts and students get to their feet.

The professor mentioned parallel universes... like the Realm, that misty, space-time puzzle I'd had the misfortune to visit? The professor can't know about that part of my life. Does he know about my mother's shifting sense of reality... about her descent into madness? Or maybe that look and grin a moment ago meant nothing and I'm looking for connections where there are none. I already have enough to be tetchy about.

As we move out into the hall, Kellen touches my arm. "You okay?" she asks. "You look kind of spacey."

I bring myself back with a quick smile. "I'm good."

"I enjoy the professor's classes," she says, pushing her black glass frames back up her nose. "He makes me think." She hugs her books close to her chest as she considers more. "Perception is reality. I get it. It's like choosing to be either happy or sad."

We pass a set of lockers where a geek with a massive overbite is obsessing over an opened textbook. There's a look of panic (or is that exhilaration?) on his face.

"It's not that simple," I say.

"It's how you decide to look at things," Kellen says, sounding as if she's trying to convince herself more than me.

My friend makes the most of what she has. She refuses to let anything dampen her spirit. I have to admire and even envy her for that. Where I might find a sinking ditch, Kellen finds a rainbow.

So, where's the rainbow in this warlock dilemma of mine? Maybe if I chose to accept a different perception...

Scary, but maybe this is all in my mind. I certainly have the genes for it.

Now, someone calls out my name. I recognize the voice before I turn around.

Since the cafeteria incident, Nick King hasn't gotten close enough for us to talk. If ever our eyes meet, a strange vacant look comes over his face, similar to the dazed expression Dita had that afternoon when she lobed up on my doorstep and Bae had placed a hand on her shoulder to make her forget.

But Bae was doing more than erasing Dita's memory. Apparently warlocks and demons can take over a mortal's body. When Bae had made physical contact with Dita that day, he was making sure that she was not, quote, *possessed*. He's checked out an assortment of my acquaintances since then, too: Kellen, the Professor... most particularly Nick King.

Although Nick was cleared of possible warlock possession, Bae keeps him at a distance from yours truly. Just the other day when I was on my way to the library, Nick was headed straight toward me. Sure enough, that strange, zombified look came over him. But this time he didn't walk on by. Rather, his jaw tightened and he forged on, like he wasn't about to give in. Then some inexplicable force (oh, let's say Bae) *physically* dragged him back, as if an invisible hand had grabbed Nick's belt and had literally wrenched him away.

As I watch Nick striding up now, he's not slowing down. No dazed look, either. He appears confident, cheeky, like he had that first day.

Biting my lip, I scan the area. As promised, Bae has come to school every day. No one sees him other than me. But this minute, I can't find him around anywhere. In fact, come to think of it, I haven't seen Bae all day.

When Nick pulls up in front of me, he offers a smile that would melt most girls' hearts. Gorgeous sandy-colored bed hair. Dimples and dark, dreamy eyes. He is incredibly cute.

Just not as cute as Bae.

"You've been avoiding me," Nick says in a deep, teasing voice.

"I haven't meant to." *Honest*.

"Hi, Nick," says Kellen, sweeping a length of her perm behind one ear. "Are you enjoying the professor's classes?"

Nick notices Kellen. "Oh, hi. How you doin'?"

She curls more hair behind that ear and smiles an extra wide smile.

Nick shifts his grin back to me. "So, I was wondering. There's a party on tonight."

"At Dita's place," Kellen pipes up.

Nick blinks at Kellen but quickly returns focus to me. "I was wondering if you might like a lift."

I sense Kellen holding her breath. Lifting my chin, I link my arm through hers. *Sisters before Misters.* I'd already promised. "Thanks, but I'm going with Kellen."

He looks at my friend harder now and then shrugs. "How about you both do me the honor then?"

"Take us *both* to the party?" Kellen asks, somehow growing taller.

"Sure." When Nick's open gaze roams my face, I feel it like a touch. Nice. A little forbidden. "How about it?"

It'd sure make Kellen's day; she obviously likes Nick King. And I can't see any harm in it. Bae mustn't either or he would've swooped on Nick by now.

I nod. "Sounds good."

"I'll pick you up first," Nick says to me.

"Actually, Kellen's getting ready at my place. You could collect us both there, if that works."

I give Nick my address and he strides off to his next class.

Meanwhile, Kellen is gaping at me. "I'm getting ready at your house?"

We head off again. "I have new makeup I want to try out, if you're game."

"I don't wear makeup."

"You don't need it, either." Her skin is a landscape of peachy flawlessness. "I just thought you might want to experiment with a little lip gloss and mascara."

Her spreading smile says she most certainly does.

---

LATER THAT DAY when I get home, the place is dead quiet.

I check out the living room. Empty. The kitchen. Ditto. I run upstairs to Bae's bedroom. *Our* bedroom. No sign of my warlock anywhere.

Forget he wasn't at school today. *This* has never happened. It was weird at first, but now I'm used to having him in this house. I'm so comfortable with it, in fact, that I invited Kellen over so I could possibly (re)introduce them.

Even his gorgeous scent is missing.

I have a creepy thought, one that's been playing around in my head a lot lately, particularly after the professor's class this morning. Seriously, what if these past few weeks with Bae have been nothing but a delusion? What if I'm losing it like my mom? She never seemed to know what was real or sane or normal.

But I can't accept that's the case here. Bae is just too real to me. Too... necessary.

"*Bae!* Quit hiding. Come out already!"

I'm about to hurry downstairs for another look around when the ruby on his dresser catches my eye. Every night that stone glows a little brighter. I've asked Bae about its meaning, its purpose, more than once. He only frowns and looks away.

Behind me, a deep familiar voice rumbles out.

"You're seeing that boy tonight."

My heart thumps against my ribs as I spin around. Bae is standing by the door, wearing the pirate breeches I hyperventilated over a couple of weeks ago. No shirt. After spending so many restful nights lying alongside of him in this room, I shouldn't be so affected by the sight of his broad bare chest. And yet I can't help but trace with my eyes the power of demon-flesh covered brawn.

Wait a minute.

*He knows about Nick?*

"So, you *were* at school today," I say with some satisfaction. Watching over me. Listening in.

Tugging on leather gloves I've never seen before, Bae only casts a glance out the window. As my heart pumps harder, I edge a little closer. I try to sound upbeat but he's acting weirder than usual, if that's possible.

"Are you going somewhere, too?" I ask.

He flexes the fingers of both gloved hands at the same time his chin lifts and veins in his neck visibly swell. "I have something I need to do."

"Wow." I try to make light. "Sounds ominous."

He grabs a shirt off the back of a nearby chair and pulls it over his head. I wait as he buttons from the bottom all the way up. Wait as he folds up the stiff cuffs of each sleeve on his forearms.

I try to act cool, stay calm, but I need him to share.

"Talk to me, Bae. What's going on?"

He flashes over a look, his eyes narrowed and intent, before he sits on the bed to slide on his boots. He's stubborn, like me, but this is just plain dumb. I'm not a child. If something's going on, I need to know.

I slump. "At least tell me when you'll be back.'

Boots on, he moves to the dresser and studies the ruby, which is pulsing, alive with red light. He runs a finger down the stone's side. "I can't say." His voice lowers. "I don't know."

My stomach pitches. Does he actually *want* me to worry? I set my jaw, ground myself. "Do you know what you're being? You're being obtuse. That means you're—"

He growls, "I know what obtuse means."

A battle-scarred black leather jacket appears in his hand before he cuts the distance separating us and cups my cheek, warm and incredibly gentle. As he searches my eyes like he wants to find some kind of answer there, my throat clogs up with a host of emotions. If he won't tell me what's going on, damned if I'll say that I'll miss him.

That I'm scared.

As I lean into his touch. I expect him to murmur, "Be careful. Be watchful." But he only gives a wistful smile and whispers, "Goodbye, Brin."

Before he can disappear, I grab his hand.

"Bae..." My throat convulses. Every hair on my body is standing on end. I know I have a pathetic look of desperation on my face but I can't change that even if I want to.

I will my lips to curve up at the corners, a weak smile, as I plead with him. "Don't go."

He closes his eyes and his shoulders lift almost imperceptibly, like he's trying not to flinch with pain. Then he inhales and focuses on me again with an inner-strength that grips my heart.

"I'm sorry..."

I hold his hand harder. "When we first met, you mentioned a witch. Someone you were... fond of."

His eyebrows fall together and he cocks his head. "Yes?"

"Who was she?"

"That was a long time ago."

"Just... she was a witch, right? Not a warlock."

"Different species."

Looking into his beautiful eyes, I hesitate and then ask, "Was she beautiful?"

"Long flaxen hair down to her thighs. Her skin was smoother than silk. She was a vixen, but vulnerable, too." His lips twitch. 'Like you."

That overflow of emotion is backing up my throat, to my eyes. I try for a grin. "I'm a vixen?"

"Spirited." His gaze skims my hair. "Beautiful."

I need to ask the question because something tells me I might never get another chance.

"Were you in love with her, Bae?"

His chin kicks up and he winds his hand away from mine. "I have to go."

And then, with a single stride toward the window, my warlock vanishes into thin air.

# CHAPTER 10

WHEN THE KNOCKER slams on the front door three times, echoing through the house, I gather myself and gradually make my way downstairs.

Through the peephole I see Kellen, cheeks pink and smile wide. I let out the breath I've been holding. Everyone needs a friend like Kellen. Always supportive and upbeat. Exactly what I need right now.

When I open the door, Kellen extends an arm. "I save it for special occasions," she says, offering a bottle of nail polish.

I check out the label. "*Lilac Glitter Shine*. That could work."

I make an effort to push Bae further from my mind. Whatever he's up to, wringing my hands over it won't make a difference. I simply need to have faith.

"What are you wearing to the party?" I ask as I search Kellen for a carryall or overnight bag.

Kellen's monobrow lowers as her cheeks pink up more. She looks down. "I thought maybe this."

Oh. The same outfit she'd worn to school yesterday and two days before that and repeat. I tack up my smile. We can fix that.

Stepping inside, Kellen looks around. She's way more polite about the lack of light and goth interior design than Dita had been.

"It must be amazing having this whole place to yourself until your aunt moves in."

Just as Bae had promised, Kellen doesn't recall any of the weirdness from the day in the cafeteria and later in the rain. She doesn't remember having met Bae or my introducing him as my roomie. Given Bae has disappeared, I let Kellen assume it's just me in the house.

I hook an arm through hers and we head off. "We'll use the downstairs bathroom. It's got the best light. We could maybe do something a little different with your hair, too."

"My father always says a change is as good as a holiday."

In the bathroom, I seat her on a breakfast stool set in front of twin angled mirrors. She doesn't shrink from her reflection. There's no reason to. Kellen has been blessed with blemish-free peachy toned skin. Her eyes are wide and sparkling. Lips, cupid-bowed and lush.

I tap my chin. *Hmm.* "We need color and volume."

"Leena likes coral lipsticks."

"I was thinking more a pink nude."

Kellen shifts a little awkwardly in her seat and then gives a firm, brave nod. "Nude pink it is."

Hers hands are laced tightly on her lap, her plump shoulders are squared and I bet her toes are curled in those scuffed black flats. She's anxious but she only conveys dignity and trust.

Kellen is one of the coolest people I know.

When we finish, Kellen has been transformed. Those crimpy waves are gone, replaced with a shimmery river of rose gold. With the help of shadow and mascara (and a light wax between the brows), her already pretty eyes have become captivating jewels. Her full lips now appear bee-stung and glossed up. Those cheekbones whisper *diva breaking out!*

After my suggestion of faux leather panel leggings, Kellen decides to stick with her black A-line skirt, which we unzip a little and fold down a couple of times until the band rests just above her hips. We swap her white blouse for a black sequined midriff top with longer chiffon split-at-the-side underlay.

Bonus that we're the same shoe size. She's shaky on platform heels at first, but females and great shoes always find a way. As she stands in front of my bedroom mirror, I am speechless. I had meant to ask whether she had any contacts, but those black frames have taken on a whole new preppy meaning.

She teeters around, showing off her stuff, and then exhales at the mirror. "I look nerdy."

"Guys love pretty nerds."

Her chin pulls in. "Pretty? *Me?*"

I laugh. "You dope." I look over her shoulder into her reflection's wide gaze. "If I were a boy, I'd date you myself."

She presses her lips together but nothing can hide that grin. She touches her hair, runs a fingertip between her separate eyebrows and then slants her head like she's not uncertain as much as curious.

"Brinley, can I ask a stupid question?"

"My aunt says no question is stupid."

"Have you ever been kissed?"

I sit on the bed to slip on my own killer heels. I've gone with jeans and white crop top with the slogan: *Eat, Tweet, Party Hard, Repeat.*

"I went steady with someone for a while last year. We broke up before I moved here." I twirl my hair into a messy bun and secure it with diamante pins. "His parents didn't like me."

Kellen's jaw drops. "What the hell's not to like." Then she stammers, embarrassed, because she never gets angry. "I-I mean... you're so pretty and smart."

"His parents found out about my mother... how she died." Gruesome, alone, and by her own hand. "They didn't want any soot to rub off on their son."

Imagine if they'd known about the *demon blood running through my veins* thing. Too weird to think about.

"I haven't dated anyone." Kellen places her hands on her hips and squeezes. "Leena says I need to lose my baby fat. It's crazy to think that someone like Nick King would ever..." Her hands drop to her sides. "Well, you know."

I smile at her blush.

*Yeah. I know.*

I turn my friend back toward the mirror and smile. "What the hell's not to like?"

Peering at her reflection, we both break into laughter. Despite her constant glass half full mentality, how long has it been since she'd truly felt good about herself. Maybe not since gas-lighting Leena had swooped onto the scene. Not since her beautiful mother had died.

*Always smiling. Always sweet.*

Like my own mother had been that long ago Christmas. The week I learned to paint, and hope, and even believe.

How different would my train wreck of a life have been without my mother's illness constantly tearing us apart? Knowing now that her mental state wasn't about genes or disease or some chemical imbalance made it even harder to accept. My mom had made love with a warlock. *Cue the descent into madness.*

Every night when I snuggle down beside Bae, I remind myself of that.

Just then I hear a car engine outside. I grip Kellen's shoulders. "Show time!"

A moment later, I find Nick standing on the porch, hands wedged in the front pockets of his jeans, lopsided grin hanging on his handsome face. Then he sees Kellen and he literally staggers back, like someone socked him in the chest. He shakes his head and frowns like he thinks he might be dreaming.

"Kellen?" he says. "Is that you?"

I can't believe what my friend does next. Oh so casually, she slips off her glasses and polished the lenses on the hem of her chiffon, all the while keeping her gaze fixed on Nick's. Did those spectacles really need a clean or is she milking the moment for all it's worth?

"You look nice tonight," she replies in her cheerful steady way.

Nick gets his gaping mouth to work. "Y-You too."

"Shall we go?" I suggest, giving myself a high five. Makeovers are so much fun.

As we girls move out onto the porch, Nick links his arms through both of ours. Remembering the door, I turned back to close it. Before I can, as if shoved by a gust of wind, the door slams shut by itself.

# CHAPTER 11

LATER, I watch Dita prance around her party-lit backyard shouting—"Make out contest! Volunteer time!"

I slink back behind my friends.

Kellen, Nick and I arrived an hour ago. Of the fifty or so here, a few are knocking back beer and mixes, but no one's flat-out misbehaving. The music is thumping at a respectable volume. Given the occasional funky smell in the air, someone's smoking. But no raucous drinking games or even dancing has broken out.

But the night is still young.

Dita descends on our circle... that's me, Kellen, Victoria Teebs and Sondra Cleary, girls from our English Lit class. Nick's off somewhere clowning around with guy friends.

"Okay, ladies," Dita coos. "Make out contest. Who wants in? I'm up for same sex couples as well as trios."

Kellen whispers across at me, "She wants girls to kiss girls?" She doesn't sound shocked as much as uncertain.

"It's a statistical fact," says Dita. "Females are more likely to have an attraction toward either sex. But feel free to step up for the regular boy and girl version."

At the same moment Kellen sends me a covert "as if" look, Nick passes by and Dita grabs him over.

"Make out contest," she tells him. "I already have your partner."

As Dita grins across at Kellen, I know Nick misunderstands. His gaze has landed on *me*. By the gleam in his eye and the way that he straightens, he's up for it.

"Sure," he says, shucking back his shoulders again. "Count me in."

Dita pushes Nick in front of her while she snatches up Kellen's hand and tugs her along. By the time all three reach the dance floor-come-stage and an eager Nick turns around, Dita is practically throwing Kellen into his arms. His eyes widen before he snaps a look over Kellen's head. As he sends me a *what happened?* face, I wave encouragingly.

I'm not sure how Kellen feels about it all. If it's too much too soon. But if she wants out, she's strong enough to speak up for herself.

Dita holds up her hands to get everyone's attention and then introduces the four couples who have come forward. There's one guy-with-guy pair, who are already performing to stir up the crowd, as well as three regular couples, including Nick and Kellen. She is gazing across at him from beneath her smudgeproof, volumized lashes, like he might be the prince from every fairy tale she's ever read. Nick is proving he's a stand-up guy. He's gazing across at her like he's more than okay with the situation. And why wouldn't he be? She's gorgeous!

When Dita at last announces Nick and Kellen, he theatrically sweeps Kellen off her feet and whirls her around before setting her down on her teetering heels. The crowd cracks up, laughing and applauding, including me. Overwhelmed, Kellen staggers back. As Nick catches her, the cheers go up again.

*Guess we have our favorites.*

"Is everybody ready?" Dita shouts, wiggling her prominent micro-mini rear as she strides back and forth in front of the contestants.

I close my eyes and mentally cross my fingers. All these people... Kellen's first ever kiss...

*Please let this be amazing.*

Dita signals to the jock who's in charge of music. But before he can press play, another sound zings out: a brief, near deafening riff from a superbly tuned electric guitar.

But where's it coming from?

Everyone's looking around, curious, confused. Has Bae dropped in from wherever in the guise of a rock god? Snippets of our earlier conversation play around in my head. I'd called him obtuse. He'd said he couldn't stay. I asked him about love. Of course, he'd clammed up. And then I'd hated myself for sounding interested. Sounding needy.

I don't want to *need* anyone.

But when a guy in tatty jeans steps into the crowd's view, belting out a solo that gives me goose bumps it's so good, I ease out that breath. Not Bae.

I can admit... I'm really starting to miss him.

People move closer as a base guitarist appears, too, and then a guy with a mic who has the audience cheering, his voice is so strong and pitch perfect. Nick takes Kellen's hand and they gravitate over with the rest to the show. Soon, practically everyone's dancing, jumping, spinning, twerking and slut dropping.

Then the most magical lightshow begins. Stars of silver and red start to float out from... I don't know where. They come to me on a wavering stream, some bursting into sparkles as they approach my space, others seeming to pass right through me. After a mediocre start, this party is smashing it now. Still...

I just can't get into it. I keep thinking about Bae, where he is. Whether I might never see him again.

I wonder about pulling Kellen aside to say I'm walking home, but I don't want to be a drag and interrupt her flow. She deserves this time. And so, while the band segues into an even louder head-banging song, I send her a text she'll get later and then walk around the side of the house alone.

I pass a bunch of guys I don't know. The smell of body odour makes me wince. One dude is ridiculously tall with oily black hair and a hook nose. Two gangly others clearly enjoy a staple diet of *nothing nutritious*. The fourth has his eye on the ground... on a cat slinking out from beneath the house. This fourth guy has a mean look about him. Poxy face with lips a little too red and eyes a little too small. As the cat scampers between them, fourth guy grins and lifts back his boot.

One guess how this will play out. Poxy-face will slot his boot up poor kitty's behind. As the cat flies through the air, screeching in pain, Poxy will chuckle and the other deadheads will join in. That cat isn't asking for trouble. He only wants to escape the noise.

Pursing my lips, I narrow my eyes on that boot as it swings forward. Then I spread my fingers wide by my sides for some reason I can't explain. I narrow my eyes, concentrate hard.

And Poxy's boot misses kitty completely! Its toe flies up and spears oily-hair guy right in the gonads. Oily-hair drops his beer, keels over and howls like his tonsils have been torn out the wrong hole.

I don't want to know about being a warlock, having any special powers. I definitely don't want to know about complications that will no doubt follow if it's true. I want to be left alone. Like the cat. But, if I'm in some way responsible for Poxy's goof... Yeah, it was fun.

With a swagger in my step, I head on down Watsons Road. The houses are spaced well apart. The live music coming from Dita's place dips more in volume the farther I walk.

A few minutes on, an overhead streetlight flickers a few times. A chill, or is that a thrill, trickles through me. Then a deep male voice warms my neck from behind.

"*Boo.*"

My stomach jumps and I spin around.

The guy smiling at me isn't Bae, although the iridescent color swirling in his eyes and impressive build are eerily similar. His scent is immediate, too... subtle and somehow haunting. Definitely drugging.

Dressed in black with hair the color of polished mahogany, his confident expression oozes magnetism. His nose is long and sharp, his mouth beguilingly soft. As his gaze grows lidded and he blinks slowly once, every part of me is drawn like a lemming to a cliff.

"It's grand to finally meet you, Brinley."

"Who are you?" I could have said *what are you*, but I'm not an idiot.

"I'm a friend of Ruarc," he says, circling me like prey. "A friend of *yours.*"

When he smiles, I hear broom straw scuffing over sandstone again, like I had that night standing in front of the incarnation of my mother's grave.

"I'm not sure what you want," I say, holding it together despite the fact my legs suddenly feel like jelly. "Whatever it is, I'm not interested."

"You should be."

He sounds so smooth, so... predatory.

Time to go.

But when I move to walk away, he's there again right in front of me; I literally slam into him. He feels rock solid like Bae, but while my warlock is always toasty warm, this guy is stone freaking cold. Looking into those eyes is enough to give me frostbite.

Looking down, I concentrate as hard as I can. Send out a silent cry.

*Bae, where are you? I need you. Come quick!*

"Your warlock isn't coming," he says at the same time a SUV drives up the road.

When the vehicle stops, I recognize the driver. It's Lance Foley from school. Lance whirs down his window and slants his head at me.

"You okay?" he asks. "Need a lift or something?"

For a second, I wonder why Lance isn't reacting to my rather conspicuous company. But I'm guessing he's gone the invisible route, like Bae does at school now. No one else can see this dude but me.

For Lance's sake, I make out everything's fine. No one else needs to get involved. I don't want anyone hurt.

"I'm enjoying the walk," I tell Lance. "Going to Dita's place?"

"I can hear the music from here." Lance narrows his eyes at me while the invisible guy checks out the starry sky like he has all the time in the world, which, in a way, he does. "Sure you're okay?"

I wave it off. "Absolutely."

Lance shores up his smile before he shifts gears and the vehicle glides off.

I cross my arms, peg out leg and get serious. "You need to leave. When Bae finds out—"

"He'll be upset. No doubt. But right now he's busy... negotiating."

I frown. "Negotiating what?"

"What we're to do with you, of course."

Something in his voice grates up my spine, making me shiver to my core. The street is quiet. There's no sign that Bae might magically snap onto the scene. I'll just have to handle this on my own.

"You want to try to abduct me again. Take me back to that Realm place," I say straight out. "I figure that's why you're here."

His sinister laugh echoes through the night. "Don't blame us for that episode. That was Ruarc. His strain. Not mine."

My heart bashes even harder against my ribcage, and my head is spinning because I know it's not true. Bae would *never* lie to me, betray me, like that. But Bae also said this kind of thing could *never* happen. That he would protect me against the other strains no matter what.

Willing my voice not to break, I try to bluff my way through. "I have things to do," I say, trying to walk past.

He laughs again, only this time the sound rumbles across the ground, trembling under my feet. I strike out my arms like a tightrope walker to keep my balance.

"You're like your father," he growls. "We were friends, too."

As he reaches out, I want to dodge but I'm frozen to the spot. Nothing in my body will move except two eyeballs rolling around my head. I can't run, can't talk. If I really had powers, if I possibly could, I'd reduce this douche to a pile of ash.

Some kind of a circle—cold and hard and thick—locks around my neck with a *click*.

"Don't be afraid," he says as he winds an accompanying leash to my collar around his wrist. "It's for your own protection. We won't harm you. We only want to know you better."

He tugs the leash and I wince at the same time a colossal tumble of dried leaves as high as a house comes hurtling toward us. While they roll right over me, the leaves hitting his back sound like shrapnel slamming against a brass dome. As he is pushed to the ground, the collar disappears from around my throat.

Heaping mussed hair away from my eyes, I frown into the jets of hot wind crackling over my skin. Then, as the leaves settle, Bae appears. His chest is heaving, fists clenched, shadowed jaw thrust forward like he's ready to lunge and tear someone to tiny shreds. As the other warlock struggles up onto one elbow, Bae growls down at him.

"Cohen, I told you to stay away."

"We've waited long enough," this Cohen guy growls back. "All of us. We'll find out what we need to know and then finally move on."

*Find out what we need to know?* And what does "move on" mean exactly?

Bae's features change—suddenly he looks ferocious, even to me. Steam emanates from his body, surrounding his frame in a ghostly crimson glow.

"Leave," Bae snarls. "Leave *now!*"

Cohen shakes his head like it's all so amusing and unnecessary. But as he pushes to his feet, he changes, too. Not the whole *morph into another creature* thing. I've heard about shape-shifters and it's not that. His body grows, his back curves, and hair springs like a thick tuft down the center of his head; I imagine raised hackles all the way down to a hidden barbed tail.

His green glowing eyes shrink into his skull. The corners of his mouth cut back toward his ears. His leer gleams iridescent white, eye teeth elongated to points so sharp, I can almost feel them pierce my skin. His smell has changed, too—something that reminds me of damp dirty rags.

He steps back on one hind leg, and then springs, a blinding full-body lash.

The resulting fight is so savage, so fast, I can't keep up with who's on top, who's mauling who, whether either one of them will survive to crawl away. I'd wondered whether warlocks have blood. They do. Red is flying everywhere. Some even slaps my face.

I search around madly hoping to find... what? A lump of wood? A rock? As if that will do any good. I can only stand back while the battle kicks into overdrive. Fences, trees, parked cars... everything in their path is smashed. When their bodies hit the pavement or asphalt, gaping craters are left behind. Around me, outside lights flash on. People edge out onto porches only to herd younger children back inside away from the carnage.

Bae is thrown into the air. Coming down, he strikes me and I'm knocked aside like a bowling pin. I hit the ground hard enough to see stars. Pain shoots through my chest like I've broken a rib or three.

Then, as quickly as it had begun, the battle ends, like a hurricane suddenly unplugged from its source of wind and thrashing rain. Cohen is gone. Bae is crouched on his knees and one set of knuckles. His head hangs as he wipes blood from his bruised and battered mouth.

Wincing, I struggle to my feet. Tasting blood and grit on my tongue and my teeth, I hear an emergency vehicle siren roaring closer. I ache all over. I can't imagine how broken Bae feels. But he doesn't look beaten. Pushing to his feet, he looks as determined as ever... to always protect me... to never back down.

As he brings me close and his arms wrap around me, my throat thickens and tears leak from the corners of my closed eyes. He feels so good, so strong, and how could that Cohen dweeb ever think I could swallow that Bae had lied to me about who was behind my unexpected visit to the Realm? I know who my friends are, and Bae stands head and shoulders above them all.

He cups my cheek and searches my eyes. "I'm sorry," he groans.

I hiccup out a laugh. "For saving my life?"

"I was late. It won't happen again."

I give a cheeky, wobbly grin. "So you're hanging around a while longer?"

His smile is slow and sexy. "Just try to get rid of me."

Then his head angles, his gaze drops to my lips and his hand on my cheek seems to draw me closer. A thrill rips through my body; despite the scrapes, I feel so alive, I could be vibrating. I've been kissed before, but never by Bae. This minute, I want that more than my next breath.

I feel that he's curious. Maybe even ready. So... I lean in...

But before my eyes can drift shut, over Bae's shoulder, I catch sight of something flying toward us. A blast of energy. A huge doomsday fireball. A screech pierces my eardrums at the same time Bae spins around and squares me away behind him.

I don't think. It's not planned. It's pure reaction. Maybe instinct.

I step away from Bae and thrust out one arm. Rapids of glaring energy explode out from the palm of my hand—from the broiling, pissed-off pit of my soul.

# CHAPTER 12

AS PLUMES of dust and debris waft to the ground, that fire truck and its siren roar up... and then continue speeding right on down the road.

On shaky legs, I dust myself off and scan Ground Zero. Instead of panicking and screaming, people are calmly moving back into their houses. Outside lights are switching off. There is no sign of Cohen or his fireball, only the destruction left behind.

Bae is gripping my upper arms. His smile says he is outright amazed as well as grateful *and* proud.

My brain catches up as I cough against the dirt invading my lungs. "Did I really do what I think I just did?" That kick-ass retaliation blast came from me?

His eyebrows slant, chiding but also teasing. "You'll need a few lessons in control."

I grin and cough again. "Don't want to blow up the world or anything."

Bae's smile slips. "Precisely."

I have this crazy urge to laugh. Because this is so *unbelievable*. This cannot be real. It seems like a moment ago I felt as if I would always be *Looney Brin*. Always on the outer. Heck, maybe I'm already locked away in a padded psychiatric ward cell, rocking back and forth, grinning as I escape into the twisted tunnels of my mind. Maybe this is one of Professor Hinkley's parallel universes. Maybe, after a good night's sleep, I'll wake up and find it's Christmas Day when I was eight and this has all been a dream.

I close my eyes, give a sigh. When I open my eyes again, there's no more pain and we're home, in our bedroom. I'm dressed in my PJ's and Bae is standing near the dresser, his broad bare back facing me. After all the excitement of the evening, I am so ready to lay back and chill-ax. I'm too physically and mentally exhausted to want to quiz Bae about anything now.

There is, however, one question I need to ask.

"That truck didn't stop. Those people shut their doors and went back inside like nothing had happened."

"They'll have no memory of the battle. The damage has already been reversed."

He turns around holding the ruby in the palms of both hands. As he walks over, he opens his fingers. Like a flower blooming, the ruby shines out, brighter than ever before.

My heart melts and I smile. "It's so beautiful," I murmur.

"That glow means you're truly becoming one of us. That you're unique and growing... getting stronger."

I arch a brow. "Complicated."

He nods. "It's enough that you accept it."

"After tonight, I don't guess I have a choice."

"You have nothing but choices ahead of you. And in time, you will reconcile who you *were* with who you were always meant to be."

My eyes drift shut and I feel as if I'm dissolving. Next thing I know, I'm in bed with Bae lying beside me. The ruby is back on the drawers. As the lights magically fade, the glow from the stone illuminates the room with a soft cherry glow.

I roll onto my side to face him. He's never looked more sexy, more handsome. I can't believe he's here... that in a way, he's mine.

"Tell me you won't go away again."

For the first time ever, Bae reaches out to curl me into the hard steamy heaven of his chest. "Don't worry," he says. "You're safe."

Snuggling in, I sigh and through drowsy eyes watch our ruby. But something has changed. Propped up against the wall near the stone...?

It's a painting. One I thought I'd destroyed eight years ago.

My beautiful reindeer kissing the snow.

And then that wall becomes a canvas all its own, a brilliant water color with pictures coming to life. I smell a fire crackling in the hearth, see snow falling outside the window, hear silver bells tinkling on the Christmas tree, feel a mother and her daughter hugging... talking...

Laughing.

As a tear slips down the side of my face, I murmur, "Thank you."

Bae's warm lips press against my brow. "You're welcome."

Real or not, as I watch those cherished pictures from my past, I feel a shift deep inside of me. Sure, it's weird. Confusing. But it is what it is. I am who I am. Whatever's to come, I'll need to accept my fate.

I'm actually looking forward to what might happen next.

---

More Young Adult books by Robyn Grady:

Thunderstruck—coming soon!

---

Turn the page to read *Dangerous Honesty* by Ebony McKenna...

# DANGEROUS HONESTY

EBONY MCKENNA

# CHAPTER 1

I CAN DO THIS. I can fake my way through this and everything will be fine. All I have to do is remember every single lie I've ever told. If I don't, my carefully constructed reality will rip apart like a pair of Nike knockoffs.

Then I remember something else, just as I open the door to head in to Homework Club. I need some new lies in my back pocket, just in case. Because if my friends are here—and some of them are bound to be here—they'll ask me why *I'm* here, and I have to be ready with an excuse. Which is just another word for a lie.

Not that studying is anything to be embarrassed about. Our school must have the biggest Homework Club in Orlando. Homework is expected, we all do it, it's not cool to fail. But as I said, if my friends saw me here, they'd be wondering why someone who'd previously claimed to have a private tutor was studying at school.

What's the fresh lie in my back pocket? My tutor is sick, but it needs to be more than that, I suspect she's been lying to me for a while now and—this is the cherry on top—she must have a new boyfriend and she's all loved up and irresponsible. It's a believable story because I put in the extra embellishment. Plus I'll get sympathy for being abandoned. Perfect.

Don't judge me. Lying is a victimless crime, I'm not depriving anybody of a living or getting something extra that I'm not entitled to, OK? So spare your judgmental curled lip and have a good hard look at yourself why don't you? Admit it, you tell lies all day. Little fibs about how early you went to sleep last night (because if you told the parentals what time you really fell asleep, they'd drag you before a therapist.) How your best friend's new hairstyle looks awesome (even though it makes her ears stick out) not to mention the biggest lie of all, "my phone must have been dead".

So why *am* I going to Homework Club? Because failing is about the most frightening thing that could ever happen. It will not happen to me. My parents didn't put everything on the line to get me into this school to see me fail. So I won't fail. I'll come to Homework Club for help. It's that simple. Which means a few more lies. In the grand scheme of things, what's one more?

There he is, the nerdiest boy in physics class (and there is serious nerd competition here) solving college-level problems with his nerdy friends. They are going to be rocket scientists for sure. They are captains of the Physics Club (of course we have one of them), they make robots in their spare time and are on first-name basis with the NASA crews who live down the end of the freeway.

Obligatory throat clearing happens on my part as I approach their table. The three of them look at me as if I'm some kind of alien species.

"This is a little embarrassing," is my opening gambit. "I need help with physics and this is Homework Club and you're all here, and... here I am."

It's only a partial lie, I'm not the least bit embarrassed but I do need help. I'm not this pathetic normally, but I'm sure they need me to sound a little helpless. It triggers the knight-in-shining-armor response. They'll fall out of their chairs to help me.

One of them, I have absolutely no idea what his name is, twitches his shoulder and turns bright red. This is going great!

"Fine. Sit down," Nerd Leader says. I know his name is Malcolm, because he writes the physics column in our school newspaper every month.

Yes, we have one of them, too.

"Thanks, Mal."

The other two look at him with betrayal writ large in their expressions. He's letting a non-geek into their personal space.

Well, I am virtually a stranger. I guess I never have spoken to them before. Time to make introductions. "I'm Bianca. I need help with physics homework so I came here looking for the three of you." That was the absolute truth, but I did kind of "cute-up" my voice to sound ever so slightly helpless.

"Noah," one of them mumbles. "Ed," the other says. I know that can't be their real names—it's their Americanized names their parents gave them to enroll in school. Not that their background bothers me one bit. A brain is a brain, and I need theirs.

As I take the seat next to Malcolm, he looks me up and down and says, "What will I get out of this?"

A brain exchange is exactly what I was expecting. "I'm happy to help you with another subject you need help with, like English or something." My English is rock-star.

"I excel at English," he says with a sneer.

Whoops, time to back it up. This is one of those occasions where lies take a back seat to diplomacy. Although diplomacy is kind of lying to keep your temper in check, and make the other person out to be better than they are so they get to save face.

"I'm sorry. That was accidentally racist. I was just thinking of something non-sciencey that I might be able to help you with. It was the first thing I thought of. Again, I'm sorry." I really didn't mean to sound so rude. I might be a liar out of necessity, but I don't ever want to be known as "the other B-word".

Generally speaking, most people who are awesome at math and science struggle with humanities, and vice versa. By the time we get to our year level, everything is elective except English. If you're big in the arts, you can cruise your way into a degree without ever facing another math problem. But if your English sucks, your whole life sucks.

"I'm not struggling with any of my studies," Malcolm says. "I chose subjects where I shine."

Confident, isn't he? We have a year and a half of high school left. Some of the übersmart students are already doing final year studies. We'll find out our college placements all too soon, which is why I need to get on top of everything right now. I feel like my future is wobbling like that bridge in Tacoma in a strong wind.

In both cases, because of bad physics.

Time to lay on the flattery. "I'm incredibly grateful you're excelling in physics, because that's where I'm falling down. I thought it would slip into my head like all the others. But some days I feel like my brain has installed a physics-proof fence and nothing is getting through."

He looks at me, like he still hasn't accepted the fact I've sat down and opened my laptop. With a shrug he says, "Fine then. I charge by the hour. What nights do you need me over?"

Burning embarrassment roars through me. I can't afford to pay him (not that anyone knows how little I have—another brilliant lie I've managed to maintain). There's no way he can come to my house either. Then he'd find out too much. It would be far too dangerous for anyone to find out the truth about me.

"That's not how Homework Club works!" I sound like I'm warming up for a tantrum. It's not far from the truth. "We're supposed to help each other out, based on need." Don't I sound like a right and proper little socialist?

Noah and Ed sit there with their mouths open, hardly believing the exchange going on. I check to make sure my mouth's closed as well. This is not going the way I thought it would.

In English Lit, our teacher, Doctor Jenkins, said to keep an eye out for signs of power in relationships. She said the person who held the power was the one who cared the least. Right now, Malcolm cares the least and holds all the power.

Dr Jenkins also said Shakespeare's Macbeth wasn't really about Macbeth, it was actually all about Lady Macbeth, because without her there'd be no story. Then she spent a whole class banging on about needing to smash the patriarchy.

I miss Doctor Jenkins.

Her words are in my head now because I'm the one that needs help and Malcolm needs nothing from me. This means I have no power and it's spreading horrible lumps of fear-fail through me.

A confident smile plays over Malcolm's face. "You can't help me, can you? So if you want to pass physics and rent my brain, you'll need to pay."

If I'd had the money I would have hired a real tutor in the first place and I wouldn't be in this mess. If my parents had money, we'd be living together in a proper house. My Saturday bakery job barely covers some of the debt. But there's no way I'm letting him in on my hideous secret. Which means trading the only thing I have left. With a shrug I say, "We can date or some-thing. I'll go out with you."

His jaw drops. Because I totally said it and he heard it. So did Noah and Ed.

Then something strange happens. He cracks up laughing. Huge gusts of cackling blurt out. Everyone in here, and I mean *everyone*, turns and looks at us.

When he stops, his voice drops to a conspiratorial whisper. "You are hilarious. I can't believe you said that. Like I need some kind of pity date. Hate to break it to you, but girls love geeks, and I don't have any issues in that department."

I find myself apologizing.

Again!

Which has to be one of my favorite little fibs. Saying sorry, early and often, loses face but gains trust.

Shaking his head, he says, "Did you really think that would work?"

Well, yes I did. And now I have nothing. We've been here twenty minutes and I have yet to look at a single physics problem because I've gone and fallen into a Malcolm-sized problem, right up to my neck.

"This was a stupid idea. I don't know why I bothered." I pack my things and move away. I'll sit by myself. I'll search YouTube videos to see if someone else is posting physics life-hacks on line. I bet someone is. I bet I never need Malcolm and his smug nerdy friends ever again.

"Hey, Bee, come and sit with us." It's Mandeep, calling to me from the other side of the room. Am I glad to see her! Welcoming faces greet me. Most of my friends are here. They even have their books open, so they must all be studying.

"Hey Mandy, what happened to your tutor?" I ask.

"She got deported," she says with a shrug, like it's no big deal.

Instantly I feel sorry for the tutor, even though I never met her. Also, I wish I'd thought of that excuse. Now Mandeep's said it, I can't use it.

"How about yours?" she asks.

"She phoned in sick."

"I thought your tutor was a boy?"

Yikes! Have I mixed up a lie? Not possible. Maybe she's testing me? "You must have heard wrong." Denial is a liar's best alibi. "Anyway, she left it to the last minute to phone in sick and then she was supposed to find me a substitute and yadda yadda, I think she's got a new boyfriend and is all love-struck, which leaves me completely in the lurch." Play the sympathy card. "Upshot is, I really need help with physics. How about you?"

*Nice save, brain. You've earned chocolate.*

Mandeep gives me a confident smile. "Sit down and join in. We'll muddle through it together."

I love Mandy so much. I know exactly when she's telling lies too. Takes one to know one, right? She's never called me on mine, and I've never called her out either. We have an understanding. And no, in the three years we've been in high school together, she's never been to my place.

Nobody has ever been to my place. If anyone saw where I lived, who I live with, everything would unravel. Absolutely everything.

Even the lies that aren't mine to tell.

# CHAPTER 2

SATURDAY MORNINGS FIND me at the bakery in the mega-mall. I'll let you in on a secret. The words "baked fresh today" on the sticker means we've taken the loaf out of the freezer and put it in the oven. In effect we have baked it; we just haven't made it from scratch. Anything left over at the end of the day gets donated to the food bank. Proper good little citizens that we are.

Some other bakery secrets: The blueberries in the blueberry muffins are fruit-flavored bits, not whole blueberries. Possibly made from apple and pear paste. The "three-chocolate brownies" are made by mashing up the entire range of chocolate chip cookies that didn't sell the day before.

Also, everybody demands healthier options on the menu but nobody buys them.

I wish they were the worst of the lies in this place, but it's not safe to talk. Maybe in a few years, when things settle down and we're out of this, I can tell you. But not now.

While taking out a batch of super-goo salted caramel crave cookies from the oven, I hear the ding of the counter bell.

A male voice says, "Never trust a thin cook." It takes me an extra second to realize it's Malcolm. I hardly recognize him out of school uniform. He looks so sloppy and relaxed, sun-faded clothes that are either hand-me-downs or from a charity shop. I know, because my clothes are all from charity shops. If you go to the right ones, you can get some decent labels.

"I'll take that as a compliment." It's a survival instinct, so that I'm never accused of eating the produce I'm supposed to be selling. That was drummed into me during induction, and I've never forgotten it. Of course, I can buy the cookies and muffins at a staff discount, but they're already garnishing my wages by two thirds, so I can't really afford the empty calories.

It could be worse. I've heard stories about places that take all your wages, even the tips.

Malcolm has arrived during a sudden lull in customers. It can be five deep during hungry hour, but he's timed it perfectly. "How can I help you?"

"Can you cook?" His face is full of intensity, his usually full and relaxed lips are tight and tense.

I make a showroom wave of the equipment behind me. "It's my job."

"Good. I need help with cooking."

Oh really? Things are suddenly interesting. "I thought you didn't do subjects you couldn't ace?" Because to cave in immediately would spoil my fun. He was rude to me in Homework Club, but now he needs me, I'm enjoying his discomfort. I'm also enjoying the sudden power shift. Thank you Doctor Jenkins.

"I'm not doing food tech," Malcolm says, "and don't pretend you're not interested because I know you need me."

Food Technology is one of the most popular classes in school. The principal says this is the result of so many cooking reality shows. Not that any student I know has time to watch anything, what with coursework, sports, extra-curricular and part time jobs.

Back to Malcolm. He's not being straight with me. Because I'm the expert on bending the truth. "Why do you need to know how to cook?"

"I need to feed myself. For a month."

"Frozen dinners. Two minutes in the microwave. Done." Honestly, why is he trying to be nice all of a sudden? I made an idiot of myself in front of him and his friends during the week, and now he's asking for my help. What, so he can set me up to fail again? "Have you made some kind of weird bet? Is that why you're asking me?"

A shrug. "The worst kind of bet. My parents won't take their holiday unless I can prove I'll still be alive when they get home. I'm not allowed to cheat either. I have to make everything from scratch."

"And in exchange?" Because there needs to be something in this for me.

"Fine, I'll let you go out with me."

The smugness! Throwing that back in my face. I give him side-eyes and wait for the real offer.

"I'll help you with physics homework."

Nice one! It's like somebody pulled back the curtains and the sun shone into my life. I want to punch the air I'm so happy.

As enjoyable as this newfound relaxed attitude between us is, more customers are arriving and I can't draw this out any longer. Plus, I can feel my supervisor, Crystal, burning holes into my head with her eyes because I'm talking to someone and not selling anything. "I finish work at one, come back then."

"Do we have a deal?" he asks, shifting his weight from one foot to the other. "Physics for food?"

He's so different and appealing when he's trying to be nice. But I'll deny that if you ever bring it up. "I'll tell you after my shift is done."

---

AT FIVE TO ONE, Malcolm is back, sitting at the plastic faux-cane garden setting outside the off-brand grocery store.

"Is that your new boyfriend?" Crystal asks. She has the world's worst imagination, always thinking people are up to something. She'd know all about that.

"He's my new homework buddy." As I say it, I realize that's exactly what he is. Woot! I'm getting help with physics!

"He's not an investigator sniffing around?"

I sigh. "Not unless they're hiring high school students."

She turns back to the ovens muttering something about spies coming in all sizes, and not for the first time I wonder what Crystal might be like if she didn't have to be constantly paranoid.

I guess it's a bit like me wondering what I'd be like if I didn't have to lie all the time.

The moment I take my apron off, Malcolm is up from the garden setting and strolling over to the bakery, his stride somewhere between jaunty and jittery. Wow, his parents must have really scared him.

"Let's get started. I'll even help you with physics first, then do some cooking," Malcolm says before I can draw breath. "Your place?"

"Er, no, I can't..." Hell no, he can't come to my place. Nobody can come to my place. "But I can come to yours."

"But you don't have your books with you. Do you?"

"You've got the same books, and logically, if you want to learn to cook, you're better off learning in your own kitchen, getting used to your own oven and pots and pans and all that."

Bullet dodged.

"Fine, whatever." But there's no matching shrug, so I can tell he's still really uptight about everything. "My car's in the lot."

Amongst a sea of sedans and SUVs, his is a shiny blue auto. "Nice wheels."

"Sarcasm becomes you," he shoots back.

"I mean it, it's a really nice car." Why doesn't he believe me?

"It's a Mom-car." I swear his eyes are rolling, just from the sound of his voice. "She just wants me to be safe."

Isn't that what all parents want for their kids?

It has all the safety bells and whistles. It won't stop bleeping until I put my seat belt on. Then it makes more bleeps as Mal reverses.

What do I do now? Small talk feels weird, but I have to say something. In the nick of time it starts raining, and the wipers come on automatically. I'm starting to wonder if Malcolm is the beneficiary of a substantial trust fund.

When we pull into the drive, his house is e-freaking-normous. I have to act cool and pretend it's not all that, because around here, everyone lives in big houses. It's right on the artificial lake that meanders through the whole development. "Do you ever go fishing?"

"Pretty sure it's only a drainage basin."

That's a shame. So many lakes, so little use. "Ever get 'gators?"

"I think there are people to take care of that."

Entering the house, I'm getting the distinct impression Mal is an only child, because the family portraits on the wall are of the three of them.

No wonder his parents are worried about leaving him to look after himself. I can't get over the huge house for only three people. I don't even know what many of the rooms are for! We pass one on the way down the hall that looks like it's an office, but I dart a quick look and all I can see are couches. Maybe the desk was behind the door somewhere?

The kitchen is another world. This is better equipped than the restaurant my father used to work in. Admittedly, he worked in a dive, and everything else was divey too. Not that I can let Malcolm know this either. It's all keep-a-straight-face, act cool and focus on homework.

But the kitchen! We're here to cook, right? I'm gonna have so much fun in here.

I thought we'd be studying at the kitchen table, but Malcolm has a whole other room upstairs, just for him to do homework and read books in. It has a gorgeous timber bookshelf utterly groaning with novels and trophies, two couches and a desk with an adjustable platform for his computer so he can stand up to type. "That's like the ones we have at school," I say, more for something to say instead of "Wow, your house is huge!"

There isn't a television in here. That's in a whole other room all to itself.

He pushes aside previous papers and other textbooks, and makes room for me at the desk. OK brain, stop thinking about how big this house is and let some physics in.

Truth be told, cooking is so much easier than physics. With cooking, it's mostly all set out for you. If you follow the instructions, you get a result. It doesn't feel like that with physics. I'm looking at the diagrams and formulas Malcolm is drawing. I'm copying them down longhand on spare paper, hoping it reinforces some kind of paper-pen-hand-brain-memory circuits. I'm even trying to think about cooking as a metaphor for physics. The problems are the meal, and the formulas are the ingredients and methods for achieving the chocolate cake with butter frosting and dark cherries.

---

IT WOULD HAVE BEEN a great metaphor if I had actual chocolate on hand. I'll have to visualize the chocolate melting on my tongue, then firing up my reward centre in my brain, giving me a temporary high.

Sometimes it even works.

At the end of half an hour of achieving not very much, Malcolm pushes back in his chair. "Why did you sign up for physics if you suck at it?"

"You need to work at your social skills."

He raises an eyebrow and waits for a real answer.

I blow air out the side of my mouth. It sends some of my fringe flapping off my forehead. "Because I... thought it would be really good, and I didn't know how hard it would really be. But girls have to stick with math and science to keep their options open. I am good at math. But I figured specialist's math would be too much of the same-old as regular math, but now I wish I had... Why are you looking at me like that?"

He smiles and shakes his head. "You're kind of making sense. What do you want to study in college?"

"I thought it would be so cool to do aerospace engineering, but mechanical engineering is my fallback. What are you doing after school?"

"Robotics club, then tennis."

He said it with such a straight face. "I mean where are you going to college?"

"I have literally no idea."

That pulls me up. "That's not possible. You can't have *literally* no idea. Your brain hasn't stopped functioning."

He touches my ear and looks behind it, as if there's some kind of switch behind it. "Are you sure you're not on the spectrum?"

Malcolm's the one asking me that? With a shrug I say, "Everyone gets a few freebies."

I can't believe we're bantering like this. This is the first time we've just talked, hung out. It's kind of nice. Plus I'm looking forward to teaching him how to cook. I bet the pantry is groaning with food.

"Earth to Bianca." Malcolm waves his hand in front of my face.

Uh-oh.

"You're a regular space-cadet."

"Sorry, was thinking of something else."

"Mmmm. I think I've worked out why you're not doing so great with physics."

He's spot on with that. "OK, I promise to apply myself."

For the next half hour we work hard. Really hard. I mean, I'm making so many notes and writing things out, my wrist is killing me and I'm developing a callus on my rude finger from where it presses against the pen. I'm not sure any of this study tonight has gone in, but at least I've tried and if we try again tomorrow, some of it might penetrate my brain and settle in somewhere.

"OK, we'd better stop there. You look wasted," Malcolm says.

"I'm feeling it."

"Don't tell me you're too tired to cook?" he says.

That would be rude, and it would make me out to be someone who goes back on her word. That's something I don't do if I can possibly help it. "I'm good. Cooking uses a completely different part of the brain anyway. Let's see what kind of ingredients you have."

Downstairs in the amazing kitchen—did I mention the extraction fan looks like a chandelier?—I open the double-door refrigerator. There's a distinct echo coming from inside. "Well, there's your problem!" There's nothing in here. How can someone have so much money and so little food?

There's a pizza box with one slice in it, a side shelf full of sticky condiments (probably a year past their date) and a quart of milk with barely anything in the bottom.

"Told you I need help," Malcolm says with a shrug.

"You need an intervention."

"It's not that bad. There are instant noodles in the pantry."

If I wanted instant noodles for dinner, I would have stayed home. "Instant noodles are an insult to my people."

"No way, really? I had no idea your parents were from..."

I love this game. Stepping back from the refrigerator, I give him ample time to study my face.

"...um, Europe... maybe Italy?"

"Nearly there. Fourth generation Portuguese via California. My folks came for the gold rush and stayed for the women." Honestly, I could pretty much pass for anything and people believe it. But Portuguese is also the truth. Mostly.

"So why did you move from California to Florida?"

Lie number four hundred and eighty seven. "We needed the rain."

His head tilts back and he laughs so hard he snorts. But we can't stand here laughing and not eating. "Grab your money, I'm taking you food shopping."

WE ARE NOT SHOPPING in the big brand supermarket, because I know a much cheaper place. Today the staples are on special, which puts me in a good mood. Potatoes, rice and beans are the way to go, but we won't be wrapping anything in lettuce. "That's nearly three times the price from last week," I say to the clerk.

"Too much rain—we've got a short supply," she says with a shrug. "If the rain holds off the prices will come down again in a few weeks."

Malcolm gives me a nudge, "I don't think my parents are that fussed about the price."

Uh-oh, my poverty is showing. "It's the principle of the thing. You have to haggle, otherwise they don't take you seriously."

"I'm seeing it now..." Malcolm says with a slow nod.

My eyebrows shoot up. What's he seeing? What have I let slip?

"...Haggling is *such* a stereotype." Ah yes, the southern European thing. Not really racist, is it? I'd let out a sigh of relief except it would give me away.

It wasn't raining when we arrived at the market, but it's thumping down now, so we dash to the car, shielding the paper carry bags with our bodies. Once we're back at the house, Malcolm grabs me the most enormous towel I've ever seen and cranks up the heating like it's no big thing.

I swear there's steam coming off me as we wash the ingredients in the double-sink and get chopping. There's a second sink in another room, by the way. They call it a Butler's Pantry, and I'm starting to wonder if his family have an actual butler.

Maybe they should get one to take care of Malcolm. Poor fool, he can't even hold a knife the right way. "You're going to slice your thumb off. Dry your hands and dry the handle, too, otherwise it'll slip and you'll cut yourself. Now put the tip of the knife onto the board like this, so you're angling the knife down, and slice, see?"

He tries it my way, then gives up and goes back to hacking at the celery.

"I'm serious. If your parents walked in right now, there's no way they'll leave you alone with knives. Hold it like this." I move my hands on top of his and physically demonstrate. "You have to hold it by the handle, don't put your finger over the top of the knife, you're not getting enough pressure. Honestly, it's a wonder..."

It's a wonder I can even concentrate. I don't know why but I'm holding his hands and something weird is going on in my brain because I can't get my next thought right.

He clears his throat and makes this weird cough, like this is really uncomfortable and suddenly things are super awkward between us for no good reason.

Emergency distraction. This kitchen is stunning. I think the benches are actual granite, and they've got these little sparkly flecks in them. "I'll do the onions." It wouldn't be fair to make a beginner chop them; they'd throw in the towel. "Do you have another wooden chopping board?"

He hauls one out from an extra-wide pot drawer.

"This is going to be the onion and garlic board from now on, OK? Don't chop anything else on it, or it will stink to the Andes and back." I've launched into assertive mode because this is so weird between us and his messy wet hair looks adorable and I need to create some kind of distance between us.

*Hang on, did I say Andes or Rockies?*

*Move on, don't dwell on it.*

"I'll share the best secret about chopping onions. Cut them in half and lay them on the board face down, so the worst of the juices soak into the board. Now do something else for a few minutes, so when you get around to cutting them you don't cry."

The detergent hiding under the sink is one of those extra lemony ones, so I give my hands a good wash to get the worst of the smell out. From the corner of my vision, Malcolm has gone back to chopping the celery the wrong way. He slices them with such force it sends a slew of chunks rolling onto the bench and tumbling to the floor.

"I'll get them." I scoop the stray chunks off the floor and into my palms, then take them to the sink to wash them clean.

"You're not serious?"

Dammit, I'm looking poor again, aren't I? Wait, there's a good reason for this. "Wasting food damages the planet," I trot out like a good little environmental crusader. "If you'd chopped them properly, you wouldn't have been feeding the floor in the first place."

"Why do you get so defensive?"

"Sorry." Because he's right, and I do not want to go down that route of why I'm being defensive every time he gets anywhere near the truth. Having friends is one thing, but being too friendly runs the risk of people finding things out about me. That would be beyond stupid. "I'll chop the rest of the celery if you like."

He tilts his head to the side. "But I need to learn how to do it for myself, don't I?"

"True. OK, try again. Put the point of the knife on the board and hold the handle at the end, then you get the best pressure, which you would already know because you're so good at physics."

He forms a half grin and then concentrates really hard at the job. It's slow going, and kind of painful to watch, but he has to start somewhere.

The urge to take over is killing me. Plus I'm getting hungry, so there's that too.

I grab a pot and flick the controls on low just to warm it up. The pantry has several fancy bottles of cooking oils so I choose the one that brags the highest smoke point. I chop the onions as fast as I can but still end up with the sniffles. Ah well. Knife must have been blunt. The ground beef goes in next and I jab at it with the wooden spoon, breaking it up. We're making the most "bog-standard" Spaghetti Bolognese, because if Malcolm can't cook this, he may as well give up.

He should be stirring things in the pot by now, but I can hear him still slicing the celery. So.

*Chop.*

Very.

*Chop. Chop.*

Slowly. I. Want. To. Grind.

*Chop.*

My. Teeth.

"Throw it all into the pot and give it a good stir."

Most of it even makes it into the pot as he scrapes it in.

"I'll do the carrots because they need to cook for a long time so we'd better get them in."

"What about the tomato..." He picks up the jar. "What is *passata* anyway?"

"A fancy name for puree. No, don't put that in before the meat cooks, otherwise it goes all mushy and weird. Right, how are we going for time?"

It's nearly five. We need to crank this up if we're going to get any more homework done. Which I figure we can do while everything is simmering. "We've got about an hour and a half before your parents get home. Text them and tell them you're making dinner."

"You're so bossy," he says, fishing out his phone.

"I'm not bossy, I have leadership qualities."

---

THE SIMMERING SMELLS of dinner make is super hard to concentrate on our textbooks, but some of this might actually make its way into my brain if I can just focus. Unfortunately, I seem to only be able to focus on Malcolm's hands. I don't know why. I only know that his skin looks kind of amazing and his fingers aren't long and gangly, nor are they short and stubby. They're just kind of... perfectly proportioned, which is an odd thing to say about hands. I mean, they're just *hands*, right?

The rain is hammering down outside, so loud it sounds like stones bashing the roof. "Wait a minute, is that—"

"Hail. Yeah, I think so." Malcolm gets up.

"This I gotta see!"

We walk out to the decking area to get a better view—it's under the roofline, so we're protected from the worst of it. Real hailstones the size of pennies are bouncing off the ground and spilling into the deck like candies out of a piñata.

As I move back I slip.

"Steady." Malcolm grabs me and holds me up.

The hail is so loud it drowns out just about everything except my thumping heart. Thumping because I nearly fell over. Not because I can't stop looking into Malcolm's dark, dark, gorgeously dark eyes that I'd never noticed were so dark before, they're so dark.

"Wow," I splutter. "Good reflexes."

It would be so very wrong of me, seriously wrong, to want to get friendly with him, because this is not what I'm here for. I'm here to study hard, work harder and pay back the family debt as fast as I can. I'm not here to mess around with boys and get distracted. That would be dangerously stupid.

And yet he's so seriously distracting. In the grand scheme of things, what could one little distraction *really* do?

Steady on my feet again, before I can counsel myself against it, I lean in and kiss Malcolm. Bliss bombs go off in my head as he starts kissing me back. He's gorgeous, he's so freaking smart and ohhhh, he is such a very good kisser. I could totally lose my mind kissing him.

"Sweetie? What are you do— Oh! Hello, there!"

Heat roars over my face, then a fast chill takes over, caused by us pulling away all of a sudden. I make a hash of clearing my throat.

"Oh. Hi, Mom," Malcolm says, all super-casual.

He might be *mas que nada* but I am super-fried. That kiss. There was truth in that kiss, and it's scaring the hell out of me.

# CHAPTER 3

"COME on out of the rain and tell us what's going on in the kitchen," Malcolm's mom says.

I hadn't even noticed the hail turn back to rain. Bit distracted.

"Mum, this is Bianca, um, Bianca, this is Mom."

I can't call her that.

"Gloria," she says, opening the bi-fold door wider to guide us back inside.

Stepping over the threshold, Malcolm leans down to my ear. "Don't ever tell anyone Mom calls me 'Sweetie'."

"I promise."

*She calls him "Sweetie"? That's money in the bank.*

"You're home early," Malcolm says at the sight of both parents in the kitchen.

"You said you were cooking," the man who must be Malcolm's dad says. "We got worried and came as soon as we could."

"That would explain why I'm here," I chime in, all smiles and nice-nice. "I'm teaching him how to make dinners. I promise he won't burn the house down."

More awkward introductions follow. I learn Mal's dad is called David, and he is utterly freaked out that his son has put match to stovetop.

"Dinner will be ready in about half an hour. I promise you it's safe to eat," I offer. Is this super-awkward or what? His parents walking in on us? Rookie mistake!

David bustles about and sets the table with linen place mats and bowls and wine glasses (for two of them). I show Mal how to measure spaghetti. "Put your thumb and finger into a circle—that's two serves. You'll probably get a little left over. Leftover spaghetti is even better." I'm babbling now because his parents are here and they're watching me. They can't believe Malcolm is listening to me and taking it all in.

"Maybe we will get that holiday," Gloria says.

"We haven't eaten yet," David says, then suddenly looks at me and adds, "No offence."

The atmosphere is so home-ish, so relaxed and a bit teasing. Like a real family. I've gotta pull myself together before memories leak in. It's like a dam, holding it all back, holding it steady. My lies are a strong dam wall, looking solid. I can't let anything form a crack or the memories are going to flood out and I'm going to cry in front of these lovely people. Or worse.

This is why I shouldn't even be here. I should be back at my place, eating and studying by myself so I can get through until the end of next year, and then everything will be more settled and I won't have to worry about what I say or what I think, or what anyone else thinks, because it will all be sorted out and paid off by then.

The four of us eating dinner together should be relaxing, but if anything it's making me more tense as I try so hard not to enjoy being in a normal family situation. It only reminds me of what I could lose.

That's why this can't go any further. Being friendly is far too dangerous. I'm gonna trip up and accidentally tell the truth and then everything will turn to crap. Not just for me, but for everyone.

The hailstorm is gone, but it's still raining at the end of dinner. The rain doesn't bother me, it's no big deal, but Gloria insists on being the perfect mom.

"You've created such a lovely meal, I insist on driving you home."

No no no no no, oh good lordy no. "Honestly, I'm fine. I always catch the bus."

"Not in this weather," she says.

"I can drive you home," Malcolm offers.

"You know how I feel about you driving at night," his mom says. "I need to get some things at the store anyway, so that's settled, I'll take you home."

The only thing settled is the ball of anxiety in the pit of my stomach. Instead, my mouth says, "Thank you so much, you're too generous."

JUST AS I THOUGHT, Gloria does the "getting to know you" patter that can lead to so many mistakes. I have to bring my A-game to this, but all I want to do is sleep.

"How long have you and Malcolm known each other?"

"It's kind of hard to say. I mean, we've known of each other for years at school, but we only recently started doing homework together." The trouble is, this is the truth, but I don't know what kind of truth Malcolm will tell his parents. I'm hoping he does the teenage boy thing and grunts at them and goes to his room. But I was in their house, kissing their son, and making myself at home in their kitchen. I owe them pure politeness. "I am finding physics really hard going, and he's so smart."

"He is a very smart boy. I wish he'd apply himself more. Maybe he'll listen to you because he stopped listening to his father and me ages ago." Gloria finishes with a half-chuckle, as if she's making a joke. But there's a kernel of truth in there. Then she adds, "You'll let me know in plenty of time where to turn off, right?"

I sure will, because this is where I catch the school bus. The second one. There's a mall across the road where I use the bathrooms to change into my uniform. "You're good. It's a right at Johnson Avenue. If you hit the toll road you've gone too far."

"Your parents were clever—you're just inside the school zone."

Flop-sweat trickles under my bra. Who keeps a map of the school border in their heads? "Sounds like you're on the board of governors."

"David is, and I help him out whenever I can." She takes a right into Johnson. "Which house number did you say it was?"

My head is humming. Am I breathing harder? Everything is going fuzzy but I have to act like everything is normal. Malcolm's dad is on the board of governors? Could I pick a more dangerous family to know? I am so deep-fried. *Quick girl, steady your heartbeat.*

"It's number fifteen, but it's behind a monitored gate so you'll have to let me out front and I'll walk through. Next time I'll organize a visitor pass for you. If you give me your plates it'll be no problem." This way I'm moving on to the next step, instead of making them worry about dropping me out here, virtually on the street. I even get my phone out and get ready to tap in the details, like it's really going to happen.

Gloria gives me her number, and then I ask for Malcolm's car plates as well.

She looks warily at me before reluctantly telling me. "I must sound like an overprotective TigerMom, but I don't like him driving at night, and especially not in the wet. And you're a lovely girl but I don't want him to get distracted when he's doing so well at school. How serious are you two anyway?"

Could she fire any more questions at me? Maybe this is for the best, maybe she'll decide I'm not right for her son and I should stay away, and then she'll do her best to forget all about me.

That would be great.

Except I'll fail physics.

"We-e-e-e-ll, we're not serious at all." Because I can't get serious with *anyone*. "I promise you, that won't happen again. We really are just homework buddies. Speaking of which, I'd better get back to mine. Those assignments aren't going to write themselves!"

"No, they're not. Nice meeting you, Bianca."

"Nice meeting you, too." I slide out of the car and make a line for the gate, waving over my shoulder. It's a huge relief to see the glow from her lights turn around as she heads back towards the mall. I thought she'd never let me go.

The app on my phone says there'll be a bus in about fifteen minutes. I can't go down and wait there though, because Gloria might drive past and wonder what the heck I was doing there. I've become an expert at hanging around without arousing suspicion of loitering. Sometimes it involves looking at my phone for a while, because that's what everyone does. Then I go to the gas station and buy a stick of gum—that can burn up a few minutes. Then I walk somewhere near the bus stop and stare at my phone, only walking there at the last moment, getting on quickly so nobody sees me.

If they ever do, I have that lie ready to go. "Had to go to the bathroom. Too much soda this morning. Sorry if that's TMI."

# CHAPTER 4

THE NEXT DAY I don't see Malcolm until lunchtime. He sidles up to me in the food line.

"Did Mom freak you out last night?"

Up this close I can't help but notice his gorgeously dark eyes—I may have mentioned this before. After my heart settles down I manage, "She's your mom, she cares about you."

"I'll take that as a yes. Don't worry, by the way, you passed the test."

That's a relief, but I'm being super careful not to show it. "There was a test?"

"She took last night's leftovers for her lunch today. You passed."

He follows me to a table I normally share with friends of the girl variety. Like Mandy, who is half way into her vegetarian slop. The girls all scooch down and silently look from me to Malcolm and back again, saying everything and nothing.

"We've got a pop-quiz coming up Friday," he says, shoving a tater tot into his mouth. "You gonna be OK?"

"They let you know in advance?"

"Every third Friday we get one. Haven't you noticed the pattern?"

I haven't, because I've been so busy with spinning all those plates on bamboo sticks that is my life at the moment.

He gives me a sympathetic look that makes him look completely adorable. "Will you be OK or do you need to study more?"

He's my kryptonite. I don't want to want him, but I don't seem to be able to help myself. Especially when he's being so nice. Wait a minute! I just realized what he's really trying to say. "You want more cooking help, right?"

He's all nonchalant, shrugging his shoulders, pretending it ain't no thing. "It wouldn't hurt to prove that one meal wasn't a fluke."

"Fine then. How about tomorrow night?"

"Sure. But my parents will be home early so we'll have an audience. Unless you'd prefer to study at yours? Might be less stressful?"

"How about Homework Club then?" Did I say that too quickly?

His brows come together. "Something wrong with your place?"

Time to reach into the backpack of lie supplies. Something that will put him off ever wanting to visit. I drop my voice down to conspiracy levels. "You have to promise you'll never tell a soul."

"Cross my heart and hope to die."

Is anyone else on the table watching us? Listening? Doesn't matter if they are. In fact, it would be better that way. "Mom's a hoarder."

"What, like the TV show?"

"Worse."

Judging from the look on is face, he's bought it. "Is that why you're such a minimalist?"

Double-take time. "In what way?"

"Your pencil case. You only have one of each thing. Most girls open their pencil cases and Walmart shelves fall out."

"I... I guess I am..." That would make perfect sense, if my mother were hoarding things, I'd rebel against that. Instead of the reality, which is that I don't have a dime. Thanks, Malcolm.

---

OVER THE NEXT week or so, we get into this supercute pattern of going to Malcolm's after school to study first, cook second. But I don't stay for dinner with the family, because it's simply too intimate and intense. I take a portion home with me, even though I've been tasting as we cook, because you always taste as you go. I can't deal with any more repeats of them driving me home, because I just know they're the kind of people who want to come in and meet my family.

So not going to happen.

Plus, I have other homework besides physics. I can't let the rest of my subjects slide.

We're getting pretty good at this cooking-slash-studying thing. Tonight we're doing something a bit lavish. Tonight I'm trying French, because we may as well eat our way around the globe. Malcolm and I are most likely over-confident in our abilities, but we'll cheat a little. Store-bought vol au vents are perfectly acceptable as long as we make the filling from scratch. It's so nice taste-testing the rich, creamy chicken and asparagus sauce. Malcolm is cutting the chives into set lengths for the garnish.

I know, it's totally cheating. But also, taste-testing chives isn't anywhere near as good as this pot of cheesy goodness.

The main will be beef with *Béarnaise* and *gratin dauphinois*. There is no way I'd ever, ever be able to afford eat like this, so it's as much a treat for me as it is for Mal and his family.

It's YouTube to the rescue here. Malcolm is watching frame by frame as he separates the egg yolks for the *Béarnaise*. I'm so glad I put Saran wrap over the keyboard before he started. What a mess!

Meanwhile we have chocolate mousse in the refrigerator, ready for dessert. If anyone has room.

When the potatoes are in the oven and everything else is set out, ready to cook, I give myself permission to stretch my shoulders and have a rest.

What a day.

"You want to know your result from the test this morning?" Malcolm has the high school page open at the student portal.

"I'm sure you got one hundred percent." I try not to sound mean. Of course he'll get one hundred, that's why I need his brain. When I look, I see it's ninety percent. "Your parents are going to kill you. You're slipping!" I hope they don't blame me.

"That's your result, not mine."

"What?" I swivel the laptop around to get a better look. "I got ninety percent on a physics test?"

"You sure did!"

An excited scream leaps out of me and I grab Malcolm in a fierce hug. I'm kissing him all over his face. "You," smooch, "are," shmack, "totally amazing," mmmmmm.

"OK."

It's the best make-out session a gal could ever want.

Oh no, the Béarnaise! The eggs are just about to turn solid as they sit there amongst the tarragon and white wine vinegar. I grab the whisk and give it everything, taking the bowl out of the boiling water and sitting it on the marble bench top. "Quick, throw in the butter."

Malcolm drops the diced butter in and I'm begging the eggs to behave themselves.

"I need ice, get me ice."

"Yes, ma'am."

Malcolm's just about to pour ice into the bowl and I pull the bowl away just in time. "Not in the sauce, into the sink!"

Confusion reigns, but he does what I say. I sit the bowl on top of the ice so the mix has a chance to cool. "That's the trouble with eggs, they keep cooking even when you take them off the heat."

A frantic few minutes of whisking ensue. More butter goes in the sauce, more ice goes into the sink. "I think we've done it."

Malcolm glides a teaspoon through the surface and has a taste. His face! His eyes close and he's making the softest moan. "That is so good," he says finally.

He puts the teaspoon down, grabs a fresh tea towel and dabs at my forehead. "You did it, Doctor Bee, you saved her."

"I had an excellent assistant, Doctor Mal."

Relief and excitement are coursing through my body. He wraps his arms around my waist and pulls me in for a magnificent session of kisses and feels. He's walking me backwards towards one of their sofas—I'm glad they have so many—and we crash onto it in a tangle of limbs.

Of course his parents come home far too early. Probably just as well.

I stay for the first course and to cook the steaks, because this is the most expensive cut you can get and I'm not letting Mal stuff this up.

David tries hard not to "work" but he's got his tablet on. "Don't fill me up so much, I'll fall asleep at the meeting."

"What meeting is that?" I'm only pretending to be interested.

"School council. Say, you can help me."

Oh geez, why did I open my mouth?

David keeps talking. "Gloria told me where you live. There's a big development going in next door. We might have to change the school zone. It won't affect you, of course, you're already enrolled, but it's something we have to seriously think about. The school's splitting at the seams as it is.'

"Do you work at the development?" I hope that didn't come out as a squeak. I haven't seen anyone who looks like David on the lot. Flop-sweat trickles under my bra. I hope my top lip stays dry.

"I've just had a few meetings with them, helping with contracts, that sort of thing. I know most of the builders from the work they did on the freshman wing at school last year."

"Well then, if they're your friends, can you get them to reduce the number of floors? It's going to be so tall it will block out the sun." Hey brain, nice save!

THE NEXT SATURDAY MORNING, my supervisor Crystal has the most amazing news.

"All going well—and this isn't absolutely certain so don't quote me on this —but your parents could be here in as little as three months."

My face feels like it's going to explode with joy.

"You can't tell a soul, obviously," she says. "I have to get to the other store. You'll be fine here by yourself, won't you?"

"Sure!" This is so exciting! Three months! My parents could be here in ninety days! Even if it's six months, that's far sooner than I ever imagined. I was thinking a year would be optimistic. Three months? That's so insanely great I want to samba on the rooftops!

Twenty minutes later, I scorch my thumb taking out a tray of brownies, but it doesn't hurt because I'm so happy.

"Looking good!" Malcolm is at the counter.

I turn around. "Thanks!"

"I meant the cookies, obviously," he says.

I'm so full of happiness I volley back a full serve of sass. "That kind of sweet-talk will sweep a gal right off her feet!

The urge to share my wonderful news with him is bursting out of me, but telling anyone about it would be to put everything at risk.

Here I am, surrounded by people who I'm sure would be happy for me, and I can't tell them anything.

I'll just have to be excited on the inside.

I can do that. If I have to, I'll lie my ass off if it means my family will be together.

---

THAT AFTERNOON we're making chicken paella. Obviously we're at Malcolm's house but it's the weekend and both Malcolm's parents are home. David is somewhere in his den on a computer, doing something official and stressful, judging by the way he's taken the coffee maker with him. Gloria is wandering about, reminding us she's there, without saying anything. "Don't mind me," she says for the eighth time. If she wants to make sure we don't start kissing again—or even remotely flirting—she's nailing it. We can't so much as share a joke without Gloria wandering in just as we're about to laugh. Darn open-plan houses!

"Smells delicious, I'm getting hungry already," she says. Then adds with a wink at me, "You're a keeper."

I think that's a good thing, but I'm a mess. We studied before we cooked (it's a sensible pattern, because then we eat our lesson) but sitting beside Malcolm and not touching him is driving me insane.

Also, my family could be here in as little as three months! It will probably be six, or even nine, but how am I supposed to concentrate when I'm so freaking excited?

I want to tell Malcolm my news. He must know something's going on, but he's being far too polite. With any luck, he'll think my weirdness is related to his mom helicoptering about.

But I want to tell him so much it hurts.

What if he promised he wouldn't tell? He said he wouldn't tell anyone my mom was a hoarder and he's kept his word so far, so if I told him— Wait. Back up brain, just wait a minute. He thinks your mom is crazy, now you're going to tell him she's not even around. He won't believe me. He'll think I'm a liar.

Worse than that. He'll *know* I'm a liar.

I don't stay for lunch. I can't do the whole "normal family" sit around for a meal. I was crazy to ever think I could just slip in to a new family situation.

I have to think about my family. I have to put them first, and if that means cutting other people off, I'm going to have to do that.

Starting now.

"It's been great but I'd better get the bus. There'll be one in five minutes."

Of course Malcolm isn't going to make it easy for me. "I'll get my keys."

Aw man, why does he have to be so darn nice?

"It's raining again, so I'll drive," Gloria says.

Now they're fighting over who is going to drive me home. How am I supposed to juggle all this niceness? I just told myself I had to get away from this ridiculously wonderful family and they're making it impossible.

Malcolm jingles the keys in his hands. "Mom, if I don't drive in the rain every now and then I'll never learn. It's only light rain." Then he wraps his arm around my shoulder and leads me to the garage. "If you let Mom drive you, she'll want to meet your folks."

He's trying to spare my feelings. What a sweetheart!

Once we're in the car, Malcolm starts priming me for conspiracy. "We'll have to come up with a reason to keep my parents away from yours. What do you suggest?"

"I'm trying to think of something." See, it's good to make it appear as if I am not good at this lying caper.

"What about we say they work night shift or something, so they sleep during the day?"

"Maybe, I don't know. Is this something I should be worried about?"

"Oh yes," Malcolm says, as he takes the turn just before the toll road. "It's the burden of being an only child. They get way too involved in everything. I think it's an overcompensation thing."

"Lucky you." I take a big breath and drop a sincerity bomb. "Whatever we do, we can't tell them the truth." I mean that on every level.

He pulls his car up and looks at me. "Mom said you had to give the gatehouse my plates to get in?"

"Dangit, I forgot! Just let me out here and I'll walk in."

"Do you want me to come in—not into your house, but just to the front door?"

A smile cracks my face. "You being a 'Southern Gentleman', walking a lady to her door?"

He shrugs and looks a little guilty. "Something like that."

"You can tell your mom you delivered me home safely. I'll even text her and say what a respectable young gentleman you were." Stupid me, I don't know why but I lean over and kiss him on the cheek. Except I meant to kiss his cheek but he turned, too, and we end up locking lips and it's all too stupidly perfect. Even as I tell myself I cannot be doing this, we start making out in the car like starving people at a buffet. It's so beautiful I want to cry.

Stupid, stupid, stupid, wonderful.

# CHAPTER 5

"YOU LEFT YOUR CHARGER BEHIND." Malcolm taps me on the shoulder as we settle into physics class on Monday.

If a wave had knocked me over I couldn't feel more flat. That's where it was! At his place. "Thank you so much—phone's been dead for a day and I feel like someone's cut out my tongue. I was searching everywhere for it."

"I guess it must be hard finding things at your place."

That's right, Mom's a hoarder. "That's about it." I look around for a power socket. There is one over by the wall, so I get up and plug in, then lean my bag against it so it doesn't look like I'm sucking juice from the wall. The school frowns on that kind of thing. Can't have a thousand students draining the power all day. I know exactly what he's going to say next because Malcolm is such a decent guy.

"I tried to bring it back yesterday," he says. Yep, right on cue. And now for the kicker, "The woman at the gate said you didn't live there."

"Sorry, what?" I'm tapping my phone and trying hard not to look up. I knew this would happen. I knew it!

"Talk to me, Bianca. What's going on?"

"I can't, not in a crowded classroom." The teacher will be here any minute.

He drops his voice so low, but I know exactly what he's saying anyway, because it's the natural conclusion anyone would come to. "Are you border-hopping?"

He thinks this is about school? Oh Malcolm, I can't stand lying to you, but you know I'm going to have to. "Take it down a notch from Defcon four. I'm not border-hopping school zones. I do live there, but Bianca isn't my real name. I changed it for school—and don't tell me your real name is Malcolm, either, right?"

He kind of nods and shakes his head at the same time.

"My family all call me *Elivre*. Because they're crazy European but it makes me sound like a Mexican."

He tries out the name. "Elivarey."

"Close enough."

"How do you get Bianca from Elivarey?"

Excellent. He's completely forgotten about accusing me of being in the wrong neighborhood for school. Mind you, now he might think I'm an illegal alien, so I'll have to be extra careful. "They both mean the same thing in English."

"OK." He creases his brows and makes to ask me something else, then stops and unloads his notebook and tablet onto the desk instead.

I know that look. I've hurt him. Now I feel like crap.

After the lesson is over, Malcolm takes my arm and guides me towards the wall, away from the torrent of students pouring past us to the cafeteria. It's a protective move, but he also pulls me closer, making it harder and harder for me to avoid those eyes of his that make me want to tell the truth.

"Bee, you're asking me to take you on trust, without giving me anything in return." His hand points back and forth between us. "I thought maybe something was happening here, but I can't trust you until you tell me what's really going on."

"I told you my real name." It really is my real name, and it is European, but it's also far more common when you're from way, way south of the border. Like me.

The hurt look on his face doesn't fade away. "I guess I have to wait until you're ready to tell me then?"

*Deus meu!* "OK, OK. Come to my place tonight to study." Before I can stop myself, I grab my phone and dial Crystal. It's gonna require some fast talking, and if I don't get this right everything will blow up in my face.

"*Olá Mãe.*" She'll think I'm calling her my mother, and I pray she catches on superfast. I've never spoken to her in anything other than English, so it's gonna be one of the strangest conversations of all time. In rapid dialect I ask her, "I need you to do me a huge favor, please. *Eu preciso levar para casa um menino após escola hoje.* So we can study."

I'm counting on Malcolm not understanding my kind of Portuguese.

Down the phone Crystal says, "I take it you're in a tight spot and you need to prove you live in the house?"

"*Eu disse a ele sobre o seu problema com o lixo segurando.* He's OK with that."

She says, "My *what* issues?"

I revert back to English, for Malcolm's benefit. "I told him the truth. That our house is piled high with junk."

"And exactly where am I gonna get piles of junk at such short notice?"

Which was exactly what I was also thinking. *Que irritante*! Then she comes up with something fabulous, and I know I'm going to owe her, big time. Like I don't already!

"Tell him I've had a team of people sorting the place out. We've shifted three dumpsters of garbage this morning. I'm on medication to stop me going into meltdown. I will be at the house after school. You better be ready."

"*Obrigado, muito obrigado.*"

At which point Malcolm turns his phone around and shows me what I've just said on his screen. Oh, shit!

Cold heaviness drags me down until I see that it's in mangled Spanish. He thinks I've said, "applied" instead of "thank you". Phew! Wrong side of the Andes.

"I still have to work the bugs out." He shrugs.

"What? You just hold it in front of someone speaking another language and it tells you what they're saying?"

"When it's finished it will."

"You're gonna put thousands of spies out of business with that." My heart is trying to leap out of my throat in panic. I thought I was safe speaking my mother tongue. "No keeping any secrets from you, hey?"

"I started it because my parents speak in Creole when they want to talk about me but not with me."

Laughter burbles out—it's my defense mechanism. "Do they know you're working on this app?"

"Nope!" It's his turn to laugh and offer a goofy grin.

The school bell rings through the air and it's time to get a move on. I wink. "Your secret is safe with me."

IT'S THROWING down rain when school finishes for the day. We dart through the parking lot, kicking up sprays of water with each step. By the time we get to his car we're both soaked.

"I'm going to ruin the seats."

"Relax, it will dry out," Malcolm says. "Wow, you look really nervous!"

"I do?"

"My driving's not that bad, is it?"

"No, you're good." But it's getting foggy in here. A horn blasts behind us as he narrowly misses two other cars in a fender bender. "OK, maybe we should wait till the rain stops?"

A grimace and a shrug are his answer, but he cranks up the heating and the air con to blast mist off the windows. He checks his phone; the weather radar is showing an enormous band of heavy rain covering nearly all of Florida. OK, he's gonna have to drive in the rain, even if his mom doesn't like it.

At least it never snows here. "I've never seen weather like this," Malcolm says, as he takes a turn at the lights.

I swear he's leaning closer to the steering wheel to see better.

We pull up at the gate and—because I texted his plates to Crystal—the gate keeper lets us through. Hurdle one, done and dusted.

This might just work.

Getting out of the car, we hear the diggers and dozers from the new housing development next door. The storm water runoff drain they've built is already bigger than a lake. It's so flat around here that when it rains, the whole city turns into Venice.

"Look how close the water is to your place!" Malcolm says.

It's lapping at the side of the garage. "Wow, that is a lot of rain!"

Meanwhile, the heavy vehicles nearby keep right on trucking.

"How do you study with all the noise?"

"I've been at yours so much I'd forgotten." I look out over the expanse of dirt streets and housing lots that will one day become an estate that I'll never be able to afford.

"Aren't you going to open the door?" Malcolm asks, as we stand under the front porch. He's pulled the mosquito door closed behind us.

I fumble about in my backpack, knowing full well I don't have the keys in here. I do have a set of keys, but not the right ones. Luckily for me, "Mom" opens the door.

"What are you doing here? You're supposed to be at your father's. I could have been *entertaining* someone."

Holy hell! Is she drunk!?

This is like the worst ever improv of all time, and I have to stand here and agree with everything and all of it is awful. With an audience of only Malcolm, Mom is putting on a magnificent performance. Her face is red and blotchy, across her forehead and cheeks. She has little devil horns of red wine stains on the corners of her lips, and she's staring me down like I'm the most disappointing daughter in the world.

"You know I don't like drop-ins!"

"Mom, I called you today and asked you if it would be all right."

"That was last week!"

The house, by the way, is suspiciously clean and relatively empty, which does not bode well for our "hoarder" story. It's only the front room, though, and it has that lived-in vibe. You can tell from the earthy mix of bodies and cooking smells that people live here, but nothing is rotting or moldering, which is what you'd expect in a hoarder house. Everyone knows cockroaches love stacked newspapers, but there isn't even a trace of vermin poop on the floors or windowsills. Which, ordinarily should make someone like Malcolm question my story, but he's so transfixed and nervous about the raving drunk woman, he hasn't said a thing.

"Did you bring dinner? I'm starving." Mom tops up her wine. She's drinking out of a plastic twelve ounce red cup. Classy, Mom.

Hang on, did she just ask me for dinner? "We'll get takeout. Malcolm and I need to study, OK, so we'll stay out of your way."

At the mention of his name, Malcolm leans over to me. "Actually, I think I left my um, calculator at home. Maybe we should... "

"Leave?" Mom says, glaring at Malcolm. "You only just got here."

"Mom? Can I talk to you for a moment?"

"Sure." She leans her thigh on the kitchen bench and crosses her arms. Steadying herself in place.

"In private?"

"I see no reason why we can't talk here. Unless I'm embarrassing you and your boyfriend."

I use the phrase guaranteed to rile anyone up. "Just calm down, OK?"

Mom screams, "I am calm!"

This is excruciating! Poor Malcolm doesn't know where to look. Brilliant!

I hike my school bag over my shoulder. "OK, why don't Malcolm and I go out and get some burgers. What would you like us to bring back for you?"

She gulps at her wine and says, "Can't wait to run away, can you?"

Under my breath I say, "When you're like this." I reach for Malcolm's hand and mouth "sorry" to him and make for the front door.

"That's right, get out," Mom hollers after us.

It's still pouring with rain out here. The diggers are still digging, making a ruckus. We dash for the car, and for a moment we simply sit inside it, breathing. Our wet hair and breath makes the windows fog up. Eventually Malcolm says, "No wonder you don't want folks coming over."

"Can we just drive?"

"Sure. Where to?"

"Anywhere. Just as long as it's away from here."

He drives to the mall and parks under cover, but I don't want to get out. I just want to sit in some peace and quiet and clear my head. Everything is completely insane right now.

Gently, Malcolm puts his hand over mine, then gives a squeeze. "I'm sorry for putting you through that."

"I'm sorry too." With my free hand, I wipe my face.

"I understand now why you lied about your mom. You say what you have to, to keep people away, right?"

"Yep," I say on a shudder. It's the truth, but I still can't tell him why.

"Maybe you should stay at my place tonight?" he offers.

Whoa, this is moving way too fast. He must see my shocked look. "That came out wrong. We have a spare room. I won't touch you, I promise. I mean, only if you want me to. No, that came out wrong, too."

Whatever expression my face is doing, his is doing double as he backtracks and flip-flops. In the end we both laugh and I lean forward and kiss him again. That's what we should have been doing all along. Parking and kissing. Isn't that what normal kids do? The ones without all the baggage? I don't care, I just want to keep on kissing him, and he is holding my face so tenderly and kissing me back and being so fabulous. And I want to tell him the truth so badly it hurts.

His stomach makes a rumbling sound and we break apart with a shy laugh.

"That sounds like a food alarm."

"Yeah, come on," he says. "My treat."

We eat at BreadLake and it's perfect. Not too low-rent and, importantly, not too expensive. He said he'd pay but I don't want to end up owing him. I already owe too much of my life to Crystal the-supervisor-stand-in-drunk-Mom.

A stray thought lands on my brain. I wonder what she owes to the people above her?

Malcolm and I feed each other bread sticks dipped in mozzarella and just for a while, I feel like I could be a regular American teenager whose only worry is whether this gorgeously cute boy wants to take what we have to the next level.

At least I don't have to worry about that last part. Not when he rubs his thumb across my chin to wipe away cheese drizzle. Then we're kissing again.

"Get a room you guys!" We spring apart to see Mandeep walking past with the rest of the gang.

We are well and truly found out, and I honestly don't care.

Before we leave the restaurant, Malcolm grabs a takeout chicken salad for Mom.

"Peace offering?" I ask.

"Something like that."

The rain hasn't let up as Malcolm pulls up outside the gates on the street.

He's stopping out here? "You can drive in, it's OK."

"I... think it's best I stay here."

Wow, Mom's episode has really done its job. "All right then."

"You gonna be OK?"

"Sure."

"Seriously. Don't brush me off like that. I'm worried about you."

Dammit. He's doing that wonderful thing again that makes my stomach flip. "I've got your peace offering. I'll be fine."

"Call me, doesn't matter what time, and I'll come get you. You got that?"

I don't know what to say so I kiss him again. Even as I do, I think about how much he's going to hate me when this is over. "Thank you for everything. See you at school tomorrow."

I run through the rain, sheltering the takeout box with my school bag.

When I turn to see Malcolm off, he's already turned his car around and is waving me goodbye.

He's such a decent guy, I can't help falling a little in love with him.

And he is going to hate me when he finds out the truth.

# CHAPTER 6

I DIDN'T HAVE to wait long for everything to turn to crap. The very next morning, before I crammed my poncho into my locker, I have friends asking me if I'm OK.

Sure, I hadn't slept much, but did I look that bad?

Mandeep runs up to me and hugs me. "We were so worried! I'm glad you're safe!"

"Worried?" What could she be worried about? Malcolm's an upstanding member of the school community. "Malcolm's a total gentleman."

"What?" Her face creases into puzzlement. "Not him! Your house!"

My jaw drops open. "He told you already?"

"He didn't have to. It's all over the news!"

Buzz saws spin in my head. I might as well be walking in mayonnaise.

Adding to the recipe for crazy, Malcolm jogs up. "You're OK! How about your mom? Do you need anything? A place to stay?"

This is doing my head in. He told everyone and now he's acting all concerned? The stupid blabbermouth!

I ditch Malcolm and grab Mandy by the arm and haul her into the girls' bathroom.

"What the hell has Malcolm told you about Mom?"

Mandy jerks backwards, looking totally confused. A quick shake of her head, then she reaches for her phone and clicks on a news file. Live reports are coming in of a collapse at a housing development. The incessant rain overfilled a run-off drain, causing nearby older buildings to slide off their foundations.

On the screen, the toppled building looks exactly like the house next door. The house where people think Mom and I live has water lapping the top step. Everything is taped off, the drives are filled with news vans and emergency workers.

It's utter chaos.

Mandy clears her throat. "You walked straight past all that and didn't even notice?"

"Well, I mean, I got really wet," my brain stutters. This is too much. "I was running late for the bus. I mustn't have..."

Mandy makes a crease between her brows. She's going to make a terrifying lawyer one day. "Your neighbor's house fell over during the night, and you didn't notice?"

I look at the video, gawping at the size of destruction. Nobody's going to believe anyone could merely sleep through that.

"It's been so noisy lately, I've been wearing ear plugs!"

The bell chimes in the hall. I try not to sigh with relief as I turn to head out. Mandy grabs my arm and quizzes me again.

"I'm here for you, OK? You can tell me what's going on."

"Nothing's going on." Stupid me, I said that far too quickly.

---

LUNCH WILL BE fine because I can shove food into my mouth so I don't have to speak. I walk into the cafeteria and there's Malcolm standing near the registers. Everyone is standing or sitting, watching him, listening to him.

And what he says rips my heart to shreds.

"...on the news, luckily it wasn't Bianca's house that fell over, but it was the house next door. We've been checking the news, and the four houses along the boundary with the development next door are being condemned. The soil has washed out from under her driveway and foundations, so she can't even get into her house. Most of you know Bianca, she works hard and studies even harder. Let's get her and her mom back on their feet as soon as we can."

Guilt and fear roil in my stomach. I have to stop this. "Malcolm, why are you doing this?"

"Because I care about you. We all do. We know how much this could disrupt your education so we want to help you out as much as we can."

Mouth turning to ash, I squeak out, "I don't want to take charity."

Because sooner or later, people are going to figure out that it's impossible to sleep through the house next door collapsing. That people don't simply "miss" massive clues like lakes of water all around your house. Or half the driveway missing. Malcolm steps down from his makeshift soapbox (several food trays stacked on top of each other) and pulls me into a hug.

"Please, Malcolm, I'm so embarrassed. I can't deal with all the attention."

"I'm sorry Bee, I just want to help."

This is all spinning out of control. Those imaginary spinning plates are crashing at my feet. "Can we talk in private, please, without everyone watching?"

"Yeah, sure. Just let me grab some food first."

"Me, too. I can't think straight on an empty stomach." This will give me more time to think of something believable.

Because of my changed circumstances, students let me cut to the front of the line and I get crunchy wedges and a burger that hasn't dried out too much yet. Malcolm and I move outside. It's still raining, which is phenomenal for Florida, so we sit really close to the wall.

"So what did you need to tell me?" Malcolm's face is pure honesty and concern.

"I didn't notice what happened last night, because I didn't stay there."

This is some of the truth. The real truth is I never stay there.

"Why not?"

"Mom and I had a huge fight." This is not the truth, but it's believable because "Mom" was surly and drunk in front of Malcolm.

"Why didn't you call me?"

"I wanted to, but she took my phone off of me." A total lie.

I don't want to lie to Malcolm but I have to. If I tell him the truth, he'll feel compelled to tell his parents, and they'll find out I don't live anywhere near the school zone. And then the shit will really hit the fan, because they'll find out I'm not even a citizen. Because every facet of my life has been carefully crafted with the very best fake documents on the market.

"I stayed with my *avó* instead. My grandma."

Malcolm leans back. "Your *avwah*?"

I love the way he tries to say it back to me. "Yeah."

"Riiiiiight."

He doesn't trust me. He can see the word "liar" on my forehead. Who knew being friends with a safe geek boy would end up being so stupidly dangerous?

"Where does your grandma live?"

"Are you gonna report me for living outside the zone or something?" Wow, that came out so bitchy.

"I'm trying to help."

We eat in silence, the food sticking in my throat. After a while, Malcolm checks his phone again. "Looks like you'll be staying at your gran's for a while then, because according to this, everyone's being evacuated. Oh, fresh update, the owner is being investigated for running an illegal rooming house."

Pulsing, whooshing noises swirl through my ears. There is no connection between my brain and mouth. Everything has shut down.

Malcolm raises one eyebrow. "I don't suppose you'd know anything about that, would you?"

I jump to my feet and run for the bathroom. Thank God there's a free cubicle because I only just make it. I throw up so hard a bit of pee comes out.

*Estou em tantos problemas. Muitos problemas.*

By the way, that's Brazilian Portuguese for "I am in so deep I can't get out."

At some point, I guess after the bell rings, I make it to English. Malcolm isn't in this class. I can't avoid Mandeep, who's saved me a seat next to her.

"We're gonna look after you," she says.

"No, really, you don't have to."

"Course I do. We do." She indicates the girls sitting on her other side. My friends. The friends I've been lying to all this time. They are going to hate on me so much after this.

MISTER FAROOD GIVES me a patronizing smile which I can only assume means he's heard about the house-toppling-sinking-debacle. I smile back and then, so help me Jesus, I gave him an OK-sign to show I'm fine. Honestly, what student does that?

Part way into class, the principal sticks her head into the room.

Who's got two thumbs and is about to be expelled? This gal!

If there was anything left in my stomach, it would fly out right in front of everyone. Instead, this horrible retching sound comes out, like a belch trying to climb down instead of getting out. The class laughs at me. The principal then gives me a beaming smile as well. Confusion sends my pulse to the sky and my stomach to the floor. So much chaos in my body, it's a wonder I can walk straight. Is she leading me to the executioner's block or what? She should totally stop smiling like that. As if she's happy to be rid of me!

"We'll talk in my office," which is down a hall and through the middle of other teachers' offices—and they're all smiling at me as well.

Who knew bad news could travel so fast?

Crystal, my supervisor, is sitting in the principal's office waiting for us. She looks like a mom who bakes apple pie every afternoon instead of crawling into a bottle. She gets up and embraces me in a hug. "I can't believe it—you studied so hard you slept through a house falling down! And in the morning you were already gone for school! Oh, my girl, I'm so worried and proud all at once!"

If that's our story I'll play along. In fact, I'll just nod and shrug and stuff, like a regular teenager. She's thrown me a lifeline and I'm hanging on.

Mom's got this sewn up. She does all the talking, thanking the principal for being so wonderful, caring and understanding. I think I can hear kissing noises. She's such a suck-up.

"Our top priority is student welfare. I'm so glad Bianca has such a caring mother to support her during this disruptive time. Bianca, for the rest of term I'm prepared to give you extensions on your assignments, and if you need assistance in college applications I'll gladly help."

I feel so guilty to feel so happy. This could all work out OK after all.

---

WHY DID I ever think this would turn out OK? Malcolm takes me by the hand after school and says, "You're coming with me."

"But I'm fine, I have somewhere to stay, it's all good." It's the same place I've been staying all this time. Not having to stop at the mall and change clothes is going to save me about an hour a day. I'm living out of zone for a proper reason now. I can't be found out, because there's nothing to find.

"This is for your own good," Malcolm says as he leads me to the car.

Does this guy have a white knight complex or what?

Wait? Is that racist?

As he drives us out the school gates, I see a police car turning in.

"You have a good reason to be paranoid," Malcolm says. "They really are coming to get you."

"You're joking, right?"

"No. I gotta hand it to you, your Mom did a great job of making me walk straight out your house and not look back. But I should have stayed."

"She pulled herself together today. She met with the principal. It was like she was a different person."

Malcolm shoots back, "Because she was never drunk in the first place, was she? That's just an act to make people leave. So she's not a hoarder, and she's not a drunk. Why do you lie so much, Bianca?"

"Why are you accusing me of all this?" The best defense is attack.

He purses his lips and keeps right on driving. We're taking the roads to his house, not mine. "Are you kidnapping me? What's going on?"

"Your mother, if she's really your mother, has been charged with running an illegal rooming house. Hoarder, boarder, whaddya know, they rhyme. I should have stayed last night and helped you with your homework in the next room. But there would have been mattresses all over the floor instead of a table to work at, am I right? The police were coming to school to arrest you on suspicion of being an illegal alien. I've spared you the indignity of being dragged out in handcuffs. In exchange for that, you're going to tell me the truth."

That whooshing, pulsing sound is blocking my ears. Nothing is coming out. My body curls into a ball and I can't see properly because I think I'm crying. That noise won't stop. I can't hear anything else. I don't know if we've stopped or if Malcolm is still driving or if I've died and gone to hell.

Whoosh, whoosh, my pulse rushes through my ears.

Then this howl. This horrible, wailing, messy howl comes out and I'm not crying for me. I'm crying for my real mother and father, my sisters and brother, somewhere in Sao Paulo waiting for their turn to get here. I'll never see them again and it will be my fault. All I had to do was be good and say nothing and they would have been here and everything would have been all right.

I've ruined everything.

Everything.

# CHAPTER 7

WHY AM I TREMBLING? My hands are shaking so badly I'm smacking my face instead of wiping the tears away.

Malcolm nudges my shoulder. "Can you please stop crying? People think I'm kidnapping you."

Eventually the car stops. Between my fingers I see him pull the keys out of the ignition, so we must have stopped. Vision still blurry from tears, my ears are thumping. He comes around to my side of the car and helps me out. Something pulls me back. The seatbelt is still clicked in. Jeez I'm a mess.

"None of this was your idea, was it?" he says as he helps me to my feet, taking shaky steps towards the house. The world is kind of swirly today. Things are weaving in front of my face. His arm is around me and he's helping me through the door. That room with all the armchairs and the big windows is right here, and he pulls me over to a seat.

"Not here. It's too pretty—I'll cry on the furniture."

"I'll make you a hot chocolate."

"No." I'd spill it. I croak out, "Sippy cup?"

He makes a funny sort of snort and shakes his head. "Come on, kitchen then." He holds his hand out and walks me down the hall. I end up slumping against the benches and sliding to the floor. Sitting on the kitchen floor feels safe. The lower I get, the safer I feel.

"My parents won't be back until six at the earliest. Talk to me. I promise you I won't tell anyone else. But I can't help you until you tell me what's going on."

It comes out in a vomit of words. Places, names, dates, details, some in Portuguese and some in English and some in a mix of tears and wails and all of it a mess. At some point he gets me a fresh hand towel and I wipe my face on it. There's also a box of tissues that appears in front of me, and a garbage pail.

I hear him saying something but it's all sounds and noise, although I swear he said the word "lawyer".

"I can't afford a lawyer."

"My dad is a lawyer, that's why he's on school council."

"Huh?" I'm imagining the school being sued for something. Or worse, them suing me because of all the lies I've told. What if Malcolm's dad is the one to send me to prison? I wonder if it's as bad as Orange is the New Black?

"He's a contract lawyer, you know, for all the building projects and employment."

"The school has its own lawyers on call?"

"No." He looks at me like I'm soft in the head. "It's part of the firm's outreach program. They work in the community pro-bono for a hundred hours a year. I bet there's someone at the firm who could help you."

For a bright, shining moment, maybe this is what I need to stay. But then reality crashes in on my next breath. This is real life, not some TV drama where everything gets tied up in a neat bow just before the credits roll. "That's a dick move, offering me hope like that."

"I'm trying to think of something. My parents will be home later. I was thinking if we cook them something insanely great, it will put them in a wonderful mood. Then you tell them what's wrong and they'll offer to help."

"I'm going to wow them with food and they're going to fall at my feet?"

Malcolm sighs. "Do you have any better suggestions?"

Nothing but crickets in my head right now, so I guess cooking might be my salvation.

"OK, let's give it a try."

"That's my girl."

Ahhhh, if only I really was.

SERIOUS COOKAGE IS GOING on in this kitchen. I am giving this everything I've got. My shoulder is cramping from whisking the white sauce so it doesn't get lumps. Malcolm is chopping the vegetables and, I gotta hand it to him, I think he's getting better at it. Only five chunks end up on the floor instead of fifteen.

We've set the table for four and I stay for the whole meal. I'm so tired I don't have the energy to ugly-cry in front of them. Instead, Malcolm and I explain everything to Gloria and David, and I pretty much throw myself on their mercy.

David is appalled. Gloria is silent. I can't blame them. We've made dessert but nobody is hungry.

MALCOLM DRIVES ME HOME, not to the flooded collapsed mess next to the estate but to my regular home in the next county over, right into the middle of the next school zone.

"This is the street," I say, looking at the familiar clapboard houses.

"It looks terrible." Malcolm locks the car doors as he drives slowly towards the correct house number. "Oh no, is this it?"

It only looks like a crack house. Inside it's really nice. Well, my room is nice, I don't really bother about the other rooms.

"But, why do you live all this way?"

"I did start in the other house, which was in the zone when I first enrolled, so I wasn't cheating. Well, only a bit because I'm not a resident. Then after a few months my supervisor moved me here, and it's cheaper here because she doesn't take as much of my wage anymore, so I can send more home to Mae and Pai."

"So she starts you off in the good school zone, knowing you'll love the school and do your very best to stay. Is that what she does?"

"I guess so." Now that Malcolm spells it out for me, I can see exactly what she's done. Set me up in a situation where I'm too scared to mess up, so I have to behave myself and do everything she tells me to.

Malcolm takes another look at the house. "I'm not leaving you here. You're coming back with me."

"No, really, I'm going to be OK, everything's—"

"—Not OK." Thank God Malcolm hasn't stopped the car, because as he's talking, some official looking people are walking out of the house with all my housemates, and their wrists are in cable ties.

"Stare at them, pretend we're rubberneckers," Malcolm says, moving the car past the house at glacial speed. Every instinct has me wanting to floor it and get the hell out of here, but Malcolm's right: if we look like we're driving past a car crash and having a good look, we'll be OK.

If we make a break for it, we'll look guilty.

And they'll come after me.

---

THE NEXT DAY, I get up early and head to the markets. Fish and prawns go into the trolley, along with tomatoes, onions and coriander. Yellow and orange bell peppers too. Coconut cream, yes please. I'm making *Moqueca*, the food of my people. I'm going to make Portuguese tarts for dessert, because who can resist baked egg custard? We'll have to opt for virgin *caipirinhas* to drink though, because the very last thing I need is to get arrested for buying alcohol under age.

Today I'm going to show Malcolm and his family the real me.

I just hope they like her.

I don't let Malcolm help me in the kitchen. I can't think straight when he's too close, and as his parents are here I think it's best they don't keep walking in on us kissing.

Cooking is keeping both my hands busy as well, even though I'd rather be running them over Malcolm's body on one of the couches somewhere.

Lunch is a massive food-fest.

"Bianca, oh my goodness, you cook like an angel," Gloria says as she dabs the napkin at her lips.

"Better than resort food," David says. "Maybe we'll have a stay-cation instead."

"Now that you've brought that up." Gloria takes a sip of her drink. I can tell it's too sweet for her, but she's being so lovely about it. "Mal, Bianca, I think we might need to delay our vacation for a while, just until all this other stuff blows over."

The "other stuff" is me living in the house. We have no idea if the authorities will knock on the door and drag me away.

But if they go on holidays and I'm here? Well, I can see from their point of view they'd be a *leeeetle* bit concerned about what mischief their son might get up to. Honestly? I wouldn't leave me home alone for two weeks with a cute boy either.

"We need to confess something," Gloria says, looking at David. "We, ah, never, um, well… there isn't a holiday."

Malcolm's jaw drops. "You lied to me?"

"We needed you to lift your game, son," David says.

Malcolm's face swivels back and forth from his mom to his dad. "You made the whole thing up? Why?"

David creases his mouth and then says, "Because you needed to grow up and start showing a little more independence. You can do so much more for yourself and you were never going to get there unless we… created a little motivation."

"You lied!" Malcolm shakes his head and looks like he can barely process it.

Should I say something? I feel like I'm caught in the middle. Then again, I should keep quiet. I'm hardly one to lecture about honesty.

But still, lying to your own kid?

"We did it for your own good," David says. "If we hadn't, you'd still be burning water."

"But hold on, you said I had to learn how to cook, or you wouldn't take the holiday," Malcolm says. "But you were never going to take it, so you were setting me up to fail?"

"You should be on the debating team," his dad says.

Gloria puts her hand over David's. "We were trying to be good parents. We're trying to build a little more resilience in you. And nobody got hurt, so what's the harm?"

As opposed to my lies, which… well, I'm hurting and scared for my family, but I don't think a judge is going to shrug it off as one of those "victimless crime" things.

---

OF COURSE I can't sleep. It's too noisy in my head. I sneak out of the spare room and think about which way to turn. I find myself in that fancy front room with the couches. In the darkness, I sit here and breathe in the quiet. This might be the last quiet time I get for a very long time.

The sound of footsteps down the hall has me squishing into the cushions, as if I can hide here.

Malcolm comes around the corner. With a whisper he says, "This is Mom's favorite room. Even I'm not allowed in here."

Thank goodness it's him and not his mom, then. "I'm sorry, I'll go."

"Just kidding. Couldn't sleep either, huh?

"Something like that."

"Shove over, my feet are cold."

He brought a blanket with him. It's just the two of us on the sofa, squished together. His arm rests over my shoulder and I burrow into him. Just sitting here, breathing slowly, feeling drowsy and numb. Malcolm's breathing slows as he succumbs to sleep, then he semi wakes and kisses the top of my head and cuddles me closer. I feel so safe and protected, I nuzzle in that little bit more.

Voice coming out in a croak, I whisper, "I love you."

I hope he didn't hear it, I just wanted to say it.

His hand gives my shoulder the faintest of squeezes as he mutters, "I'll remember," before his hand drops away and his whole body softens into sleep.

# CHAPTER 8

JESUS, I'm in the principal's office. I'm gonna vom till there's no tomorrow.

There *is* no tomorrow.

I'm so dead, I may as well be literally dead. They know where I really live, they know I'm a liar and they know they can ruin my life in the next five minutes.

This must be how the aristos in Revolutionary France felt as they waited for Madame Guillotine's blade to fall. But there is no Scarlet Pimpernel coming to my rescue.

"At first we were concerned about your living circumstances, because your house and those in the block, have been in the news," the principal says. "We ran a check of students addresses in the database and we've discovered we have five student families all claiming to live in the same address.

"Naturally, we don't believe you all live there together."

"There are five more?" I blurt out. Oh shut up Bianca, don't say anything!

"So you didn't know about that?" The Principal gives me a steely glare.

"No, I didn't. I mean, I knew it was a rooming house, and I really did live there for a while when I first enrolled, but... I have no idea what's going on there now."

Malcolm's mum, Gloria, is sitting beside me. We haven't been able to find Crystal, but it's unlikely she'd want to be here. Maybe she got arrested. She hasn't texted me and I haven't texted her.

"We are not going to expel you," the principal says, looking down over her reading glasses. For a second I can breathe as hope surges faster than my ribs can expand. Then she kills me. "But we are going to ask you to look for alternative enrolment. And we have notified the authorities."

*Slice.*

My life, cut off in one sentence.

Nothing makes sense, it's all

White noise

White noise

White noise

White noise

Gloria is rubbing my back but it isn't doing any good.

I can't tell the school that my real parents are in Brazil. That the woman who enrolled me in to school isn't my mother but my sponsor. Actually, she's probably not a real sponsor now that I think about it. Because sponsors don't take your wages under the guise of paying off some kind of personal debt to the immigration authorities, do they? The school doesn't know any of this. They're going to kick me out anyway, so why tell them anything?

I mean, I've still got my job at the bakery in the mall, unless they've shut that down. I should go and check, but I don't want to hang around in case the cops are watching. Maybe I'll just stay away. I've still got some friends and I've still got my brains and everything I've learned so far, and I can still go to school somewhere around here. Then I'll sit my exams. Nobody knows I'm an alien, except Malcolm, and he's keeping my secret.

But wait a minute, she said "the authorities". Which ones? Education or Immigration?

I should be bawling my eyes out but the tears won't even come. Everything feels numb.

It's over, it's over, it's over.

My life is over.

***

GLORIA AND DAVID have gone to a meeting with other lawyers in the office. We're under strict instructions to be quiet and not open the door to anyone.

The moment the front door closes, we hold each other so tightly I wish we could superglue ourselves together. Desperation bursts out of me, "I love you so much, I can't let you go."

They could be coming any minute now, the police or the feds or immigration officials or anyone, really. I can't leave with this unfinished.

"Oh God, baby, me too." He's kissing me like we're never going to see each other again. Which only makes me more desperate to make this count. It could be our last moments together.

I'm pulling his shirt out of his waistband, exposing his skin to the air, running my hands over his back. Then it's the buttons at the front that have to come away. Because I have to get close to him.

"Whoa, Bee, lemme catch my breath."

"I don't want to stop."

"You're gonna have to slow down or I won't be able to stop."

"Maybe you didn't hear me. I want to keep going. I need this."

"Alright, alright, hang on."

We kiss and stumble-walk to his room. I push him on to the bed and I'm so crazed with love and lust and desperation that everything has gone blurry. When this is over we'll both be utterly wrecked.

I need the oblivion.

---

AN HOUR LATER, we're in his bathroom, tidying ourselves up a little.

"That was intense," he says, running a towel over his face.

He has this goofy grin like he can't believe what just happened. I put that there. I put my stamp on him. Whatever happens to us from this day, I'll always have this memory. This precious time where it was just us, in our own little world.

Our lips are swollen and our eyes are dilated. His look even blacker than usual.

"You're handling this amazingly well," he says, wiping his face again. "What the hell do we do now?"

"Now we get dressed, head downstairs and cook dinner for your folks. That way we'll be busy when they get home and they won't suspect a thing."

"My mum will know. She knew that time I pretended to be at soccer, and I'd been smoking with friends instead."

"The smell does tend to be a giveaway."

"And the singed eyebrows," he says.

"I'm going to cook anyway. If they come home and there's no food, they'll know we haven't been cooking."

Garlic. Garlic and lemon and rosemary. Now there's a stink that could cover up a crime scene. Into the pan they go, along with Arborio rice. We'll have risotto, and for good measure it will be salmon. It will stink the house out for a week.

His parents still aren't home, so we slap the bag of fish on the bench and get straight back to kissing. It sets everything off inside me again and I have to tell myself to slow down or we'll burn dinner. I'll just have to stew quietly until we can have some more alone time, whenever that is.

His parents walk in on us kissing and instead of springing apart, Malcolm holds me even tighter.

He whispers in my ear, "Go along with me."

I don't have time to wonder what he means by that before he says, "Mom, Dad, I have the most amazing news. Bianca's pregnant so we're going to get married!"

*The what now? Whoa, Mal, steady on we've only just done it.*

Dad takes a step back like he's been punched.

Gloria sucks in a room-full of air and squares her shoulders. "Oh no you are not!"

"Fine, you don't have to come to the wedding," Malcolm starts.

This is so crazy, I'm walking in mayonnaise.

"This is insanity! You've never even had a serious girlfriend before and now you're telling me you got her knocked up? What kind of fool does that? What are they teaching you at that school?"

David's covering his mouth in shock, holding it all in like he doesn't trust what he's going to say.

Gloria's talking with her hands. "Are you all right Bianca? Have you told your parents? This is all so sudden, I can't even think!"

"I don't know why you're making a drama about this," Malcolm says. It's possibly the most unhelpful thing anyone could say in this situation. Of course his parents are going nuts.

Gloria's voice comes out low and angry. "I can't believe you could be so stupid as to not use protection. You've just ruined both your futures." Then turns to her husband, "Your son is an idiot." Then she whirls on me and I wonder what she's going to bring down on my head. Instead, she shocks me sideways and asks, "Are you all right sweetie? Do you need to sit down or something? We'll make the best of things don't you worry. Oh My Lord when the ladies at the club find out they'll never stop laughing."

Her concern utterly breaks me. "You haven't called me a slut or anything." Tears make my vision blurry.

"He's the slut," David mutters.

"Hey!" Malcolm shouts. Suddenly the three of them are wailing on each other.

I shove my hands over my ears. "I can't stand this! Stop fighting everyone. Please! I'm not pregnant!" Although their reactions to the news were really impressive. I mean, seriously, Gloria is amazing.

Gloria stops, mouth open mid yell, and stares.

Malcolm turns, gives a frightening glare just for me and hisses, "Yes you are."

It can't go on like this.

"No. I am not. Malcolm, that was, wow, I did not expect that. And now I think I've learned just a little more than I was supposed to. Gloria, it's good that you're protecting your son. He's just trying to help."

"In his own inept way," David says, rubbing his forehead with relief. "I am far too young to be a grandpa."

I have to get this out before I chicken out. "I'm not lying any more. Gloria, David, I am absolutely not pregnant. I promise. And therefore Malcolm and I are not getting married. He was only saying that so that I could stay."

"So you're not pregnant?"

"No."

Gloria's eyes narrow. "And there's no chance that you could be pregnant and not know it?"

Malcolm slips his hand over my mouth to keep me silent. "She's gonna plead the fifth on that one."

---

I HAVE A LAWYER, which is the most bizarre development out of so many bizarre things that have happened to me in the past month. I'm living at Malcolm's house in the spare room, but some nights we sneak around because, oh my lordy, I cannot keep my hands off Malcolm, or the rest of me. And yes, we are being careful.

I cook dinner for them nearly every night. I may as well, because I have plenty of time, what with not going to school any more. It's super annoying, but at least I can still sit my exams—just not at Malcolm's school. The school said that as I'm definitely not from around here, let alone the zone, letting me back in after all the lies I told would set a bad "precedent".

I'm under strict instructions not to answer the door or phone. It's kind of like house arrest. Or *mansion* arrest I guess. They don't want me going out in case I'm pulled over.

Tonight at dinner, David announces he's quitting school council. "From now on, if they want my legal advice, they can pay for it."

"What's happening with Bianca's case?" Malcolm asks.

"It's on a go-slow," he says.

"So I'm in limbo?" I don't know what's happening to me, and I don't know what's happening to my family.

"Go-slow is good," David says. "It means we have plenty of time to keep gathering evidence and every day we delay is a day you're not deported. Looks like your supervisor, what's her name, Carol?"

"Crystal."

"Yeah, Crystal. She has a set date. If you testify against her, it could work favorably in your case."

I need to squeal on her to save my own skin? I don't know if I can do that. "Can't she inform on whoever is pulling her strings? Won't that be good for her, too?"

"I do believe they're offering just such an incentive."

"We could totally still get married," Malcolm says.

It's so hopelessly romantic of him. Emphasis on the hopeless.

David shakes his head and launches on a lengthy explanation of immigration law. It's all word salad, something about section two-forty-five, something about being in the country for more than one hundred and twenty days but less than a year and ending with some horrible regulations about me having to leave the country and not come back for up to ten years or something.

I am so deep fried.

Thank God I have Malcolm. But for how long?

# CHAPTER 9

O̲NE YEAR LATER

T̲HINGS WENT ABOUT as bad as they could in Florida. I try not to think about it too much because it's all in the past. I have to build a future here, back in Brazil. We all do.

Malcolm's parents could see the writing on the wall. They did as much as they could to help, but the law is the law and my case came up right when people were going to re-election and they were campaigning against illegals.

The timing was terrible.

Still, I made it onto the news as an example of an innocent but hard-working youngster trying for a better life.

Yeah, I didn't buy it either.

I still have my health, so I've got that going for me. I also have my family. They're safe. We don't live in Sao Paulo any more. We're nowhere near any of that. We're living in Foz do Iguacu, most all of us working at a big tourist hotel. Except for my little sister who got into high school. I'm so proud of her.

I got a job in the kitchens. I'm not a chef yet but I'm working my way up through the ranks and they know I'm good.

Before I got deported, Malcolm set me up with a crowdfunding account and that has helped enormously. That's how we were able to move somewhere safer—which was the whole reason we were trying to get into the USA in the first place.

In the long run, we'll be OK. We're making the best of a pretty bad mess.

I miss Malcolm so much it hurts. We skype. We send cute text messages. But it's not the same. We're on different continents now.

There was a time when I was kind of hoping I might be pregnant. Then I'd be able to take a little of Malcolm back home with me. But then reality slaps me upside the head and tells me I'm crazy. I'm lucky things turned out as well as they did. It could have been awful, all things considered. The authorities in Florida could have made an "example" out of me and sent me to prison if they really wanted to.

So I have to make do with my memories and my limited cell-phone budget to skype each other.

Every time I cook *Moqueca* it reminds me of Malcolm and his family. And I make at least two dozen batches of it every day.

I'm in the middle of making bowl number eight and it's only six in the evening.

One of the waitresses comes into the kitchen and calls out to me. "Bianca! Somebody's asking for you."

"As soon as I finish chopping these peppers."

"I can do that," a familiar voice says behind me. "A really smart person showed me how."

It can't be? Sweet Jesu it is!

The knife clatters out of my hand and I run for him, wrapping my arms around him. He looks just as cute as I remember and in the next heartbeat we're kissing like we never want to let go.

There's some whistling in the kitchen, someone calls out that I have to get back to work. Which is true.

"Where are you staying?"

"Right here."

"What about school?"

"It's winter break."

I've lost track of the seasons—such as they are in Florida—that I forget it's winter for him and summer for me.

He's here. He's here in my arms and I can't let him go. Then again I could lose my job if I don't get back to work.

"What room number are you in?"

"I didn't come alone, my folks came too. Between you and me, I think they're worried I might do something stupid."

They never did get that vacation I guess. "I finish at three, I'll come up then."

"In the morning? Yeez."

"I'll tap softly on the window to wake you."

"I'll set my alarm."

He gives me another one of those knee-melting kisses before he sneaks out of the kitchen.

I'm sure I had a brain at some point, but for the life of me I wouldn't know where it was right now.

Malcolm is here.

I could just about cry.

Except it would make the *Moqueca* too salty.

---

A DATE at three in the morning isn't suspicious at all. That's why I'm tiptoeing around outside his apartment, wondering how I'm going to tap on the window loudly enough to wake him, without waking his parents.

I hear the most ridiculous "pssst" behind me. What the heck is Malcolm doing out here instead of in his room?

"The stars are so beautiful here," he says, "I couldn't sleep so I got up."

"The falls are pretty beautiful too," I offer. "People come from all over the world to see Iguazu Falls." Why the hell am I babbling? We should be kissing already.

"I don't need stars or falls," he says, stepping closer and wrapping his arms around me. "I just need you."

"I am so sorry I made a mess of things."

"Aw, babe." His kisses. Kisses in real life. I have missed them so much.

As quietly as two horny teenagers can manage it, we sneak into his room, into his bed. This is the best day of my life. Or the best pre-dawn of my life.

In a few hours the sun will be up, but until then we have the intimate seclusion of the darkness making the most wonderful cocoon. We are the only people in the world. No boundaries, no legal issues, just the two of us wrapped in each other. If feels so right.

My hand is stroking the back of his head and he's doing the same to me.

The kisses are so fierce and tender at the same time, they're killing me. Between kisses he mutters, "I am never letting you go."

"Me, neither."

Every kiss is like the most perfect agony, each touch a reminder of how much I have missed him. And how much I will die inside when he leaves. A tear slips out and we taste it mingling into the kiss.

"Bee, what's wrong?"

"Don't talk, just love me."

"I'm making you cry, what have I done?"

I have to be honest, even though it's killing me. "I love you so much Malcolm. Leaving you once was hard enough, I don't know if I can do it again."

He stops kissing me and pulls back. "Are you planning on leaving me?"

"Very funny." Why is he being deliberately dense?

"I mean it, are you planning on loving and leaving me?"

OK, he is being deliberately dense. "Not if I can help it."

"Good, because I don't think you heard me properly the first time. I am never leaving you."

"But... I... what about your home? You can't just up and leave?"

"Yeah, I can."

"No, you're going to college next year."

"Don't bore me with details." His hands start trailing a path over my body. Kisses trail down my neck and I'm so far gone my breath is jagged. "I have the most gorgeous woman in the world in my bed and she says she loves me. And I said I loved her right back and then we had the most amazing night and we lived happily ever after."

"Oh really?" It ends on a gasp because his kisses move further down and I want to squeal. "This dream has a happy ending, huh?"

"Very happy."

I think I am the happiest I have ever been in my life. And after all the crap I've gone through, and everything I've put Malcolm through, I think we both deserve a little happiness.

"Now, I have to tell you something, and you can't tell my parents," he says.

"Please, no more secrets." I can't stand secrets any more.

"This one's a good one."

"Really?"

"Yeah."

He runs his hands down my thighs and I can't think straight. "You're not playing fair."

"I know. So I'll tell you what it is and then you can decide if you want to keep it a secret."

"That sounds... fair." I have no idea.

"Do you remember that app?"

"Hmmm?" I can barely remember my name at this point.

"The one that tells you what language people are speaking, and translates it for you in real time?"

"Oh, that app." The one where he nearly ripped open all my secrets.

"Well, I ironed out most of the bugs and... it kind of broke the internet."

He's about to break my mind if he keeps doing what he's doing with his... hands. Oh sweet oblivion.

Wait? "Your app is out live now?"

"Yep."

"And your parents... don't know."

"Yep."

A dirty chuckle sneaks out of me. "That is a good secret."

---

MALCOLM IS HOLDING my hand as we walk towards my family's home. It's not a big place, but we're happy here and I can't wait for him to meet my family. I'm so in love I can barely feel my face. His parents are right behind us, bringing a suitcase full of who knows what. The fact they're coming and they're bringing gifts is wonderful. I just hope it's something simple like booze. My parents will love that.

Just because I didn't end up getting everything I wanted—my whole family didn't get what we wanted—we do have everything we need. My family are safe and they have jobs. I have a job, and I have Malcolm. But what I don't have is even more important, because I don't have to tell lies anymore.

No more stories and convoluted scenarios. No more exhaustion from having to remember it all.

We are here, we are all together. The future will be what we make it.

More Young Adult books by Ebony McKenna:

*The Ondine Series*:
The Summer of Shambles (Book 1)
The Autumn Palace (Book 2)
The Winter of Magic (Book 3)
The Spring Revolution (Book 4)

Lara's Christmas Gamble (short fiction set in the world of Ondine)

1916-ish

Robyn and the Hoodettes—coming soon!

# MORE YA BOOKS BY THE AUTHORS

SARA HANTZ:

Written In The Stars
The Second Virginity of Suzy Green
Will The Real Abi Saunders Please Stand Up
Falling For The Wrong Guy
In The Blood
Running Out Of Time (a Murder in Mind novella)


MAREE ANDERSON:

*The Liminals Series*:
Tangent (prequel)
Liminal (Book 1)
Phase (Book 2)—coming soon!

*The Freaks Series*:
Freaks of Greenfield High (Book 1)—free at most eBook stores!
Freaks in the City (Book 2)
Freaks Under Fire (Book 3)
The Freaks Series (Books 1-3)


VANESSA BARNEVELD:

Live Fast, Die Young
This Is Your Afterlife

ROBYN GRADY:

Raising Hell
Thunderstruck—coming soon!

EBONY McKENNA:

*The Ondine Series*:
The Summer of Shambles (Book 1)
The Autumn Palace (Book 2)
The Winter of Magic (Book 3)
The Spring Revolution (Book 4)

1916-ish
Robyn and the Hoodettes
The Girl & The Ghost (2018 RUBY Finalist)

# ABOUT THE AUTHORS

SARA HANTZ

Sara Hantz originally comes from the UK and now lives in New Zealand. She writes contemporary young adult fiction, including: *Falling For The Wrong Guy* (Entangled Crush), *In The Blood* and *Will The Real Abi Saunders Please Stand Up* (Entangled Teen), and the award winning *The Second Virginity Of Suzy Green*. Sara lectured for many years before deciding to devote more time to her writing and working in the family hospitality business. She has two grown-up children and when not writing, working, or online with her friends, she spends more time than most people she knows watching TV.

sarahantz.com * twitter.com/sarahantz * facebook.com/sarahantzauthor

MAREE ANDERSON

Maree Anderson writes paranormal romance, fantasy, and young adult books. She lives in beautiful New Zealand, home of hobbits, elves, and kiwis —both the fruit and the two-legged flightless variety. When she's not writing, Maree's got her nose in a book... and can often be found debating whether to wrestle with the espresso machine or settle for a plunger coffee. Her debut novel for young adults, *Freaks of Greenfield High*, was optioned for TV and currently has over 2 million reads on Wattpad. *Liminal*, the first novel in the *Liminals* series, was an iBooks Store "Best Books of August

2013". She recently released the third book in her *Freaks* series, featuring cyborg heroine Jay, and is currently working on a second novel-length *Liminals* story.

mareeanderson.com * facebook.com/MareeAndersonYA * twitter.com/MareeAnderson

### Vanessa Barneveld

Three-time Golden Heart® finalist Vanessa Barneveld lives in Australia. Her debut Young Adult novel *This Is Your Afterlife* (Bloomsbury Spark), won Oklahoma Romance Writers of America's National Readers' Choice Award. Vanessa's pastimes include baking, iPhonography, and traveling the world on a quest to find the world's greatest fries.

vanessabarneveld.com * twitter.com/vanessab73 * facebook.com/pages/Author-Vanessa-Barneveld

### Robyn Grady

Robyn Grady has sold millions of books worldwide and features regularly on bestsellers lists and at award ceremonies, including The National Readers Choice, The Booksellers Best and Australia's prestigious Romantic Book of the Year. When she's not tapping out her next story, she enjoys the challenge of raising three very different daughters as well as dreaming about shooting the breeze with Stephen King during a month-long Mediterranean cruise. Robyn knows that writing is the best job on the planet and she loves to hear from her readers!

Keep up with news on her latest releases at www.robyngrady.com.

### Ebony McKenna

Ebony McKenna is the author of the internationally acclaimed 4-book *Ondine* series, about a teenage girl whose pet ferret, Shambles, starts talking with a Scottish accent. Her most recent novel is The Girl & The Ghost, which is a 2018 finalist in the Romantic Book of the Year.

www.ebonymckenna.com